E·A·R·T·H K·I·N·G

EARTH
KING

Michael Youssef

CROSSWAY BOOKS • WESTCHESTER, ILLINOIS
A DIVISION OF GOOD NEWS PUBLISHERS

Note to the Reader

This is a work of fiction. As such, it intends to give a general picture of events surrounding the Last Days. It is not meant to be, nor should it be taken as, a detailed exposition of Biblical prophecy or any particular school of End Times thought.

Cover illustration by R. DiCianni
Book design by K. L. Mulder

First printing 1988
Second printing 1988

Printed in the United States of America

Library of Congress Catalog Card Number 88-70692

ISBN 0-89107-502-X

To Paul and Jane Meyer,
a source of inspiration.

It is with deep gratitude I acknowledge the contribution of Cecil Murphey to this book. Thanks also to John and Inez Bolten of West Germany and Victor Oliver who read the manuscript and made very helpful suggestions, and to Jan Dennis and the Crossway Books editorial staff.

P·R·O·L·O·G·U·E

On May 14, 1948, the day Israel became a nation, a boy was born to a Russian-Jewish family named Gad-Erianko in Moscow. His father was Jewish and his mother Gentile. They called him Joshua in honor of the famed leader of Jewish history.

"He is a special boy. He will achieve great things," said his father, Johan Gad-Erianko.

"Hah! Because he is your son? Because you want great things for him?" chided his older brother Abner.

Johan's dark eyes peered into the distance as if searching the horizon. "I know what I know. He is destined for great things. It has nothing to do with me."

"It had better not have anything to do with you!" Abner slapped his shoulder.

"Perhaps despite me, then." Johan forced a smile onto his face. His brother laughed and so did the boy's mother. But Johan knew. Something within his own heart told him. All morning he had known this secret—this terrible secret—of Joshua's greatness. He had tried to explain, but no one had listened, considering it only the babbling of an old man, nearly fifty when his first son was born.

"We shall see," he mumbled to himself as he left home. It was time to return to his classes at the University. Yet throughout the day his thoughts returned to that newborn. He knew that his son was destined for greatness no matter what anyone said.

Joshua Gad-Erianko amazed everyone who knew him. He walked at seven months, started to speak in full sentences by the time he was a year old. At three he picked up his grandfather's violin—the only heirloom his parents had carried with them to Chernogorsk, Siberia.

"Show me how, Papa," he said. "Show me how to hold it and I can do it, too."

Johan had been a child prodigy but now turned to music only for relaxation. In reality, he had not pursued his gift because his talents never matched those of his own father. He laughed. "Perhaps you wish only to have an early start, huh?" He tucked the violin under the left side of his chin and took the bow in his right hand. "Notice. The arm must always be straight and the right wrist relaxed." With deft fingering and virtuoso technique, he played several bars of Rimsky-Korsakov's *Sheherazade*.

Joshua's eyes focused on every movement of his father's hands. He applauded gleefully when the performance stopped. "I could do that, but my arms are too short."

"Ah, you can do this, huh? It took me until I was eight years old to play this!"

"Let me, Papa. Let me try."

Johan shrugged and handed the boy the polished violin and bow. The boy, unable to reach to the top of the violin, compromised by tucking the instrument under the front of his chin, and his father held it in place. He played eight bars without a mistake.

Johan stared at his curly-haired son. "I could never have done that before I was at least six, perhaps seven." He shook his head. "What kind of son do I have?"

The boy put down the violin and held out his arms for his father to pick him up. "Know something else? I can play the piano, too."

"Is that so? You decide you can play and so you play?"

Joshua snuggled into the beefy arms. "No, not like that. Mama goes to the piano when she thinks I'm asleep. I hide and watch while she plays. When she goes out for her walk, I go to the piano and play, too." He paused and kissed his father's rough cheek. "Did I do wrong, Papa?"

"No, you did not do wrong. And you may play—anytime you wish."

By the time Joshua was five, Johan could say with both honesty and pride, "My son has mastered two musical instruments."

Johan's father had been one of Lenin's close associates and a leader in the 1917 overthrow of the Czar. Johan, therefore, enjoyed privileges not normally given to a man like himself. He, like all good citizens, had joined the Communist party and performed the responsibilities given to him. His obvious indifference to Soviet socialism brought his name before government officials often. He was becoming an embarrassment.

Giorgi Versky, a member of the Politburo, agreed to make an arrangement with him. "Because your father was my one true friend," Versky said, "and because of him I did not die while fighting Germans in World War I, I wish to help you. I made your father a promise that nothing would happen to you."

"Yes? And what will you do?" Johan said, being young and strong-willed.

"I am preparing to send you and your family to Siberia. We have an adequate house for you, a position on the faculty of Chernogorsk University."

"I've never heard of such a place."

"Exactly. An obscure university. Far from the purges

that come daily to more populous areas." Giorgi, who never smiled, made a special attempt to soften his features and to express affection as he added, "It will also provide a little more freedom than I could allow you to enjoy in Moscow."

"It is exile, then?"

"Let's call it a promotion." Giorgi's eyes bored into the younger man. "If you refuse, your situation is out of my hands. I can no longer protect you. I may not even be able to protect you there."

Johan had shrugged, knowing he had no choice, and refusing to let his late father's friend totally win the day. "If that is the way it is to be, let it be so."

Johan and his wife Magda had arrived in 1937—in the middle of the Stalin purges. Only later did he realize that had he remained only a few months longer in Moscow, Stalin would have killed him along with 60,000 other Russian citizens.

Both an intuitive and shrewd economist, Johan could have provided immeasurable help to the Soviet government in Moscow. They could not allow him to voice his opinions in Moscow because of his indifference to politics, his distrust of Stalin and those who surrounded him, but mostly his professional opinions. More than once he had confronted top leaders of the nation, showing them with irrefutable proof that their expedient economic measures would bring chaos later.

At one point he prepared a twelve-page report showing the waste and the foolish policies of land development. He correctly forecast the years of wheat shortage for the years ahead. He brilliantly laid out plans to reverse the present policies. Even Stalin, had he been a more secure leader, would have implemented the agricultural reforms he proposed. He reaffirmed his original position, making it clear that he would tolerate no dissent.

At first Johan made no secret of his opinions of the

national policies and his veiled attacks of the Kremlin. This infuriated Stalin who, surprisingly, did nothing to shut him up. At Chernogorsk, Johan taught faithfully and brilliantly at the University. By 1940 Johan had learned to keep his views private. He presented the party line to students, careful not to express his opinions except to a select few. That saved his life the second time.

Johan almost lost everything in 1950. At age sixty-four, his health seriously deteriorating, he turned with fervency to Judaism for consolation. Although his own father had renounced religion early in his life, Johan's mother had remained devout. She was ninety years old when Johan knelt beside her bed and received the timeless blessing that Aaron of old had pronounced:

> The Lord bless you and keep you;
> The Lord make His face to shine upon
> you, and be gracious to you; the
> Lord lift up His countenance upon
> you and give you peace.

Johan made many attempts to instruct his only son Joshua in the Jewish faith. The boy listened, learned, and repeated every answer correctly. Yet both of them knew that Joshua believed none of it. His mother being a Gentile didn't help either.

The boy continued his brilliant growth. He excelled in everything he attempted. His talents brought him to the attention of the Politburo. They lavished upon the young boy the best of everything. Despite Johan's protests, they took the boy to Moscow where he lived in his private dacha. Tutors came to instruct him. Within months he grasped all they had to teach him and moved on, immediately replaced by new ones.

By 1968, Joshua had received his fourth doctoral degree and could have excelled in any field he chose. He chose economics as his father had chosen before him.

On the day of receiving his fourth doctoral degree, the Soviet government released the first of eight textbooks he would write before his twenty-third birthday. All were monumental in scope and all evidenced a lucid reasoning that astounded world-class thinkers in economics, physics, chemistry, and mathematics.

Joshua's remarkable talents, especially in mathematics, catapulted him into prominence, as he had anticipated. He appeared on Soviet television regularly, demonstrating that he could compute numbers faster than modern computers.

Soviet officials sent their prodigy abroad, visiting not only Communist nations but the non-allied countries. "This," they boasted, "shows the brilliant work going on in our educational institutions."

Joshua used that brilliance in mathematics as his means to come to public attention. The world knew his name. It was only the beginning.

B·O·O·K
O·N·E

O·N·E

"Today I begin," Joshua said on his fourteenth birthday. "Today I use *it*."

Although long aware of his one unique talent, he had tested it privately and discreetly, never allowing anyone to know of its existence. Then, at fourteen, Joshua knew he must plan his future. He had known for as long as he could remember—perhaps he had been born with this knowledge—that he had a special destiny in the world. A destiny only he could fulfill.

Joshua laughed, thinking how easily he had gained access to the prominent and inaccessible people in the world. They had sought him, and in so doing they helped to prepare him for his ultimate triumph.

From childhood, renowned leaders, ranging from politicians to scholars to entertainers, talked freely around Joshua. Even the most secretive and reticent sensed an understanding resonance from the quiet, dark-haired boy who immediately grasped their most esoteric concepts or private thoughts. Occasionally Joshua made an incisive comment that helped the speakers to solidify their thinking. He encouraged their ambitions by silent approval or a nod.

In those days, Joshua listened but said little. Although no one ever noticed, Joshua seldom voiced a direct opinion. Joshua spoke each comment in an impersonal and detached manner, his features immobile, and his body straight to the point of rigidity. His non-judgmental, non-intrusive presence and full attention provided a sacrosanct atmosphere.

The ambassador to the United States once said to Joshua, "When I am with you, I trust you as I have never trusted another man in my entire life. You have the ability to make a person like me know that it is safe to speak from his inner heart."

Joshua nodded. He also knew far more about the ambassador than the information he divulged.

He stored the voluntarily given information in the recesses of his mind, awaiting the moment when he would have use for it.

At age fourteen, he began to use what he had learned. Furthermore, he knew that no one could resist him.

Joshua spent the night hours planning his future. In the special room he allowed no one else to enter, Joshua Gad-Erianko wrote with clear precision on the specially constructed north wall. Originally designed by Joshua to lay out mathematical problems, the entire wall resembled a giant white chalkboard.

Beginning the evening of May 15, 1962, using an ink he had invented that would disappear within eighteen hours, he laid out the years through 2048. He would then be 100 years old. He did not expect to die that year. He would wait until he had entered the next century before he set into motion his plans for the second century of his life.

Writing with an accuracy as if he had copied the information from his writing manual, Joshua wrote with the thirty-two-character Cyrillic alphabet. Although equally proficient in writing and speaking eight of the world's major languages, he preferred his first language.

Without pausing to rest or to reconsider, Joshua wrote down each goal and its purpose, followed by precise statements as to how he would achieve it. His plan lacked only the specific names of men and women who would become his pawns. He could decide on them as need arose.

While he worked, his mind fully concentrating on his task, his fingers moved rapidly from line to line. He never erased, never revised, and he never hesitated. During the nine continuous hours of work, Joshua felt a keen sense of excitement, much like the sexual stirrings he had read about. He wrote on, fully covering the entire wall, never once doubting his choices.

An observer might have called him inspired.

Or possessed.

Joshua stepped backward toward the south wall. He read each line carefully, imprinting it all upon his memory. Once there, it could be instantly recalled. Joshua's memory never faltered. Had Joshua truly believed in a god of any kind, he would have paused to give thanks. Instead he said, "Joshua, I salute you. Tomorrow you begin to fulfill your destiny!"

Tomorrow he would start with Ivor Kalinin.

T·W·O

On the afternoon following the formulation of his plans, Joshua finished playing the piano duet with Ivor Kalinin, who sat across from him at an identical grand piano. They had played nothing but the works of Sergei Rachmaninoff, beginning with Kalinin's favorite, the Third Symphony. They followed with the Fourth Piano Concerto and Rhapsody on a Theme of Paganini. At Joshua's suggestion, they concluded with *The Isle of the Dead* with its asymmetric rhythms.

Kalinin paused and stared at his pupil. "Never, never have I heard anyone play Sergei's music so well. Joshua, were Rachmaninoff alive today, he would bow to you as his greatest interpreter."

Joshua nodded. He found the words neither flattering nor significant, only true. He knew the extent of his great talent. He had heard the highest of all praises all his life. They meant nothing to him.

"And I am tired," Kalinin said. "Even with music as beautiful as this, I can become fatigued."

Joshua shrugged. It made no difference to him. He had

memorized the score of all the published works of Rachmaninoff—an effortless task.

Following their daily custom, they stopped when the waiting housekeeper brought in Georgian tea. Minutes later they went out for their brisk two-mile walk.

Once outside the dacha, Ivor Kalinin paused to take in the scenery, as he often did. It had stopped snowing an hour earlier, leaving everything looking clean and freshly laundered. Behind him stood the dacha, a large white building constructed in the modern style, surrounded on three sides by a perfectly landscaped terrace overlooking the road below. The Kremlin had employed their best architects and carpenters in constructing the living quarters for their brilliant citizen. Built out from the hillside, its spacious garage underneath escaped notice until people got close. It housed a Chaika and a Zis limousine, with uniformed drivers always available.

Joshua appreciated—as much as he could appreciate any man—his teacher's brilliance as a musician and his sharpness of mind in discussing philosophy. Kalinin had proven to be the most capable of his instructors. For that reason Joshua had chosen him for his first action.

Kalinin pulled his ankle-length greatcoat tighter, then tugged at the earflaps of his hat until they fit snugly. The bitter cold wind whipped through his clothes, although, as usual, Joshua hardly noticed the weather.

The surface splintered under the impact of their boots like eggshells. Joshua paused next to his teacher and stared intently into his deep-brown eyes. Joshua had done that on many occasions lately. Their eyes met and locked. In one instant, Joshua knew Kalinin had finalized his plans. It was as he expected. He could now make his first strategic move.

"Come," Joshua said. They continued their walk through the wooded estate. Joshua's eyes never left the other man.

Finally, Ivor, disturbed because the intense gaze never left his face, asked, "Something is wrong?"

"You have a secret, Ivor. I know what it is."

The teacher's face registered momentary shock. "Secret? What kind of secret?"

"It will do no good to lie. I know." The penetrating stare of Joshua's dark eyes never flickered.

"How could you—? You're guessing, surely!"

"No, Ivor, I do not have to guess and you do not have to be afraid. In fact, I am telling you that I know because I have decided that I shall help you."

"Joshua, what are you saying?"

"You wish to emigrate, don't you? Or should I call it defect? No, let's keep it simple. You want to leave the Soviet Union."

Ivor gasped as if someone had knocked his breath out of him. He turned and laid his arms on the boy's shoulders. His whole face tightened in fear. "I have never told a soul. Not a single soul in the world."

"It won't work," Joshua said. "Your plan, I mean. In fact, I am surprised that a man as brilliant as you would attempt such a foolish scheme. Don't you know that when you travel on the cultural exchange *they* watch you every second?"

Ivor's face reddened. "You know! You do know! But how could—"

"I told you I knew."

"But how? How could you know this?"

"That is not important for you to understand. I have told no one else. I have no need to tell anyone, do I?"

"Joshua, I beg you! Please, please, I'll give up my plans. I won't leave you—"

Joshua knocked the professor's arms from his shoulders. "Don't be stupid! Listen! I can help you leave. Obviously you desire to leave what you consider an oppressive system."

"Help me? I—I don't understand what—I'm confused. I—"

"Don't bother to understand, Ivor. Now . . . if you want to emigrate, I can assist you. Simple, really."

Joshua pushed the teacher away from him, and the man spun around, falling to the ground. He lay motionless in the snow too stunned to move. Joshua continued his walk, picking up his stride. He listened until he heard the teacher rise to his feet. His heavy footsteps crunched the freshly fallen snow as he raced toward him along the path lined with snow-laden birch and fir trees.

Joshua had already lost interest in Ivor Kalinin. He felt an exhilaration he had never experienced before. He *knew* the thoughts of this man and Kalinin had verified it. He knew exactly and totally. Although quite certain before, he had never confirmed it.

Joshua didn't have to turn back and stare into the teacher's eyes again. He could feel the confused reasoning going on in Ivor's mind. It was as if he could actually hear Ivor analyzing his plans, asking himself questions, such as, Is this a trap? Has the KGB detected something—and also hear Ivor answering his own questions: I cannot believe the KGB has had reason to suspect. I have been discreet.

Joshua reached the fence that surrounded the dacha and waited. Ivor would overcome his confusion and questions and then he would beg for help.

He stared at the snow-carpeted countryside. Had Joshua been a sentimentalist at that moment he might have believed in the propaganda of the communal serenity of the USSR.

Ivor hesitantly approached him. "Yes, help me. I want you to help me." He was trembling and Joshua liked the diffidence in his teacher, a trait he had never displayed before. "You are right that I cannot escape using my plan."

"It is simple for me to get you out of the country."

"Then, please, Joshua, I beg you. Allow me to leave—"

"My friends," Joshua said, "at the Komitet Gosudarstvennoi Besopasnosti would hate to know the subversive thoughts you carry in your head."

"You—you would not tell the KGB? But you—"

"This is our secret," Joshua answered. "Only ours."

The teacher, twenty years older than Joshua, fell in step with Joshua as they veered from the path and their fur-lined boots crunched the snow beneath them. His voice sounded old and extremely tired. He stumbled, sprawled face-forward on the ground, and turned over, and looked up at Joshua. "I beg you, do not play with me—"

"Get up!" Joshua said, tired of the game. "Prepare to leave the Soviet Union. You must tell no one, you understand. I shall see that you have your passport within a fortnight. Just one thing, Ivor . . ."

"Anything—"

"Don't be too quick to promise. I may ask of you more than you wish to give."

"If you get me out of this country, ask anything and I shall do it."

"That is exactly what I want. A promise. Nothing more. One day I shall contact you for repayment. It will not happen for many years, but I shall come to you. Then you will repay my kindness."

"Of course! You will be saving my life." He crawled over to Joshua, grabbed his hands and kissed them feverishly.

"That is premature. Get off your knees."

"What? Premature—?"

"Never mind. Stand up. Let us continue to walk as I explain what you must do."

As Joshua's fame spread throughout the Soviet Union, he had met every top official along with those second-line individuals who aspired to the top. He had systematically pulled out the secrets of their inner hearts. At first he had played it like a game, seeking only to discover how much he could learn. By staring into their eyes, using his total powers of concentration, he willed them to think of their secrets. Their minds suddenly concentrated on their deepest moments of shame, guilt, wrongdoing—acts they had committed but would do anything to prevent their coming to light. Even those purportedly without conscience held their secrets as tenaciously as the others.

Joshua had learned much, remembered it all, and confided in no one. Now he would bring a second secret into the open.

Joshua made his selection with deliberate care. The object of his choice must meet two requirements. First, the man had to have enough power to guarantee the departure of Ivor. Second, he must be a man that Joshua would not have to use again.

The next day he asked for and received an appointment with a second secretary of the KGB. The official, pompously dressed in his colonel's uniform with an array of medals dangling across his massive chest, smiled with a contrived benevolence at the youngster who stood before him. They met near St. Basil, the most famous cathedral in Moscow.

"I am honored, Joshua," he said. "First that you wished to speak with me. Second, that you would select such a public place." His hushed voice reveled in conspiracy.

"Thank you," he answered. "Ivan the Terrible planned this cathedral and had it built. I assume you know that."

"But of course—"

"Money was no object for the czar, was it?"

"I suppose not," the colonel answered, confused at the line of conversation.

"I thought it best to meet within the shadow of the Kremlin walls, yet where ears do not hear our words," Joshua said. He started to walk away from Dzerzhinsky Square.

"You are most wise." The colonel strolled casually nearer St. Basil's. His furtive glances made certain no one followed them. A frown covered his massive forehead.

"Ah, do you not find your heart beating with loyalty?" Joshua asked with a touch of mockery in his voice.

"Right here at Red Square," the colonel's sonorous voice rose, "masses of people from every republic in the Soviet Union as well as people from countless nations walk down this street."

"Well done, with just the right amount of patriotic fervor," Joshua answered. "Exactly as I have heard you say it before."

The security people scarcely noticed the uniformed officer and the boy walking together. They preferred to watch the civilians who massed before Lenin's tomb and waited for the changing of the guard.

"I was flattered that you should wish to see me. For our nation's greatest intellectual to contact me—"

Joshua held up his hand. "I have come to ask a favor of you, sir. In return, I shall do you a favor. Does that not sound agreeable to you?"

"It does sound—uh, equitable." His voice sounded strained and he cleared his throat. "What kind of favor?"

"I have a friend who wishes exit papers." Joshua took his hand from his pocket and gave the colonel a single sheet of paper. On one side it contained information about Ivor Kalinin.

The colonel stared blankly at the information. "You do not understand. I wish to help you, but I simply cannot issue exit papers for people to—"

"Turn the paper over, Colonel." Joshua faced St. Basil's. Dusk had come to the city. Powerful lights suddenly lit up the dome of the cathedral, and it appeared to glow.

The colonel gasped. "How—?"

"That is not important. As you can see, this is not guesswork. I know the number of your account in Zurich as well as the balance—give or take a few rubles. Or should I convert it into Swiss francs? American dollars? German marks?" Joshua pointed to St. Basil's. "Perhaps not quite enough to build an edifice like this, but at your rate of accumulation, in four years, you will have enough."

The colonel swore as he tore the paper into two strips. "How dare you think that you can blackmail me—"

"Please don't tear up the information about Ivor Kalinin. I am asking a favor of you. One faithful patriot and Communist to another. A simple favor. Once you grant my friend his exit papers and he is safely out of the country, I shall have a serious attack of amnesia."

Ten days later Ivor emigrated to the United States.

For the next thirty-five years, Joshua assisted others to move within the Soviet Union or outside the Eastern bloc. Joshua himself traveled throughout the world from 1970 until the late 1980s. He manipulated events and individuals so that his name became associated with compassionate care for needy, desperate people.

Yet Joshua did not limit his sphere of help.

One Japanese embezzler needed half a million dollars in cash. Within three days Joshua provided, binding the man's loyalty to him forever. He advised politicians in England, the United States, and Australia, giving them expert advice that assured their elections. Sometimes their tactics included blackmailing opponents or members of the opponent's staffs. Yet without exception, all of them came into office.

Once Joshua built up his cadre of indebted leaders, he implemented Goal 2 of his strategy. These activities would lead to his recognition as Israel's champion in the world. As his first step, he selected nine Jewish dissidents, all brilliant in their fields of specialization, who wanted to emigrate to Israel. He arranged for their exit, asking only that they inform the Prime Minister of Joshua's efforts on their behalf. "And one day I shall ask a favor of you," he added.

They, like the others before them, made unreserved promises. "You have only to ask. Everything I have is at your disposal," said one of them.

Three months after the release of the dissidents, Joshua traveled to Libya, "and made a personal plea for the release of five Israeli intelligence operators" (according to a *New York Times* article).

Joshua allowed eight weeks to lapse before he intervened in a purging of Jews who lived in Syria. He arranged for their safe exit to Israel. During the next year, Israeli citizens learned of eighteen specific incidents where Joshua Gad-Erianko preserved the life of Jews in the world.

"You are now a full citizen of Israel," read the formal letter signed by the Prime Minister and every member of the

Knesset. "We have marked May 14 this year as a day of double celebration. It is the birthday of our country. It is also the birthday of our great friend and hero."

The letter did not elicit a smile. Joshua had expected it to happen—down to the last detail.

By the time Joshua turned forty-five, he was considered not only the most brilliant man inside the Soviet Union, but in the world. He privately claimed no allegiance to any political philosophy, although he was careful never to speak against the policies and practices of his own country.

Joshua never married and no one ever linked his name with any woman. Nor was there the slightest hint of any sexual deviation. Joshua's energies lay in other directions.

In one month, he would show the entire world where his true passion lay.

T·H·R·E·E

The afternoon sun streamed upon the western side of the Nile Hilton Hotel that faced Egypt's famous river. The horns of a thousand cars blared in a cacophony of orchestrated disruption. As they passed Kornaish el Nile Street, the vehicles seemed to make an endless and unbroken chain. As usual the street filled with an array of sleek American cars, smaller European and Japanese models, carts pulled by donkeys and horses, bicycles, motorcycles, and pedestrians attempting to dart between them.

Zechariah Kalif stared down from the balcony and saw a fight between a car driver of a Mercedes and the driver of a beaten-up Toyota truck. It took no special ability to realize, even from the height where he stood, that their shrill tones and violent gestures involved who had the right of way.

Slowly Zechariah turned his head, wanting to avoid going back into the room. To the right a policeman was writing a ticket to a Fiat driver after the policeman's patience had run out waiting for a baksheesh that was not forthcoming. In spite of himself, Zechariah Kalif smiled and shook his head. No matter how Egypt progressed, Egypt stayed the same.

Turning slightly as he stood on the top floor of the Nile Hilton Hotel, he appreciated, as he always did, the breathless view of the river and the sailboats that streamed to the right and to the left. He leaned forward as if he might catch a clearer view of the great pyramid, partially obscured by this beautiful yet dusty and dirty city.

Unable to prolong his diversion, Zechariah turned fully around and faced the other nine people. All of them had remained seated around the mahogany table in that spacious and well-furnished room. He had hoped they would have reached enough of an agreement to dismiss until dinner. "No such luck," he mumbled under his breath and squared his shoulders. He stepped slowly forward, aware that the eyes of the other seven men and two women scrutinized his features. They hoped for a telltale sign of his thinking. Even the slightest grimace would be enough. They were experts in the area of negotiation.

"We shall begin the bargaining again." He knew the Israeli delegates did not like to call it bargaining. They preferred terms such as negotiating or discussion. Zechariah Kalif would have preferred to say, "throat-cutting," but that would have antagonized everyone, especially his fellow Egyptians.

The Israelis exchanged covert glances but in such a way that he could not read their expressions. Yet his intuition at the bargaining table told him that they displayed glum, serious expressions for the benefit of his fellow Egyptians. They not only showed great suspicion and distrust, but behind the facade they expected to beat their opposition.

Changing his approach from the diffident moderator, his dark eyes bore into the face of Gideon Wittstein, head of the Israelis. "Taba belongs to Egypt and you know it."

"But that is not the point," his counterpart answered, switching from the hard-line approach to quieter tones that he had shown earlier. "Israel has invested large sums of money in developing a sandy, deserted place. A place in which you had no interest until we intervened."

"So, you believe that gives you territorial rights? We are talking reality, not science fiction!"

"Science fiction," said Gideon Wittstein, an avid reader of the genre, "is for recreation. But I wish to remind you that we are not attempting to enact any Arab fables either." His teeth gleamed in his most persuasive smile.

"Despite the sharpness of your wit," Zechariah said, "you are surely thinking in less than non-fiction if you have the slightest hope of obtaining anything—"

"Slightest hope! We have far more than a slight hope! We have come here—"

"Sir!" Nagila Levy's voice interrupted. It was the first time she had spoken since the meeting started that morning. Although an Israeli, her features fit none of the stereotypes. Her small, straight nose, pale-blue eyes, and ash-blonde hair swept into a knot at the back of her head made her appear out of place among these typical-looking Middle-Eastern delegates.

"You have something to say," Zechariah smiled, his eyes carefully noting her soft complexion. Even from several feet away, his sensitive nose caught the delicate fragrance she wore. Subtle. Not too much. He liked that in a woman.

"I came here hoping we could settle this matter like civilized, educated, and intelligent people, not like—"

"Ah, yes!" Zechariah nodded. "I forget your western training. You aim for the jugular vein. Is that not the expression?"

"We aim for results!"

He waved her words aside. "Yes, but Americans and women!" He shook his head.

"Sir, I did not come here for you to patronize me." She said the words softly, and they had a stronger effect on Zechariah than he wanted to show on his face.

"I underestimated you. That was my error. Forgive me."

"Your error," interjected Shaheen Ahman, "lay in trying to cross swords with a beautiful woman who uses her words as cleverly as her charms."

"Shaheen, I resent that!"

"But is it not true?" Shaheen Ahman smiled, showing his straight teeth.

"It is not! And may I remind you that you came as part of *our* delegation," Nagila said.

"Against your personal objection." His dark eyes stared into hers.

"Now anyone can see why."

"But our government prides itself on recognizing the rights and opinions of non-Jews. Or . . . does it?" He smiled again. A shock of his tight-curled black hair, cut long, kept falling over his forehead, making him look like a mischievous little boy.

Nagila first met Shaheen Ahman two years earlier. At that time he worked for Shin Bet—counterpart to the American FBI. Shaheen resigned over the murder of two captured Arab terrorists. He stated that only barbarians killed their captives. After that he went into civil service, concentrating on educating and employing the poor and handicapped. His outstanding training program at Taba earned him the right to be a delegate.

"Before my colleague interrupted," Nagila said, "I simply tried to urge us to discipline ourselves to get to the point immediately. Frankly, you know what you want. We know what we will settle for. Let's get to the bottom line."

"The bottom line—yes, an American expression—and we know precisely what we will settle for."

"Shall we begin there?" Nagila asked.

Zechariah Kalif made his second mistake. He did not answer immediately. That pause gave others the opportunity to interject. Once that started, both Zechariah and Nagila knew it was a matter of sitting and listening to every argument spelled out again and again. Delegates would go back to the days of Mohammed, Moses, or Abraham and work slowly, painfully, and argumentatively toward the present.

Zechariah Kalif felt a twinge of resentment as he watched the slightest smile on Nagila's cheeks. She had not gotten what she wanted, but she had wrested control from him. He half-closed his eyes, as if listening intently. But it was already too late. She had caught his momentary slip and discomfort. However, he reminded himself, he would assume control again.

The flood of arguments, interlaced with interpretive theology of Islam or Judaism, permeated the room. One by one, the delegates rose to speak, their voices and gestures bellowing as if speaking to hundreds. Pandemonium broke loose when an Israeli challenged an Egyptian's flimsy argument. A second Egyptian, who happened to agree with the Israeli, however, broke in to support his brother. Naturally a second Israeli joined in the melee. Other than Zechariah, Nagila, and Shaheen, they all gesticulated wildly as each tried to outshout the other.

Out of courtesy for old customs and culture, and reminding himself that four of the delegates were old men, Zechariah Kalif allowed the cacophony to continue. He needed the total support of his own delegation. They would be easier to control in the long haul if they had freedom to screech and to pull out all the slogans from the days of Nasser. Once out of their systems, they would listen to his persuasive reasoning.

Zechariah Kalif's eyes surveyed the other members. All strong delegates, all determined to have their country come out on top, they sometimes lost sight of the overall situation. Shaheen Ahman, the one token Muslim on the Israeli delegation, puzzled him.

But then Shaheen Ahman had always amazed him. Born an Arab, he had been raised by a Jewish family in his own tradition while they remained Jews. Kalif could never understand how that might be possible. He remembered also that in his later years the father converted to a Christian sect. Shaheen married a Western-trained Jewess who converted to the "true faith of Allah." They had lived happily together except that they could never have children. Then, three or four years earlier, the wife had died in the Syrian bombing of an Arab-populated village in Israel. The planes struck at night and mistakenly thought they destroyed an Israeli kibbutz.

Zechariah Kalif had followed the career of Shaheen.

The young man burst into prominence at age twenty-two as a voice for moderate Arabs in Israel. People listened to him—Arabs, Jews, Christians—even though no one fully understood him. Once he gained the support of the moderates, he slowly shifted into radical views that alienated most of his Jewish followers and all of the Christians. Shaheen embraced a mixture of Islamic faith that included a commitment to Russian communism, and an open intolerance of Jewish and Christian religions. Despite his quirks, Kalif knew that above everything else Shaheen Ahman was a man of deep feeling—"a typical Arab."

Kalif allowed himself to smile. If the antagonism between Shaheen and Nagila Levy continued to escalate, he would have the support of one Israeli delegate on their side. It might be easier than he had anticipated.

After another hour, Zechariah's fist pounded the table. "Order!" Then, changing the tone of his voice, he bowed his head toward Farouk, to indicate his respect for the older man's experience, but also to announce that he was in control. "We can achieve nothing if we keep talking *at* each other. We must talk *to* each other, and one at a time, please, so that we can hear each other's argument."

"Look how far we have come," said an Israeli delegate as if intended as an aside. "We fought three bloody wars, during one of which I lost my only brother." He turned his face slowly now that he had the attention of everyone, his eyes shifting from face to face. "Then we had Camp David. Since that time we are no longer at war with each other. Let us build on this for the future of our children. We must not allow a small piece of land to destroy all that we have accomplished so far."

"We agree," said an Egyptian delegate. "However, this small piece of land, as you call it, is *our* land. It represents more to us than a 'small piece of land.' It represents our heritage and our pride."

"You may keep your pride. You are welcome to your heritage. But do not overlook what we have done for you," interrupted Shaheen Ahman.

"What you have done for us?" Farouk asked, surprised at the outburst. He sighed, realizing that the man must have a great struggle going on inside of his own heart to be a Muslim brother and to have to support Israel. "Yes . . . yes, you have done something for us. You have occupied our land for years—land you took from us by force, by treachery, by bribing the consciences of the world—"

"Despite your rhetoric," Nagila Levy said, the firmness of her voice so surprising Farouk he did not attempt to interrupt, "we are all well aware of how you interpret the past. And as you well know, we interpret it differently. We remind you that our country came to that barren portion of land and developed the oil fields in the Sinai. We spent a lot of money. Then, without force and in good faith, we handed it all to you on a platter. Is that not so?"

"But nobody asked you to develop our land."

"True."

"You have prospered, have you not?" Shaheen said. "And so have both sides. Is that not also true? Has it not benefited the Republic of Egypt? It makes me wonder if we ought not to declare Taba an independent—"

"You speak like a fool!" snapped Nagila.

"How wise of you to notice," he said, smiling as if delighted he had aroused her anger.

"Besides," Farouk said, his hand sweeping away Shaheen's last remark, "we were in the process of developing these oil fields ourselves when you took our land. By force."

Gideon Wittstein shook his head. "I must be in the wrong place. We came here with good intentions—"

"Hah!" Farouk said as he folded his arms across his chest. "Does not the jackal say that to the chicken before eating her young?"

"That is unfair—" Gideon stopped himself from falling into the old trap of being baited and prolonging the very thing he wanted to stop. "Forgive me, Farouk, for my lack of control. I simply wish to point out that we are rehashing old arguments that the Camp David accord settled years ago. We have an agreement. Please, let's not bring up all these futile arguments. We shall make better progress if we put that behind us and concentrate on the matter at hand."

"Yes!" said Farouk. "At last! It comes down to one question. When do you plan to return Taba to us? Give us your timetable and we shall return to our homes."

"We cannot just return to you one of our most popular holiday resorts willy-nilly," said Gideon, his face showing surprise at the naivete of Farouk's outburst.

"What do you mean by 'willy-nilly'?" said Farouk. "You insult us again?"

"Insult you? We did not come here to insult," Nagila said. "We came to talk, to understand, and to agree." She opened a manila folder and glanced at a printed page. "We should like this body—this delegation representing Egypt— to lease this resort—"

"Lease our own land? Surely—"

"Or we could consider the option of selling it to you."

"Our land? Sell *us* back our own land? The land of our fathers? Do you not realize that since the time of our great prophet, our people have lived—"

"But, surely," Nagila said, "you do not expect us to hand it over to you freely. After all we have done for this land."

"Do we Arabs not say that a gift that costs us nothing is worth nothing?" Shaheen asked.

"How can you lease to us our own land?" said Farouk shaking his head and ignoring Shaheen. "Or sell it to us?"

"You insult us first," said a small Egyptian with an extraordinarily deep voice. "Now you provoke us. Is that your plan?"

Shaheen Ahman stood. "Obviously, you Egyptians are not serious about a peaceful agreement. Forgive me for thinking you were." He took a few steps as if to leave the room.

Farouk, despite his weight and wide girth, pulled himself up so that he stood facing Shaheen. "Peaceful agreement? If I were not a man of peace would I have come to this conference? If I were not a man of peace I would slit the throat of a brother who consorts with infidels."

"But wouldn't a jackal say the same thing to a chicken to put away any suspicion?"

"Now I am a jackal? Is that what you say of me? Of us?"

"No. I only used your own proverb—"

"No! No! No!" he bellowed. "You are saying that we, the Egyptians, are not serious about peace! About agreeing with you! That is what you are saying! We who love peace so much. We who do everything possible to bring peace into the Middle East! Ha! You Israelis have now invaded Lebanon. You refuse to return Taba to us. And you can come into our beautiful land and talk about peace?" He pushed himself away from the table, brushed Shaheen aside, and stalked toward the door.

"Wait, please," Zechariah Kalif said, beckoning Farouk to return. "Do not leave us. We need the wisdom of your counsel."

"I shall not sit among infidels and be insulted—"

"Please," Kalif said, embarrassed as he became aware that he was pleading.

If Farouk left, it might ruin everything. He had received precise instructions. No matter what the others wanted or what his government insisted upon, he had to bring about exactly the right agreement. Until minutes ago, it seemed as if everything would fall neatly into place. Silently he swore at Shaheen. *If he continues to antagonize us, I'll fail.*

The thought of failure momentarily paralyzed Zechariah Kalif, and he gasped for breath. He had no idea what would happen if he failed. *He knew only that he could not— must not—fail.*

F·O·U·R

Farouk opened the door, stopped, and pretended to listen. Anger burned inside his chest like a blazing fire. In another place or time, he said to himself, I would have killed that faithless Muslim who deserves neither an Arabic name nor heritage.

He stopped, trying to decide how to go back inside without losing face. He waited. If someone did not speak, he would have to humiliate himself and go back inside. He had his orders and he could not risk failure.

"Why should you take my words as insults?" Shaheen said. "I am a man of many different thoughts and I speak accordingly."

"Oh, that you do. First you sound like a true believer. The next minute you speak like—like one of them." Farouk turned and faced the group. Shaheen had not apologized. Farouk waited a few moments, realizing nothing further would come as an apology. He decided he would accept this as close enough. The man had not been brought up properly as an Arab, so he must make some allowances for him. He walked toward the heavily cushioned chair he had sat in earlier.

"I spoke what I believe is true," Shaheen said. "Must I not speak truth because it offends?"

"Offends?" Farouk said as he squeezed himself into the soft pillows. He knew that he must continue to play out the charade a little longer and did not like it. "Every time you open your mouth, you speak with the tongue of the serpent!"

"Ah, yet I do not feel insulted when you speak that way. Why do you hear my words as insults when they say less? And I spoke without venom."

"And I speak with venom? Is that it? When you speak, the words come out with sincerity, but when I—"

"Enough!" Zechariah Kalif yelled. He had gotten Farouk back into the room and he could not allow another incident. He pressed a button. "It is time for coffee. Perhaps if we drink coffee together it will calm our nerves and bring us closer to understanding one another."

The remaining nine got up and gazed out the window, looking again at the view of the Nile with the city of Gizeh lying like a beautiful yet dirty tapestry.

An Egyptian waiter entered the room, interrupting their silence. He wore the traditional Arab dress: a long green flowing caftan with a colorful, wide silk belt wrapped around the waist. His head was covered with a round cap made of the same color material as the belt. "*Itfadel*," he said as he served each of them a small cup of thick coffee. Next, he placed before each delegate a plate of baklava. A deafening silence filled the air, and no one wanted to be the first to break it.

Gideon arose. "Friends—and I hope that before we leave we can use this word and mean it—we must pledge to each other to fight the temptation to bring up any of the past arguments. Sadat and Begin dealt with these issues. Let us leave them behind as part of the past. Let us leave this room tonight vowing to come back tomorrow with this determination . . ."

"I agree." Zechariah lifted his cup as if to toast Gideon. He silently thanked Gideon for taking the initiative.

Had he done so, Farouk would have chastised him later.

"Let us not open the wounds of the past," Gideon said. "They have been bandaged adequately—"

"But not healed," Shaheen said. "Obviously."

"Yes, it is obvious that they have not healed *completely*," Zechariah said, stressing the last word and giving his most magnanimous smile to Shaheen. It was becoming more difficult to treat him with civility. "But at least they are bandaged. Let us leave them there. Allah heals."

"Let us break bread together tonight," Farouk said, now pacified with food and the lighter mood. "We Egyptians have a saying, 'Aish-wa-Milh,' that means when we eat bread and salt together, we can be friends."

"Ah, if only it were so easy," Shaheen said softly. Everyone studiously ignored his comment.

While the others sipped their coffee in silence, Nagila Levy tapped Shaheen Ahman lightly on the arm. She nodded, indicating she wanted him to follow her to the now-deserted balcony.

Shaheen came out, his eyes able to make out the silhouette of Nagila. She was beautiful, he admitted. He wondered if she were too attractive for this line of work. He immediately felt ashamed of himself for thinking that way. He had long supported the equality of women. "Yes, Ms. Levy. Or is it to be Nagila?"

"Call me what you like," she said calmly. "You always manage to find a way to insult me."

"Is that how you perceive my words?" He caught a whiff of her perfume. It reminded him of the soft fragrance of orange blossoms that he smelled when he walked in the garden with his adopted father.

Ignoring his answer, Nagila stepped forward, keeping her voice low and not wanting the others to hear. "I am asking you to stop."

"Stop? Stop speaking? Stop breathing? Stop drinking coffee?"

Even in the dark he could see her features tighten as she fought to retain self-control. "We came here to speak as one voice. You know that."

"I made no such agreement," Shaheen said.

"You intend to be disloyal to our government? To stand with the Arabs against—"

"I mean, I shall stand with my conscience and not settle for agreements that rob the poor—"

"You agreed to abide by the majority decision."

"I did, yes." He smiled and wished he could see her features clearly. For a second he wondered how he could be thinking about her as a woman when his responsibility lay primarily in negotiating for his government. "I have not changed my mind."

"Then why do you antagonize us? Me in particular?"

"You think I have singled you out?"

"I think you purposely throw barbs at me. Why? Because I am a woman? Because you resent—?"

"If I have singled you out," Shaheen said, "and I was unaware that I did so, I have a reason for what I am doing."

"That delights me. Please, may I also know?"

"Simple. You see only the economic gains of Israel. Not only for the state but for the wealthy. I wish to negotiate in a way that benefits the poor as well. Poor Israelis. Poor Egyptians."

"Poor Arabs!"

"Have it your way." He shrugged. "I care deeply about the poor and the downtrodden no matter what you may think or how you may interpret my position. I care about them, regardless of their origin—"

"Sorry, Shaheen. I know you genuinely mean—"

"But I do particularly antagonize you. Yes, yes, you are right. I admit that."

"But why?"

"I have trouble relating to two kinds of people. Those I dislike intensely and those I like too much."

"And which am I?"

Shaheen turned and walked back into the room.

F·I·V·E

"You think you have become bigger than Mother Russia?" taunted the barrel-chested man.

Joshua stared back at him, refusing the bait. He had flown into Moscow's Sheremetevo Airport that morning, and immediately entered into the Chaika limousine where Povin Michaelov waited for him.

"I received your message," Michaelov tried again. "I have waited for more than two hours."

Joshua ignored him, peering through the half-drawn curtains. He disliked riding in the slow-moving Chaika even though it stayed in the center lane, reserved for official vehicles. When they reached Arbatskaya Square, Joshua told the driver to stop. He exited from the vehicle with the bulletproof glass in the small windows. He did not turn around to see if Michaelov followed.

Joshua's footsteps crunched the snowy cobblestones with Michaelov hurrying to stay beside him. Joshua's even rhythm contrasted with the irregular thudding of the limping Michaelov.

"My left leg. In the Afghanistan thing—" He stopped

trying to explain. They walked in silence through the wide Arbat Boulevard in the gray mist of the city.

After passing the Lenin Library they turned into the wide side street. Michaelov's office, a kilometer from Red Square and across from the KGB headquarters, kept him out of the public sight, allowing him to operate without officials constantly passing his door. Just the way he liked it. From his office he looked upon the lean spire of Moscow University.

"As I told you," Joshua said without any trace of a smile, "it is time for me to leave the Soviet Union. I have accomplished my objectives here."

"Oh? So you think you can come in here and leave an hour later with exit papers? Like that, huh? You walk into my office and explain that you are now ready to leave and I must jump." He spat contemptuously.

"Not quite that simple," Joshua said. "However, I tell you this only because I am offering you the opportunity to leave as well."

"You *are* serious, then?"

"But, of course. Have you ever known me when I was not serious?"

The older man shook his head. He had not liked Joshua when he first met him as a five-year-old prodigy. Even then he saw the body of a child but the calculating mind of a man without human emotions.

"Then you are ready, Povin Michaelov?"

"No. Twenty years ago perhaps. But not now. No, I choose to stay here. I am getting on in my years and—"

"Then you do not understand, comrade. I have a need for you. Naturally I can find others. I prefer your expert services."

"I am flattered—"

"I do not flatter. I approach you because you are the best in your specialty. Nothing more."

The man raised his drooping eyelids and stared into the face of Joshua. "You have no human feelings, do you? You do not like me. You are without compassion or—"

"I do not like you. I do not dislike you. I selected you because of your suitable skills. More precisely, I came to Moscow today because I wish to make use of your considerable terrorist abilities."

"You know about—?"

"Of course. I know of all your activities since you blew up the American attache's car in Lebanon in 1968. If you like, I can quote to you details of your specifically planned terrorist activities. All 134 of them."

"That many? There have been that many?" He smiled, showing his missing back teeth that gave him a sinister look.

"I have not included your current but unexecuted plan for Thailand."

"How could you know? Only the *Troika* and I—"

"Come now, Povin Michaelov, you have no secrets from me. None at all."

The old man stared, his mouth open. Making a last attempt to retain his dignity, he said, "You are more diabolical than I had imagined."

"Your opinions of me mean nothing," Joshua said. "I have four projects for you. They must be completed within the next eight days."

"Eight days—impossible."

"Not at all. I have planned them. I shall put all the available resources at your disposal. I need only your personal touch and your, ah, employees."

"And if I turn this down?"

Joshua shook his head. "You will not. If you turn it down, you will have noplace in the world to go. When the Kremlin learns of your hand in the meltdown at Chern—"

The man cursed and stopped suddenly, breaking into laughter. "It is a pleasure to work for a demon worse than me. You are the better man because you have outwitted me. I accept."

"Naturally."

"And about the passport and exit permits, I assure you—"

Joshua waved him into silence and stared blankly into

the distance. He did not tell the man who worked as the unofficial terrorist for the Soviet government the purpose of his plan. They would both leave Russia. He would go to Israel. Povin Michaelov would perish in the execution of Joshua's last project.

On the second morning of the Egyptian-Israeli talks, camera clicks and bright TV lights swooped over the delegates when they arrived at the conference room in the Nile Hilton. Reporters repeated their frenzied demands of the previous day. The delegates faced the babble of questions from the reporters. "Have you made any progress?" "Is it true that Israel will return your land for 200 million American dollars?" "Is there any truth to the rumor of a joint ownership of the resort plan?"

Both Israeli and Egyptian delegates responded with forced smiles that to some, at least, felt like a cracking of the olive skin of their faces. They rushed past the journalists and photographers, none of them making any comment.

Shaheen Ahman and Nagila Levy walked twenty paces behind the others. They had started to talk socially after breakfast, and moved into voicing their differences. Both had grown angry and yet neither wanted the Egyptians to hear their arguments.

"—and I warn you," Nagila said. "You stay in line."

"In line? Behind you perhaps? Allowing you to usurp authority? Is that it?"

Both of them automatically stopped when deluged with reporters. The same questions poured out a second time.

"Please, please," Shaheen said, "we wish we could tell you everything, but we cannot."

"Can you tell us anything? Have you made progress?"

Shaheen stared at Nagila. "No, she staunchly rejects me."

An Egyptian reporter barred Nagila's path. "He is saying that you two talk romance while the other delegates argue over Taba? Is that it?"

Nagila glared at Shaheen. "Definitely not. You see, Mr. Ahman *thinks* he has a sense of humor." She moved around the reporter and raced ahead.

"Does that not prove my point?" Shaheen said as he followed Nagila to the room.

When Nagila, followed immediately by Shaheen, entered, Zechariah Kalif stood and watched them in silence. He did not like what he perceived happening between Ms. Levy and Shaheen Ahman. If only they had continued to disagree in front of the others. But, with an intuitive insight that came from years of negotiating with immotile faces, he sensed that something had developed between the two of them. An alliance? An agreement to thwart the Egyptians? He could not be sure. He would watch them carefully and find out.

He smiled benevolently at each of them, the way a kindly teacher might react to tardy pupils. "Day two begins. Back to the serious business. I think it might be well if we review—"

"Mr. Kalif," Gideon Wittstein said, "I talked to our Prime Minister over the phone last night. He continues to give us his full support. He is determined that we must find a solution to our dispute for the sake of our joint future—"

"Our President is just as determined!" Farouk hissed.

"But, of course," Gideon said. "Therefore, let us come up with acceptable plans that we can present to our respective governments by the end of this day."

"Taba cost us five billion dollars to develop," said Nagila. "At today's prices, it would—"

"Ah, yes, but you made profits from the tourists," said Zechariah.

"We remind you that we started with useless land," Shaheen said. "Furthermore, we gave employment to 1,052 Egyptians who would otherwise have had no income."

"We acknowledge that fact," Kalif said, hoping it sounded more gracious than he felt.

"Our government wishes to make an equitable settlement. I shall insist that, no matter how we conclude our
agreements, those 1,052 be retained in their present positions." He smiled at Nagila as if to say, "Is this being in line?"

When Nagila returned his smile, he winked. She turned
her head away.

"You cannot ask for such a guarantee," Farouk said.
"That is not yours to decide."

Shaheen leaned forward, his face only inches from the
rotund delegate. Farouk's garlic-flavored breath threatened
to overpower him and he pulled back slightly. "Sir, I have
known of your dealings elsewhere. You, in true Arab style,
advocate nepotism—"

"What? What insult do you make?" Farouk leaned
back and Kalif defined the word. Farouk smiled. "But of
course that is the case. We Egyptians must care for our own
families first."

"But what of those who have no wealthy families behind them? How will they live if you displace them?"

"We shall settle that in our own way. After all," Zechariah Kalif said, the smile plastered on his features, "they are
citizens of the United Arab Republic.

"They are also people. People who will starve!"

The debate started. It continued from mid-morning
until sunset. Finally they agreed to present to their respective governments the following solution: Israel would return
Taba to Egyptian sovereignty. Israel would manage the resort
for 50 percent of the profits. Israel would train, and the
Egyptians would guarantee to employ, a minimum of one
thousand people, based on their need for work and their
qualifications.

Shaheen had insisted that the Egyptians could not hire
anyone not fully trained by the Israelis. The Israelis, caring
nothing for Egyptian nepotism, would at least offer a fair
plan of employment. Shaheen had first struggled to convince
his own delegation in private session. Nagila Levy had, surprisingly, supported him early in his presentation. With Nagila as an ally, Shaheen easily won over the others.

Three days later both the Egyptian President and the Israeli Prime Minister met at the Taba resort to sign the agreement.

"We have resolved the final obstacle to a lasting peace between our two nations," said the Israeli Prime Minister as he mustered his most engaging smile for the cameras. "Today we can truly quote the words of our ancient prophet Isaiah, 'And they shall beat their swords into plowshares and their spears into pruning hooks.'

"Today we call upon Jordan and Syria to join in this peace movement so that the entire Middle East can experience tranquility as never before. We wish to see the fulfillment of that prophecy by the same ancient prophet who predicted, 'A highway out of Egypt to Assyria . . .' We, in Israel, long to be that highway that connects Egypt to Assyria."

Meanwhile, demonstrators in the streets of Tripoli roared, screamed, and threatened. Within minutes sheer hysteria gripped the mob. "Death to Egypt!" roared some. "Death to Israel!" replied a second group. "Death to America!" They screamed in unison while they paraded up and down Tareg al-Thourah, the main street of Tripoli.

Similar demonstrations took place in Teheran and throughout Iran. The crowds, soon out of control, smashed anything that belonged to foreigners from America or Western Europe. The people in both Iran and Libya, listening to harangues by Qadhafi and Khomeini, grew even more wild.

The following day the Libyan leader flew to Teheran for a consultation with the Iranian prelate. After two days of discussion, they issued a joint communique that shocked the world. Neutral Arab nations hastily considered their position. The Point-Four Manifesto, as they called it, appeared in every nation of the world.

THE POINT-FOUR MANIFESTO

1. The peace established between Egypt and Israel with the possibility of Jordan joining in violates the

principles of Islam. Allah has said in the Koran that the house of Islam must never sign a treaty with the house of war.

2. Egypt and all Egyptians, as well as Israelis and Americans, must be treated as enemies. This announcement constitutes a declaration of war upon these nations with the understanding that Muslims may without penalty kill any infidels wherever they find them.

3. Iran and Libya call upon all Muslims in Egypt, the United States, and the rest of the world to intensify the bombing and destroying of public places, and to consider those governments and their people as enemies of the true faith.

4. Libya and Iran, because of the cooperation with our true ally, the U.S.S.R., are now preparing nuclear bombs to rid this earth of infidels and those who have destroyed the true faith.

TO ALLAH BE ALL THE PRAISE, AND
GLORY TO ISLAM

S·I·X

Joshua Gad-Erianko sat in his private room, staring out the window. He put in a long-distance call on his private line—one of only six telephone lines in the entire Soviet Union that the KGB never bugged. He dialed direct to speak to Solomon Bronski, Israel's Prime Minister.

Bronski's secretary, upon learning the identity of the caller, explained in an eager voice that Mr. Bronski would return his call within minutes.

As Joshua waited, he turned toward the window and stared at the countryside. On the other side of the house, a dog howled and he knew the cook had arrived. Michaelov's employees would be completing their final project and returning to Moscow. It was late February, hardly a month for most people to travel. In the major cities, the streets would be cleared by now. The narrow ones would still be thick from last night's snow.

Joshua had been awake since daybreak. The single window in his private room faced so that he could see the first light of the Arctic dawn as it insinuated itself like a thief through the thick bars. He hated daybreak, preferring the hours of darkness that made him feel as if he alone existed in the world. Sometimes he drew the heavy drape and enveloped the room in darkness. Joshua thought better when nothing diverted his attention.

"Tchach," he mumbled in disgust. Bronski, while no fool, played his role as Prime Minister cautiously. Perhaps too cautiously.

Returning his thoughts to the issue at hand, Joshua felt twinges of impatience over the unfolding of events. Occasionally he wondered if he should not have shortened the process. Ah, well, he decided, it will come out the same. A few months makes little difference to me.

When the Prime Minister returned his call, Joshua Gad-Erianko plunged directly into his purpose for calling. "Since you and the Knesset have made me a citizen of Israel, I take my duty seriously—"

"We are delighted—"

"Therefore, Mr. Bronski, I wish to inform you of a plot against Israel by a coalition of seven South American states. They have quietly amassed atomic weapons and secretly trained soldiers for such a plan as this."

"We have heard rumors. Nothing the Mossad could verify—"

"Mr. Prime Minister, I can give you a plan to prevent their taking any further action. The elimination of four key people will totally sabotage their well-laid plans."

"Eliminate? You mean to imply that—?"

"Sir, please do not effect such shock in your voice. We are discussing the survival of Israel."

The Prime Minister swallowed before he replied. "Tell me what to do."

"You must have the unanimous consent of the Knesset in secret session. Once you assure me of that, I will tell you precisely how to eliminate these four people in a way that involves no danger to Israel and will guarantee the elimination of any further threat from the nations of South America."

"I shall call you back within the hour," Bronski said confidently.

"In much less than an hour," Joshua said after hanging up the phone. "Much less."

Apr 7, 1992. *Tel-Aviv:* Following an emergency session, Ethiopia announced its willingness to join the Iran-Libya-USSR alliance. Iraq is expected to follow. Saudi Arabia declares itself neutral despite threats of Muslim extremists.

Apr 7. *Berlin, East Germany:* Patriots marched through Tripoli today, chanting, "We will throw Israel into the sea." Soviet officials announced that they have begun to provide technical aid to Libya to enable them to mass-produce nuclear weapons.

Apr 8. *Washington, D.C.:* President Douglas Alexander Whilhite, at a special news conference with the Senate and House members present, warned the USSR that if they aid "Muslim terrorists, murderers, and extremists, we will have no option but to install nuclear missiles in Israel and Egypt to help them to defend themselves. America stands firmly with her friends and just as firmly for world peace."

In a barely-controlled voice, ABC anchorman Stanley Cott, Jr., shown with Beijing, China, in the background, spoke rapidly. "Yesterday, about 2:00 A.M. here, The People's Republic of China extended its borders and deposed all leaders in Taiwan, what they once again are calling Formosa. Their soldiers have marched into North and South Korea. Unconfirmed reports say they have also invaded India. They have offered Japan an opportunity to surrender or be annihilated by nuclear bombs. The government of Japan is now in session.

"Rumors fly constantly. Unofficially, Pakistan, Goa,

and Afghanistan have already sent envoys to Beijing, asking for peace."

He paused and the camera focused on the scene behind him of marching soldiers parading the streets, complete with armored vehicles, military bands, and crowds of flag-wavers.

The camera turned back to Cott. He was perspiring profusely. "I do not know if they will allow any further broadcasts. I can only say that I would never have expected this to happen. It is as if the nation has been waiting and preparing for this moment. Yet the rest of the world had no idea of their plans."

Almost immediately the face of Victoria Nichols flashed on the screen. "I am speaking from Montevideo. Two hours ago in the most unprecedented act of history, every nation on the continent of South America proclaimed its unification with Jose Garcia del Gato of Peru as the Premier of the entire continent, now called the United Republic of America.

"Unconfirmed reports say that the countries of Mexico, El Salvador, Costa Rica, and Nicaragua have all undergone bloodless coups within the past twenty-four-hour period. The new leaders have also proclaimed their nations as part of the new United Republic of America."

In Washington, President Douglas Alexander Whilhite sat with his Joint Chiefs of Staff. His grave features and sleepless eyes expressed his deep concern to everyone present.

"Thank you for coming." His blue eyes shifted slowly from face to face. "By the time this day finishes, we can expect our world to be divided into four distinct portions. The largest belongs to China, who now controls the entire South Pacific. Second, the coalition of the USSR, Iran, Libya, and Ethiopia, with all the Arab nations behind them—except Egypt. Third, Del Garcia controlling everything in the Western Hemisphere except the USA, Canada, the British Isles—"

"What about Europe—Western Europe?" General Marlin Freeman asked. "It seems to me that if we mobilize our forces with those nations now, without delay, we could—"

"Do what? There is nothing we can do to prevent what has already happened. Further, if we mobilize, don't you understand what that would mean? The other three federations would go on alert. *They might even take the initiative and strike us first.*

"Besides, if my information is correct, and I have no reason to doubt it, German chancellor Karl Schell has proclaimed himself President of all Western Europe along with all non-Arab countries of Africa and Australia. We expect to hear of the official capitulation of each of those governments within the next few hours."

He sighed and added, "That's the only good news we have, unfortunately. I have communicated with Chancellor Schell. We have verbally affirmed our mutual agreement to assist each other."

"You mean," General Freeman paused as the enormity of the situation struck him, "that leaves only us and Western Europe against the Muslim-Russian coalition and the Chinese world?"

"And likely the United Republic of America would oppose us as well."

"That's most of the powers of the world against us." Admiral Gerald Coker shook his head. "How can this be? How did it happen? What—?"

"Forget trying to figure out how it happened," the President interrupted. "The reality is that we were asleep at the wheel. At this point, our preservation lies in our alliance with Canada, Britain, and Western Europe." He sighed and pulled down a map. "That leaves only Israel, Egypt, and Lebanon not controlled—"

"Excuse me, Mr. President," said Benjamin Cartledge, the Secretary of State. "Lebanon has shaken off Israeli control. Arabs assassinated the Christian President—" Cartledge paused, unable to recall his name. "Anyway, Arabs are now running the government."

"What kind of world are we now living in?" the President asked bitterly. "What kind of world has this become?"

As he posed the question verbally, others were silently wondering how this could have happened. Despite the best espionage system in the world, the United States had detected no movement toward these three alliances.

It had been done in total secrecy.

S·E·V·E·N

Most people would have overlooked the news item if it had not radically changed the world's economy: A team of world-renowned geologists, on a grant from the Gad-Erianko Foundation, discovered malgamite in Israel.

The New York Times carried the item at the back of the first section:

> A team of renowned geologists and scientists, attempting to develop a means of providing abundant and inexpensive fuel to replace fossil fuels, has discovered a new source they call malgamite.
>
> Extracted from limestone, yet found in abundance only in Israel's Negev Desert with minute amounts in Jordan, malgamite provides the necessary ingredient for a new form of fuel.
>
> Through a revolutionary process, scientists claim they can extract the ore with no serious

effect on the ecological balance. Israeli soil contains the world's largest and most accessible supply. Scientists estimate that the malgamite potential in Israel would provide fuel for the world's transportation needs for approximately 500 years.

Most readers bypassed the small article. Oil producers in America and their counterparts across the world ignored the item because they had known of the discovery for over a month. Stanley Cott, Jr. reported from Beijing: "China's burgeoning automobile industry immediately began the process to convert to malgamite fuel. Their cheaply made but highly reliable new cars flooded the western world, virtually wiping out markets previously controlled by the Japanese.

"Their revolutionary vehicles require virtually no parts replacement, no need for fossil fuels, cause no environmental pollution, and operate at an average cost of under two American cents a mile. The Chinese are prepared to revolutionize the transportation industry, making conventional vehicles obsolete within three years. In China-dominated countries, governments declared all fossil-fuel engines, including airplanes and ships, illegal in four years.

"By making an elaborate financial and nonaggression agreement with Israel, China has guaranteed itself a major place in the international transportation industry. The Chinese, in turn, have allowed limited use of malgamite by the Russian-dominated nations. The United States, paying prices almost double that of the Russians, has entered headlong into the new venture."

The nation of Israel now had more money than it had ever thought possible. Unlike some of the Arab nations that had received money in abundance and used it profligately, the Israeli Knesset maintained strict control of finances and on all mining of malgamite. Using a highly complex system, they allowed all citizens to profit from the financial windfall.

"We can control the transportation industry," Solomon Bronski said. "The entire world must come to our door and deal with us."

"Just one thing," Bronski's clerk said. "We don't own all of it. The malgamite-enriched land."

"We don't? Where else have they found malgamite?"

"No, not that," he said shaking his head. "I realized only this morning that 12 percent of the malgamite-productive land belongs to Joshua Gad-Erianko."

"We can certainly not allow—"

"Sir," the clerk interrupted, "a few months after the Knesset gave Mr. Gad-Erianko honorary citizenship, you may recall that he asked for the privilege of purchasing land in Israel."

"Unusable land, he said. A place no one wanted. It was a gesture—"

"We sold him a large tract in the Negev." The clerk unrolled a map and pointed to the area circled in black.

"That was more than three years ago . . . before anyone knew about malgamite or had the slightest idea—" Bronski shook his head. "How could he have known?" And then to answer his own question, he said, "He did not know, naturally. Just one of those strange things that happen." Yet his mind did not rest. It was too much of a coincidence.

"Bring me his letter," Bronski said. The clerk, in anticipation, had a copy of it ready for him. Bronski skimmed the letter and read the innocent-enough request. Gad-Erianko had asked for permission to buy any portion of unwanted land, and "I would certainly not mind if shepherds allowed their flocks to graze there. I have no desire to build or to grow anything. I wish to own a portion of land that ties me to the heritage of my fathers."

The Knesset, using their powers, sold him a totally useless portion of land, confirming that he would never be allowed to construct any permanent building on the site, and that the shepherds who had long used it for grazing would continue to do so. As a concession they had stated that the soil and anything that lay beneath it would be the property of Joshua Gad-Erianko.

Prime Minister Bronski had considered that an especially brilliant move at the time. Over a twenty-year period, a multiplicity of teams had surveyed the very land they sold to Joshua Gad-Erianko. Every survey declared the land contained nothing but limestone. They found nothing of commercial value.

Joshua Gad-Erianko had accepted the purchase price of one million American dollars and had generously added another million "as an act of appreciation."

When Bronski realized what the Knesset had done, he shook his head. "Who would have guessed that land would be useful for anything?" As he asked the question aloud, a serious doubt of Joshua Gad-Erianko's integrity slipped into the back of his mind. He bent forward and, using his desk calculator, estimated that Joshua Gad-Erianko would earn the two million dollar purchase price back within six months. A shrewd bargain.

Immediately Bronski rejected such thoughts. Joshua had proven to be nothing but the greatest friend Israel had in the world. He, of all people, would certainly not play a double-sided game.

"Do you realize the income he will derive from his land?" the clerk asked. "In this year alone—"

Bronski waved his hand. "It does not matter; we shall pass a law that taxes private ownership and assess it highly."

"You cannot do that in his case," the clerk pointed out. "You yourself, when you heard of Gad-Erianko's generosity, agreed that no taxes *of any kind* would ever be levied against his land."

"Hmm, so I did," Bronski said dejectedly. He also assumed that a kindly man like Gad-Erianko would likely allow for some kind of renegotiation.

"We are in the most excellent financial shape since we began in 1948," Solomon Bronski stated the next day on public television. "We have never been stronger as a nation than we are right now. We are now one of the wealthiest nations in the world. We no longer will need to depend on financial aid from others."

Despite his cheerful words and optimistic smile, he had two concerns. First, the nagging suspicion that Joshua Gad-Erianko had known of malgamite or anticipated it. He had purchased the land three years before the first experiments with malgamite had begun. Despite the logical answers Bronski gave himself, the niggling question would not leave his brain. He felt guilty and uncharitable for having such thoughts.

His second concern he dared not voice either. Israel owned the world's greatest deposit of limestone-enriched malgamite, but it would take only one invasion from a superpower to grab it from them. With four great powers aligned around the world, any one of them could control the economic future of the world.

The Prime Minister no longer slept well. Had he known, neither did others in the cabinet who silently shared his concerns. Although they kept their faces smiling to the public at large, they worked feverishly in private to prevent the takeover of their nation. They had concluded years earlier that Israel held an indefensible geographic position. Any major power could easily destroy them. Their secret to victory lay in pitting one major power against another. And, as they learned through the discovery of malgamite, they could use this product as the great bargaining chip.

Their willingness to sell malgamite to the Chinese gave them protection against any Russian-Arab takeover. Their ongoing friendship with the United States held the United Republic of America in line. Temporarily, at least, they were safe.

Bronski knew that the situation could change at a moment's notice.

Joshua Gad-Erianko was making certain that it changed.

E·I·G·H·T

The heat blistered the already tanned skins of those who lived in Tel Aviv. Nagila Levy, oblivious of the azure blue sky and the soft ocean breezes, felt chilled inside. She could not figure out how her project had failed.

She walked mechanically toward the university library, her mind weighted down by the impending danger to Israel, and her own role in reversing it. A week earlier her network, fully functional, had started to transmit the first vital information. Then it stopped. Everything fell apart.

Nagila Levy, at twenty-nine, had worked hard to overcome the prejudices against her gender, as well as the suspicion of some that the American CIA had recruited her to spy against Israel's Mossad. She had worked energetically and faithfully. As a result of her valued input in the Taba Accord, she had received the promotion for which she had been trained and to which she aspired. She ran her own team of agents as well as agents-in-place.

Although officially part of the delegation involved with Egypt, Nagila Levy's real work had been with the Mossad.

Even during her college years in America, she had worked for the Mossad. Her dossier contained three letters of merit from her student days overseas.

She had reveled in her first major assignment to recruit high-level nationals in Russia already in strategic positions. Because of their earned positions and accessibility to confidential or secret information, they could warn the Mossad. They would take no active part in circumventing the USSR's plans to invade or to destroy Israel. Yet their knowledge proved invaluable to the Mossad in their decisions.

Weeks before Nagila had flushed with pleasure when she announced to her supervisor her well-placed team.

"It has every chance to work well," he said.

She had made these contacts during her graduate studies in Germany. She worked part-time for the Israeli Ambassador and turned up as a hostess at many diplomatic social events. She had worked carefully through trusted contacts. She had expected nothing but success.

Her agents-in-place had done a splendid job on behalf of Israel for more than a year. Then it fell apart. Exposure. Not as agents, not even together. Yet three of them within a period of weeks disturbed her. Not only did it curtail her supply of information, it left her wondering how much the KGB knew.

Nagila decided to go to the university library because she expected it to be nearly deserted. Right now she wanted to get away from everyone. She had lost three of her five top agents. Those three men should never have been exposed. The Mossad had contacted them more than twenty years earlier, paid them generous sums, waiting until they reached levels of leadership where they could help.

Someone had leaked the information of her agents-in-place. She had no other explanation. Worse, Nagila Levy had no idea who had betrayed them or why.

She forced herself to push aside her depressive

thoughts. After all, she reminded herself, these agents had known the dangers they faced. It still did not make it any easier for her. It made the situation hopeless for Israel. She had counted on them to help counteract the Arab-Russian threat against Israel.

Nagila Levy squared her shoulders and demanded control from herself. She must figure out new methods of infiltration. She had only two high officials left—neither knowing of the other—and both having access to the same information. One provided an excellent check on the other. All this, and she knew it still was not enough. She needed to uncover the right people for other strategic levels of the Soviet power structure.

For a moment her thoughts reverted to the Arab threat. So far she had received only advance information. She had not yet figured out defensive methods. That fact scared her as she sensed that the Arab-Russian alliance would soon take offensive action.

Newly installed loudspeakers broke through the normal silence of the day, disrupting Nagila's concentration as she walked. The Knesset had finally decided that they must tell the citizens the truth of what was awaiting them. They replayed the Prime Minister's broadcast. Nagila had heard the message twice since arising that morning. The Knesset would continue to have it played for forty-eight hours.

As his first words penetrated her consciousness, Nagila felt tears rush to her eyes. She had known and had ignored the implications. She had chosen not to think or to feel anything. But now, in an unguarded moment, the words reached her deepest level of consciousness. It was true: Israel stood alone. Israel against the world.

The Prime Minister's speech attempted to galvanize the nation. Those old enough to remember the experiences of places such as Buchenwald and Dachau saw the threat as one more attempt by the *goyim* of the world to destroy God's special people.

"We shall survive!" Bronski's voice said with unshakable authority. "We shall remain in our land and we shall fight to the last man, woman, and child! We will not be defeated. Nations have risen against us for thousands of years and they have ultimately failed! We shall stand alone if our allies do not come forth and march beside us. But we wish the world to know that we, the people of Israel, will never, never surrender!

"We shall survive! God is with us. Do not give up heart . . ."

Nagila did not want to hear any more. She feared that she would break down with a flood of tears. Time to cry later, she told herself. Now is the time to work.

She ran the last twenty yards to the library and rushed inside. She forced herself to walk through the main section and into the reference room. She picked up books at random and placed herself and her papers in an unobtrusive corner. She spread out the books, giving the impression she was doing serious research.

Nagila had found it helpful to get alone in times like this. She allowed her brain to come up with ideas—preposterous or not—and write them hurriedly on paper. After half an hour she would then go over the ideas, one at a time. She quickly came up with twenty-two ideas, but in the refinement process, rejected most of them. She filled sheets of lined paper with her notes.

Twice tears came near the surface, but Nagila willed them back. Now is not the time to despair, she told herself. Now is the time to plan and to prepare.

If we can only figure out enough ways to protect ourselves, we can survive. I know we can. Nagila tried to direct her thoughts in positive directions. Several times she wondered how her ancestors felt when waiting for the Assyrians or Babylonians to overpower them. Or how they stood up centuries later when the Romans surrounded them.

She paused from her tortured thoughts to pray to Yahweh, the covenant-making God of all Jews. God had called them to be a special people. To God she must now appeal for wisdom. *If you will help us, we can outwit our enemies and survive. Help us, your special people.*

When she finished praying, Nagila opened her eyes and saw Shaheen Ahman coming toward her. He raised a hand in mild greeting and smiled.

She gave him the briefest of nods, not wanting to encourage him to come closer. Yet, she realized in a moment of truth, he had disturbed her. Shaheen frequently disrupted her thoughts—and she found it uncomfortable.

He was handsome with his tall, straight body and almond-shaped eyes. His quick mind had always impressed her and she felt she usually came off second best in their verbal exchanges. Nagila had been aware since the conference over Taba that she liked Shaheen more than she ought. He was a Palestinian Arab who advocated communism and she was a neo-orthodox Jew and capitalist. Neither of them would ever cross the line.

Nagila bent her head, showing her intense interest in work. She breathed more slowly when she realized that Shaheen had not come closer. For an hour longer she forced herself to keep her vision focused on her immediate area. In one careless moment, however, she glanced across the room.

Shaheen sat directly across from her, holding a book in front of him but obviously staring at her. He smiled.

Hardly aware of what she had done, Nagila returned the smile, then dropped her gaze. Seconds later she heard the distinctive sound of Shaheen's footsteps as he approached her study table. This time she glanced up and into his face. When Shaheen smiled, she realized that his whole face lit up. She dropped her head again to signal that she chose to ignore him. She could still sense his presence and her discomfort grew.

"Heard the great news?" he asked.

Nagila checked herself, refusing to allow him to upset her. "What great news?" she asked in a flat voice, her arm covering the paper she wrote on.

"The great news that Israel finally will no longer be a Jewish state." His eyes focused on her. "But a state for all people or any religion—"

Nagila looked up at him and turned her face back to

her paper. "Nothing happening these days surprises me." She wanted her voice to sound indifferent. She would not allow him the satisfaction of knowing that his words had upset her.

"Do you mean that finally you agree with me that Islamic communism is the only hope for the world?"

"No, I don't mean that! I mean that our prophets foretold this sort of thing hundreds of years ago."

"Is that so? Just what did your prophets say?" He leaned on the table, lowering his voice although only the two of them were in the reference room.

"It surprises me that a man of your great knowledge would not know," Nagila said. "I suggest you read Ezekiel chapters 38 and 39 for a starter. But of course it would not make any difference to you, would it?"

"One never knows," he said. "The thirst for knowledge—for truth and understanding—these matters keep us curious and open."

She nodded. One part of Nagila wanted him to move away from her, to leave. Another part of her wanted him to stay and talk.

"One more thing," he said.

"Yes?"

"Would you have dinner with me tonight? You could read the words of your prophets to me. That is, if we found our conversation at a lull."

"I'm busy. Far too busy."

"Perhaps I could help you complete your task then—"

"Besides," Nagila said, ignoring his interruption, "a man of your intellectual abilities should have no trouble reading and understanding. That is, since you are eager for truth."

"But of course you are correct." He smiled and gave her a mock salute. "I thought only that a person of your spiritual and mental acumen might offer insight that we benighted Arabs could grasp. How could we possibly understand? After all, your God rejected us and made you the chosen people. Or don't your prophets say that?"

Nagila's clear eyes looked into his. "Shaheen, you're trying to bait me. I cannot find such things humorous when the world—our world—is at the brink of chaos."

A seriousness spread across his face. "It is at times like these that we *must* turn to laughter and humor. If not, what else do we have to take our minds from the potential deaths of millions of people?" He turned and walked from her table.

Nagila felt the sting of his words. She still did not know Shaheen well, but enough to know that he was a man of deep compassion for human life. He cared deeply about people, all people and not just other Muslims. His final words had thrown her into confusion. She sighed. Shaheen had managed once again to come out on top.

That afternoon the Knesset met in emergency session. They had received word that the major powers were amassing their forces, surrounding Israel on three sides. Ships were racing across the Mediterranean to form a blockade around Israel's ports.

The air forces of Iran and Iraq, adequately supplied by the Soviet Union, would occupy the airspace so that no plane could go in or out of Israeli aerial territory.

Under Soviet General Gorki, the cooperative nations had scheduled the massive attack to begin in fifty-six hours.

Prime Minister Bronski stared down at the assembled members. Memories flooded his thoughts as he considered the ominous situation before them. Hopeless. Utterly hopeless. Was this always to be the fate of the Jews? As hopeless now as it had been for his people half a century earlier.

Is this the way it must always be for us? Must we always be hated? Threatened? The situation, although different than it had been during his childhood, seemed the same in many ways. In German-occupied Europe the Jews never had a chance. He could not see that they had much of a chance now.

While he waited for the session to begin, his mind

pushed back the elapsed fifty years. It seemed as if it had happened only days before. He remembered when the Germans erected walls around the Warsaw ghetto—for "your protection," they stated but fooled no one. Later, intent on liquidating every Jew, troops surrounded the long-blockaded area, with every inch of the walls fortified by German artillery.

It had been a hot day like this one when the Germans came inside the walls of the ghetto. Methodically they searched each building, shooting first, taking no survivors, wanting nothing except to rid themselves of "Jewish lice." And Solomon Bronski, a mere ten years old, had escaped.

Yes, he had escaped, but what a price he had paid. It was a terrible secret that Solomon Bronski had lived with—and remembered—every day of his life.

N·I·N·E

Joshua Gad-Erianko received the second message from Prime Minister Solomon Bronski. If not delivered with enthusiasm, at least it contained the important summons to come to Israel.

Over the telephone Joshua forewarned Bronski of the impending invasion, giving him an additional twenty-four-hours' notice. Knowing Bronski's nature, Joshua had correctly perceived that the Israeli leader would not know what action to take and, consequently, would do nothing to take advantage of the information.

Joshua had not expected him to do anything. The message had one purpose—to make clear to Israel's leaders that in Joshua Gad-Erianko lay their hope for deliverance.

At the end of their brief conversation, Joshua Gad-Erianko said simply, "I shall arrange to arrive at Tel Aviv tomorrow. Is that satisfactory?"

"Yes," Bronski said, "but what could you do for us? Meaning no disrespect, but you are, after all, only one man and—"

"You perhaps know the story of King Saul's fear when confronted by the Philistines? Only one person stood up fearlessly against them and willingly opposed the giant Goliath. The people called it a miracle."

"You are such a miracle?" Bronski asked with skepticism in his voice.

"Sir, Israel is in a desperate situation—"

"I know that—"

"What would it take to save Israel?"

"A miracle!"

"I shall arrive tomorrow at midday."

Nagila was scared. Her legs felt rubbery and she wanted to get off the street. An irrational idea propelled her onward. If she could get into her car and drive to her own apartment she would be safe. She knew that considering anywhere in Israel as safe was irrational. Yet she had to do something to alleviate this fearful anxiety that would not let her go.

Nagila hurried, aware that rumors and bits of information had spread all through the city of the soon-coming invasion. Around her she saw business as usual. And yet it was not usual. The voices sounded shrill and the activities too frenzied. People who had previously waved and called out greetings seemed not to see her. Their faces, plastered with smiles, held a tightness about them. They went through the mechanics of daily routine, but fear gripped them, filling their minds with nothing else. At least I'm not the only one who's afraid, she thought.

Perhaps, Nagila reasoned, the common strangling fear affected everyone differently. She slowed her pace, determined not to give in to the hysterical fear bottled up inside.

Ordinarily she might have stopped to buy vegetables on her way home. Today she had no appetite and she did not want to make the effort of small talk with the vendors. She sensed that their forced gaiety held a fear deeper than her own.

"You notice it, too, do you?"

She whirled around. Shaheen walked a few paces behind her. "They are frightened," he said. "They try to ignore it or to treat it philosophically, of course—"

"So now you are a psychiatrist!" As soon as she said the words, she heard the harshness in her own tone. "Forgive me. That was unkind—"

"Everyone's frightened. No need to apologize."

"Even you? A Muslim?"

"Bullets and bombs do not understand the difference between the children of Allah and the infidels."

"You could leave Jerusalem. Go back to—to wherever you're from."

"I suppose I could," he said. "Except that I have no place to go. I was born near the Golan Heights. I could not get within a mile of a home that no longer exists anyway."

"I keep saying unkind things to you, Shaheen. I don't know why. I don't usually—"

"It does not matter." He took her arm and propelled her forward.

Nagila did not resist. The strength of his hand and the power of his fingers digging into her skin made her suddenly aware of herself. The presence of another calm person and his easygoing talk soothed Nagila. She snapped out of her own frightened stupor.

"I don't know why I allow this fear to make me sound hysterical," Nagila said. "Our people have lived with fears and bombs and—"

"Yet this time . . ." He picked up the pace. "I want you out of here—away from this."

"Is there any place in Jerusalem or Israel where we might be safe from the fear? Safe from destruction? Safe from—?"

"Nagila! Stop!" His voice snapped at her. "Do not give in to this."

"What should I do?" Tears filled her eyes as they approached the Temple. She saw a large mass of people on the outside. Some knelt, praying aloud. Nagila had never seen so many people at the Temple before.

"It would seem to me," Shaheen said, "that if you are a good Jew and you believe in your God, is this not the proper time to show your faith?" He propelled her across the street, hurrying from the cries behind them.

"You're trying to anger me? You think I have no real faith—?"

"I think you are too frightened to understand what you are doing. I want you to get hold of yourself, Nagila. I am with you. Surely Yahweh is with you, too."

Nagila stopped, turned, and stared up into his eyes. "Thank you, Shaheen, for reminding me." She shook her head. "Strange that a Muslim must remind me of the faith of my people in this time of crisis."

"Crisis? The word sounds somehow inadequate for the present situation. How about holocaust?"

"It is all the same for us, you know. We have long known suffering and have come to expect it."

"Why do you Jews do that to us?"

"Do what?"

"Speak and behave as if you are the only people who have ever suffered. You are so filled with your sense of self-pity that you do not know—perhaps do not care—about other—"

"We know Hitler killed six million of us—"

"And what about thirty million Russians—good, peasant Russians—systematically murdered under Joseph Stalin only a few years before Hitler? Most of them were not Jews. Did you cry for them, Nagila Levy? Did you ever feel their pain?"

"I—I wasn't born then."

"Nor were you born until after the holocaust in Europe!"

"Now you want me to feel guilty on top of all—?"

"No, Nagila," he said. "I want you to put life into perspective. You suffer. We all suffer. If you think Muslims have not suffered, you do not know history. If you think anyone is exempt from pain—"

"I suppose you're right—"

"Forgive me, Nagila, I have taken out my own frustration and anger on you."

Nagila stopped again and they looked intently at each other. She saw pain in his eyes and it touched her. "Shaheen, I am sorry, too—"

"No, it's not your fault. My family, a Jewish family that raised me, said the same things. Growing up I heard them. Day after day after day they cried and wept and groaned about the destruction of Jews. When I tried to speak about the suffering of *goyim* they wouldn't listen. My father who could be kind and tender, who could weep in moments of sorrow, would harden himself and say, 'God's curse' or something like that."

"But they raised you?"

"Oh, yes. And they loved me in their way. I am grateful to them. But, Nagila, they could never understand the suffering of other people. One day I showed my father the history book of the Hungarian revolt against Russian domination in the late 1950s. May I tell you what he replied?" Without waiting for her answer, Shaheen said, "He told me that I should not trouble my mind about such unimportant things."

Shaheen's eyes filled with tears and he tried to blink them away. "He could never conceive of the truth that they were human beings like himself."

In that fraction of time, Nagila Levy's heart grasped the pain and compassion of this handsome Muslim who stood in front of her. Until that moment she had never thought of his suffering. She had known of the death of his adopted parents by fanatic Arabs. She had heard of the death of his beautiful wife, Zaynab. Yet she had never connected the loss and suffering to Shaheen Ahman. Perhaps, she realized, because she had never cared to know. Or even because Shaheen had never allowed her to get close enough to penetrate his defensive wall.

"Shaheen, I am sorry." Her hand, in a gesture of sympathy, touched his left arm. Instinctively he responded with his right hand clasping hers. She felt herself drawn to him and their eyes locked. In that instant she intuitively knew that, as long as they remained alive, they would no longer be enemies. She understood him in a way she could never have described in words. "Truly, I am sorry."

"I know."

In Nagila's awareness, Shaheen also recognized a kinship they had never shared before. He felt a stirring inside himself, emotions he had thought himself incapable of since the death of his beloved Zaynab.

Shaheen felt his breathing constrict as he stared at the face of Nagila Levy, and yet his thoughts moved backward in time to Zaynab. He decided he could like this woman and that liking her would not make him untrue to Zaynab's memory. They could be friends, perhaps good friends. Yet Zaynab would always hold a place inside him that no other woman would ever dislodge.

"I never thought about your troubles before," Nagila said, aware of the quiver in her voice.

Shaheen bent toward her, surprised at his own desire to kiss her, to touch her soft skin.

"Shaheen! Shaheen!" A voice from across the street called. The traffic filling the streets blocked the view so that it took several seconds before they saw the tall figure waving at them.

Shaheen waved back. "Come!" he said to Nagila, taking her by the arm and edging toward the curb. "I want you to meet someone."

"Who is that?"

"Nasief Habib. But to everyone he is simply Nasief. An old friend and a fine adversary. However, you'll like him." Without waiting for her further questions, Shaheen led her as they darted between the vehicles that crawled in the bustling afternoon traffic.

Nagila Levy stared at a rather ordinary looking older man. His clothes hung loosely as if he had purchased them two sizes too large. She walked beside Shaheen to meet him, unaware that he would change the direction of her life.

Bronski sat with the phone in his hand for a long time. He experienced a newer, deeper level of fear in the pit of his stomach. The news of the amassing of troops around Israel numbed him. In his mind he saw them as he had seen row after row of German soldiers marching through the streets of Warsaw during his childhood. No one who lived behind the ghetto wall had expected to survive. Many despaired, crying out that Poland would never know freedom from the Nazis. But the Germans melted into the past. Surely it would be the same with these enemies.

He wanted to believe in Israel's survival. The threat of annihilation concerned him, frightened him. But it did not compare with the terror he experienced when he thought of Joshua Gad-Erianko.

After their conversation, Bronski allowed his mind to retrace everything they said. The man had made no threats. He had not forced himself on Israel. For the past dozen years he had become a true patriot of Israel, winning the respect of the entire nation. The Mossad had checked him thoroughly and had never produced anything to his discredit. Yet something about his voice—ominous and a portent of greater evil than the amassing of troops on Israel's border—made him know this man was the greater enemy.

Momentarily, Bronski laughed at himself. Maybe I'm jealous because of all he's done . . . all he can do.

Jealousy? Is that it? No, he decided, something stronger, more powerful. He brooded several more minutes, trying to label the emotion that knotted his stomach and filled his stomach and throat with bile. The emotion had a name, but he did not want to say it to himself.

His contacts in Russia had investigated Joshua Gad-Erianko and found him to be above reproach. He recalled an old proverb: Can a man sleep with dogs and not have fleas? Joshua Gad-Erianko moved in the highest circles and personally knew some of the most unscrupulous people in the world. That had always troubled Bronski.

As a young man, Gad-Erianko had visited Israel on several occasions. He had given the nation help in a variety of ways, from lavish financial contributions to private information that allowed Israel to take advantage in world trade. He had advised them in the design and production of the

Merkab, which had just become the world's most efficient vehicle run on malgamite. The Merkab had placed Israel as the number three auto manufacturer, behind China and the United States.

On and on ran the record of Joshua Gad-Erianko's achievements and contributions for the good of Israel. He could detect nothing that hinted at doing it for his own good. The Russian-Jew had never asked for anything in return. Polls in Israel showed that Joshua Gad-Erianko had, for the past four years, been the most admired man in the world.

"Perfect," Bronski muttered. "Too perfect and too good. Surely—" He could not say the words that his suspicions had aroused.

He laid the telephone in its cradle and pushed himself back from his desk. Gad-Erianko would arrive the next day. Bronski had only hours to see that the proper welcome awaited him. He leaned forward to press the button to call his secretary. As he did so, Bronski uttered the one word he had tried to hide from his consciousness.

The one word was fear.

T·E·N

Two days before Joshua Gad-Erianko arrived in Israel, the American President debated with himself and his staff over sending aid to Israel. For more than a week he had stalled, waiting for what he called "the right wind to send out the fleet."

If America sent aid and the Arab-Russian coalition took over the production of malgamite, inevitably the new owners would treat them unfavorably. The aid they promised would not be enough, by itself, to save Israel unless America declared war. The country had opposed the draft and the use of American soldiers for more than twenty years. This step would make him the most unpopular President in thirty years.

The dark rings under Douglas Alexander Whilhite's eyes showed clearly that he had not slept well for a week. His divided staff only confused him. Congress railed at him for his lack of declaring himself. No matter which way he went, his growing number of opponents—even among his own party—would escalate.

When coming into office two years earlier in the election of 1992, Whilhite reaffirmed America's support of Israel following the tradition of his predecessors in the Oval office for the last fifty years. If he remained true to his promises, he would have given the order a week ago to send American ships and troops to Israel. The polls showed enough sympathy for Israel that he could even have asked Congress to declare war.

Despite his powerful physical size and a persuasive personality, Douglas Alexander Whilhite was a coward and had always been a coward. He feared a nuclear holocaust. He feared that the rhetoric of the Soviets and Arabs indicated the prelude to immediate war. He feared the ire of the American public. He feared his name would go down in history as a failure. And above all other things, Douglas Alexander Whilhite wanted his name to go down in history as one of the great Presidents.

"Mr. President, sir," Benjamin Cartledge said, "I refuse to delay." The Secretary of State spoke with a firmness the President had never heard from his long-time associate before.

"I'm not sure—"

"You must give the order. Today."

"Ben, what if—"

"Mr. President, not 'what if' at all. You must. It is your duty." The short, slightly built man started to walk away but paused, turned, and faced the President. "I have been a good Secretary of State."

"You have been more capable and efficient than I had the right to expect."

Cartledge held up his hand. "I wasn't asking or hinting for a compliment. I want you to understand that I am speaking to you as firmly as my office allows. Mr. President, I plead with you to send help to Israel. We owe it to them."

"It's far more complex—"

"Sir, forget the Russians and the Arabs and the Chinese and everyone else. Sometimes we have to ignore expediency and follow our sense of integrity. And honor."

"The situation has become so many-faceted," Whilhite said. "I must be careful—"

"No, sir," Cartledge interrupted. "That's not the case!"

A startled President gasped. The man had never spoken to him that way before.

Cartledge's face reddened. He focused his attention on his shoes and said softly, "Unless you act with courage and integrity, Mr. President, you will have my resignation by noon tomorrow."

Douglas Whilhite blanched. "Ben, I've known you for more than thirty years. We've been through a lot together—"

"Sir, with all due respect, for thirty years I've also known how scared you are at making tough decisions. You prefer to wait until it's out of your hands or someone makes the choice for you and you get credit for your grand strategy. I've been around to pick the fall-guy when you made bad decisions. I've covered your tail hundreds of times and never complained, have I?"

"You've been loyal and—"

"Today I'm giving it to you straight. If you don't send aid, I shall personally leak to the press—unofficially so that no one can trace it to me—exactly why I resigned. I can no longer support a man who cares more about how history regards him than he does about integrity and doing what he believes is right."

"I cannot believe that you, of all people, would talk to me like this." The deep-blue eyes hardened. He dropped his hands into his lap so that Cartledge would not see them shaking.

"Mr. President, I can't believe I've waited so long to finally say it." Cartledge, emboldened, stepped forward and leaned across the desk. With his head only a foot from the President's, he said, "I won't cover for you if you fail on this one."

Whilhite opened his mouth, but no words came for several seconds. He shook his head slowly. "You would— you really would—do that?"

"I would and I shall."

The President continued to shake his head. "Ben, Ben, you always know what needs to be done. Don't you ever have doubts about the rightness of your decisions?"

"Often. But I refuse to let myself be paralyzed with fear, sir."

"How dare you—"

A slight smile crept across Ben's face. "Sir, you are the one who reminded me of our thirty years of knowing each other. Surely that entitles me to tell you what I think. At least once." He walked toward the door.

"Ben, how do you know what's right? If I send in those troops and the Russians use their nuclear missiles—"

Ben came back to the President's desk and leaned forward. "Mr. President, let me tell you something." Ben pulled a chair close to the desk and sat down. "You don't know much about me personally. You've never cared."

"Ben, of course I care. You are like a family member."

"No, Mr. President, you are a man committed to your career. You are at your best when you stand before an audience. You are a man who exudes power. You are also a lousy human being when it comes to relating to people as individuals."

President Whilhite wanted to interrupt and to argue. He did not only because he knew the man spoke the truth.

"When I was a boy of fifteen, I had a religious conversion. I promised God and myself that I would always try to do what I believed was right, regardless of the consequences."

"Admirable—"

"And for a long time I did that. Then, by the time I was elected to the Senate, I had begun to deny my integrity for the expedient. It has to be done for the good of the country, for the good of the party, for the good of somebody, I told myself."

Ben leaned back in his chair and said softly, "I am not blaming you, sir. I made the choices. I covered for you and I did anything necessary. And you know that—"

"I certainly do—"

"But that's changed, sir. A few weeks ago I became so disgusted with my life I wanted to die. I hated what I had become. And you know what pulled me out of it? My granddaughter. She's in fifth grade, Mr. President. She lives in Pennsylvania and I visited with her. She said to me that she thought I was the most wonderful grandfather in the world."

Ben Cartledge put his hand up to prevent the President's interruption. "She read me a report she made on the Secretary of State and one simple sentence in that report says, 'And he would not do anything wrong because he is a good man.' That statement hit me deep. And frankly, sir, I have decided that I am going to be that kind of man."

"Ben, Ben, I'm delighted for your self-examination. I believe that you will make an even finer Secretary of State because of your renewed—"

"Don't treat me like one of the voters," Cartledge said. "I have renewed my integrity and my faith in God. I have promised myself that I will speak up when it is appropriate. I will do what I believe is right."

"Regardless of the consequences? Without considering that you may be wrong?"

"Sir, as part of your campaign pledge, you made a commitment to Israel. Two months after taking office, you publicly declared to Israel that the American people would stand by them. You have a debt of honor."

"Many things have changed in the past two years."

"All the more reason for you to show stability. *And integrity.*"

"Sometimes I wonder if *you* ought to have been elected President." He forced a smile.

"The temptation to lie and double deal are heavy enough for the Secretary of State. I would never make it as President."

Whilhite's eyes hardened and he felt the anger building up inside. His stomach muscles tightened and a vein in his right temple started to twitch. Pulling together all his reserves of willpower, he held his emotions back. He breathed deeply several times and mumbled, "Send the aid. And may God forgive me if I'm wrong."

"May God forgive you for delaying so long, sir!"

E·L·E·V·E·N

Solomon Bronski, through the Minister of State, arranged the grand welcome for Joshua Gad-Erianko. Despite the lack of time for preparation, the event took place, complete with banners, wide news coverage including an array of cameras and microphones, cheering crowds, and a handful of impressive officials. It carried just the right amount of pomp until a surging mass of students converged.

The schedule called for a motorcade to parade Joshua Gad-Erianko through the streets of Tel Aviv at 12:30. The following day, Bronski had arranged for a larger parade as Joshua drove into Jerusalem.

He did not plan to go to the airport. He carefully arranged pressing matters that precluded his presence. The marshalling of troops along the nation's borders gave him the perfect excuse. Had he been present, his level of fear and anguish would have intensified. Bronski was not ready to face that.

Joshua stood calmly on the airplane ramp while the excited crowd applauded. Though he never made any secret that he was in his forties, no one could believe the youthful features and agile body belonged to anyone over thirty. He spoke and the power in his voice convinced even the skeptical that a charismatic leader had come to Israel.

"I have come to aid my adopted country. I have come to the land of my forefathers. I have come as one citizen. I have come as one man. I have come to offer my help. We can defeat those who boast of tossing us into the sea. No, we *will* defeat them! We will triumph!"

The crowd burst into hysterical applause and clapping. One student raced forward to the microphone and started a chant:

> Saul has slain his thousands,
> David his ten thousands,
> Joshua his millions.

Immediately other college students echoed the three lines. Soon the crowd, caught up in a frenzy of patriotism, picked up the distinct cadence of the chant. The young man, a resonant baritone, improvised verse after verse. When he paused, the crowd broke into the chorus again, clapping, and some swayed in time to the music.

The young man finally raised his arms and waited for calmness to descend. "No one invited me here. We came—" he paused and pointed to his fellow students who cheered and clapped—"because we want to be the first to welcome Israel's man for the hour. Israel's David to slay Goliath. Israel's secret weapon against aggression and tyranny! Joshua Gad-Erianko!"

"Yes! Yes! Yes!" boomed the students, and the rest of the audience, caught up in the excitement, thundered back with them, "Yes! Yes!"

"Joshua! Joshua! Joshua!" The man started a chant and the voices erupted in feverish pitch.

"Make him the head of our nation!" screamed a voice near one of the microphones.

"Put Joshua Gad-Erianko in charge and we'll see real action!" shouted a high-pitched woman's voice.

"Enough rule by old men who're afraid of their shadows!" called out a woman. "Give us real leaders!"

For more than two hours, the chanting and singing continued. As soon as one exuberant person stepped down, another hurried into place.

Solomon Bronski frowned as he listened to the telephoned report of the police escort. Logically, he admitted, Joshua deserved a hero's welcome. The event, led by college students, might naturally get out of hand. He doubled the police escort.

He wondered if Joshua had arranged his own cheerleaders and hearty welcome. All the while his mind examined this, Bronski's stomach twisted in knots. A sour taste filled his mouth and a wave of nausea swept over him, making him want to vomit. He used all his willpower to suppress it.

Three hours after his arrival, Joshua Gad-Erianko and the escort left the airport. Meanwhile, Solomon Bronski proceeded with the emergency session of Knesset behind closed doors. He finished reading everything except the concluding statement of his hastily prepared report. He now prepared to give them detailed information about the size and potential of the troops along each of Israel's borders and the impending sea blockade.

A shuffling noise interrupted him and he glanced up to see the door close behind a tall, dark-complexioned man. For the first time in his life Solomon Bronski saw Joshua Gad-Erianko in person. A rivulet of fear shot down his spine and he felt his body jerk. He dropped his papers and his hands shook as he bent over to retrieve them. His pudgy arms, filled with perspiration only seconds earlier, now turned cold as if an Arctic wind had whipped across the room. Clasping his report to his chest, Bronski stood rigidly erect. Aware of his body, he bent his head forward and stared above his half-moon glasses at the tall figure.

The guest of honor raised his hand for silence. "Forgive this unannounced intrusion!" He started to walk forward.

"You may relax," Joshua Gad-Erianko said to them. "There is no danger from me. None at all."

For a moment the eyes of the members of the Knesset darted from Joshua to Bronski and then back to Joshua. Then, without a word, they lowered their defenses simultaneously. Their eyes followed him across the room, but they did not change position.

Ignoring his audience as if they no longer existed, Joshua Gad-Erianko walked toward the podium. He stopped, turned and faced the members of the Knesset. His eyes moved slowly across the room, lighting momentarily on each face. He already knew them all by their pictures and dossiers, and though he had not yet met any of them, that did not trouble him. He knew enough already.

"By now you have received word of the Arab-led plans to invade this country, I assume."

A startled Bronski hissed, "Yes."

"It is true information. As a matter of fact, I can offer you even more specific information, including the number of troops and the amount of military equipment. The figures do not really matter, you know. They have enough to destroy you completely. They do not plan to spare survivors." Joshua spoke Hebrew with only the slightest accent.

His eyes roamed slowly across the room. "I have come to offer you the way to save yourselves. To save the entire nation and to bring honor to Israel at the same time. I—and only I—can deliver you from this hour of destruction."

"That is quite a boast," Bronski said. He hoped his low voice sounded more menacing than he felt.

"Not a boast at all. It is true."

"How dare you?" Ilina Shemail, known popularly as the Iron Woman because of her tough attitudes, pounded her fist on her desk. She rose and accidentally knocked her briefcase to the floor. She did not bother to look down. "You must be a lunatic! I resent your bursting in here without an invitation. I want you out of here before I call the guards to escort—"

Joshua walked to the woman. She was tall, an inch over six feet with heavy features and a large but well-proportioned body. Her hair had been gray since her early teens when she escaped from Russian control in Lithuania.

"You *do* know who I am." He peered into her strong face and her dark eyes were mesmerized by his intense gaze. He laid his hands gently on her shoulders. For several seconds he said nothing. His eyes seemed to penetrate to the depths of her soul.

He dropped his arms, leaned toward her and whispered, "Anton." He turned to walk away.

"What did you say? What did you say?" Her voice had begun in a whisper but ended in a scream.

"I have said enough," Joshua answered calmly, his back to her. "Unless, of course, you would like me to tell everyone what I whispered."

Ilina Shemail backed away, shaking her head. "No. . . no . . ." she whispered, "Only the Devil—only the Devil himself—"

Joshua whirled around and slapped her twice on the face. The noise reverberated through the chamber. "You are hysterical! The news of war must have temporarily unsettled your mind!"

For a moment she stared in stunned silence. "Yes," she said weakly. Tears flowed from her cheeks. "But how? How did you—?"

"Do I need to say anything more to you?" He stepped forward. "Surely your nerves are on edge."

"No. I mean—" She shook her head. "I am all right."

"Then tell them," the softness of his voice belied the authority in his tones, "tell them to listen to me."

Ilina Shemail, her cheeks now deathly pale and her eyes listless, said, "Listen to him." Her normally strong voice trembled and she sounded like a child. "Joshua Gad-Erianko is the only one who can help. The only one."

At her side again, he asked softly, "Is this the voice of the Iron Woman? I assumed her strength overcame anything. *Tell them to listen.*"

"Please . . . please listen to him." She paused, closed her eyes and willed the strength to flow through her once again. She faced her peers and in her booming voice, long familiar to them all, she said, "I am convinced that he knows what to do. He has served our nation faithfully in the past, never asking for anything in return. I, for one, believe him." She returned to her place and sat down. She never looked at him again.

"Joshua! Joshua!" shouted one of the ministers.

"Yes, Joshua!" echoed another.

"Is it not possible," said Marcus Zelig, "that God might be performing a great miracle in our midst and we are too proud or too dim-sighted to perceive it?" He paused and surveyed the other members. "Think of our rich history, ladies and gentlemen! Remember! When God's covenant people came to desperate straits and they cried out for help, God answered. God raised up a Moses. A Gideon. A Deborah or Jepthah! A Judas Maccabaeus!" He sat down abruptly.

"Excuse me," Joshua Gad-Erianko said. "I came here unannounced and uninvited. If I have been improper, please forgive my breach of manners. However, we find ourselves caught up in the midst of extraordinary events when manners seem unimportant!"

"Hear! Hear!"

"I do not wish to waste your time or mine," he said. He walked back to the podium. "I have come here to tell you of more than the imminent danger to your country. You will be under siege in two days' time. You have no hope of escape—except through my plan. At the risk of sounding like a demented person, I am informing you that I am the only person who can save this country."

"Hah!" shouted a voice from the far side of the room.

"You come in here and expect us to believe you are some kind of superman who can win against the combined forces of our enemies? You surely must have escaped from some mental institution—"

"Sit down!" cried out another voice.

"I shall not be silenced! We are grateful to the services of our friend from the Soviet Union. On many occasions he has aided us and we're thankful. But to place him in the same category as Moses and—"

"What you call me at this point does not matter." He snapped his fingers. A tall man wearing a blue pinstriped suit stood just inside the door. None of the ministers had noticed him before. He walked to the back of the room and opened up the large black case he carried. He reached into it and pulled out a slide projector. He plugged it in and a map of Israel flashed before them.

"Here are the exact spots where Israel's enemies will converge tomorrow. Your Prime Minister and a few select others," he nodded toward Bronski, "can verify this information. Is this not so?"

"Yes, but then—"

Joshua waved him aside. He pointed to each of the strategic points at Israel's borders. He rattled off the figures as he broke down the complement of soldiers and specific types and amount of equipment. He sounded as if he were reading a computer list.

When he finished, Joshua said, "You may not believe me. I do not expect that all of you should at this point. One of your ministers referred to our heroes of the past. If you wish to refer to the days of our ancestors, I shall do that also. In the days of old, prophets came and spoke to kings and legislative bodies. These prophets foretold events and often gave a sign to back up their oracles. Today I am going to give you a sign. Two signs in fact. Their fulfillment will transpire within twenty-four hours. That will convince you that I can do what I claim."

"And then what?" asked a voice.

"Then you will know who I am and what I can do."

"But surely you want more than that?"

"You will receive me accordingly."

"Accordingly? What do you mean by that vague statement?"

Joshua turned away from the questioner. As he did so, a tinny voice cried out, "You're Joshua Gad-Erianko! You are God's deliverer for us!"

"We know how to receive you," stated the Iron Woman with an attempt to sound like her normal self again.

"Yes, you already know." Joshua nodded. "My first sign: Within six hours you will have a report from an impeccable source of the assassination of three of the nine leaders that form the military coalition. The three top men from each nation. Nothing will connect their elimination with any terrorist group. They will simply be found dead—each will die separately."

"You plan to—to murder—?" cried out a voice.

Joshua laughed at the voice. "Come now. Your government, working through organizations such as the Mossad and Shin Bet, has been doing this for years. The difference is that in your case no one publicly acknowledged it as happening. Therefore it did not occur.

"I promised you a second sign. The supreme commander of the forces surrounding Israel is General Gorki, as you may well have suspected. By nightfall he and his chiefs of staff will have become the victims of an unfortunate accident. An experimental bomb will detonate unexpectedly."

Joshua paused and his eyes swept the room once again. "I expect this to remove any question about my role in the salvation of Israel."

"You want us to look upon you as our Messiah? Is that what you are trying to say?" Solomon Bronski came around and faced him. "How dare you, sir!" His voice shook, but he could not hold back his words. "How dare you come here today and—"

"Silence." Although spoken quietly, the force behind the word pierced Bronski's bravado.

Bronski blinked at Joshua, hardly believing that anyone

would dare to order him to silence. He stood a foot shorter and outweighed Joshua by sixty pounds. Physically Joshua represented everything that Bronski was not. Bronski had made it a point to triumph over the handsome and the physically virile. The two men stared at each other like two prize fighters, each waiting for the other to deliver the first blow. The seconds of silence were all that Joshua needed. His eyes narrowed and focused on Bronski's face.

Fresh shivers of fear ran down Bronski's spine. He would not let Joshua see this and determined to tough it out. "Sir, I can overlook your rudeness. Many are frightened in this hour. But—" He shook his fist at Joshua. "I do not know where you received this information, nor do I care. I shall not today or tomorrow or any other day give you the kind of—of tribute that you seem to believe is your due! I am not altogether certain who you think you are, sir, but I wish you to know that I shall not allow you to disrupt our parliament. While we owe you a debt of gratitude for what you have done for our nation, I want to remind you that the people of Israel have elected us to our offices. We hold our positions because of public trust."

Joshua stood quietly, showing no emotion and giving no indication that Bronski's words had any effect. His indifference angered the Prime Minister.

"Sir, you will not be allowed to return tomorrow. I shall have you shot if you attempt it."

Joshua walked over to the nearest desk, took a sheet of paper and wrote three words. He folded the paper, handed it to Bronski and walked out of the large room. "I am staying at the King David Hotel," he said over his shoulder.

Bronski, completely unused to having anyone thwart him, stared in bafflement. His clenched jaws and fists attested to his barely controlled anger. Only as the doors closed behind Joshua and his pinstriped assistant did Bronski look down at his hand.

In his agitation, he had wadded up the paper. He unfolded the single sheet and read the scrawled message. Seeing those three words, a sharp pain raced through his heart.

As he staggered backward, everything went black momentarily. Bronski thought he was going to faint and he grabbed for the corner of the desk. He held on, steadying himself.

How could Joshua know? How could he possibly know?

T·W·E·L·V·E

"Gentlemen and ladies," he said, finally regaining a measure of control. "This has been an—an unfortunate experience . . . and yet . . . ," he swallowed hard, "if . . . if events happen as he says, I am willing to step down and . . . to declare him . . . the sole authority and power in Israel."

Solomon Bronski, the single sheet of paper gripped in his fist, turned and shuffled out of the room before anyone could stop him. He heard none of the voices of confusion and protest. He opened the paper again and reread the three words on the paper. His rapid and shallow breathing made him feel he might collapse in the hallway. He tried to walk faster, suddenly afraid he might fall dead before he could retreat to his private office.

Once inside his own chambers, he stared at the writing. Hours later his secretary knocked discreetly and getting no response, opened the door. "Sir."

Bronski looked up, confused. He turned his face away and stared at his wrinkled hands. He could not understand what was happening. Despite all his efforts, his mind refused to find a rational explanation and therefore made no sense.

Worse, he could not focus on present events. The power of those three words had hurled him backward. He was a boy again. A skinny boy of ten who had not experienced a full stomach for more than a year.

Momentarily he pulled himself back to the present. Aware of his present surroundings again, he focused slowly. "Yes?"

His secretary, keenly aware of the strange look on the Prime Minister's face, hesitated to interrupt. She did so, carefully remaining at the door. "I assumed you didn't want to be disturbed, sir, but I thought you would want to know the good news. General Gorki and his entire senior staff, along with fifty foot soldiers, died a few minutes ago. Reports tell us that they were witnessing a demonstration on how to deploy a small, nuclear-powered device. The demonstrator accidentally dropped it and it inadvertently detonated. Only four people in the room survived, and none of them is expected to live."

"Thank you," he said without emotion.

"The Arab armies are in total disarray. Thousands have deserted. Confusion is rampant throughout the armies. For some reason we cannot understand, the retreating soldiers say that they are afraid of *us*." She kept adding details in a hurried, excited voice.

Bronski had stopped listening. He had known as soon as he read the three words that everything Joshua Gad-Erianko said, would happen.

"Thank you—thank you," he said when she paused. With a nod, he dismissed his secretary. He stared again at the paper. In clear letters, written in German, he read aloud: "Heinemann, Warsaw, Betrayal."

Solomon stared at the glass in the window. He could see the outline of his own features. Somehow this man—this demonic and despicable person—had found out. How could he have known? He asked himself that question again and again. Not another person alive could have known.

Just before midnight he had slipped over the ghetto

walls of Warsaw. As on hundreds of other darkened nights, he had sneaked past the guards, gone to sympathizing Poles for food, and returned to the ghetto before morning.

Colonel Heinemann, who seldom visited the ghetto walls, had been present that night. He had stood in the shadowy silence, not because he expected anyone, but because he decided to view the ghetto walls himself. Solomon had slid softly down the wall, and only an alert soldier, turning the corner and seeing him, caused his capture.

Colonel Heinemann had personally interrogated him. Solomon Bronski gave the Germans a false name, and he had no papers on him to prove otherwise. They questioned him without letting up, and constantly threatened him. For three hours the colonel worked the boy over, careful not to harm him physically but to strike at his fears and weaknesses. The boy and all of the remaining inhabitants had known they were doomed. Yet they pledged to remain within the walls until the Germans killed every one of them.

Colonel Heinemann finally persuaded young Solomon to give him information—somewhat general—on the number of Jews still alive, where they hid, and how much ammunition and food they had. In return, he promised a safe passage for Solomon Bronski and any other member of his family. Solomon was the only Bronski still alive.

In a moment of weakness—that was how he later explained it to himself—he told the colonel everything he knew. The Germans provided him with a generous amount of food and sent him back to the ghetto. He was to return to the Germans in two days with more accurate information. At that time, they would give him his freedom and provide him with safe passage to Switzerland.

The boy, frightened by the Germans and scared of his own people, lived in a state between disoriented confusion and abject fear. He finally reminded himself that if he did as the Germans asked, he would live. He could go free and live to fight again somewhere else. They were all doomed anyway. No members of his immediate family survived. He might even do his people a favor by getting it over quickly.

Colonel Heinemann had said those words to him over and over again. If they continued to hold out, the Germans would starve them to death.

In the end, Solomon told Heinemann everything. He knew the location of the 112 people still alive. The colonel convinced the boy that if he gave any wrong information, he would know and would kill the boy anyway.

The day after Solomon's return, the Germans began the final assault on the ghetto. Within a week it was over. All dead. Colonel Heinemann, true to his promise, released the boy.

Young Solomon, tortured by his guilt and his betrayal, did not leave Warsaw. He took the four days' food supply the colonel had provided him, rationed himself carefully, and hid outside the city. He slept among rubble during the day and foraged at night. He bided his time for a week.

On the eighth night he crept silently through the streets of Warsaw. He knew exactly where to find the colonel. He had not figured out how to get into the officer's quarters and would have to decide that when the time came.

Shortly after midnight he saw the staff car drive up. The colonel got out. He staggered toward the building he had commandeered for both his office and living quarters. He waved aside the driver who offered assistance. The colonel yelled in a slurred voice, "I am a German officer. I need no help from anyone."

The car sped away. The colonel staggered onward, paused at the door, and fumbled with his key. Young Solomon slipped up behind him. Summoning all his strength, he struck the officer repeatedly on the back of the head with a lead pipe. The drunken colonel tried to struggle with him but could not coordinate his own body. Long after Heinemann stopped resisting, Solomon kept striking, all his rage poured into that single act. The rage against his own weakness, against the death of his people, and against the colonel for corrupting him.

Solomon reached for the officer's holster, unsnapped the cover, pulled out the luger, and pressed the gun against the officer's chest. He fired twice, surprised at how little noise the gun made.

With the gun still in his hand, he ran away. Within a week he was out of Poland. He made his way across Europe with the idea of going through Spain and into Portugal. Instead, he spent the rest of the war years working with freedom fighters in Holland. He kept the luger throughout the war. He often told the story of killing the officer, carefully omitting details of his betrayal.

How does that man know? No one could know. The colonel had not even known his name. He had been careful not to give his true identity. He had never told anyone—not one person in the whole world.

Yet Joshua Gad-Erianko knew.

T·H·I·R·T·E·E·N

At 9:48 P.M. the telephone rang in Joshua's hotel room. "Yes?" He lay on the bed, fully dressed, waiting. He had known it would come before midnight.

"This is Solomon Bronski." He hoped that his voice betrayed nothing.

"Yes, Mr. Bronski?"

"We have received confirmation of the—of the events that you informed us of this afternoon."

Joshua remained silent. He could visualize Bronski's discomfort in making the call. He decided to let him sweat while he completed his assignment.

"Our government has . . . has capitulated. We . . . accept your demands."

"Capitulated? Demands? I made no demands."

"Wishes, then." Fear mingled with his words and Solomon felt a loathing he had not experienced since his childhood in the Warsaw ghetto.

"My wishes? I only want what is best for Israel."

"For the good of Israel, then, the Knesset would like to have you meet with us this evening. That is, if you are ready."

"I am always ready."

"Whatever your demands—desires—we are prepared to agree."

"As I said, I only wish to be of service to the land of my fathers."

"When you are ready to meet with us, and if you'll be good enough to let us know, we'll send . . ."

"You may call for me in twenty minutes."

"That is fine . . ."

Joshua's fingers tightened their grip on the telephone. He knew the unspoken question. He hesitated several seconds while he made his decision. Yes, he had stretched Bronski as far as he dared. Otherwise the man might emotionally collapse. "You need have no fears about the Warsaw incident. It need never come up."

"But how did you—?"

"I am prepared to allow you to remain in the cabinet, Mr. Bronski, provided that you are as willing to cooperate as I am sure the others will be."

"You may believe this or not, but the good of Israel is foremost in my thoughts."

"Naturally I believe you. Because I *know* you speak the truth, I am prepared to keep you on. You can still make worthwhile contributions to Israel. Several. I shall explain further to you in the days ahead."

Joshua laid down the phone. He had accomplished the largest hurdle. In coming this far, he knew he would fulfill the rest of his plan. No one could stop him now. He smiled as he thought of the writing of the prophets his father had quoted so often—"No weapon raised against you will prosper."

He lay back on the bed, his arms under his head. He had spent a long time in preparation, but now everything was set. He relaxed, knowing that by now most members of the Knesset were scared or at least confused. He liked the feeling of power he had.

Twenty minutes later Joshua permitted himself a smile as he walked through the corridor of the King David Hotel.

An escort of ten soldiers flanked him, providing the utmost protection. In front of the hotel, a bullet-proof Lincoln Continental awaited him.

Joshua Gad-Erianko's only surprise came when he saw a cadre of reporters gathered around the vehicle. Someone in the Knesset had leaked the word. He did not mind. It could only help. He planned to take advantage of the public coverage, and it was starting earlier than he had expected.

He nodded to the reporters and paused while they snapped pictures. Seven microphones appeared, all thrust in his face at once. Questions came to him in four different languages. Being multilingual, Joshua was equally proficient in answering.

He fielded their questions by making a statement about his purpose in coming to Israel. He called it the land of his forebears. "I decided that as a true son of Israel, it is my duty to be present during this difficult period."

"Mr. Gad-Erianko, is it true that you single-handedly killed General Gorki?" an American reporter asked.

"We have heard that you went into the enemy camp and won victory by yourself." The Jewish reporter pushed the microphone closer. "Is that statement true?"

"Sir, can you confirm the rumors we have just heard?" asked one female reporter in Arabic.

"How can I confirm rumors? I have heard no rumors."

"But is it true—?"

"Please excuse me, but I cannot give you any statement at this moment. I am going to the Knesset now at their summons and at the invitation of Prime Minister Bronski."

"But you surely know something," said an English reporter.

"After I have met with the Knesset, I am certain we shall be able to tell you everything you want to know." He nodded for the driver to open the door for him.

"Is it true that you are going to head up a new government—a revolutionary council perhaps?" a Frenchman asked.

"Please," he said quietly. "You have my word that I will

answer all your questions just as quickly as I have them
answered for myself."

"I may be crazy," a female reporter yelled in Swedish,
"but for the first time I believe a politician."

"I am not a politician!"

"Perhaps that is why I can believe you!" she shouted.
"Good luck!"

Joshua got inside the car. *Good luck? Luck has nothing
to do with this. Each step has been carefully planned.* He
laughed silently, realizing that for some people the word luck
described anything they could not grasp.

By midnight the message went across the nation of
Israel. TV stations showed pictures of troops massed at six
different places. Taken a day earlier by Russian photographers, the film emphasized the coordination of troops and
the vastness of their strength. The clip ended and a reporter
explained that the next ninety seconds of film came from
Israeli sources.

The public saw Arab and Russian soldiers breaking
ranks, discarding ammunition, and fleeing. One Arab officer
shouted commands to the troops to reassemble as they
rushed past him.

Immediately the TV studio camera cut in to Prime
Minister Bronski standing in front of the Knesset. He stared
unemotionally into the camera as he announced that the
Knesset had made a revolutionary decision in an extraordinary period of Israel's history. The Knesset had taken the
authority upon themselves and appointed Joshua Gad-
Erianko as the King of Israel.

The statement released by Solomon Bronski live and
reprinted the next day in Israel's newspapers said in part:

> . . . We live in extraordinary times and our nation
> has been at the brink of extinction. Through the

remarkable efforts and unparalleled vision of one
man, Joshua Gad-Erianko, our nation has been
saved from imminent destruction.

Once again the God of Israel had raised up a
David who has slain the giant Goliath . . . It can
now be told that our enemies had begun to amass
troops along all our land borders with ships
blockading us from the sea. They were bent upon
our total elimination as a nation and committed to
destroy every person of Jewish blood. Joshua Gad-
Erianko single-handedly stopped the planned
slaughter . . .

We have, therefore, without authority from
the people and yet from the dictates of our
conscience, taken an unprecedented step. We have
unanimously declared Joshua Gad-Erianko King of
Israel! We believe we are once again living in a
period when only a single person at the head of
our government, an individual appointed by God
himself, is the answer. The only answer!

To the surprise of only a few, the people did not raise
an outcry. Crowds filled the streets of Jerusalem and Tel
Aviv, from the northernmost parts of the country to the
south. Without opposition, they supported the appointment
of King Joshua.

The next morning King Joshua appeared on television
and the message went throughout the entire world:

"I, Joshua Gad-Erianko, King of Israel, have declared
freedom and prosperity for the people. We have met our foes
and we have conquered them. They now flee in total disarray! Although they outnumbered us forty-five to one, it has
made no difference. Although they possess weapons we do
not have, we fight with a greater strength. Although they
have military strategists leading them, we have a superior
guidance. Although they breathe destruction, we do not fear
them. We have prevailed! We shall continue to prevail!

"We are the chosen people of the world! We have suffered defeat in the past. It shall never happen again. We have suffered untold affliction from Arabs, from Russians, from misguided Christians and benighted Muslims. All peoples of the world have seen Jews as their target of derision and destruction. We will not allow this to happen to us again. We are here to win and nothing can stop us! We will cast all our enemies into the sea. They shall perish as the Egyptians who opposed Moses!"

Joshua's voice, normally low and well-modulated, took on a shrillness and, as if under a hypnotic spell, he launched into what Nagila Levy considered a kind of theatrical diatribe. Yet she also knew it packed enough emotion to stir the people of Israel. His voice, his eyes, his gestures mesmerized the people. He spoke the words that they had long wanted to hear and had been afraid to say aloud.

"We live in a new day and a new age! I have brought you hope and prosperity. Our nation and our people have been attacked, hated, slaughtered, murdered, exiled, despised, and persecuted. Sixty years ago the Germans attempted to wipe us from the face of the earth. Through the centuries other nations have tried to exterminate our race from this planet, and none of them has prevailed. None of them will. Our enemies cannot triumph! They will not triumph over us! None of those who raise their hands against us will prosper!"

For forty-three minutes Joshua spoke in terms that filled Jews with pride and erased the vestiges of doubt. This was the man they wanted—that they needed. Even though he never said that he alone could save Israel, those who heard him speak knew his intent. Most of them felt as if Joshua spoke directly and personally to them. Joshua would save them, perhaps even the entire world from warmongering politicians and imbecilic puppets of big business.

Nagila Levy listened to the TV broadcast as she drank a second cup of coffee. When she analyzed his speech, she concluded that he had actually provided little substance although he had spoken passionately. He had majored in generalities. The emotional impact of his speech captivated her despite the repetitious rhetoric. Watching King Joshua in action reminded her of watching newsreels of the tirades of Adolf Hitler. Mentally she compared their methods and message. They sounded amazingly alike. But after that the similarities ended.

Joshua was one of the handsomest men she had ever seen. He exuded a kind of sexual attraction that pulled women toward his strength and vitality. Yet his strength, rather than offend men, appealed to their pride of country and aroused a strong patriotism. At one point in his speech he praised Jewish males and their willingness to defend and to die for their families.

Beyond his remarkably handsome features and his strong presence, Joshua Gad-Erianko was a man of great power and persuasion. Through a sometimes rambling message, Joshua Gad-Erianko ceased to be a figure on a screen. He communicated directly to Nagila in a way that made her feel she knew him. Even more surprising, she had a strong sense that if they ever met face to face he would be even more personable. He would pay no attention to anyone else in the room. Nagila laughed at her own feelings because she suspected that millions of other Jews responded the same way. Men of Joshua's caliber were made to rise to the top in periods of fear and uncertainty.

Only once did she feel a shudder within her body. *What if he, like Hitler and other orators before him, should use this ability for evil?* Immediately she regretted thinking that way. "This man saved our nation," she reminded herself.

Nagila videotaped the entire episode, especially wanting to reevaluate Joshua's speech when she was no longer caught up in the emotion of the moment. "King Joshua," she said aloud and the words felt strange to her lips.

Nagila had been so completely absorbed in the newscast that she jumped when the phone rang. By stretching carefully she pulled the phone off the wall hook. "Yes?"

"Nagila Levy?" asked a man's flat voice.

"Yes, it is."

"Hold, please."

A moment later she heard his voice speaking to her for the first time. "Good morning, Ms. Levy. This is King Joshua speaking."

"Good morning," she said as she wondered why he would call her and at the same time she noted how easily he used his newly bestowed title.

"I assume you have heard the newscasts?"

"Yes, I have."

"Good. Then I need to explain nothing there. I am calling because I wish you to come to my office this morning at 9:30. This will not inconvenience you?"

"No—no—" she stammered. A request of this nature precluded inconvenience.

"I have an assignment I think you will find interesting. A car will call for you at 9:15." The phone clicked.

Nagila held the phone in her hand long after the call ended. He had called her. How did he know she existed? She had worked for the government eight years—since her college days—yet she had never done anything of prominence enough to call any special attention to herself. In the negotiations with Egypt she had done most of the background preparations that made the meeting possible. She had provided the subtle persuasion behind the scenes. Gideon Wittstein had pushed her contributions into the background as she had expected.

At 9:15 a limousine pulled up in front of her apartment. The driver held the door open and waited until Nagila came outside.

When the vehicle stopped in front of the Knesset building, a soldier with an automatic machine gun slung across his shoulder opened the door. He escorted her inside and to a small anteroom.

A uniformed woman carrying the same style machine gun said, "I shall have to search you." Without waiting for Nagila to give permission, the woman's hands moved quickly and lightly across her body. The other soldier took her purse, rifled through it just as thoroughly and handed it back.

The woman said, "Follow me, please." She led the way and the other soldier followed Nagila down the hallway.

Minutes later Nagila came to what was now the office of King Joshua. A male secretary looked up. "You may go in."

The woman who had searched Nagila opened the door and closed it behind her. Nagila stood just inside the room, waiting for instructions.

Joshua had been gazing out the window and turned around when she entered. "Please. Sit down." He indicated a stuffed chair. "I believe you take your tea without milk with only a little sugar."

"That's right. How did you know?"

"I make it my business to know these little things," he said. He handed her a cup of tea and sat down across from her. "Incidentally, you are far more lovely in person than your photograph indicates."

Nagila Levy felt her cheeks flush and she took a sip of tea quickly to cover up her discomfort.

"We have won a war," he said, as if he had been talking to her previously. "It is not the last war. It is the prelude to other skirmishes. The Arab-Russian coalition is, even now, preparing to sign an alliance with the Chinese."

"Not this quickly surely."

Joshua focused on her blue eyes. "I do not offer supposition. When I speak, I assure you that I am giving you facts that I can verify."

"I didn't mean to—"

"I wish you to know," he said, ignoring her attempt to apologize, "that they are meeting secretly in Albania at this moment." He paused before adding, "Of course, in your position with the Mossad you may already know most of this."

"Actually, I know little," she said. "I learned of a high-level Soviet meeting only yesterday. I have had no word that any Chinese would be present."

"Which brought you to my attention. No one else or their operatives learned of this meeting except you. You have set up a model of efficiency. Despite the limited number of agents under you."

"Thank you—" Nagila felt herself flushing again. "Will they join together? China and Russia?"

"Yes. That is part of the reason I called you to my office. You are the Mossad operative for six people of secure status among the Arabs. You have only two such people with the Soviets. Correct?"

"Yes, but how do you know so many of these things?"

"My sources are not important for you to know. I merely want your confirmation of the truth."

"I have been trying to recruit additional help."

"Yes, of that I am aware." He picked up a sheet of paper and held it so that she could read it. It contained ten names followed by a single word. "All of these people are in high Soviet positions. You undoubtedly recognize the name Alesander Sasanov of the Politburo."

"Yes—"

"These ten will be your sources. You are to memorize their names. Next to their names is the code name I have assigned them. I have named Sasanov *Child*. From this point on, no one but you and I will know their true identities. They will report directly to you." He leaned forward and gazed into her blue eyes. "Only to you. If you encounter interference from coworkers or superiors, you will appeal to me. These are the people for whom you are responsible. Later I shall inform you how to contact them. Any questions so far?"

"None."

"My staff is preparing an office for you two doors down from mine. I have splendid plans for you, Nagila Levy."

"You do?"

"You can be of great service to me. And to Israel."

"You mean if I choose to work directly for you. I have not yet decided. I could choose to leave government ser-, vice."

"Forgive me. I supposed you would have made that choice."

"Israel is still a free country, isn't it? I can choose to decline the honor?"

"This is an honor I offer to few people. You would be wise not to refuse my offer."

Nagila stared uncomprehendingly. She started to get up.

"Wait. Do not leave. You may refuse without impunity. I seek only those who wish to serve Israel. We need more people of your ability."

"Sir, uh, King Joshua, I do not like threats—direct or veiled. For you to offer me a position with the opportunity to decline is one thing. For you to intimate that my refusal would be unwise troubles me."

"I intended only to convey that I need your level of energy and efficiency. For the good of Israel."

"If you put the needs of our nation foremost, then I have no hesitation. Otherwise—"

"Ah, a woman of spirit." He leaned still closer, his face only inches from her own. She did not flinch or pull back. His eyes bore into hers. For several seconds he concentrated before he pulled back. "You are an extremely complicated woman. I do not understand you."

"I'm not certain I understand myself completely—"

"No, not like that. You are—multi-layered. Complex. I have never had such an experience before."

"I have no idea what you're talking about."

"Yes, yes, I did not make myself clear." Joshua stood abruptly and walked across the room to his desk. He tried to hide his confusion. Only once before in his entire life had he failed to grasp the inmost secrets of a person.

From Nagila Levy, he received a mixture of confused images but could come up with nothing clear. He could not comprehend this response and needed time to work this out. "Please leave now and I shall call for you later this morning."

As soon as Nagila Levy walked out of the office, Joshua slumped in his chair. How could this be? What had prevented him from gaining the hidden information? Everyone had secrets, sometimes insignificant, but secrets just the same.

Only once had he failed. He had assumed she was not coherent enough to bring her secrets to consciousness. Or perhaps she had been too brainwashed with the teachings of her religion. They called the young woman Lidia. She was a Russian Christian, a Baptist, as they called everyone who did not belong to the Orthodox faith.

Lidia had undergone a hunger strike for twenty-eight days. From her 100 pounds she had shrunk to a mere eighty-four. Lidia, barely five feet tall, dark hair and complexion, with enormous gray-green eyes that protruded from her emaciated face, stared back at him. She showed a total absence of fear. He had not impressed her with his presence. She lay on a hospital bed, being fed with an IV. The obvious courage in her own eyes prevented him from going into her soul. She, like Nagila Levy today, had resisted him. He could not understand why.

In his lifetime he had now met two people who did not fear him. "Why do I let such things trouble me?" he asked aloud. "Hundreds have yielded to me. Soon millions will fear me. I can easily destroy those few like Nagila Levy if I choose."

Joshua Gad-Erianko's self-composure returned. He turned to the papers on his desk. He did not need to look at his own copy of the list he had given to Nagila because he knew each person well. He laughed drily as he thought of each of the ten code names he had used. He had chosen the code names carefully. Each one subtly reminded the agent of a deep-seated secret that he or she did not want the world to know. With Sasanov it was his preference for young girls—very young girls. Each time Nagila used his code name it would remind him and would bind him more completely to Joshua's will.

Joshua leaned back. It was all coming together smoothly. He had experienced less problem with the Knesset than he had expected. That old fool Bronski could be controlled easily, even though his enemies called him implacable.

It had taken him only thirty seconds to subdue the old fox. None of the other members of the Knesset posed any danger.

Since he arrived in Israel, not a single person had created a problem. Except Nagila Levy. By having her close by, he could keep his eye on her. Joshua silently vowed he would find the way to read her inmost secrets as well.

F·O·U·R·T·E·E·N

King Joshua avoided Nagila for the first three days after she started to work for him. Through his secretary he sent instructions and messages. He determined to sort out his thinking before he allowed any personal contact with her again. He thoroughly read her personal file. He could find nothing that hinted of any secret past. Yet he believed that no one, no matter how carefully prepared to conceal, had a past without secrets. He also knew that no one had successfully kept back those secrets from him. He had learned from reports of Nagila's friends the hint of a short-lived affair with a man of twenty-four when she was barely sixteen. Joshua snorted. In this day, that sounded almost virtuous.

No, he reasoned, there had to be at least one secret, a dark part of Nagila's life she wanted no one to know about. He also determined to discover what prevented him from penetrating her defenses. He had sensed no resistance on her part. She had liked him. At least, she had not disliked him. That told him that she had not consciously withheld her shameful secrets.

For the first time, Joshua recognized that he had a

personal interest in Nagila. She intrigued him. His mind returned to her constantly. He wanted to be with her, to touch her, to kiss her. He could not understand such desire and emotion. Perhaps, he reasoned, because he did not have true objectivity with Nagila, it kept him from penetrating the depth of her soul.

Joshua wanted to accept that explanation. He wanted to believe it. Only one thing prevented his easy acceptance. He kept thinking about Lidia.

Mentally he compared the two. He could not marshall enough facts to correlate. Lidia followed an obscure Christian sect, Nagila the Jewish faith. He had never encountered problems getting to the depths of Jews before, even among the most pious. Solomon Bronski or members of the Knesset: none of them had presented any challenge. It had to be something else—something stronger.

In Lidia's case, he wondered if it had been a combination of her weakened condition after a month of fasting. Yet his mind told him that ought to have made her just that more accessible. With Lidia, he had eventually concluded that it was not just her faith, but her particular kind of faith—the fanatical fringe of her strange sect—that had somehow fortified her. The same could not be true with Nagila. She was, by all he could learn of her, a practicing Jew who attended worship regularly. But that fit many others whom he had already penetrated. Nasief Habib fit in there someplace. Did he have an effect on her? What about Shaheen Ahman? Where did he fit in? Several facts remained hidden from him. He would soon find out.

He buzzed his secretary. "I wish Ms. Levy to come in immediately."

She arrived in less than one minute. He motioned for her to sit down and he remained on the other side of the room. She wore a light-weight wool suit of tan with threads of green running through. The green blouse made her blue eyes look aqua. She wore her hair loose and its natural curl emphasized her clear complexion and a face that required little makeup.

"Miss Levy, I wish to ask you a few questions. They have nothing to do with your position, you understand." Joshua spoke with the sincere tones that never failed to put others at ease.

"I don't mind answering anything," she said.

He noted the lack of rigidity in her body. No matter how well people tried to hide tenseness and fear from him, he could always detect it in the neck and shoulders.

"As I expected. First, I understand that you are a close friend of Shaheen Ahman, a Muslim."

"I wouldn't call him a close friend. I know him, of course—"

"How well do you know him?"

"Have I done something wrong? Or has Shaheen? Is he in trouble?"

"How well do you know Mr. Ahman?"

"I suppose I'd have to say not well."

"How well is that?"

"I knew of Shaheen because of his work with Shin Bet. His name appeared often in the media because of his work with the poor. We both served on the delegation in negotiating for Taba. That was when I first met him."

"I understand you opposed his being a member of the delegation?"

"I did." She paused, wanting to protect Shaheen if he was in trouble. Yet she did not want to lie. Nagila decided to be open about what she knew. "First, he's radical in his beliefs. He's one of those people who find it nearly impossible to compromise. I knew he would be difficult to work with on the Taba delegation. He was difficult indeed."

"You said 'first,' so I assume you had other reasons?"

"He's Muslim. Frankly, I did not believe it would serve the best interests of Israel to have a Muslim on our delegation since we were negotiating with Arabs. If he had been more sympathetic to our official position, I wouldn't have objected."

"I see," Joshua said. Her openness pleased him. "Since then—the Taba Accord—have you been in contact?"

"We've run into each other. Once at the library. I've spoken to him several times."

"Any romantic attachment to him?"

"Certainly not! I'm Jewish."

"Yes." He paused and tried to decide how to proceed. He felt strangely uncomfortable. His methods had never failed before. Once others came under his influence (the word he liked to use with himself), he often had to restrain them from talking too much.

"I understand you also know a man named Nasief Habib."

"Yes."

"A Christian?"

She nodded.

"He teaches his anti-Semitic lessons—"

"Not anti-Semitic, sir. I mean, he's not against Jews or any other faith."

"Oh? I understood differently."

"Not unless I've misunderstood. He's not opposed to other religions. He is a Palestinian Christian, you know."

"Yes, I know. But if not opposed—?"

"He told me that he thinks of both Judaism and Islam as paths that can start people toward a fuller life. At least that's the best I've understood. He teaches several classes right here in Jerusalem. But I suppose you know that."

"Yes. And you have attended his classes?"

"Did I do something wrong by going? I have no intentions to convert."

"Does Ahman attend those classes?"

"Yes. Regularly. As a matter of fact, he introduced me to Nasief—"

"Who then invited you to his study class."

She nodded. "And I attended."

"Why? As a practitioner of the Jewish religion, I would think you had no interest."

"Ordinarily not, I suppose. Frankly, the topic intrigued me. I had never heard such a teaching before."

"What kind of teaching?"

"About what Nasief believes will happen before the end of the world comes." Nagila showed an obvious embarrassment and Joshua sensed he was getting closer to the answer he sought. "They believe that their Messiah will return charging to earth on a cloud or something like that."

"What does Nasief say will take place before the end of the world?"

"I don't understand it all and I'm not certain I can explain what I did hear. I've been there only a few times—"

"Four times."

Nagila nodded and smiled. She rested her head against the stuffed chair. "Obviously you have all of that in my file. Perhaps if you tell me exactly what you want to know, then—"

"No, please. I was only corroborating your statement. I am pleased that you have told me nothing that I cannot substantiate. Now, explain to me the teachings of Mr. Nasief."

"As well as I can understand, he expects the end of the world to take place here, right here in Jerusalem. He keeps quoting things from the Christian Bible. He also believes that powerful rulers will arise, all of them evil. One in particular, far worse than the others—he calls that man Antichrist because he will attempt to destroy the Christian people."

"And what will happen to this—this Antichrist?"

"I'm a little vague there. Nasief has all kinds of charts and keeps explaining that some students differ from him. Essentially, they all believe that Messiah is going to come back to Israel, take all of the good people to heaven—"

"And—?"

"And destroy this planet, I think. Destroy it with fire. Nasief believes in a nuclear holocaust."

"I understood they believed in some kind of destruction of the earth by fire."

"Nasief said that the prophets wrote about it thousands of years ago and they did not know of modern weaponry and nuclear warfare. That by using the symbol of fire, they explained their understanding in terms they and the people of their time could grasp."

"Has he concluded when this person—this Antichrist—will come? Or has he already arrived? Who is he?"

Nagila rethought the statements at the study the night before. She had asked the same question. "Nasief said that it is still a little too early to tell."

"Too early? Why is that?"

"This figure will have a lot of power. He will control the armies of the world or most of them. But, you see, Nasief pointed out that at one time many people believed Hitler was the Antichrist. He did control Europe and almost defeated the Russians—"

"Quite true. So Nasief says people must wait before they identify this Antichrist?"

"Before they start pinning names on anyone. His exact words." She did not mention that he had hinted that they needed to watch the King of Israel's activities. She also assumed that his spies had reported that.

"Do you believe his teachings?"

Nagila's blue eyes stared unflinchingly at his. "I don't know." She shook her head slowly. "I really don't know."

"But you would like to believe?"

"Nasief is so sure. So convinced of what he teaches. That certainty—that inner calmness he has received from his faith—that appeals to me." She laughed self-consciously. "I've always assumed that I didn't have that kind of spiritual capacity. You know, some people hear about God once and they embrace it all without doubts or hesitation."

"I see." Joshua walked across the room and pulled up a chair next to Nagila. He sat in silence and stared at her. This interview had been only partially satisfactory. He gained the information he had sought about Nasief Habib. In the meantime, he began to feel even more uncomfortable over his inability to read Nagila's secrets.

His eyes took in her whole appearance. He had a strong urge to take her hand and to touch her soft skin. He wanted to press his lips against hers and to hold her. Joshua pulled his thoughts out of that track. It confused him because he had no reference for such an attitude. Desires of this type had never troubled him before. He had read of other men who experienced such sensations. They had spoken openly of their weakness for many women or sometimes for only one.

Joshua, now in his forties, had never experienced sexual feelings toward any person in his life. The first longings of desire stirred inside him and refused to be silent. This added to his confusion.

"Nagila," he said, "one question. Are you in love with Shaheen Ahman?"

She stared in surprise. "That could never happen. A Jew and a Muslim?"

"That is not exactly what I asked. Your personal feelings for him, what are they? Love? Affection?"

"I don't know. I try not to think of him in that way."

"You try not to? Then you do think of him that way?"

"I didn't mean it like that. I simply want to convey that I could never convert to Islam. He would never become Jewish. With those formidable barriers, I have refused to speculate about any emotional involvement."

"I see." He stood up and walked toward the window. He needed to free his thoughts and stop staring at her. "Do you have feelings of love for any man at present?"

"No."

"But you did before?"

"Of course."

"You were married?"

"I was. As my dossier will show. I lived with my husband in a kibbutz in Galilee. Arab bombs killed seven people. My husband happened to be one of them. We lived in Northern Galilee and we knew the risks." She paused. "I suppose it sounds unemotional for me to talk this way. It happened many years ago. I worked through a lot of pain and bitterness."

"Against Arabs?"

She shook her head. "Not anyone personally. I simply

lost a part of myself in Northern Galilee. Since then, I haven't allowed myself to think of love again."

Joshua stood as if the interview had finished. He turned slowly and asked, his emotions overcoming his better judgment, "Will you think of it again one day?"

He faced her, staring down into her face. Automatically Nagila got out of the chair.

"Will you?" he asked again and stepped toward her so that only inches separated their bodies. He liked the subtle fragrance she wore. He wanted to wrap his arms around her and pull her tightly to himself. "Would you perhaps one day think of someone else? Someone like me?"

Nagila lowered her eyes, covering her surprise. "I . . . I don't know . . . I had never thought of you . . . in that way."

"Please think of it." He took her hand in his and held it. Joshua had never made a romantic gesture before and he felt unnerved. His own fingers tingled and the physical sensations generated within his body surprised him. He lifted her hand and kissed it. "Never have I known a woman like you. I doubt that I shall ever know another."

"Sir—"

"You may call me Joshua—please."

"Jos—Joshua," she said, her own breathing constricted. His presence was powerful. She felt herself being sucked into a vortex of swirling emotions along with an overwhelming dizziness. His presence, his words, his lips against the back of her hand, all conspired to pull her to him. Yet intuitively she sensed that to yield to Joshua would be a serious mistake. If she yielded, she would be like the proverbial fly enticed and entangled in the web of the perilous spider.

Nagila backed away; her hand clutched the doorknob. "I—I shall think about it."

Later that evening, Nagila relaxed in front of the TV. The events of the day were still fresh in her mind, and she wondered why Joshua had acted as he had. Was he in love with her? Or was he merely flattering her, trying to bind her more closely to him? As she sat mulling over these thoughts, the familiar face of Gary Lefmann, TV reporter for America's Cable News Network and the only American allowed to remain within Beijing, came on the screen:

"After four days of secret meetings, top officials emerged, with flags unfurled and bands playing loudly in Tiananmen Square. Here in the world's largest open-air square, which can contain several million people, I have never before witnessed such a flurry of activity. The enthusiasm, patriotic slogans and military presence makes it seem as if they are preparing for war."

Lefmann paused while the Forbidden City loomed in the background. The camera moved toward the middle of the square, focusing on the imposing tomb of Chairman Mao where his body lay in state for viewing. Along one side stood the Great Hall of the People. In front of the hall the camera zoomed in on more than two thousand parked bicycles. From there the viewers saw the beginnings of a ceremony of great pomp on a dais.

"From the north a military band leads the Russian hammer-and-sickle flag unfurled. Three top men from the Soviet Union march behind the flag. Twenty-four rows of precision-trained honor guards come next, separating the Russians from the delegates of Libya, Iran, and Iraq. Each country displays its own flag.

"From the opposite direction, a more passive march has begun. Chinese soldiers are escorting Chairman Chou Chung, the Chinese Premier. Behind him I can see delegates representing the nations who are now part of what we loosely refer to as the Chinese Federation. I have never seen such enthusiasm among the Chinese people!"

The camera focused on Lefmann's broad face. He tried to erase the grave concern from his features. "None of us knows what this means. The Arab-Russian combined forces recently surrounded Israel and then retreated. These leaders, we hear from reliable sources, plan to galvanize the masses of the world against Israel and her allies. Although not specifically stated, they obviously referred to the American-Western Europe coalition and the Republic of America.

"What happens next? We can only guess. However, I have heard one portentous word that crops up whenever Israel is mentioned: *holocaust*.

"Reports have come to us that this new coalition of over half the world's population plans a fiery holocaust to utterly destroy anyone of Jewish blood or ancestry from the earth's surface."

Gary Lefmann hesitated and, his journalistic sense winning over his caution, said, "Here is a secretly filmed interview between Chou Chung and Amparo Marina. Two days after this interview, she died, the result of a hit-and-run accident, according to the government." The sneer in his voice made it obvious what he thought of the report.

Across the screen flashed a head shot of Amparo Marina, a beautiful and intelligent reporter from Colombia, South America. The film then focused on Marina as she asked the Chinese leader, "Are you aware that others have tried to destroy the Jews? They have ended up destroyed themselves and the Jews continue to live."

The other reporters who heard the question marveled at her courage. A Swedish reporter tried to interrupt before Chou Chung received the interpretation. The Chinese statesman held up his hand to silence the man.

A deep frown crossed the unlined face of sixty-year-old Chou Chung. He recovered quickly and said, "When I was a small boy we had ants outside our humble village. They were a nuisance. They brought harm. They did nothing of benefit. We tried many ways to rid ourselves of them. It took many years. Today, if you should go into the mountain country to my village, you will find no ants remaining. Need I explain the analogy?" he asked, giving his most gracious smile.

Ms. Marina, already emboldened, did not wait for him to recognize her a second time. "Sir, we have heard that the armies—and particularly those backed by Chinese funds—

that surrounded Israel only days ago have now retreated in disgrace."

Ready for this question, the Russian delegate stepped forward. "As you may have heard of the unfortunate accident to our chiefs of staff, we have decided to withdraw—temporarily. We have accomplished our purpose to show the Israelis our strength and our intent on peace and sharing of the world's resources. We would be most pleased if they would act accordingly. Because the Israelis cannot cooperate and live in peace with the rest of the nations, we cannot allow them to stir up troubles and play mischief makers. We promise that if they voluntarily leave the land, we will not exterminate them. We agreed only a few hours ago to set aside sufficient land where all people of Israeli blood or religion can live."

"But, sir, you must know that would never be acceptable. They don't want just a place to live. They want the land they believe God gave them."

He shrugged. "We propose a humanitarian and compassionate expression. Should they choose to refuse, it absolves us of any further responsibility."

"Where is this land?" the reporter persisted.

"It is a place where we," he paused with his arms spread out, indicating that delegates from all of the other nations agreed, "believe they could live and not harm other nations."

"On the Russian-Mongolian border? Is that it?" she asked. "Somewhere in the Arctic circle?"

"We are not prepared to mention specifics." Chou Chung stepped forward. "We are people of concern for others. We wish to live together on this planet. We believe in treating others fairly—even those who have set themselves against us."

The delegation marched on and soldiers barred Amparo Marina and others from following.

Still photographs showed the historic march in Tiananmen Square of the Chinese from one direction, meeting the

Russians and Arabs who marched from the opposite side.
The ceremonies concluded with the delegates standing in a
circle. They linked arms as a symbol of unity.

The next day, the Russian news agency, *Tass*, carried
the following story, picked up and translated by UPI:

> After four hours of speeches, special music, and
> frequent bursts of applause, Chou Chung of the
> Chinese Federation announced that those gathered
> represented 62 percent of the people in the entire
> world. They had come together for peace,
> prosperity, and for the benefit of all people of the
> world—especially the downtrodden and enslaved
> people. They pledged to free the rest of the world
> from capitalism and totalitarianism.

B·O·O·K
T·W·O

O·N·E

Chairman Chou Chung, a man of ascetic habits, had only one weakness. He liked Turkish coffee, served in a brass pot, and drunk from brass demitasse cups. He allowed himself two cups every afternoon at 3:30.

At 3:28 on October 8, 1996, Chou Chung's personal guard looked up to see a man carrying the tray covered with a white cloth over the tall pot. The steward paused, removed the cloth for the guard to examine.

"I have never seen you before," the guard said.

"No, you have not. This is my first time of being so honored to bring coffee to our noble leader."

The guard eyed the man with suspicion. He had learned in all the years of working with Chou Chung to trust his intuition. Something about the man disturbed him, but he could not pin it down. An uneasiness, a flicker of warning, but nothing definite. He stared at the steward. The man's eyes met his and held only a second before he looked away.

The guard felt a little more assured. Hardened enemies of the regime would have stared him down to assert their innocence. This man acted perfectly normal by looking away.

"Set the tray on my desk and lean forward."

The steward obeyed. While stretched in this awkward position, the guard checked him thoroughly for concealed weapons but found nothing. He picked up the cup and the pot. He even ran his fingers across the bottom of the tray. Nothing.

Yet his suspicions would not go away. He could think of nothing more to check. He eyed the steward again, stalling for time while his brain sorted out the confusion.

"Something I have done wrong, perhaps?" the steward said, his Mandarin having the slightest accent.

"You are not from Beijing?"

"No, I come from the northeast. The far side of Manchuria."

The guard relaxed slightly, still not completely satisfied. That could explain the variable. "Pour yourself a cup."

The steward hesitated. "For myself? But is this not—?"

"You drink first. That is why you have brought two cups."

"I do not like coffee," the steward said. "However, if it is an order—"

"It is."

"Then I drink, but I do not have to like coffee, do I?" He grinned and showed spaces between his front teeth. He poured himself a cup of the scalding liquid and drank it in one swallow. "It is better to take such a detestable drink in one motion than to take it drop by drop, I think."

"Yes, that may be so." The guard rechecked the tray, the cloth cover, the cups and even the pot. He could not dismiss the ominous feeling. Something still bothered him and he did not know what it was. "Take the coffee back to the kitchen."

"Back? Why must I do that?"

"Send one of the other stewards." The guard dismissed him.

A few minutes later a steward whom the guard recognized came into the outer office of Chou Chung. The guard checked the contents of the tray, and watched while this steward drank. This man sipped the coffee slowly, fully relishing both the taste and the aroma.

"Take it to him," the guard said. Yet with all his suspicions satisfied, something continued to bother him and he could not decide what it was. This steward was trustworthy, of that he was sure. His intuition had never failed him before. He reminded himself that he had checked the first steward thoroughly and everything he carried.

He closed his eyes, relaxed his conscious mind a few seconds. He would allow his unconscious mind to speak. In his concentration, he shut out every distraction around him. He let his mind float, knowing from his vast experience that it would lead him to the answer.

He had almost given up when a moment of insight came and he felt a flash within his skull. He knew what troubled him. The bottom of the coffee pot! It was different from the rest of the pot. For half an inch around the bottom, the metal was smooth and silvery and not delicately embossed with designs on the brass like the pot.

He rushed to the door and swung it open. He screamed back at the steward, "Get away from the coffee!"

Unfortunately, he yelled one second too late. From outside the building, the first steward, no longer wearing a servant's uniform, pressed the detonator. Early that morning he had carefully molded the bottom of the brass pot with the plastic explosive FOAM-X. A jarring clash erupted, followed by three other powerful explosions. The noise temporarily deafened everyone within the confines of the great palace.

The assassin had placed enough FOAM-X to destroy the entire wing of the building. The impact tore down the heavy walls, crushing Chou Chung. The steward, only feet from the tray, had no chance. The guard received multiple head injuries and died seconds later.

Hours earlier, the assassin's leader had carefully instructed their man, providing him with a uniform, including a pair of shoes. Inside the heel the leader had hidden more FOAM-X. The final destruction, noise activated, occurred through the pre-programmed detonator. The smaller amount of FOAM-X ripped a gaping hole into the nearby building, and pitched the body forty-two feet into the air.

When Chinese investigators discovered the assassin's body, they connected him with the death of Chou Chung. They also assumed he had made a mistake in his use of plastic explosives and had killed himself as well. They had no suspicion that this, too, had been part of the plan.

Investigators found the man's picture and prints in their files. They knew he had been in the pay of the Arabs.

Within twenty-four hours, the Chinese began to plan their retaliation against the Arabs. Yet, as one of them remarked, "We Chinese are people of great patience. We can wait for the appropriate time. When our enemies least expect it, we shall strike."

King Joshua instituted a number of changes within the first six months of his reign. First, he changed the official language of Israel to English. "English is the *lingua franca* of the world. We must not only speak it well, we must speak it as precisely and as idiomatically as Americans, Canadians, British, or Australians." The Knesset approved the measure without negative votes.

All civil servants had to speak idiomatic English within one year or face termination of employment. Schools immediately switched their language curriculum to English.

The King brought in tax reform that equalized the burden of the poor and the rich. The common people praised him because it gave them more spendable funds. Among other reforms, citizens of Israel received a greater share of the malgamite income. He cut the wealth of the rich by as much as 40 percent. They did not protest. He pacified the wealthy through private (if questionable) arrangements.

Joshua produced plans for a palace. He laid out the

five-story building in the form of a castle with all modern conveniences, including advanced protection devices. Eight hundred workers began the construction of the palace and finished it fully by early 1998. An American architect announced over CBS TV in America that it cost the Israeli government the equivalent of 150 million dollars. Two days later, information leaked to the public media of the world that the palace in Jerusalem had not cost the Israeli taxpayers anything. The full cost of the palace had come "from private contributions."

The newly completed edifice with lighted fountains, well-kept gardens, and ample private grounds befitting a king became the envy of international royalty and the dream of the middle class. A broad, well-lighted street allowed visitors to stare at the magnificence of the palace.

Israel had started in 1948 as a religious state. The government limited citizenship to those of the Jewish faith. Some had embraced Judaism as a cultural choice, others had converted to other faiths after becoming citizens.

King Joshua made a shift in the policy of Israel. He had the Knesset declare it illegal to teach any religion contrary to the teachings of Judaism.

While everyone knew of the statute, politicians quickly assured everyone that religious discrimination would not happen in Israel. They enacted the legislation, they said, to root out fanatical sects that attracted the youth and involved them in drugs and extreme metaphysical practices.

Nagila Levy sat in on many high-level meetings Joshua held with the top international advisors he had recruited. She laughed to herself at the title "Administrative Advisors." They comprised a group of international experts who found themselves at a complete loss in coping with the world situation. They met with Joshua for his advice. No, she thought, he directed them.

She marvelled at his calm, self-assurance. Never once

using notes, looking at the information on the desk in front of him, or asking Nagila for verification, he pointed out the situation in every corner of the world. He knew the military power, the exact count of stockpiled weapons, and each country's own projections and strategies.

None of these experts ever brought him information he did not already know. Occasionally they brought misinformation and Joshua corrected them, pointing out the source of their misinformation. Usually it came through double agents who distorted true facts only enough that it could bring confusion.

After several meetings, each delegate made a report and waited for Joshua to add information, which he invariably did. From that point on, no delegate had anything more to contribute.

The meetings normally lasted four hours. Joshua Gad-Erianko spoke nonstop for most of that time. He never encouraged them to speak, although he did nothing that prevented their input. They sat stiffly in their chairs, eying him much like awestruck and fear-ridden students might appear before a formidable teacher.

After the third month of sitting quietly in the room, Nagila realized that he had never corrected her information. Twice he had held her up as an example of efficiency and thoroughness.

While Nagila listened, she also observed. It became clear to her that no one had ever argued with Joshua or offered the slightest protest. No one ever would. No one questioned facts about anything Joshua said or proposed. She also realized that Joshua never made personal references, offered opinions, or tentatively suggested anything.

Previously these eight people, six of them men, had never agreed among themselves. They represented a wide spectrum from far right-wing viewpoints to extreme liberals. She had known some of them to argue for hours over minute details. Yet in the cabinet office, restraint and silence prevailed. Other than, "Yes, your excellency," the most Nagila ever heard was, "I am not clear on what you mean, sir."

Nagila perceived another fact—one that troubled her.

For lack of a better term, she called it a glaze of fear. When King Joshua's attention turned to one of them, the expert stiffened slightly and then a look—a shroud of fear—covered the eyes. It never failed. The more she observed, the more she became aware that they sat in mortal fear of Joshua. She wondered why. She had no such feelings.

This puzzled Nagila. Joshua never threatened or belittled. He never hinted at removing any of them. Yet it was there. As soon as Joshua directed his attention elsewhere, the person's body relaxed slightly and the eyes hooded over. Not one of them looked directly at the others. They kept their gaze either directed at Joshua or upon themselves.

Her recognition of fear began with Bronski. She had never liked Solomon Bronski's heavy-handedness or his authoritarian tones. Yet in the meetings with the King, he sat with downcast eyes, his head slightly forward. When Joshua addressed him, his eyes—more than those of the others—registered stark terror. Most of the time his hands shook when the King spoke.

Once Nagila perceived the element of fear in Bronski, she noticed the same response from the others. These brilliant leaders of the world now became mere puppets, subservient and unquestioning.

The biggest surprise for Nagila came with the appearance of Zechariah Kalif. He had, months earlier, headed up the Egyptian delegation when they discussed the matter of Taba. She had argued publicly with Zechariah more than once. His staunch commitment to Arab solidarity had always been his blind spot. Nothing was more important to him than solidifying a base on which all Muslims in the world could work together.

Nagila Levy had been working directly under King Joshua almost a year when Zechariah Kalif appeared at the palace where King Joshua now conducted all affairs of state.

"Zechariah Kalif," she said and walked toward him with eager greeting. She held out her hand to him. Although not friends, they had always respected each other.

He nodded his head and said, "Ms. Levy, it is good to see you once again." He stopped and stared at the opulence of her office. All four walls, paneled in narrow strips of olive wood, contrasted with a desk and four chairs of handcrafted teak. The soft beige sofa at the far side enabled visitors to view the enclosed courtyard below.

"You are looking fit," she said.

"So do you and, ah, yes, you have come far. Quite far." The conspiratorial gleam in his eye momentarily disturbed her. "I had not expected—but then, I have had many surprises of late."

"Are you implying that I moved into this position because of something other than hard work?" She felt her face flush, hardly believing his words.

"But, of course," he said. "I would imply nothing else. After all, what would a fine woman like you have in her past?"

"What are you talking about?"

"Nothing," Zechariah Kalif said. "I beg your forgiveness. I think I was in error."

"Of course," Nagila said. Yet something about the way he had stated his apology failed to convince her. At the same time she wondered why he had even had such thoughts.

"Could you spare me three minutes of your time, Nagila?"

"Three minutes for an Egyptian to speak? Come, now, Zechariah—"

A sly grin appeared, making him seem like the old Zechariah Kalif. She pointed to a chair and he sat down. He refused tea.

"I come immediately to the point," he said, lowering his deep voice. "I have valuable information for King Joshua, but he is in conference now and unable to see me." He waved aside an explanation before Nagila had a chance to speak.

"It is only that I have urgent information." He placed his hand inside his jacket pocket and revealed a large envelope, folded in half. "I cannot wait. I must leave immediately."

"I suppose you could leave it with his secretary. As soon as he breaks—"

"No. With you." Zechariah's eyes searched Nagila's face as if sizing her up for the first time. "I asked if there is anyone he trusts. No one can answer that except to say that many believe he trusts you." He pulled an envelope from inside his coat. "He must have this immediately."

"Is it something I may ask about?"

"If you are trusted, he can tell you."

"I shall see that King Joshua receives the letter today."

"No, not today. He must have it now. Immediately."

"Zechariah, you know he's involved in a high-level meeting at this moment. I have never walked into such a meeting and interrupted him before—"

"Can you do it? Could you walk into the meeting and would he allow you to speak with him?"

"I suppose so—"

"Then you must do this." He waved the envelope toward her.

Nagila hesitated, her gaze shifting from the proffered envelope to his face. Then she saw the same expression as the others. Fear. She sensed immediately the powerful emotion that made her wonder if he feared for his life. He seemed pleased that she would take it, as if it meant he would not have to face Joshua in person. He had become like the others.

"Zechariah, I've always respected you. Even when we have disagreed. I've considered you a man of high character. But I have to ask you this. What are you afraid of? You and all the others?"

Confusion flashed across his face and he covered it quickly. "Fear? Do I look like a man afraid?"

"Yes. You and most of the others—" She paused as she realized she could have said *all of the others*. "I've been with the King in meetings and I can read the fear in their faces. Joshua treats them with respect, although he may make a little display of his vast knowledge. He doesn't shout or treat anyone unkindly and yet—"

"Is it not perhaps what he does not speak that says the most?"

"I don't understand what you mean, Zechariah."

He shook his head, dismissing her questions. "The envelope. I must leave. You will take it to him now? I shall wait here a few minutes while you do this."

"All right," she said. She walked unhesitatingly to the King's office.

He had told her he was meeting with non-Jewish officials who did not wish to be known. This happened regularly. Such guests came with an escort through the King's private entrance. No one in the palace saw them enter or leave. On two occasions within the past month, Joshua called Nagila into the office. She listened to them and received firsthand information.

On the second occurrence, she recognized two men from the Soviet Union's Politburo. She had seen their pictures and it surprised her. Both were men who purportedly never left the environs of Moscow, let alone the USSR. She wondered how Joshua had persuaded them to come. How had he arranged for their travel to Israel without their being missed and without a reporter somewhere informing the world?

The two guards at the door stared at her. "No one has permission to enter," one of them said.

"I shall take responsibility," Nagila said.

"But I have no authority to allow—"

"I have authority," Nagila said, not allowing herself to wonder if she had or not.

The guard moved aside, and, taking a key from around his neck, he turned and unlocked the door. He opened the door for her and pulled back, careful not to see anyone inside.

The parquet floor did not muffle the sound of Nagila's heels like the heavy carpeting in her own office. Joshua stopped speaking while she approached.

"Excuse me, your Excellency," Nagila said. She kept her eyes directly on the King, trying not to notice the others in the room. She held up the envelope. Joshua motioned for her to bring it to him.

As she came toward him, from her peripheral vision she

saw four men sitting in padded chairs, forming a kind of semicircle on the left side of his desk.

Joshua remained behind the huge desk. He reached for the envelope. "Wait," he said.

Nagila tried to keep her attention away from the visitors. Instead she concentrated on the office itself. Only two weeks earlier Joshua had refurbished the entire room, with the walls now made of highly polished teak. All the furniture in the room was handmade of teak. Only his office and hers had teak. The simplicity of the spacious room also gave it a special kind of elegance.

Joshua opened the envelope and extracted four sheets of paper, scanned them quickly, then paused to read them carefully. While he read, the four men kept their vision fixed on him, as if afraid to look around. Nagila moved her head slightly so that from her vantage point she could take in the entire scene.

Farouk sat on the far side. She had not seen him since the Taba negotiation. He was one of the last men she would have expected to see in this room. This hard-willed man influenced public opinion in Egypt, Jordan, Syria, and Arabia with the proverbial iron fist. A rumor circulated that he had once killed all members of a particular family because they had insulted him by not bringing their best food to a celebration in his honor. Nagila's sources had convinced her that it was no mere rumor.

Next to him sat Gideon Wittstein and that also surprised her. To his right sat Izzak Bermann, at one time the opposition leader in the Knesset. He had participated in the Taba agreement, although he had hardly spoken during the entire proceedings.

Nagila looked at the fourth man and it was not a face she recognized. He did not seem to fit into this odd mixture and she wondered what he was doing there.

Strange, she thought. Today I've seen four people, three of them involved in the Taba situation. As important as the event was, so many more significant things had happened that overshadowed the Taba Accord. In that moment, the full meaning of that Taba Accord struck her as violently as if someone had punched her in the stomach. Nagila gasped.

The Taba agreement had been set up. Somehow, far off in Russia, Joshua had set the stage for that, alienating Egypt from the rest of the Middle-Eastern Muslims. It afforded greater opportunity for the Arabs to vent their hatred on the Jews. That's why the Muslim world had condemned the agreement. *They—or somebody—wanted Israel set apart as everyone's enemy.*

T·W·O

"Ah, Nagila, you did well to bring this to me."
Nagila, startled by his voice, flinched.
Joshua did not seem to notice. Zechariah Kalif brought information that Solomon Bronski had entered into a secret agreement with the Russian-Arab powers to overthrow King Joshua. He smiled at the report. He had already known that information. He leaned forward and scribbled a note, folded it, and handed it to her. "I do not need to see him."

He turned toward the four men, his mind already beyond the interruption. "We are now ready for the next step in our strategy. I have marked it out for you, step by step, on the bottom of the page." He handed each of them a sheet of paper.

Nagila closed the door, her mind returning to the Taba agreement. If her suspicion was true—and she had an inner certainty that it was—that implied that Joshua had probably manipulated other such negotiations.

"What kind of man," she said aloud inside her office, "can manipulate the leaders of the world like this? What kind of king do we have?"

Citizens of Israel stared in shock as they read the news item. Even the enemies of Solomon Bronski found it hard to accept. They learned that the government had uncovered evidence that their former Prime Minister, Solomon Bronski, held a secret bank account of sixty million dollars.

The reports said that although the government had made no formal charges, the King would appoint a special committee to investigate.

The following morning King Joshua appeared briefly on television. "I have been deeply saddened at the turn of events. The honorable Mr. Bronski has served Israel well in the past. We do not wish to condemn him, however, until our investigation has uncovered all the facts."

Later that morning, Nagila saw Solomon Bronski at the palace. He waited in King Joshua's outer office for well over an hour for an appointment. Nagila passed him twice, but he never looked at her.

After a brief conversation with King Joshua he walked out of his office. Nagila, going down the hallway, almost bumped into him. He seemed unaware of her presence.

Nagila laid her hand on his shoulder. "Solomon, I'm sorry to hear about what's happened. I want you to know that I believe in your innocence."

He stared at her and slowly shook his head. "It doesn't matter."

"Of course it matters if you're innocent of the charges."

His eyes focused on Nagila. "God must have a strange sense of humor," he said. Then, as if talking to himself, his eyes focused in a stare, he said, "Innocent of one crime but guilty of a different one. Which is worse? Does it make any difference?"

"Solomon, please, can I help? I believe in you."

He shook his head. "No one can help me now . . . no one." He pushed past her and walked to the elevator.

Nagila wanted to run after him, but she had no idea what more to say. She prided herself on being a good judge of character. Whatever faults Solomon Bronski had, they did not include accumulating wealth.

She turned to go back to her office, then paused at the window. She stared vacantly, wondering if she ought to appeal to the King to help Solomon. She saw Solomon leave the building and walk over to the fountain. The central figures, spewing out water, depicted the heroes of Israel who had died fighting for the country.

Solomon paused in front of the fountain, stared at the bronze figures and shook his head. From inside his coat, he pulled out a gun and placed the barrel against his right temple and pulled the trigger. The impact of the bullet killed him instantly. His body slumped forward and into the fountain.

It happened so quickly that the final act did not register in Nagila's mind. When it did she screamed.

The next day, King Joshua announced over television that his investigative committee had concluded that Solomon Bronski had done no wrong. Enemies of the nation had set up the account in an attempt to blackmail Bronski into betraying his country.

"Abject sadness that his name be sullied with such terrible rumors caused such stress upon our former Prime Minister that he suffered a heart attack." King Joshua paused and said, "I have, therefore, declared that Israel will observe tomorrow as a day of mourning for this honorable champion of our country."

With a closed casket, at the family's request, Bronski's body lay in state for three days.

"It is always good to see you, Nagila," Nasief said as he welcomed her into his home. "You have not been here lately. I wondered if I had offended you or—"

"No, nothing like that. It is my work. It keeps me so busy these days."

"You look tired," the older man said softly. "I hope you will soon have a chance to rest."

"Yes, I hope so." Nagila said. It was not the work that caused her the problem, it was the inability to sleep at night.

Had she known him better, she would have told him of Solomon Bronski's death and her suspicions that Joshua had somehow influenced him to take his own life. She would have told him about the glaze of fear. And lately another element had begun to trouble her.

Nagila had made remarkable progress with her Soviet operatives. Astounding response. Never had she known of officials so eager to pass on information, all of it totally genuine and of high caliber.

Although other Mossad members like herself did not tell her of their activities, she had the impression that they encountered the same phenomenon. Everyone wanted to pass on vital information to King Joshua. Why, now? Some of her agents had reputations as being among the most anti-Israeli in the world.

Nagila sat down, lost in her own thoughts. She wished she had someone to talk to. After several minutes, she roused herself, pushing her troublesome thoughts aside. She observed her surroundings.

Instead of the usual fourteen or fifteen people who attended the meeting, forty-three were present tonight. Most of them brought their own Bibles in English. A few brought them in the now-banned Hebrew language as well. Nagila surveyed the room once and noticed that Shaheen was not present. That realization brought on a pang of loneliness. He had never missed any of the studies she had attended.

Nasief stood up. "The study will begin." Nasief prayed in soft tones for Yahweh, the God of Israel, to enlighten everyone as they studied together.

"Tonight I am reading to you from the Gospel according to St. Mark. I particularly wish you to pay close attention to these words. Jesus spoke them only hours before his betrayal." Nasief read:

"Take heed that no one leads you astray. Many will come in my name, saying, 'I am he!' and they will lead many astray. And when you hear of wars and rumors of wars, do not be alarmed; this must take place, but the end is not yet. For nation will rise against nation, and kingdom against kingdom; there will be earthquakes in various places, there will be famines; this is but the beginning of the sufferings.

"But take heed to yourselves; for they will deliver you up to councils; and you will be beaten in synagogues; and you will stand before governors and kings for my sake, to bear testimony before them."

A hand shot up in the front row and a voice called out, "Were not these prophetic statements fulfilled in the first century? The followers of Jesus underwent persecution—all the things Jesus said would happen."

"And through the centuries," another voice added, "haven't there been zealous men rise up who claimed to be the Messiah?"

Nasief nodded. "Yes, to both of your questions. At the same time, please understand something about biblical predictions. They have had a limited fulfillment. They await an ultimate fulfillment in the last days."

Nagila only half-listened for several minutes. Being away from the palace meant that she could think clearly. The atmosphere there seemed to prevent any clear concentration. She felt as if Joshua's spirit permeated every square foot of the building. But outside, such as here in Nasief's study, her mind cleared and she could reason things out.

"The Antichrist is coming! He may already be on the scene," Nasief said. "I warn you to watch. To be careful. In fact, I have a strong opinion that this evil creature is already loose in our world."

Nagila, suddenly alert to the statements Nasief had just made, raised her hand. "As you know, I'm not a convert, but I have a question."

"Ask away," he said with genuine warmth.

"If there is such a person as this—this evil being—"

"The Antichrist," Nasief said. "I also assure you he is real."

"If I accepted this as truth, does it mean I would also need to accept the other things—"

"To believe them? If I am being consistent with the truth, yes." He paused and added, "Years ago a British scholar spoke about what he called the ring of truth. That which is true, even when we can't verify it has a sound—a ring—a tone—that makes seekers of truth understand."

"If I should be able to say that this teaching I have heard tonight has the ring of truth, and I believe that this Antichrist exists, it logically means that your Jesus must be the Messiah, then? Is that what you are saying?"

"Precisely."

"But something more. Suppose . . . suppose this person—this Antichrist comes—"

"Or has already appeared and begun his work," Nasief interrupted.

"But how can we know? Powerful people rise to the scene all the time. Several powerful men are in strong positions in the Soviet Union. Or what about the leaders from the United States? Right here in Israel, we have a King again, after more than 2500 years. He is a man of extraordinary ability and power."

Nasief's white head nodded slowly. A thin man with a small frame, his strong voice seemed out of place with his physique. "Nagila, in another place Jesus said that we should know the false from the real by looking at the results in their lives. Or, as he put it, by their fruit. Good people do good. Evil people do evil. Whoever is the Antichrist will declare his true nature by what he does. It cannot be otherwise."

"One more question," Nagila said. "Do you yourself believe that this Antichrist has already come?"

Nasief stared into space and Nagila began to wonder if he would answer her. "It may be too soon to tell. Historically, when an event takes place, those immediately present often do not realize that it is a new epoch in the world. One must watch carefully and evaluate cautiously."

"Nasief, while that's good advice, what do you personally think? Have you really answered my question?"

"I have tried to avoid answering your question," he said simply.

"But if you know—"

"At the moment, I merely hold an opinion. I do not wish to express this until I am more certain. That is the best I can offer you as an answer."

"Thank you," Nagila said.

"Now, if we look once again at these verses in Mark . . ." In his resonant voice, Nasief explained, verse by verse, what Jesus wanted his followers to understand.

A loud banging on the door interrupted Nasief's teaching. He stopped speaking and, like all of the others, stared at the door. "Yes? Who is it? Come in!"

The pounding stopped and the door opened. An Israeli army officer walked inside. Behind him marched twelve armed soldiers.

"I have come here," the officer said, "in the name of the King of Israel." From inside his tunic he pulled out a sheet of paper, unfolded it and read, "By order of Joshua Gad-Erianko, King of Israel, all religious teaching that goes contrary to the teaching of Judaism is hereby outlawed. The Kingdom of Israel will tolerate no subversive elements that speak, teach, or work against the religion of our fathers."

The soldiers moved their automatic rifles from their shoulders and brought them forward into the firing position. Poised to fire, they waited for a command. One woman screamed.

"This is an outrage!" cried a man.

The officer held up his arm. "Because we are compassionate people, we shall not punish anyone here tonight. You understand, of course, that you cannot meet again. You must not speak of these teachings that run contrary to our faith."

Nasief walked across the room and stopped in front of the leader. "For more than thirty years I have taught the Christian faith. I do not plan to stop now."

"You are an old and foolish man," he said. "Next time, we will beat you. Perhaps imprison you. Who knows? It is misguided people like you who bring disunity to our nation."

"Disunity? When I teach of a God who loves all people?" Nasief moved closer so that only inches separated the two men. His voice stayed calm. "Surely love never brings chaos. I invite you and your men to stay and to hear what—"

The officer struck Nasief across the face. The crack of force against the cheekbone sounded across the room. A large ring on the officer's finger bit into Nasief's skin. He lost his balance, staggered, and barely righted himself.

"I'm sorry you feel forced to do this," Nasief said through his bruised lips.

"I obey my orders."

"And I obey mine. I shall continue to speak—"

A second blow struck Nasief on the side of the head and he crumpled to the floor. Nagila raced to the old man. She helped him to his feet and stood next to him, her arm around his shoulder. "Colonel," she said, "I do not know you or where you think you get such authority—"

He held out the paper. She immediaty recognized Joshua's distinctive signature.

"There must be some mistake! My name is Nagila Levy and I work—"

"Yes, I know. I expected to find you here." He nodded courteously. "My orders are to treat you with deep respect. However, I will not hesitate to do whatever I consider necessary to break up this illegal meeting."

He brushed past Nasief and faced the people. "You are to disperse. Now. Go to your homes. I am listing no names today. If you meet again, however, you will be charged with committing crimes against the Kingdom of Israel."

The people hurried toward the door, eager to be gone. The officer turned back to Nasief. "I hope you understand the seriousness of this order."

Nasief pulled away from Nagila. "As long as I have breath in my body," he winced in pain, "I shall continue to teach the truth."

"I have warned you."

"I'm not afraid of warnings! I am not afraid of brute force. I have a power behind me that will take care of me. No matter what you do! God is with me and you can do nothing unless he allows it!"

T·H·R·E·E

Shaheen pulled Nagila closer so that her head rested against his chest. His encircling arms held her with a gentleness she had not thought possible from him. "Don't be afraid," he whispered and kissed her brow. "If they come here, they come."

"Why wait for them to come?" Nagila pulled away from him and moved into the center of the room. "Quickly! Get rid of the candles. Turn on the lights! Set up chairs so that we look like friends enjoying an evening together."

She raced into another room, found two straight chairs, and hurried back with them. "Quickly! Help me!"

The others moved into action. Shaheen dragged in a stuffed chair and pushed it into a prominent place. Another brought in a small table and someone else two more straight chairs. The podium Nasief had used disappeared from sight.

As if energized by her activity, Nasief left and reappeared immediately with a television set. Someone came behind him with a table for the set. Nasief snapped on the TV and the canned laughter from an American-made situation comedy filled the room.

Nasief disappeared a second time and returned with

cups and a teapot. He poured varying amounts of cold tea into each cup and placed them on the table.

They were waiting for the inevitable sound at the door. Nagila wondered if they would force the door open or knock.

As Nagila shivered out of fear of the impending soldiers, Shaheen put his arm around her and pulled her close to himself. "I'm right here, Nagila."

Before she could answer, the pounding of a rifle butt drowned out all other sound in the room. Without waiting for a reply, the handle turned and the door flew open. An officer, not the one from the previous night, marched into the room. Six soldiers flanked him, their Uzi machine pistols poised, as if eager to open fire.

Nasief, halfway to the door, stopped. "Why do you break into my home like this?"

"You have a meeting of Christians here. I have come to arrest them."

"Is that so?" Shaheen stood. "Is that what you see? You have caught us studying forbidden books? Advocating the overthrow of our King? Or would you say we are sitting here as good citizens. Come now, what do you see?"

The captain stared at the room, seeing his mistake but unwilling to apologize. He stepped backward and his eyes surveyed the room. He turned and walked out, saying nothing.

Shaheen walked with Nagila through the Arab quarter and to the place where she had parked her car. He rode with her to the palace, despite her protests. "I have no weapon to defend you," he said, "but having another person with you surely makes it safer than being alone."

"How will you be safe after I go inside?"

"I will fade into darkness and stay off the street," he said calmly. "I have been practicing."

Nagila laughed and realized that it was the first truly

relaxed moment she had experienced in the past two weeks. "Don't you think I can blend with the blackness of night as well? I could blacken my face, change into darker clothing—"

"You may have to do that in the future in order to leave the palace when you wish."

"Come now, Shaheen. You think the King wishes to make me a prisoner?" The question stuck in her own throat.

"I don't know." He slowed down and shook his head. "There is so much I don't know about these days." He lapsed into momentary silence. "Nothing is as it used to be. Everything—everybody—different. Our leaders do not act or sound the same. It used to become boring to hear them say the same things repeatedly, but they have changed."

"You have noticed that, have you?" Nagila asked.

"It is getting late," Nagila said. "I had better go inside."

Shaheen put his arms around Nagila. "Before you do, one thing I want you to know. I love you, Nagila. I know that now."

"Shaheen, don't say that, please."

"It is true and I must tell you. I am not good at saying things like this, but I love you. I have loved you for a very, very long time. I hope you feel something for me—"

"Shaheen, I know what you'd like me to answer, but I can't."

"I am sorry. I thought you felt something for me."

"I do. I mean, I don't know what I feel. I like you immensely. Right now I'm too confused about what's going on. I love my country. I work for the King and I'm confused about my loyalty to him. These things are tearing me up so much inside that—"

"I love my country, too," he said, "but I have time for personal involvements."

"Don't press me. Not just yet, anyway—"

Shaheen pulled her body toward his own. With his right hand, he tilted her chin upward. He kissed her lips gently. "You know my feelings for you."

Before she could reply, his lips pressed against hers again and his arms encased her. Without considering her action, Nagila responded to the pressure of his lips against her own.

Nagila approached the palace, paused in front of a bright light. She waited for the two guards to recognize her. Sometimes she had to show her identification but usually not. Tonight one of the guards waved her inside. Another fifty paces and she came to the second checkpoint. The whole area, swathed by brilliant light, always made Nagila feel as if the brightness penetrated every pore of her body. She got out of her car, leaving the keys in the ignition. She handed the corporal-in-charge her identity badge.

All four soldiers on duty knew her, but, following strict orders by King Joshua, they asked Nagila to present her identity badge.

Satisfied, the corporal summoned one of the guards to park Nagila's car. He then personally unlocked the outer palace door for her. "Good night, Ms. Levy." His calling her by name sounded like an apology for the impersonal role he played.

Upon entering the palace proper, she approached the mammoth desk where three security guards worked at all times. Two of them kept their gaze on TV monitors while the third watched everyone entering or leaving.

"Good evening," the soldier said and handed her an envelope.

Nagila thanked him and walked down the corridor toward her own spacious apartment. She was one of twelve people who lived in the palace on the ground floor. Joshua had his private quarters on the fifth and highest floor. The other floors contained offices for members of what had formerly been called the Knesset. These leaders had now been named Regal Advisors.

As Nagila walked ahead, she opened the envelope. It read:

COME TO MY ROOMS. J

"The King summons," she mumbled and tried to laugh at the idea. Joshua had never asked her before to come to his private quarters. It was after eleven and she wondered if she ought to wait until morning. She decided that if it was too late, Joshua's personal guard would stop her.

The soldier who guarded the King's private elevator watched her approach. He inserted a key and moved aside. The elevator door opened. "You are expected," he said.

Nagila stepped inside, with the guard immediately behind her. An iron grill slammed shut and a heavy steel door slid silently across the opening.

"Please stand in the center." He pressed a button on the inside of the elevator; a strong light shone from the top that lasted eight seconds and then went off.

Seeing the surprised expression on Nagila's face he said, "Special detector. If you are carrying arms of any kind or plastic explosives, the light turns blue and emits signals to guards throughout the palace." He smiled. "We must protect our King. Many terrorists travel the world today, you know."

"Yes. I know," Nagila said. *And I wonder how many of them King Joshua sends.* The thought caused her a flush of consternation. This was her King she was criticizing. She had no actual proof, only suspicion. All governments employed terrorists of one kind or another. She had no right to be harsh toward Joshua.

The elevator operated so smoothly she hardly noticed the upward movement. The door opened into a large hallway. Outside the elevator stood a guard, his rifle poised at parade rest. He snapped to attention and took two steps back. Behind him stood two other guards, flanking the double oak doors of the King's living quarters.

Nagila reached for her identification, but the first soldier shook his head. "His Majesty expects you. You may enter without knocking."

Nagila entered the room and Joshua came toward her. He wore the usual black business suit. As late as it was, Joshua appeared as fresh and alert as if he had just started his day.

"Ah, good evening, Nagila." He said. He held a partially filled wine glass in his hand. "Thank you for accepting my invitation."

A streak of defiance stirred inside her. "Did I have a choice?"

"Perhaps not." He indicated a chair. "Please sit down. May I pour you a glass of wine?"

"I don't care for any."

"Pity. It is one of the first from southern France. Sent especially to me only last week. 1939 vintage—an excellent year for them." He took a long drink and drained the glass. He poured himself another.

While he finished his drink, Nagila allowed her eyes to survey the room. The walls, painted in a dull gray, surprised her. Not a picture anywhere. The furniture, although functional, might have been purchased from any retail chain.

"You expected a more elaborate setting?" he asked as if she had spoken her thoughts.

"Yes, I suppose I did."

"These things—" his arm swept out wide, "mean little. I have other things that entice me more."

"Such as power?"

"Precisely." Joshua leaned forward. "Does that surprise you?"

"Not anymore. My research indicates, however, that those who climb to positions of power want everything that goes with it. That includes riches and luxury."

"Yes, to some, ownership and possession of goods are important. I prefer to concentrate more fully on other things." He sat down in a padded straight chair and indicated the sofa for Nagila. "You are sure you want nothing to drink?"

She shook her head.

"First, Nagila, a minor issue I must bring up. I want you to know that I could have had you arrested when you congregated with that strange group this evening. I choose instead to warn you. *This time.*"

"You mean that you knew exactly where I was tonight? You have had me spied upon?"

"Spied upon? Come now, Nagila, that is unfair. I have placed you under discreet protection. You are important to me. I wish no harm to come to you. Ever."

"I see." Nagila made no attempt to hold back the hardness in her voice or to deny the resentment she felt. "It makes me feel like some kind of prisoner."

"Not at all. Further, no harm has come to any of the people who attended the teaching class tonight. I wanted to assure you of that fact. Tomorrow, however, representatives of the state will visit them and warn them of their foolishness and the danger to which they subject themselves."

"Those people cause no problems. They're probably the most peaceful people in the nation. They are serious about their religious faith. They are anything but subversive. I cannot understand why you had their religion declared illegal."

"Nagila! You question my judgment?" He stopped and smiled self-consciously. "Forgive me. One of the tragedies of being a King is that I am not used to anyone offering a contrary opinion. As a matter of fact," he smiled and touched her hand, "you are the only one who has either disagreed or questioned my decisions. You are a brave woman. I admire that in you." He leaned forward and took her hand. "However, I will not tolerate it."

Nagila immediately recoiled inside, although she carefully concealed it. "Why am I the only one?" His strong fingers engulfed her hand and closed firmly. It surprised her that his hand was so cold.

"Perhaps no one else has your courage—"

"Nonsense! You hold a kind of power over people. You make them afraid of you. How do you do it?"

"Power? Do I?"

"Of course. You instill fear."

"Did you ever read the writings of Machiavelli?" he asked.

"No, but I know a little of what he believed."

"He was a man who wanted to unite Italy and free his nation from corruption and the hands of degenerate men. He believed that a single man—a lawgiver who creates a sovereign power and writes the laws—is the basis of a great government."

"And you're already doing that," Nagila said. "And, as

I remember, he also believed that such a person—this law-giver—was above the law."

"That's true. He proposed that the function of a ruler is to maintain and to enlarge his political power. He stated that the ruler must use any means necessary to achieve his right purpose. Any means."

"You have certainly followed him, haven't you?"

"Further, and more to the point, is the issue of fear. Machiavelli said that those in power rule either by love or by fear and that fear is the greater and more permanent weapon."

"So you have found a way to make everyone afraid."

"Everyone? You're not afraid of me."

"I'm not important either."

"On the contrary, you're quite important. To me. Extremely important." He took a step toward her.

"Joshua, I have something bothering me," Nagila said. "If I'm important to you—"

"I assure you that you are." Joshua pulled up a chair next to hers. He sat down and took her hand.

"Then tell me about these leaders." Nagila wanted to withdraw from him, but she hesitated. Momentarily she wondered if she had become afraid too. "I've seen how great leaders react to you. Everyone who comes to visit you ends up afraid of you."

"Nagila, you have nothing to fear from me." Without releasing her hand, he moved forward in his chair. Their knees barely touched. "I want only your happiness, your best in life."

"I'd rather talk about the others."

"I prefer to talk about you."

"Joshua, it's late and I'm tired. I think I'd better go." She tried to remove her hand from his clasp.

"You do like me, don't you, Nagila? At least you like me a little?"

"I don't know how I feel, Joshua. Right now I can't get my personal feelings toward you sorted out because I can't figure out what's going on around here."

Joshua stared blankly at her. "I do not understand. I

wish to talk about you and me—a woman and a man. You keep returning to other people. What do they have to do with us?"

"Everything."

"I do not see any connection—"

"Joshua, the way you treat other people or the way other people respond to you, that's important. That helps me to know more about you."

"I still do not understand. You see, you have been attending those classes which I dislike. You have talked regularly with Shaheen Ahman. Yet these things do not change my feelings toward you."

"Joshua, I wouldn't love you just because you are handsome and brilliant. Any man I love would have to be the kind of person I could respect. A man I could be proud of. Part of my loving him would come out of the way he behaves with others."

Joshua shook his head. "I do not see how this should make any difference. I would always treat you with kindness—"

"Let's leave it for now, then," she said. "I can't tell you how I feel about you or anything until I figure out a lot of other things going on inside me." Nagila successfully withdrew her hand. She leaned back so that their bodies were no longer in contact.

"I care deeply about you. I want you to feel the same about me. I want your desire to burn for me as strongly as mine does for you—"

"Right now," Nagila interrupted, "right now I feel confused. I don't know what's going on and yet—and yet I know you're behind it. Not just the events happening here in Israel. Everywhere—everywhere in the world."

Joshua smiled, nodded, and closed his eyes. "You are both brilliant and beautiful. Just today I tried to decide which quality you possessed more fully. I have still not decided."

"Joshua, what's going on? You've allowed me to talk frankly, so I ask you to answer just as frankly."

He hesitated and Nagila had the impression he debated within himself to reply. He took his wine glass, refilled it, and drank it down in one swallow. He refilled it and set it on the table in front of him. "I have a destiny laid out for me, Nagila. You may not understand this, but I have things I must do and nothing can stop me. Nothing! It is as certain as if it had been planned and foreordained before my birth."

"What kind of destiny?"

"If I told you, it would sound ludicrous and I think you would laugh."

"A year ago I might have. Nothing you tell me now would surprise me too much."

Joshua gripped her shoulders and his fingers dug through the material. "I will rule the world—the entire world. This is my ultimate destiny."

Nagila stared at him. She laughed self-consciously. "You're right. I find it difficult to believe."

"That does not matter now, Nagila. I am talking openly to you because—because for the first time in my life, I have known someone with whom I wish to share that destiny."

His words came as a shock. She listened, but she did not want to accept the words. Her eyes appraised the man next to her. She knew Joshua's age, but he could easily pass for thirty with the ruddy cheeks of the young. No lines on his face indicated the aging process at work. "You make it sound so mysterious."

"Perhaps you could speak of mystery. Even I do not understand all of this and why. I know only that I came into this world for a special purpose. You will see this purpose unfold before your eyes."

Joshua stared down at Nagila. For the first time he detected fear in her. Yet not the kind of fear from those whom he controlled. He touched her shoulder and she pulled away.

"Why did you do that?" he asked. "Jerk your shoulder away?"

"I don't understand you, Joshua." She dropped her

gaze and said, "I wonder if you're fully sane. You talk like you're mad."

"Ah, is that what you think?" He nodded and considered the matter in silence before adding, "Yes, I can see why you might think such a thing. But I am sane and I speak the truth."

"In that case, I'll watch it as it takes place. Ruling the world, I mean."

"More than that, Nagila. Much more than that."

"More? What more can there be?"

Joshua knelt in front of her. "Look at my face. Look at it carefully. How old am I?"

She thought for a moment. "Hmmm, you were born in 1948, so that makes you fifty."

"Do I look fifty?"

Nagila's eyes scanned his face. He did not have a wrinkle. She could not detect a single gray hair. She glanced at his hands and they were definitely the hands of a young man. "No—no, you look—well, more my age."

"Precisely. That is part of my secret, Nagila. I will never look older either."

"Like the novel *The Picture of Dorian Gray?* The picture gets older, but you stay the same age? You want me to believe something like that?"

"I want you to believe what I tell you because I speak the truth."

"You have discovered the legendary fountain of youth. Is that it?"

"Do not make light of this, Nagila. I have discovered a way to remain young."

"A lot of companies would murder for that secret—"

"Do not make light of this. I ask you to think about it, Nagila. But also," and he leaned closer, his lips inches from hers, "I want to share this with you as well."

F·O·U·R

Long after Nagila lay in bed, she kept remembering the conversation with Joshua. In some ways it would be wonderful if she could love him. Who wouldn't want the luxuries and splendor he could offer? Suppose he had found a way to remain young. Never to grow old. Never to get crippled and wrinkled or to feel the pains of the aged.

But, she reminded herself, she did not love him. She would either love him spontaneously, easily, or she would never love him. She wanted to trust him, yet she found herself resisting. Nagila believed that he genuinely loved her. He was too awkward and unsure of himself to be putting on a false front.

It had touched her when he said, "I cannot get you out of my mind. No one has ever stirred me inside before. Not another human being on this earth. I had no feelings—no tender emotions before I met you. You have stirred up something inside me. You have made a part of me come to life."

They had stood at the door and he spoke those words to her and then he kissed her. Nagila did not respond even when he embraced her and held her tightly.

"Joshua, don't—" she said.

"But I want you to know—"

"I can't, Joshua. I just can't give myself to you like this."

"Not even with the promise of what I hold for you?"

"But I don't care about that. At least not as most important."

As Nagila's body begged for sleep, she thought of Joshua. She decided that he was so used to winning in the struggle over power that he could not grasp that other people had no interest in ruling or controlling others.

After he released her he tried one more time. "Nagila, together we shall inaugurate a true utopia. I can and shall wipe out every enemy or anyone who opposes me. I shall have the means to wipe away hunger and poverty. No one will have material needs. To my friends I shall bring peace and happiness for a long, long time."

Joshua paused and looked at her quizzically. "Does my frankness disturb you?"

"Very much. It sounds ruthless."

"Only until I achieve what I wish. But understand, Nagila, I would never wish to harm you in any way. Please believe that."

"You'll harm others. Some of them people I care deeply about. But you're saying that I don't have to have any personal fear. Is that it?"

"Yes. Even those you care about, as you say, I harm only because they defy my laws or they deserve punishment. You can forget them. You will not need them to be happy."

"Is that how you understand life? And relationships with people?"

"I don't want to understand anything more about people. As long as they do what I ask—"

"You mean as long as you control them?"

"You could say it that way."

"And control me, too?"

"To love you. That's all I want. You are different. Nagila, let me take you for myself. As my queen. My wife. My companion. Whatever you wish to be."

"I don't love you."

"This Shaheen? Do you love him?"

"I don't know."

Joshua had seen from her expression that she spoke the truth. "I do not know much about love, of course. For now I am willing to wait a little longer. I will do anything necessary to have you."

He had let her go. Now her mind kept her tossing through the night.

Weeks later Nagila reread the decoded messages from her two contacts in the Soviet Politburo. Upon receiving them, she had asked to see Joshua. She handed him the two separate messages. Both informed her that high-placed members of the Soviet Union, China, and the AAN (Alliance of Arab Nations) had met secretly in Singapore. They agreed upon the single purpose of destroying all opposition in South America and controlling the entire continent.

Joshua read the material rapidly and handed it back. "Yes? There is something you want to discuss about this?"

"Shouldn't you intervene?"

"Why?"

"If they succeed, that means that more than three fourths of the world will band together. Eventually that means they will fight against Israel. We would have only the United States and Western Europe to help us. And we have learned we can't always depend on them."

"We need no help from anyone."

Nagila stepped back in surprise. "Joshua, we are a small nation—surrounded by our age-old enemies. Rumors hint that the Egyptians are reconsidering their position."

"It must happen this way."

"I don't understand. Can't you do something to prevent it from happening?"

"Prevent it? Of course not. Nagila, we shall assist it."

She faced him, obviously unable to grasp what he was

telling her. "I thought you wanted power—that you would—"

"You must learn to trust my judgment. All things are working out for the best. Do not worry. At the proper moment, I shall save Israel from all enemies."

"You have the final decision," Nagila said, her voice filled with anger. She turned and walked out.

Back in her office, Nagila sat at her desk and replayed the conversation. No matter how she tried to reason it, she could make no sense of it. Her thoughts kept returning to the night she had gone to his quarters. Since then she had wondered several times about his sanity. Had he started something that no one could control? Were his ideas purely self-delusion? No matter how she considered everything, she had to admit that Joshua had come into power suddenly.

The latest news items never flustered him. She could tell from his responses that he had anticipated the events before they happened. Sometimes she wondered if he actually planned it and then waited for confirmation of its fulfillment. The immensity of the number of people Joshua would have to control to bring about such changes staggered her mind.

"What kind of man is he?" she asked again and again.

By midafternoon, Nagila had accomplished little because she found it impossible to concentrate for more than a few minutes on her work. More and more questions troubled her. What would Joshua do about Nasief and others? Surely he would not kill them, would he? Yet she realized that Joshua would never hesitate to destroy anyone if it suited his purpose. It also troubled her that, by living and working at the palace, she was aiding Joshua's bid for world control. Did she want to have a role in that?

If I want to leave, will he let me? Nagila came to the frightening realization that Joshua was not only capable of doing anything, he could just as easily turn on her and have her done away with.

Once she reached that last conclusion, her rational mind argued with herself that Joshua could not possibly be that amoral. He was not some inhuman creature, devoid of feeling. The other part of her counter-argued that he himself had said he had no emotions, that he had never loved anyone before Nagila.

Nagila decided she needed to talk to someone she could trust. Immediately she thought of Shaheen and phoned his office. "Could we meet? I need to talk to you about some items that have arisen since the Taba Accord."

"Of course. You name the time and the place."

Because Joshua already knew of Shaheen, she assumed that his discreet protection meant that the King had assigned men to follow her no matter where she went or how carefully she tried to elude them.

Her defiant streak came to the fore. "Come here. To the palace. We have a dining room for palace residents. We're permitted to invite guests. If you could come right away, we could take afternoon tea."

When Shaheen arrived at the palace, he had a visitor's badge waiting for him. A guard directed him where to park his car. A four-soldier, armed escort led him to Nagila's office.

Nagila dismissed the guards and led Shaheen down the hallway to the dining room. A waiter, wearing a red fez and his starched white uniform-gown, appeared as soon as the door opened. Nagila had not eaten lunch, so she ordered a sandwich for herself. Shaheen wanted only coffee.

As soon as the waiter disappeared, Nagila leaned forward and lowered her voice to a whisper. "I don't know if this place is bugged or if I'm getting paranoid or what's going on. I'm terribly confused and I had to talk to someone."

Shaheen smiled as he also leaned forward, leaving only inches of space separating them. "I like being close to you, Nagila. Talk all you want."

Keeping an eye out for the waiter, Nagila sketched the information she had picked up from her sources that possibly linked Joshua with heinous terrorist activities. She told him what she had learned about the three powers aligning themselves against South America. "Joshua supports such action and says it must happen according to his plan. Is he insane?"

"I do not think he's insane."

"What do you think?"

"I think he has a plan, a diabolical plan," Shaheen answered. "I would even say that he has some way to influence leaders around the world. I don't understand how—"

"I keep coming to conclusions I don't like. I see things here at the palace that trouble me." She stopped, hesitant to influence him with her suppositions. "I wanted to tell you, to get your perspective."

"I think, Nagila, that King Joshua is unlike any other man either of us has met before."

"Shaheen, you know something. You're holding back. Please tell me."

"It's nothing I actually know. More what I suspect . . ." Shaheen tried to decide how much he wanted to say to her. "I've been reading the passages in the Bible that Nasief recommended. He has also loaned me several books. I am somewhat reluctant to offer my conclusion—"

"I want to hear anything that could possibly shed light on this."

"You want to know what I think? And before you answer, remember that I may be totally mistaken."

"Please tell me. That's why I asked you to come."

"All right. King Joshua stands behind many of the assassinations and political upheavals going on in the world. He does this because he has some kind of diabolical power at his disposal. What Nasief calls satanic or demonic power. Power above and beyond human ability."

"Oh, come on, Shaheen."

"You do not think that possible?"

"I don't understand things like that. Even though the ancients believed in them, we of the modern world—" Nagila broke off in mid-sentence, and her hand clutched Shaheen's. "Oh!"

Shaheen followed her gaze. Two men entered the din-

ing room. The tall one was Joshua. His face registered no
surprise at seeing them together. He led the way and walked
directly to their table.

Shaheen stood. "Your Excellency." He bobbed his head
in respect.

"I have not had the pleasure of meeting you personally,
Mr. Ahman," Joshua said. "I am aware that you have ren-
dered valuable service to Israel in your work with Shin Bet,
at Taba and in your present work with the indigent and
handicapped."

"It flatters me that you would know that. It flatters me
even more that you would say so," Shaheen said. He stood
an inch shorter than the King with a slighter build. He
underweighed the King by twenty pounds.

Joshua stared into Shaheen's eyes, peering deeply. Seconds ticked by before Joshua took a step backward. "I have
underestimated you, Mr. Ahman. You are a stronger man
than I had suspected."

"I have no idea what you're talking about," Shaheen
said. "Please forgive my frankness, Your Excellency."

Joshua gave him the merest nod and turned away from
him. "Nagila, I wish you to meet my teacher from my boyhood in Russia."

"I recognize Ivor Kalinin from having seen photographs
of him. I didn't realize you were Joshua's teacher."

"Many years ago," Kalinin said. He stooped slightly,
but without disguising that he had once been tall and thin.
His sparse hair, lined face, and wearied eyes marked him as a
man who had endured much hardship.

"You left Russia many years ago, didn't you?" Nagila
asked. "You're Canadian now, I believe."

"That is correct." His flawless grammar retained the
harsher Russian sounds when he spoke. Yet his deep voice
and his phrasing made him sound almost musical.

"King Joshua must owe you a great debt," Shaheen
said. "You did an excellent job in preparing him for leadership."

"I did little," he said. "Joshua Gad-Erianko needed no

one. His remarkable intellect and drive for knowledge would have happened anyway. Outstanding always. No, it is I who owe him."

"You mean because he let you teach him?"

"That also," he said. "When I wished to leave Mother Russia during Joshua's student days, the government allowed virtually no one to leave. Yet he managed to be of help to secure my exit papers."

"Yes, we have known each other a long time," Joshua said. The hardness of his voice stifled Kalinin's further explanations.

"I have heard of your splendid work with the Canadian government," Nagila said, trying to bridge the awkwardness. "I have been told that your economic policies have set the example for much of the western world."

The teacher smiled. "I have only done my best." The smile vanished immediately. His gaze shifted to Joshua as if asking for permission to continue.

Nagila recognized the same fear in Ivor Kalinin's eyes she had seen in the others. He was different, more resigned to the life of fearful subservience. Yet he had a softer appearance about him, perhaps because he had been under Joshua's control longer. Nagila realized that she perceived not only fear of Joshua in the eyes of many but hatred as well. Ivor Kalinin was not a man who hated.

"Can you believe that I have not seen my old teacher since I was fourteen? That was when we parted, not to meet again in person until today."

"And yet, you knew he would call upon you one day, didn't you, Dr. Kalinin?" Shaheen asked.

"He made me to know that when I left Russia many years ago." He clamped his mouth shut, and Nagila saw the terror on his face.

The old man knew he had overstepped the line and moved into dangerous territory.

F·I·V·E

At exactly 3:30 A.M. in every time zone worldwide, a coordinated event took place. Specially trained men and women attacked and killed the heads of every major Christian sect, denomination, group, or organization in the world. Many received the death blow in their own beds. Through their well-planned strategy, terrorists had previously enlisted the cooperation of aides, secretaries, assistants, or anyone else necessary for them to reach the titular head of the religion.

The slaughter included outstanding leaders who, although not officials, commanded empires of wealth and influence. Among them were the Archbishop of Canterbury, Pope Gregory, Bishop Mikhail of the Syrian Orthodox Church, Bishop Makar of the Coptic Church, eleven of the world's best known "electronic preachers" from America, the heads of all the major Protestant denominations, and many prominent evangelical and fundamentalist leaders.

By midmorning, the leading newspapers and television stations in each city and country directly affected received elaborately documented evidence of the evils and corruptions of the recently assassinated religious leaders. That the material had often been cleverly fabricated made no difference. The release of volumes of pictures, tapes, videos, and documents brought about an outcry of rage against the Christian religion that spanned the globe.

English agitators demolished York Cathedral. New York City's St. Patrick's Cathedral crumbled from the effects of more than a hundred handmade bombs. Plastic explosives, placed in three strategic locations, killed a bishop, three priests, and two hundred people present at a mass in the Vatican.

The following day mobs bombed or torched every house of Christian worship. No city in the world received exemption. Even in remote sections of the Soviet Union reports came of the destruction of Orthodox churches or those belonging to Baptists.

For another four days the people of the world screamed their anger at the bondage that religion had placed on their lives. Then, in a seemingly spontaneous eruption, a systematic purge of local religious leaders began. These systematic purges, at least, took different forms. In a few instances, vengeful crowds screamed "Deceiver! Liar!" They ruthlessly murdered their victims by beating them with fists, clubs or hammers. In other areas, they settled for maiming or permanently disabling all clerics.

On the sixth day, King Joshua Gad-Erianko made a universal appeal through satellite television. In part of his message he said: "I appeal to the people of the world for moderation. Have we not had enough killing? Enough destruction of property? Enough vengeance? Is it not now the time for peace?

"I understand the anger and anguish that has burst upon the world. These men and women in whom we put our trust, to whom we gave our gifts, to whom we went with our problems, and at whose feet we worshiped deceived us. We reacted in horrified anger. We were like prisoners who broke from their bondage. These masters of deceit have paid the price for their nefarious activities. They who claimed godliness have shown their own selfish greed and their crimes have come to light.

"Impassioned people have retaliated. They have, in their own way, acted as unresponsibly and ruthlessly as those they punished. The time has come when we must put a stop to violence, bloodshed, and destruction. If we continue in this way, we are no better than they!"

Political leaders across the globe made follow-up speeches pleading for compassion and common sense. "Live and let live!" they screamed. "Allow freedom! But let us guard ourselves against such deceivers arising again! We follow the advice of King Joshua—the King of the most persecuted people on earth!"

The Prime Minister-elect and leading politician of India, Bagwan Rashid, said, "We shall never let religious zealots deceive us again, but we need not kill them either! Has not King Joshua set the example for us? He and his people who have known more hatred and persecution than any nation on this earth now offers his guidance and wisdom. Long live King Joshua!"

Similar messages filled the airwaves, newspapers, and magazines across the world. Although hardly anyone noticed, all the messages used essentially the same words with only the slightest variations.

When the mob broke into Nasief's home and his church, he was sitting by the bedside of a member of his congregation. The man, dying of cancer, had been a faithful supporter since Nasief's early days in Israel.

Nasief knelt beside his old friend's bed, refusing to leave until morning. He knelt at the bedside, praying for a peaceful death, at the moment he should have been killed.

Later that day he walked openly through the streets of Jerusalem. A man grabbed his arm and pulled him inside a nearby house. "You are Nasief Habib?"

"Yes—"

"How can you be so stupid and walk down the streets like this? Don't you know what's happening?"

"No. I haven't heard any news for two days," Nasief replied. He explained that he had been with a dying man all night.

The kindly man told him about the killing of local clerics. "If you go walking along these streets, someone will recognize you. Please, stay here until dark. Go into hiding."

Nasief thanked the man for his concern but added, "I cannot hide. I am not afraid."

"You do not have to be stupid either."

Nasief left the man and walked toward his home. He now realized he might be attacked at any time. He had become one of the best-known figures in the nation. Even those who had long opposed Christianity had respected him because he never belittled Judaism or Islam. He became known as a man who helped those in need, regardless of their religious connections.

Gangs of well-trained teenage anti-religionists divided the city of Jerusalem into fifteen districts. Each gang marched through their section several times during the day. They carried banners that bore slogans such as, "Down with Religion," "No More Deception," "We Want Truth." They sang lustily as they marched from street to street, encouraging other young people to join them.

At one point Nasief saw the youthful rabble coming in his direction. He paused and watched their approach. They had not yet come close enough to recognize him, yet he knew if he turned to walk the other way or to run some of the faster young men would race after him.

A member of Nasief's church saw her teacher from her window across the street. She raced out of her house, grabbed his arm and pulled him across the street and into the shadows of her building. "Please, stay off the streets."

"I am no criminal," Nasief said. "I've done nothing wrong, so why should I hide?"

"Please, go into hiding. Your life is not safe."

"I don't seek safety," Nasief said. "If I hide am I not

admitting that these charges are true? No, I shall do the things I would do on any other day of the week."

"But if they attack you?"

"Then they attack," he said and began to walk on. "I am more afraid of disappointing God than I am of physical torture from half-crazed fools."

"But if you are taken from us, what shall we do?" The woman's eyes filled with tears and she held his arm in her tight grip. "Please! For our sakes—"

"I'm only a man—and an old man at that. God will take care of you."

The woman wept hysterically, pleading with him not to go out on the main streets. Touched by her concern, Nasief said that he would avoid public places. By the time he had calmed her, the raging mob had passed the street and moved out of sight.

Nasief allowed the woman's husband to drive him home, using a circuitous route. At their insistence, he sat low in the back seat so that no one would recognize him.

The teen gangs had razed both his house and the church building to the ground. Nasief stared at the damage, saddened at the sight before him. He knelt beside the communion table, partially burned and the legs broken. His fingers traced only the still readable words "Do this." Between fire and axes they had destroyed the rest of the statement from Jesus, "in remembrance of me." He prayed for guidance, strength, and, most of all, the ability to forgive.

Later, he stood and walked through the destruction, surveying the damage. They had been thorough, but it did not matter. Nasief had made up his mind. He would hold his Bible study here in this same place, among the rubble and destruction. The weather would not prevent their meetings. Fear might keep them away, especially participating in a study in the open. Nasief determined that if his enemies wanted to take him, they would not have to search others' homes to find him. He would make himself available to friend or foe alike.

Nasief worked methodically for hours, moving enough

debris so that people could walk around comfortably. He swept and shoveled, produced makeshift chairs, cleared space for people. It taxed him physically, but he hummed softly to himself the whole time.

While he worked, Nasief wondered if anyone would show up. He prayed they would have the courage to stand against the growing opposition. Yet he would not blame those who stayed away out of fear.

At seven o'clock, two elderly people approached. Before they could respond to the destruction before their eyes, Nasief waved them forward. "We are alive, my friends! God is still in heaven! Come and join me!"

They walked forward and sat down on the crudely prepared chairs. Nasief stood, ready to teach with as much zeal as if speaking to hundreds. He closed his eyes and raised his hands upward in an opening prayer. When he concluded, he saw that the members had doubled. Nagila and Shaheen sat next to the couple.

"Friends, we live in perilous times and I do not need to say any more about that to you. We have only to look around us. Our newspapers and television stations keep us informed on what is going on in this wicked world. The news, however, is not all bad. I bring you this message of hope. God is with us. No matter how dark the night, we have the true light to lead us . . .

"We have now reached the beginning of the end. Time is running out for evil deeds. It is also running out for us to do the works of goodness and truth. When the prophets spoke of the last days, they prophesied of what is happening right now! We must fortify ourselves to face those who hate us."

For the next forty minutes, as the darkness crept upon the small assembly, Nasief spoke with a boldness he had never experienced before. Verses from the Old and New Testaments filled his thoughts and he tied seemingly contradictory prophecies together.

"So many things must happen in the days ahead. I do not know if I shall be with you until the final days of earth. Yet, I can tell you of events that must surely happen."

Liberally quoting from the Bible, he told them of a worldwide famine that would affect one third of the earth. Wars would escalate. Plagues and diseases would spread across the land, claiming the lives of millions and affecting another third of the world. He said that, as he understood his Bible, eventually ten world leaders would emerge. Between them they would control the world. Once their power was secure, they would themselves bow to the Antichrist.

"This Antichrist will wage an unrelenting war against us, the people of God. We shall see persecution as no human eye has ever seen it before. Every true believer will have to face the moment to decide whether to serve God or the forces of darkness. But don't be afraid! These things must take place. They are the proofs to us that the end is upon us! At the darkest moment our beloved Lord and Savior Jesus Christ will return from heaven with mighty angels and destroy all evil!

"Rejoice! Our redemption is near! Rejoice! These things must happen! Remember also that our God is with us at every moment! We may not have strength or wisdom in advance, but we shall have them at the moment we need them."

Nagila, captivated by the intensity of the words and the energy of the old preacher, clasped Shaheen's hand. As his message intensified, hardly realizing she was doing so, she squeezed his hand tightly. Tears filled her eyes and slowly slid down her cheeks. For the first time, her resistance and doubts vanished. In watching this man speak, the depth of his character and the conviction of his faith found permanency within her.

"It's true," she whispered. "At last I know it's true. I believe it."

"It is true," Shaheen said. He kissed her cheek.

Nasief closed the study with a benediction upon himself and the four who had listened. "Now, go to your homes. Every minute you remain here, you open yourself to trouble. You will not need to seek out persecution. It will chase after you. At this moment I sense that danger is near. Please go. Please."

The two old people moved quickly from the rubble and disappeared from view. Nagila and Shaheen stood in the encrouching darkness, staring at each other.

Nagila opened her mouth to speak because she wanted to explain to Shaheen what had happened. Yet she had no way to tell him in words. "I believe," she mumbled. "It just happened—in an indescribable way and—"

"I understand," Shaheen said. His lips brushed hers lightly. "My own conversion came about slowly, but once I believed, I had an inner peace—"

"Yes! That's it," Nagila said. "An inner quiet. Oh, Shaheen, I tried for so long to be a good Jew. I tried never to admit to myself all of my doubts. Now, all of that is gone. I am at peace." She wrapped her arms around him and rested her head against his chest.

Nasief had listened to Nagila's words. When the couple moved apart, he took their hands in his. "Please go. It is not safe for you here."

"I would like to stay with you," Nagila said. "I'm not afraid. Really, I'm not."

"You can't. You will do more good for God's kingdom if you leave now." His eyes blazed with a glow none had ever seen before. Although his eyes focused on them, he appeared to stare through them and to look beyond. "The day will come," he said in a soft voice quite different from the way he normally spoke, "when you will have to take a courageous stand. Now is not the time."

"Please don't send me away. Not now that I believe—"

"Listen to what I'm telling you." He shook his head slowly. "Leave. Now."

"I want to stay with you. I want to be here if they come. Perhaps I can help."

"You know, Nagila, I understand how the prophets of old felt when they spoke for God. I have these words pounding in my heart. I know what you must do. As much as I would like to give in and allow you to stay here with me, I am telling you that God says you must go. Hurry! They will be here soon."

"Who?"

"Just—just go!" He pulled their arms and led them toward the street. "Don't linger for a minute!"

She kissed his cheek. "I'll leave . . . only because you tell me I must."

Shaheen grabbed her arm and they made their way quickly through the path Shaheen had cleared from the rubble. He watched until they disappeared from sight.

Nasief sat down and sang quietly in his strong baritone voice. He could feel the enemy coming. He would wait.

Minutes later he heard the sound of marching. Nasief did not stop the hymn. He closed his eyes, his face lifted upward, and raised the volume of his voice as he sang:

"God, give me grace to sing a thousand songs,
That tell the world of your great love divine.
That I may spread to ev'ry tribe and throng—"

"Stop!" commanded a voice.

Nasief stopped singing and opened his eyes. In front of him stood a uniformed officer and twelve soldiers with submachine guns. The officer's revolver pointed at Nasief's heart.

Nasief smiled. "I am honored that you would have so many to come for one old, harmless man."

"You are Nasief Habib?" the officer yelled, even though he stood four feet away.

Nasief sank wearily to a plank. "Yes, I have been expecting you."

"Stand up! You are an enemy of the people!"

"As you say." The strain of working in the ruins all afternoon had tired him greatly. It seemed like such an effort, but he stood up again. "But, of greater importance, I am a friend of God."

"Silence."

"Surely you are not afraid to let me speak?"

The officer struck him across the face with the butt of

his revolver. Nasief staggered and crumpled to his knees. The hard blow left him dazed, but he determined not to pass out.

"Stand him up!"

Two soldiers came to Nasief, each grabbing an arm. They lifted him, more gently than he had expected. He barely made out their features. All of them were young. The officer couldn't have been older than twenty himself.

Nasief shook his head slowly. "Sad. So sad to see your hardened attitudes and you are yet so young—"

The officer, using an open hand, slapped Nasief across the cheek. Nasief reeled backward. The two young men held him.

"Bring him with us," the officer said. "Drag him feet first if you must, but bring him." He turned toward the rest of the troops, giving curt orders. Each soldier snapped into action. They marched forward in a box shape with the officer leading and the others on all four sides of Nasief.

Nasief watched when they moved into place. He felt the strength of his two captors as they propelled him forward. One of them whispered, "If you're tired, relax; we're strong and we'll carry you."

"May our loving God bless you for your kindness."

"I'm not doing this for God," the man said, a sneer on his face. "I feel sorry for an old man."

By the time they reached the street, Nasief felt new life pouring into his frail body. The pain from the heavy blow of the revolver still hurt. He instantly felt strong—stronger than he had felt in many years. He released himself from the grips of the two soldiers. "I am able to walk myself."

"It must be four miles—"

"I am strong enough."

Nasief straightened; a sense of triumph flowed through his whole body. He believed that, in this moment of need, God had infused him with physical strength. He knew he would be less tired at the end of the march than his captors.

Nasief marched silently, wondering why anyone would consider him important enough to send all of these soldiers after him. "Captain—officer—where are we going?"

"You need have no worry about that, old man."

"I do not worry. I am only curious."

"Will you come peaceably?"

"Of course. I would not consider running away."

The officer stopped the march. He cut through the ranks. "Nasief, you don't seem so powerful now. You are the man who has caused so many problems in our city?"

"Is that so?" he said softly. "I am flattered. I had no idea of the extent of my influence."

The young man struck him across the face for the third time. Nasief fell backward and received a rough kick in the stomach. The impact knocked his head backward and it struck the concrete pavement. A searing pain raced across his forehead. He closed his eyes and lay unmoving.

"The order was to treat him rough, not to kill him!"

At first Nasief had no idea who spoke. He opened his eyes and saw the soldier who had been kind to him earlier. He pulled Nasief to a sitting position. "Easy, old man, let me help you."

"You think I have treated him rough?" the officer said. "You watch!"

A sharp blow struck Nasief on the left side of the head. Blackness encircled him like a whirlpool sucking him into its vortex. Nasief sensed he was losing consciousness. He tried to raise up by stretching out an arm, reaching for someone to help him up. Instead of help, a booted foot crashed against the front of his skull and he fell back. When his head hit the concrete a second time, Nasief had already lapsed into unconsciousness.

S·I·X

Anger and destruction did not stop with Joshua's public plea. Nor did he expect it to. Leaders assented to the wisdom of his words; in actual practice, they encouraged the beatings and destruction. By controlling the reporting to the media, the ongoing events received no new publicity. The mobs no longer did their destructive acts openly, but they continued with the same intensity.

In Paris, a young woman named Jeanne barely escaped death when hoodlums destroyed her church. Ruffians came in the middle of a special meeting the pastor called, urging members to pray for forgiveness. The gang of young men and women converged at one time, splaying bullets everywhere. One of them tossed a grenade into the chancel, and it instantly killed the pastor.

Jeanne dove for the floor and remained immobile during the shooting, screaming, and pillaging. When they left, she crawled out, whispering, "Anyone here? Anyone alive?"

Two men answered. Jeanne pulled them, one at a time,

from the rubble. Then she raced to get her car, parked a street away. She stopped the vehicle next to the broken door. She half-carried the two men inside. One of them she knew would never make it, but she refused to leave him. She staunched the bleeding of the other's chest wound.

Jeanne drove recklessly out of the city. She knew a small farm twelve kilometers from the city. When she reached there, the farmer agreed to take the one in the front seat. He said he would bury the other.

Jeanne headed back for Paris and ran into a blockade. They had become common in the last two or three days. They questioned occupants and any who admitted they belonged to the Christian faith were beaten or executed on the spot.

She quickly made a U-turn and headed her Citroen back toward the farm. Seconds later she heard sirens. From her rearview mirror, Jeanne could see that they chased her. She remembered Duclos, a young man she had attended university with who lived nearby. She raced on, making sharp, last-minute turns, hoping to elude the pursuers. They grew closer.

Realizing her only hope lay in escaping by foot, she waited until she rounded a corner and had a grassy bank on the left. As the car followed the road, she threw herself out of the car, her body tucked into a ball. To her amazement, she tumbled down the grassy incline unhurt. She heard the crash of the vehicle ahead.

Without waiting to discover what happened, she took off running across the field. She tripped over a drainage ditch and started to pull herself up. She changed her mind and lay flat in the ditch.

Voices filled the area and she heard them coming closer, but they never found her. Later she walked for almost an hour before she came to her friend's home.

She tapped lightly on the door. Duclos himself answered and held the door open.

He stared at her momentarily and asked only, "Police or gangs?"

"Both. I think—"

"Quickly. Inside." He closed the door behind her.

The two sat in the kitchen and she painfully told him everything that had taken place. Duclos listened in silence, interrupting only for clarification.

A loud banging at the front door made Jeanne jump. A look of terror filled her eyes.

"Sit quietly. Have another coffee."

Duclos answered the door, but Jeanne could hear nothing above the muffled voices. Duclos returned minutes later.

"The police are investigating everyone in the community."

"And they left? They didn't arrest you?"

Duclos smiled. "They asked me, 'Are you a Christian?' and I answered that I belonged to the religion of Aryeh."

"Aryeh? What does that mean?"

Duclos patted her hand. "It is a password that we have begun to use. It is Hebrew for *lion*. Since Jesus was born of the tribe of Judah and that tribe used the lion as its symbol, we have adopted the word in place of Christianity."

"They didn't ask you anything more?"

"He asked, 'What do you believe in this religion?' I told him that we opposed Therion and all evil. So he left."

"And by Therion—?"

He laughed. "The man was a complete fool. He understood nothing but would not admit it. Therion is Greek for the beast mentioned in the book of Revelation. The beast is the one who plots and carries out all the evil plans. Therion is another of the secret words we use."

"Aryeh for lion and Therion for beast. I shall remember that."

"Do. I suspect that within a short time, we believers will have to use such words as these in order to talk among ourselves."

Within months, Christians around the world did indeed use such terms among themselves. They pulled many words from the Hebrew or Greek, but the two Jeanne learned that night became the most widely used.

Nasief had the sensation of floating through the air, his weightless body buoyed by air currents. He decided he was being carried on some kind of stretcher. As he gained more consciousness he felt each step as they marched in fast cadence. He tried to open his eyes, but daggers of pain stabbed all through his forehead. It was not worth the effort. He lay still and the searing torture lessened slightly.

When he opened his eyes, he found himself propped up in a metal chair, held in place by ropes stretched across his chest and legs. He sensed that a lot of time had passed, perhaps even the whole night. A single bulb, hanging from the ceiling, cast shadows upon the wall. As his mind cleared, the tight ropes burned into his hands and ankles. His feet had the tingling sensation that comes from cut-off circulation. He tried to move, but he could only raise or lower his head.

"Nasief!" a voice called. "Can you hear me?"

Nasief nodded. He knew someone called his name, but he couldn't connect it to anyone he knew. Drawing upon his willpower, Nasief opened his eyes, but everything blurred. He blinked several times and tried again. Finally he gave up and concentrated on the speaker. Then he knew. He recognized the voice from listening to his frequent speeches on television.

"They only hurt you this time. Next time it will be worse. Unless you stop your illegal activities."

"Never," Nasief said through swollen lips. He did not know if he actually spoke the word aloud. He may have passed out again. He felt a stinging on his lips and a coolness against his face.

When he opened his eyes this time he could see clearly. His face hurt. His arms, chest, and legs ached.

"I want you to be clear about what I say. This is a warning. Your final warning."

Nasief smiled despite the pain. "It surprises me that you fear me. I am only one man and you are the King. A giant afraid of an insect."

"Fear you? I have no fear of you or of anyone."

"I think you do," Nasief said. His swollen lips distorted his voice, but he determined to speak anyway. "Otherwise, why do you tie up an old man? Why does the King involve himself? Why the warnings and not a bullet in my head?"

"Untie him," Joshua said and stepped back. Two soldiers appeared from behind Nasief and removed the ropes. He rubbed his ankles and hands, feeling the tingling of life returning.

"Wait outside," Joshua said.

Nasief heard their heavy steps across the cement floor, followed immediately by the slamming of a metal door. He sighed as he continued to rub his ankles and wrists. "It feels good to have blood circulating again. Thank you."

"Where did you learn your information about me? Who told you my plans? Who betrayed me? Nagila Levy?"

"No person has told me anything."

"Liar!"

"No, King Joshua. You do not like what I teach, but you know that I do not lie. No one told me anything. No one had to."

Joshua stepped closer. "Look up at me, Nasief."

The old man slowly raised his face and they stared at each other. Joshua's eyes bored into the deep-set pupils of the old man. Joshua flinched and slapped Nasief. "Who are you?"

"You know who I am. I have nothing to hide from you."

"You—you are not human. There is something about you that makes you different. Who are you? How do you know so much about me?"

"Is that what you want? Simple. I learned it from God. From our holy book."

He slapped Nasief's face so hard that the cracking noise of the cheekbone echoed throughout the room. The blow knocked Nasief backward and the chair tipped over. Nasief lay on the floor, still conscious, yet feeling no pain. A quiet cloud of light descended on him and he closed his eyes and a smile covered his bruised face.

"Don't die on me, old man! Not yet!"

"I shall not die until it pleases God to take me."

Joshua rushed to the door and banged on it until it opened. To the guard he said, "Do whatever is necessary to keep him alive. Barely alive!"

Joshua left the room and headed back toward his private quarters. He felt his hands shake—an experience entirely new to him. Never in his life had he ever felt fear. He had observed it in others. He knew how fear crippled a person's reasoning ability. Who knew that better than he?

Nasief puzzled him even more than Nagila. As in the case of Nagila, he could not read this man's soul, but worse, he sensed strength in the old man. Where would such strength come from? Nasief was sixty-nine years old. Men of that age were sometimes stubborn and strong-willed, but this man was not like anyone else he had known before.

From what his spies had reported of Nasief's teachings, the old man knew his entire plan and had even sketched it to the people who listened. How could he know? He had spoken to Nagila only in generalities. Joshua had never revealed the ultimate plan to another human being. To Ivor Kalinin he now occasionally revealed the next events to transpire. They often shocked and puzzled his old teacher. But Ivor had not learned of such things as his plan for the ten kings. How could this old man possibly have known? Yet this man did know!

The easy thing would be to have his men kill Nasief. The old man lay half-dead anyway. Joshua knew the wisdom of liquidating an enemy, no matter how small the threat.

Yet Joshua did not kill Nasief. He could not do it. For a moment Joshua felt that some strange power beyond would not let him take the old man's life. A spasm passed through his body and he stopped walking. He leaned against the wall to hold himself up. *What is happening to me? Is Nasief instilling fear in me?*

Joshua waited until he felt in full control again before he continued toward his office. Logically he knew what he ought to do. In those moments Joshua Gad-Erianko learned what most human beings learn early in life: fear is not rational.

He did not kill Nasief.

That was Joshua's first mistake.

S·E·V·E·N

Henri duPre faced a dilemma. He had considered the situation from every possible angle and he still had no idea what he should do. He picked up the reports and reread them in their entirety. It was an unnecessary gesture because he had practically memorized them anyway.

He had promised an interview to the press. What could he tell them? They wanted to hear of results. If not a major breakthrough, at least something encouraging. He couldn't even offer them that.

Ten new cases since yesterday. His quick mind calculated the statistics of the past two weeks. Exactly 1,732 case reports in eleven countries across central and southern Africa. The disease did not confine itself only to Africans but struck whites and orientals as well.

"What is it? What's causing it? What can we do about it?" He shook his head. He had been asking himself those questions for days. He sat in his comfortable office of the World Health Organization in Geneva, no more clear on what to do than the hundreds of doctors trying to isolate the disease and to find a cure.

Of the 1,732 cases, 559 had already died. So far as he could tell from the reports, all of the others would succumb. The disease followed a distinct pattern. It began with a low-grade fever that lasted forty-eight hours. Intermittent headaches began on the eve of the second day. After seventy-two hours, body temperatures reached between 107 and 111, when the patient had become convulsive.

No medicine they tried had lowered the body temperature as much as one degree. On the fourth day the temperature swung to subnormal within minutes and the patient regained consciousness. Nerve endings in the body's extremities lost all feeling. The fingers and toes turned a ghastly blackish-green. From then on, it was only a matter of time. Doctors reported watching the blackish-green seep throughout the body until it reached the heart. That last phase never took more than twelve hours.

The most extensive reports, coming from the Communicable Disease Center in Atlanta, showed they had worked with 101 cases but had been unsuccessful in isolating the virus (if it was a virus) or in suggesting a cause. No one would speculate on a cure. The report concluded that, until two weeks earlier, no country in the world had ever encountered such a disease.

They went on to report that they assumed a viral infection, giving a list of circumstantial evidence, and ruling out virtually every other method of contagion. They had no tentative conclusions as to how the virus transmitted itself.

The jangling of the phone jolted duPre, interrupting his deep concentration. He picked it up mechanically and answered.

"This is Levis Cothrell, CDC in Atlanta. We have one piece of news. Not much, but a beginning."

DuPre straightened up. "What? What have you found?"

"We know that this attacks people by blood types. That sounds strange, but only those with type O are affected."

"Not much consolation there," duPre said. "If I recall my statistics, that only narrows the target group down to 70 percent of the world's population.

"I told you it was a beginning."

"Sorry, Cothrell, I am overreacting. I am so anxious for a breakthrough. Every bit of information helps."

"I know. My staff is already trying to guess where it hits next."

"I think I can answer that," duPre said. "Cameroons. Two cases reported yesterday. Exactly the same as in Zaire, Zimbabwe, and everywhere else."

After duPre's conversation, computers brought in additional information. Forty cases in Tanzania on the east coast. Ninety-three in Libya. Four in Algeria.

Henri duPre stared at the figures. He knew that at least a million people would die before they could find the cause. The disease might kill another million before they could supply a counteractive drug in large enough proportions. He laid his head in his hands and wept.

Franklin Brackett liked the early fall. Unlike most people he enjoyed the hard winters and the isolation in North Dakota. At times it did get lonely, but he always had plenty of work to do. He had planted his wheat crop and, if things went as well as they had the previous two years, this would be the largest yield yet.

He had risen early that morning, eager to see the wheat stalks as they poked out of the ground. He liked making his regular rounds, watching the miracles of nature creep upward inch by inch.

He had no premonition of what he would find when he walked across the rising bluff that led down to the rich 108 acres.

At first he couldn't believe he saw it correctly. From the distance of a quarter mile he knew something wasn't right, but he could not figure out what it was. He raced ahead, panic in his movement. At fifty-six years old and with a strong body, he had not run for years. Yet this morning he raced toward his precious wheat fields.

He fell on the ground and his callused hands touched

the first stalk. Instead of its usual golden-tan, each stalk had turned a deep rust. Brackett had farmed all his life, but he had never seen wheat that color before. He broke off the stalk and put it to his lips. Instead of the sweet taste of fresh outdoors, as he always called it, the odor nauseated him, giving off the strong odor of rotting fish. Never had he known such a sight or odor in his life.

Dazedly he walked across his field. Every stalk the same way. As the sun spread across the sky, the plants emitted gaseous fumes that gagged him. He turned to leave the field and the odor overpowered him. He gagged, gasping for breath. The fumes seemed to suck the oxygen out of the air, making it impossible for him to breathe.

Only by sheer determination did he reach the end of the wheat field and crawl up a small hill. He collapsed. When strength returned, his lungs burned and the weakness of his body prevented him from standing. He crawled across the barren field, moving toward home. He noticed that the further he got from the ruined wheat, the less labored was his breathing. By the time he was half a mile from the ruined crop, his breathing normalized and he felt stronger. He stood up and walked slowly toward his house.

When he reached his house, Franklin Brackett immediately phoned his nearest neighbor, Philip Cartrette. His wife answered, telling him that Phil had gone to the fields at sunup.

"I don't want to alarm you, Patricia, but I'd suggest you go try to find him. Quickly." As rapidly as possible and yet keeping his voice calm, Brackett told her what happened. "It may not be the same over at your place, but—"

Patricia Cartrette dropped the phone and Brackett heard the door slam. Too exhausted to drive over to the Cartrette's farm, he did the only thing he could. He called other farmers. Then he phoned the county extension agent. No one answered. He dialed every ten minutes. No one answered all day.

By late afternoon the Secretary of Agriculture knew of the plight of the Dakota farmers. He heard about the same problem in Iowa, Minnesota, Michigan, and Wisconsin. By the following morning, the wheat disaster had spread all the way south to Oklahoma and northward into British Columbia.

"We anticipate a 100 percent winter wheat crop failure this year," the Secretary of Agriculture told reporters. "We have enough in storage bins to take care of our national needs, but we will certainly have none to export."

At the time the Americans made their announcement, Russian farmers discovered the ruin of their wheat crop.

Within a week the news had spread across the globe. Reporter Jerry Richardson on CBS had personally seen crop damage in five states. He told the sad details:

"The failure of winter wheat this year from still-unknown causes brings anguish from every sector of the world. While wheat-producing nations such as the United States and Canada can supply their own needs, this will cause a worldwide shortage for the next six to eight months.

"In grocery stores across America, flour has disappeared from the shelves. Consumers are hoarding and freezing baked goods . . ."

The TV camera cut in to show stores across the nation. In one grocery store in Chicago, riots broke out. Six women fought over the last two five-pound bags of white flour.

"Experts from the World Health Organization predict that at least two million people will starve to death, mostly in the Soviet Union. The President is urging Americans not to hoard food and to share what we have with other nations. If each of us here in America and Canada would give up half of our bread, cereal, or grain supply for the year, experts tell us that we could save more than a million lives!"

In Pakistan the rice crop failed for lack of sufficient rain. The islands of the South Pacific received their usual humid winds. They did not receive their usual rain, and all their crops failed.

Cambodia quietly sent two thousand soldiers into Thailand, terrorizing the people, and stealing all foodstuffs available. In Kenya and Uganda, rain deluged the maize fields, rusted the plants and nothing survived. In a united action the two nations marched across the plans of Tanzania and robbed every grain-storage bin in the nation. They suffered the loss of 2,000 troops and killed 9,000 civilians and hundreds of Tanzanian soldiers.

E·I·G·H·T

Nagila Levy sat in the dining room, eating by herself. She had chosen a far corner and faced the wall. She wanted to be alone and hoped her obvious position made that clear. Several times she heard voices in the background, but she tuned them out.

She held the morning paper in front of her, and the news on the front page brought tears to her eyes. She had never heard of such human suffering before on this scale. Not that the world hadn't suffered famine or plagues before. Yet these two great international disasters occurred almost simultaneously. By now, two months after the outbreak of what everyone called the Green Plague, half a million people had died. Their bodies, piled in stacks like logs, waited for volunteers to collect and burn them. Still the disease spread.

In the areas not touched by the Green Plague, starvation stalked the land, affecting every one of the Third-World countries. Her resources conservatively estimated that more than 700,000 had already died of starvation.

Citizens from Mexico raced across the border into Texas and New Mexico, slaughtering and pilfering food of any kind. Nearly 100,000 perished in the foray, most of them Mexicans. All along the southern border Americans armed themselves against invaders from the south. Some claimed their neighbors were selling hidden foodstuffs to starving Mexicans at twenty times its normal price.

Nagila folded the paper and laid it aside, then pushed away her untouched salad. She had tried to eat. As soon as the fork touched her mouth, she thought of the people who could subsist a week or longer on her lunch. She poured herself a cup of coffee from the carafe in front of her. She felt ashamed to be sitting in Jerusalem with plenty of food and anything she needed available.

Nagila sipped the hot liquid slowly. She had come to a conclusion without any direct evidence and the results disturbed her. It seemed so impossible. She vividly recalled Nasief's predictions. He said famine and plagues would happen. He did not specifically mention the Green Plague or the destruction of the wheat crops, but he did predict plagues, famine, and wars. He had said they would come soon.

She did not hear the man who came up behind her. He stood four feet away in silence, waiting for Nagila to look up. After several minutes, he cleared his throat and stepped forward. "I should like to sit down if you do not mind."

Nagila turned. "Oh, Dr. Kalinin—"

"Call me Ivor."

"Sit down. Ivor. However, I'm not good company today."

"Nagila, I want to talk—" He paused. He sat down and faced her. His gaze was fixed on her and he acted as if he had not made up his mind to continue. He shook his head slowly. "Perhaps I make a mistake. I do not know. I need to talk to somebody. To someone I can trust and a person unlike the others in the palace. I do not know you well. Actually, I do not know you at all." His stiff English seemed even stiffer because of his discomfort.

"Then why come to me? With all of the hundreds of people here in the palace—"

"I chose you because I sense that you are different. Unlike the others. I cannot tell you why I know this to be so, except that you are not afraid of Joshua. You are not?"

Nagila's fingers gripped the cup in front of her. The fear in his eyes had not changed. Yet today she saw something else, a new element, a lessening of the fear. "I am not afraid of Joshua—not personally afraid anyway."

"As I thought."

Nagila pulled a cup and saucer from the far side of the table and poured coffee for him.

"I am afraid. I have feared Joshua since he was fourteen years old. Back in Russia when I taught him. He did make it possible for me to leave the country. But he did it in such a way that although I was free from the country, he has personally kept me imprisoned—" He halted, considered the last word and said, "obligated, fearful, for all of these years."

"That's a long time."

"A very long time. Only recently we have come into personal contact again. Through these many years he has constantly let me know of his remembrance. He has—well, knowledge of certain other things about me. He wants always to keep me aware of my obligation to him."

"I'm sorry—"

"No, I do not tell you this for sympathy. I made a bargain. I obligated myself. He knows things about me—things of which I am ashamed and would choose not to have anyone else know. Ever."

"Is it the same with the others? Is that why they live in fear?" Nagila said. "Because he knows their secrets?"

Ivor Kalinin nodded.

"How does he know?"

Kalinin shook his head. "He has a kind of gift—or a curse perhaps. It is as if he can search into the depths of a person's soul and nothing remains hidden from him."

Yes, she thought, that could be it. Secrets, deep and well-hidden from others, could be the key. Secrets so embarrassing or terrible they would do anything rather than have the truth exposed. That would explain the loyalty of the others. He blackmailed them with knowledge he possessed about them.

"But now I do not wish to participate—I cannot sit by

and do nothing while these terrible things happen. These terrible things going on right now."

"What things?"

"Do you not know? People starving? Others dying? Plagues? Countries overpowering each other just for food to give to their own people?"

"Yes . . . I do know that."

"Joshua Gad-Erianko is behind it all. You did not know that?"

"Strangely enough, within the last half hour I came to that conclusion. It's the only explanation I can find for all of this destruction and devastation breaking out just at this time."

"You do grasp what I am saying! I knew I could speak with you and that I could trust you."

"You can talk with me, but what can I do? What can either of us do?"

He shook his head. "I do not know." He slumped in the chair and gazed into space. "I knew I could no longer carry this secret alone." They sat in silence, interrupted only by the humming of the air conditioning.

"It's hard to believe that any human being could be behind such inhumane things."

"Joshua is not like other people. He is a man without conscience. None at all."

Nagila stared, first in unbelief, and then she gradually comprehended. "So thousands, millions of people suffering has no effect on him, does it?"

"That is correct. Ms. Levy, I am ashamed to be part of anything that Joshua Gad-Erianko touches. Long ago I did things of which I have always been ashamed and of which he knows. As bad as I have been, it is nothing compared to this—this evil in him." He stopped, aware of the rush of his own words and then laughed self-consciously. "Even to say these words may cost me my own life." Ivor leaned forward, his hands shaking and his voice quivering. "But whatever it costs, I can no longer go on as I have."

Nagila laid her hand on his and patted it. His hand turned and his fingers wrapped tightly around hers.

"He planned this chaos in the world, you know. Every part of it."

Nagila nodded. "And yet I find it so incomprehensible. Why? Why?"

"But hard to believe or not, it is so. I can tell you one example. I heard and observed myself. Joshua instructed eight scientists to work together to manufacture a virus that would withstand every known cure. They then perfected an antidote. Joshua controls both formulas. Only he can prevent its spreading and he will not do so until two million people die. He did the same thing to make crops fail. He awaits the death of another two million."

"But why?"

"He is evil. For me that is reason enough. He says too many people now live on the planet. He will rid the world of another ten million through another plan—a plan of which I do not know specifically."

"That's monstrous!" She bit her lips to hold back the tears. "I didn't want to believe he could do this—"

"You don't want to believe it, Nagila, but you do. You know I speak the truth."

"Yes, yes . . . but what can we do?"

"I think, however, that we can do nothing about it. He has planned it. Meticulously he decided on every detail of this when he was fourteen years old. Just before he arranged for my exit from Russia. Does that not prove he is truly monstrous?"

"And we can do nothing to stop him? To change it?"

"I think not," Ivor said. "Yet I must act. I must do something. To make the gesture. To try—but I do not know what I can do."

"Ivor, do you have any faith? Religious faith?"

"You would not tell me to pray, would you?" He shook his head. "We are combating something more important than believing or not believing, or praying to a god or—"

"I don't know much about God myself. But if this God is real that I have—well, I have come to believe in, I can pray and others will pray. The man who teaches us tells us that God is greater than any other power. He tells us that God cares about what goes on in this world. If this is so, and we don't know what else to do, why not try religion? For myself, I am convinced that I and the whole world have hope only in following Jesus the Messiah—"

He shook his head. "You are a good woman, Nagila. It is too late for me to believe in religion."

"I'm not sure it's ever too late as long as you are still alive."

His dark eyes peered at her. "That may well be the trouble. I am not alive. I have been a dead man for many years. I chose not to see what he did and I ended up killing myself—my self-respect, my honor when I allowed Joshua Gad-Erianko to take control."

"How did he do that, Ivor? How could he just control you?"

Again the old man shook his head. "It is this strange power. He can look into the soul. At least he did it with me and I have observed him doing it with others. He penetrates so that he knows your weaknesses. He knows your shame. Because I could hide no secrets from him, he controlled me. Until now—I can take this no more!"

He pushed his chair back and bent down to kiss her hand. "You have been most kind to listen to my confused talk—"

"I don't think it's confused!"

"They will say so later. When I am gone. I can no longer contain my words. Joshua will know because he learns everything that is whispered. When I see him again, I will need to tell him nothing. He will know. And then—" He shrugged.

"Ivor, please—" Nagila started to get up.

He pushed her back. "Do not do anything. You have your religious faith, so you can pray. Pray that your God will not allow him to succeed in his ultimate purpose."

"What is Joshua's ultimate purpose?"

Ivor shook his head. "I have spoken too much already. I make it no longer safe for you." He walked out of the dining room.

Henri duPre hated to look at the pile of reports on his desk. He no longer wanted to know the number of cases of Green Plague. The figures of those who had died overwhelmed him and his stomach tied up in knots.

He glanced up and saw Gertrude VanderHof approaching his office. He had always liked Gertrude. A little aloof at times, a little too much of the Dutch temperament, but a pleasant woman and a hard worker.

She had brought a modicum of peace to his department in the past few months. Unlike most of the others, she had not sunk to the point of despair. Yet today, the robust cheeks looked pale and the gray-blue eyes had lost their luster.

"What is wrong?" he asked, getting out of his chair and meeting her in the doorway.

"Bad news, Henri. Very bad."

"More cases of Green Plague?"

"No, nothing like that."

"But what could it possibly be?" Yet even as he asked he knew the answer: a new disease had erupted somewhere in the world.

"Eight months ago we discovered a form of Sexually Transmitted Disease that defied all of our medical knowledge." She slumped into a chair. "That did not surprise us at first. These forms of STD have been growing steadily more virulent for the past twenty years. We keep having to find stronger drugs—"

"Yes, yes, Gertrude, I know that—"

"But you do not know of the new disease. We called it SP disease. More as a joke at first. It means Spanish Prostitute. That's how we came across it. In Spain."

"And—?" he asked waiting for the worst.

"We began with four isolated cases in Spain. Then six more. And now we have had twenty-one. All of them prostitutes. Well, originally anyway. In this last group we have two women who actually fit because both of them have had multiple sex partners. Both of them averaged more than one partner a day."

"Symptoms?" DuPre tried to keep his questions professional and to sound emotionally uninvolved.

"That's what makes it hard to diagnose. It begins with a slight numbness and then progresses to a complete loss of feeling in the whole pelvic area. One of them described it as that part of her being dead."

Gertrude recited the way SP manifested itself. It began with a deadening of nerve endings in the genital area, spreading rapidly to the central nervous system within days. From there it manifested itself at any place in the body, usually the extremities such as toes or fingers. "Eventually it attacks the brain and they die of a hemorrhage. The merciful thing, I suppose, is that the hemorrhage's severity brings on death within minutes."

"Only females?"

"Until three days ago. We have two males who are manifesting similar symptoms. Both heterosexual, both in their twenties, and both men who have multiple sex partners—including prostitutes."

"I see. And prognosis?"

She shook her head. "Our team of STD specialists has tried everything. Nothing slows down the spread of the disease. Nothing touches it, as if it is totally invulnerable to medicine."

Henri duPre sat behind his desk and stared at Gertrude. "When these things happen like this it is almost enough to make me believe once again in God."

"In God? Death of these people and you think of God?"

"I think of the wrath of God. Punishment for flagrant disobedience—"

"Not a very scientific approach."

"Not one that brings me much comfort either," he said.

Four months later Gertrude VanderHof walked into duPre's office. She dropped a stack of brown folders on his desk. "Well, that's it. The thing we've feared most."

DuPre stared at her, not wanting to know what she meant.

"We called it SP around here because it seemed confined to Spain. We checked water supply, hygiene, insects, even insecticides. Blank. Yesterday we received a report of three cases in Portugal."

"So it has begun to spread."

"Worse."

"Other places?"

She nodded. "Eight cases from Puerto Rico, six from Macao, and eleven on the island of Zanzibar. These twenty-five have only one thing in common—the tropics. Here, look at this." She pointed to the top folder and opened it. "Our research indicates it is viral, that it breeds best in tropical and subtropical climates."

"Anything else?"

She nodded. "It appears that with the spread of SP, its insidious form works more rapidly." She pointed to charts on pages four and five. "We think it took approximately a month from the time patients began to complain of lack of feeling in the pelvic area until the brain hemorrhage."

"And the time is now reduced to—?"

"Four days maximum."

DuPre shook his head. "Are we rapidly destroying our entire earth through disease? We've never had anything like this in recorded history. Even in the days of the black plague or yellow fever, it was always restricted—"

"Henri, one more salient fact. We have not gotten full reports from Zanzibar, but from the other fourteen cases, I want you to see this." She flipped to the final page of the top folder.

Henri duPre read the graphs and stared in unbelief. "All of them have had three or four or less sexual partners in the past year?"

"So they say. At least it's the best evidence we have."

"Gertrude, what is happening? It makes me feel as if we're nearing the end of the world?"

"Maybe," she said, "we need to think more about cure and less about an effete religious theory."

DuPre had never seen the level of hardness in her eyes that showed then. For the first time he saw her as an uncaring woman, a woman who had previously played the role of a compassionate but efficient administrator.

"Or perhaps," he said, his eyes meeting hers, "it is time for us to turn back to our religious heritage. Maybe we can at least receive comfort even if we don't have answers."

N·I·N·E

Stefen Gregory hummed a pop tune, "Ready, Ready for Anything," when he came into his office. The financial ups and downs the past four months had taken their emotional toll on him, but he had relaxed all weekend. As he began his new week with a sense of satisfaction, he felt like yelling the final line of the song, "I'm ready for anything."

He had no idea how wrong he could be.

The previous Thursday afternoon Gregory had wrapped everything up on his shrewd negotiating of stock transfers that would net his corporation a profit of more than a million dollars annually. He had driven to his home on Long Island and flew to Nassau for a long weekend.

He smiled as he faced whatever the day would bring. Stefen Gregory thumbed through Friday's correspondence. Now in his early sixties, with one personal triumph after another behind him, the CEO of the American Banking Corporation, he had succeeded far beyond his expectations. Another year and he might consider retirement. He had already become a legend for his uncanny business hunches.

His relaxed attitude left him totally unprepared for the hand-delivered letter that arrived at 9:12 that Monday morning. Three minutes later his personal secretary brought the communique into his office.

"This just arrived by messenger." She made an effort to make her voice sound calm. The effort resulted in a nervous twitching of her lower lip. "I had to sign for it," she said. It had surprised her because their Arab clients had never proceeded that formally before.

"About?" he asked in his customary one-word replies, only half-listening. He continued to thumb through the stack of correspondence she had laid on his desk that morning.

"I think you should read this for yourself."

"You?" he nodded, asking if she had read it.

"Yes. That's why—" She broke off, her lower lip twitched uncontrollably. "Sir, I think you'd better read it yourself."

Stefen Gregory, head of the American Banking Corporation since the mid-1980s, accepted the embossed envelope. He flicked it open, extracted the single page, and his eyes raced over the words. He paused, stared blankly at his secretary, then read the relevant paragraphs a second time. It came as a formal request, issued jointly by the King of Saudi Arabia and the Amir of Kuwait. It read in part:

"Because of the discovery of malgamite, the worldwide switch from petroleum products, and the resulting low sales of oil, we now inform you that we wish to withdraw all deposits, beginning in February 1976, made by our two governments.

"We wish to inform you that this in no way reflects upon the courtesy and service you have extended to us over these years. We face the issue of economic survival.

"We do not wish to make this difficult for you. Our figures show that we have on deposit with you the sum of 285 billion dollars. We wish to have you transmit the full amount, in twelve equal monthly payments, to the Arab Trust Bank in London."

The letter closed with the usual Muslim benediction: "To Allah be the praise and glory to Islam."

Stefen Gregory had dreaded this kind of crisis. For more than three years he had urged his own organization as well as other American banks to prepare for the rollover of these funds. On several occasions he had warned bankers across America, but they didn't listen.

"Banks. All. Crisis," he said. His secretary, long used to his shorthand-speech, immediately arranged an emergency conference call between Stefen Gregory and the heads of American Express, Chase Manhattan, the Bank of America and fourteen other institutional heads.

He snapped his fingers before she closed the door and held up two fingers, changed his mind, and added a third. "Valium."

An hour later, Stefen Gregory went into the newly decorated conference room. A telescreen measuring twenty-two feet by twelve covered one entire wall. The computer operator lit up the screen and left the room. Stefen Gregory sat momentarily in silence, his eyes gazing from one face to another. Sixteen sections filled the giant screen.

Gregory had moved ahead in his field because of his uncanny ability to read the faces of those banking magnates who prided themselves on their lack of facial expression. He seldom erred. Today, as he slowly moved his eyes from one section of the screen to another, he detected a tenseness that several of them made no attempt to hide. He had observed these same moguls under many circumstances. Never before had they betrayed their emotions so openly. It gave him little relief to see that their hands shook as badly as his own.

"Stefen Gregory," he said. He paused, knowing he would have to break his one-word statement rule. Known throughout the industry he had worked hard to cultivate his no-nonsense attitude. His refusal to speak more than one word at a time often so disturbed others that they ended up speaking far more than they would have under normal conditions. He decided to switch to a diplomatic posture. "Thank you for responding to this emergency conference—"

"Get out with it," Kendall Harris of CitiBank Corporation shouted. Gregory stared at his picture in the top-left corner. "We're all on the line because you said crisis. It had better be."

Gregory breathed slowly and deeply. He held the letter in his hands. "I am inserting this into the tele-line printer." Eight seconds later, each of those on the conference line stared at a copy of the letter.

A few cursed. Someone pounded his fist. He recognized the voice of Marsha Nybern of Chase Manhattan when she shouted, "How dare they!" Stefen silently read the letter again, not wanting to see any more of their pained expressions.

"All of it? Every cent?" asked the head of the American Savings and Loans. "That—that will bankrupt us—totally."

"Ridiculous!"

"Impossible."

"They can't make a demand like this."

Stefen waited until they had all commented before he said, "Can," reverting to his old way of speaking. "Have."

Sir Elwood V. Oliver of the British-American Banks said, "I propose a solution. We shall authorize you to communicate with the Arabs a simple explanation. They may go directly to the banks of Mexico, Brazil and the seven or eight other Latin American nations and ask for the return of their funds."

Stefen shook his head. Just as he expected, they would not—perhaps could not—face the fact. "I think, Sir Elwood," he said, "you do not grasp either the intent or the gravity of their action."

"Obvious, isn't it?" Marsha Nybern said. "They *want* to bankrupt us."

"I can hardly believe—" Sir Elwood said in his precise Oxford accent. He stopped as he allowed the realization to crystallize. "You are quite right."

"And it is within their rights to call for their deposits," Nybern said. She allowed herself a small smile. Under her leadership Chase Manhattan had begun to divest themselves of Arab money more than a year ago. She turned to another computer on her right.

Seconds later, her pleased expression fell. None of the transactions, the statement on the screen informed her, had gone into effect. The Federal Banking Commission had held up the negotiations. Chase Manhattan had as much of a problem as the others.

"Can we stall?" the head of American Express asked.

"I think not," Sir Elwood replied.

"You Americans!" Klaus Muller sputtered. "You led my country in this direction, you know! We allowed you Americans to lead our German banking interests in this folly—this—this—"

"Excuse me," Nybern said. "As I recall—and as I can prove from recorded conversations—you and your associates approached us. When you learned that the Arabs were sinking large deposits in American banks, you wanted access to the cash. Do you recall? My memory tells me that I have a letter from you personally, dated March 17, 1975, in which you asked for a meeting with our bank."

Marsha Nybern genuinely smiled. Her memory, almost photographic, always settled such issues. She sighed as she thought, That's probably the only satisfaction I'll get today.

The conversation continued for another thirty-one minutes. In the end, by unanimous agreement, Stefen Gregory sent an official reply to both the King of Saudi Arabia and the Amir of Kuwait:

. . . Our banks used your deposited funds to make emergency loans to Latin American countries. As you likely know, because of their current unstable nature, we regret that we cannot fully recover the total funds at this time.

In an emergency session, we have agreed to deposit in the Arab Bank Trust of London the sum of forty billion dollars within the next twelve months.

In carefully studying the situation, we
estimated that we shall be able to return all
monies to you over the next fifteen years, granted
that favorable economic conditions persist.

On the day of the first emergency meeting of the
American bankers, Arab delegates quietly visited Pakistan
and held secret negotiations with the Prime Minister. For the
previous decade the Pakistanis had the capabilities of manu-
facturing nuclear warheads. The Arabs, guaranteeing financial aid to Pakistan in their famine, would receive twenty-
one missiles within the next six months in return.

The Arab leaders, well aware of what the Americans
and their allies had done with the 285 billion dollars, did not
expect to have it returned easily. They did expect to triumph
finally over the supposed superiority of the Western world.

Upon receipt of the American bankers' communique,
Saudi government officials held a press conference by satellite. Spokesman for the Arabs, Fahed Akbar gave an impassioned speech to the world. He explained that they, a backward nation, had put their trust in their western friends.
These supposed friends had betrayed their trust and taken
advantage of them. "Now," he said, allowing his voice to
take on an oratorical pitch, "is the time for rectification. We
face hardships in Arabs countries. We have asked for nothing but what is lawfully ours. Is this not the way of business
throughout the world? I place money in a bank to keep it
safe for me. When I wish to have my money I withdraw.
Simple procedure.

"But not so simple for Third-World countries. The
Americans have stolen our money. They come to us like
beggars on their knees. We have misused your money, they
tell us. But we shall return it all, they promise us. We did not
know you would want to have it returned now, they say to
us. We shall return it to you in fifteen years, they claim.

"We have wearied with waiting. We have made arrangements to do what all Arabs must do to avenge them-

selves when their enemies steal from them. We must never allow them to escape unpunished for their dastardly actions. We are now ready to avenge ourselves for the glory of Allah.

"We, however, being of kindly natures, will allow our Western bankers a period of twelve months for the total return—every dollar—as we have asked. In the event they refuse, we have already prepared our action."

Akbar moved closer to the camera so that the audience saw nothing but his head. The dark eyes flashed in anger, and no one who saw and heard doubted the intensity of his emotion or the truthfulness of his threat.

"We have nuclear bombs already in place. They are aimed at the major cities of America, England, West Germany and Japan. In exactly twelve months from today, by the Arab calendar, we shall use these weapons. We shall have our vengeance on those who rob the poor of the world and waste if foolishly on their luxuries.

"Praise be to Allah and glory to Islam!"

The following news items appeared internationally:

Mexico City, Oct. 9, 1997. Western bankers began meeting today with government and banking officials. Despite the threat of Arab nuclear bombs, officials state their hope to reach a mutual agreement soon.

Mexico City, Oct. 12, 1997. Western banking officials left at noon today. "We are closer to agreement," said vice-chair Marsha Nybern of Chase Manhattan Banks, New York.

Stefen Gregory, chair of the delegation, head of the American Banking Corporation, commented, "Soon."

Brasilia, Oct. 18, 1997. Six representatives of North American concerns left today after a four-day meeting. Although none of the conferees, totalling 93, will make any public comment, rumors are circulating that the North Americans walked out in anger. Officially they will meet again in November.

New York City, Nov. 29. Secretary of State Benjamin Cartledge addressed leaders of the western banking system. In a closed meeting, he hinted of America's readiness to invade Mexico and Brazil on a 24-hour notice. He stated that American warheads are now aimed at every strategic Arab city. He claims that sufficient American missiles exist to prevent any nuclear attack by the Arabs. "At the same time," an unidentified source quoted Mr. Cartledge as saying, "We have sufficient advanced weaponry to destroy all Arab countries from the face of the earth."

Rumors circulated that vast sums of money had surfaced among the now-impoverished Arab nations. They made agreements and paid in cash for nuclear weapons in eight western countries, including United Germany and France.

Additional rumors circulated that on January 28, 1997, the Arabs had successfully placed their nuclear missiles. These missiles, aimed at forty-one major American cities, and thirty-three of the important military installations in the world, could destroy them all within a three-minute period.

The American President, Douglas Alexander Whilhite, had just begun to serve his second term. He realized now that he had made a mistake. While knowing details of the banking crisis during the last weeks of his campaign for re-election, he had not grasped the significance of the issue. Of course, he had chosen not to listen to the Secretary of State and had refused to allow his staff "to cloud the campaign issues."

Polls told him that most Americans had little interest in the Arab threat. They had less interest in the bankers' crisis. As in the past, most Americans assumed that the federal government would step in and bail out the banks.

Americans in general had not grasped that the government did not have 285 billion dollars in liquid assets. The Arabs would accept nothing but the actual transfer of funds.

"Our nation is broke," Cartledge said again. He had pounded the message every day for weeks, saying it in different ways or using various means to make his point. Until today the President had refused to hear.

"What are we going to do, Ben?"

Cartledge nodded his head. "One minor victory. You finally acknowledged we have a problem."

"We can't help the banks," Whilhite said, ignoring Cartledge's remark. "We don't have the cash or enough of our own resources left. The Arabs, Japanese, and Chinese own nearly half of our nation's businesses. If the banks don't come across—" The President closed his eyes.

He could not take it all in. He tried to visualize that history would record his name as the last President of the United States. That he had failed the nation in its moment of greatest need.

"Ben, what are we going to do? Heaven help us!"

"Maybe that's the solution. Let Heaven help us."

"Maybe it's too late for that," the President responded sharply. In the past few months he had grown tired of Cartledge's frequent religious references. He gave him a weak smile, "Making a bargain with the Devil may be our only chance."

T·E·N

In Buenos Aires the first anti-American demonstrations broke out on January 29, 1999, with a parade. Most participants displayed national flags, banners, or placards of anti-Americanism. An estimated twenty thousand chanted slogans such as, "Go home and leave us alone." "Americans, you have met your match!" "America, prepare to meet your doom!"

On February 3, fourteen African nations declared "Burn America Day." As symbolic of their anti-American feelings, they publicly burned flags and used pictures of the American President for target practice.

On March 1, the USSR announced that it would no longer purchase surplus American grain—now that they were producing wheat again. They planned to trade primarily with Canada and to buy the rest from the open market and from "other undisclosed sources," a trade spokesman said. He added, "We can no longer trade with a nation that destroys the little people of the world and denies its culpability."

Minutes after this announcement, the Soviet Premier

announced that, out of compassion for the plight of Arabs everywhere, they would provide sufficient nuclear warfare to compensate for America's threat to retaliate.

Since the money crisis came to the public's attention King Joshua had refused to make a public announcement. Israel had access to the nuclear bomb, and the world waited to hear that they would side with the Americans.

He waited for one phone call. He had expected it by March 1. It disappointed him that the call did not come until late on March 3.

"I appeal to you," the American President said, "because you are the only source I have. My advisors tell me that you may be able to use your influence—" He paused. The first part of his words had come easily enough. He could not humiliate himself further.

"Yes, I could do that," Joshua said and waited.

"And you will?"

"Do what? Specifically?"

"Lend to us or help us to locate a source to borrow 240 billion dollars." The president attempted a laugh but could not make it. "I—I don't know how to say this well. To be frank, King Joshua, I am clutching at straws—"

"And I am the final straw you have clutched?"

"You have been foremost—"

"After you appealed to eighteen allied nations who all gave you reasonable enough excuses for not standing with you." Joshua enjoyed the discomfort of the pompous American President.

"So you know what we have tried, then?"

"Yes."

"What more can I say then? America has always been Israel's closest ally. We stood with you when no other nations did."

"True. But, of course, you profited from being noble."

The President swore under his breath. "All right, I'll

say it as straight as I know how. If you have any way of intervening to prevent a world nuclear holocaust, I am asking your help."

"Asking?"

This time the President lost his control and swore aloud. He caught himself before he flew into a rage. "King Joshua, we are desperate. We plead. Beg. Is that better?"

"You shall have your 240 billion dollars by tomorrow. I shall have it electronically transferred via four banks in Switzerland."

"Where could you come up with that kind of money?"

"You have called to ask about my financial resources or for my help?"

"I apologize if I have offended you."

"It does not matter," King Joshua said. "One thing only. When I make the public announcement tomorrow, you will follow it up with a statement from the joint houses of Congress, expressing your gratitude and unqualified support for me personally and for my government."

"Of course—"

"I have already prepared a statement for you to read. The Israeli ambassador will deliver it to you at nine in the morning. I hope that will be satisfactory."

"At this point, anything."

"At this point, that is all I want from you."

"You will exact payment when? How?"

"Good day, Mr. President."

Joshua completed a series of international telephone calls. Most of them went into the Third World and of those calls, all went to Arab heads of state.

King Joshua appeared on television the following morning. "I have come to bring news of peace and prosperity. Like all good citizens of this planet, I do not desire a nuclear holocaust. The forces of the Arabs and Russians opposing those of the Americans could result in a conflict so brutal it could destroy the entire planet.

"I have been in secret negotiations with leaders around the world. We shall have peace."

Joshua stepped off the platform after giving his shortest and most perplexing message ever. He had no need to say more. His selected friends would take care of it.

"Ladies and Gentlemen," began the sonorous voice of Erik-Hans Olson, Swedish commentator, "we have cause for celebration in the entire world tonight. King Joshua Gad-Erianko of Israel has intervened in an impossible crisis. He has, in the most unbelievable fashion, removed the nuclear threat.

"In a joint statement made only hours ago, representatives of the Arab nations and those of the American banking concerns announced that they have placed on deposit in the Arab Bank Trust Company the sum of 285 billion dollars. This repays the total amount owed to the Arabs.

"A stunned and grateful world owes a debt of thanks we can never repay to King Joshua Gad-Erianko."

The American President explained to his nation that because of the wise and humane efforts of King Joshua of Israel, the world had pulled itself back from the brink of extinction. Leading senators from both political parties affirmed their gratitude and loyalty to the King of Israel.

Newspapers and television newscasts in every major city in the world reported on the diplomatic strategy of King Joshua. The Swedish government announced that, in an unprecedented step, they had decided to award the Nobel Peace Prize to King Joshua. They had not bestowed the award for the past five years.

The Russians hailed Joshua as the world's greatest leader. Leaders of Arab countries stated, "No one else in the world could have averted this disaster. He has saved our honor and our money."

Frequent questions around the world centered on the source of the funds that King Joshua made available. Economists asserted that no single nation had that much currency available without bringing about the total collapse of their own economy.

Rumors spread across western Europe that King Josh-

ua had secretly appealed to twenty nations and asked them
to lend money for the sake of world peace. Widely quoted
sources in China claimed they knew that King Joshua had
influenced the Russians and the now-prospering countries of
Africa to contribute a large sum of the money. The same
sources hinted that most of the capital had come from Arab
nations other than Kuwait and Saudi Arabia.

No one in the world knew, and only Ivor Kalinin figured out that King Joshua had amassed vast sums of gold
bullion and precious stones. He kept them secretly deposited
within the banking systems of every nation in the world. The
tiny country of Goa held forty-two million dollars worth of
bullion waiting for this day to arrive. Joshua had calculated
so that he had, by the rollover of funds, pushed every country to the verge of bankruptcy. Each political and economic
leader knew of the crisis their own nation faced without
knowing the manipulative mind of King Joshua behind it.
Had he withdrawn all his deposits, every nation's monetary
system would have collapsed.

Following all the praise and congratulatory announcements, King Joshua allowed newscasters to read the letters
from children around the world. Their simplicity and direct-
ness forged stronger links of the chain with which he would
soon bind the world.

One typical letter read:

> I love you, King Joshua, because you love all of us
> kids in the world. I am going to live to grow up
> because you helped to save me. I live in America
> but I wish I could live with you. (signed) Jackie
> Michaels.

King Joshua's picture appeared in newspapers everywhere. Below his picture, editors published letters from children. For two weeks, these letters appeared.

One enterprising writer collected the letters, and with
appropriate introductions to each geographic area, pub-

lished them in a book. *Children's Letters to the King* sold more than six million copies in its first three months. By June, 1995, the publishers stated that they had sold more than twenty million copies in English. Although English became the official world langauge in 1992, in a few remote parts of the world, the elderly held onto their own tongue. Because of contributions, the International Children's Compassion Fund (ICCF) printed and distributed another forty million copies in the Mandarin, Ukrainian, Arabic, Hindi, and Swahili languages.

An investigative reporter announced that 38 percent of all males born in the state of California bore the name Joshua or some form of it such as Josh or Yeshua. Feminine forms such as Josie and Yosie accounted for 43 percent of new births. Another large group of parents, but she did not have the exact figures, had chosen parts of his name or title such as King, Gad, Eri, and Erianko.

Other countries reported similar trends. The figures ran from 51 percent in India to a low of 29 percent in Australia.

Joshua stood on the balcony of the palace and surveyed the city in the soon-approaching darkness. He felt a keen sense of pleasure. This phase of his plan, in some ways the most dangerous, had gone smoothly. He still found it remarkable how utterly gullible the people of the world had become. He smiled benevolently at the world below him.

Everything had gone exactly as he had planned. Only one thing troubled him—an element he had never foreseen or expected back in 1962.

Joshua Gad-Erianko, at age fifty-one, had almost overnight developed human emotions. He felt an acute sense of loneliness, as he felt the difference between himself and every other human being on the earth. He would always be different and he could never fully share himself with anyone else.

Yet he yearned for that. He wanted someone to understand him, to appreciate the real Joshua Gad-Erianko. But he had no one.

The closest person in Joshua's life that bordered on friendship was Ivor Kalinin. He tried to open himself as he knew others did. He began by explaining certain aspects of his plan. Kalinin understood, admired his brilliance, but nothing more. No friendship. No understanding of Joshua himself. Joshua knew then, as he had always known deep within, that he would never—could never—develop friendship with another person. No one was his equal.

Joshua, surveying the city of Jerusalem from his balcony, began to understand why. Ivor Kalinin was an ordinary man. Brilliant in certain ways, but limited and flawed.

Nagila's face came to him. The heretofore unknown sexual longings had begun to stir within his body and psyche. He wrestled with emotions he had never known before. He found his thoughts of Nagila distracting him, tormenting him, and keeping him awake at night. She might never understand, but she could love him. Be with him. Touch him and allow him to caress her.

Or, he asked himself, was that impossible, too? Was this the price he must pay?

Sadness filled King Joshua Gad-Erianko for a few moments. He had never had anyone close to him before. Until now he had never needed anyone.

Joshua had no one—not a single person in the world—to stand by his side and to share his triumph.

E·L·E·V·E·N

"He has made a remarkable recovery," the doctor told Nasief's friends. "Even six months ago I did not believe he would pull out of this. He is too stubborn to die. By every rule of the medical book, he should have died from any of six different reasons."

Nasief Habib knew he would recover. He tried being patient during the long ordeal of weeks and months when he could do nothing. He lay immobile for the first seven months, in the hospital. Upon his release he moved into an apartment that friends rented and furnished. Volunteers came in shifts to force him to remain in bed for another three months. He remained non-ambulatory an additional two months until the multiple breaks in his legs mended.

When he expressed impatience at the slow-healing process, the doctor reminded him of his age and of his great fortune even to be alive. The medical staff encouraged him by reminding him that he would walk again. Yet Nasief knew that, as strong as he was, he would never walk normally again. From the day of his beating, Nasief was never to know one moment without intense pain.

Only when he was alone did he break down and allow self-pity—and then only for a few minutes. He was still alive. He had a message to teach. "God has spared me for this purpose. I shall not fail him."

After a full year of convalescence, Nasief insisted on teaching. Groups of twenty people crowded into his room, and he taught two classes a day. When the nurses and doctors remonstrated with him, Nasief laughed. "They help me get better."

He began by teaching from his wheelchair. Converts, taking courage from Nasief's example, drifted back to his classes. When no trouble erupted after a month's attendance, the less bold followers joined, earnestly listening and considering the message of Nasief.

Because of the limited space in a large apartment, he could accommodate eighty-three if they stood for the entire hour he taught. The numbers who attended continued to grow, and Nasief found himself teaching six hour-long classes each day. He did little in between but rest and sleep. Instead of the demand on his energy wearing him down as everyone had expected, Nasief grew stronger.

The crowds multiplied. Since his own church building had been destroyed and governmental regulations would not permit a rebuilding, Nasief rented facilities. He began with a hall that held two hundred people. Within weeks, he was again teaching six classes and running out of space. He moved to new facilities. No matter how large the seating capacity, word spread throughout the city and more people came. He moved regularly, always seeking out larger halls or auditoriums. Any building spacious enough for the consistently growing crowds, he accepted. The numbers swelled from day to day.

Nasief made it his policy from the beginning never to ask for funds and never to tell of his personal needs. Yet he never lacked money. He allowed the use of a box in the rear of the building that bore the single word, "Offering." Nasief

Habib said when asked about finances, "My work is to teach. God's work is to provide the people to listen and the money for all the needs."

By early 1999, Nasief personally addressed more than 10,000 each day, five days a week. On the two weekly religious days of Saturday and Sunday, he did not speak but encouraged the people to go to their own place of worship.

On his two off-days Nasief spent most of his time in bed; piles of books and translations of the Bible took up as much space as his own body.

Nasief began predicting catastrophic events with unerring accuracy weeks or months before they happened. He predicted the famine and the plague before anyone knew of them. He predicted wars in most unlikely places such as the Sudan, New Guinea, and Turkey. Nations invaded other nations with such frequency it became difficult for most people to keep up with which power controlled which territory. He predicted that more than five million people would die from the ravages of war. Conservative statistics listed war casualties (military personnel and civilians killed in combat) at 5.3 million.

Despite Nasief's plea for his students not to talk about his predictions, they spread the word throughout Jerusalem. Many sat with tape recorders and video machines. They sent copies to their friends all over Israel and throughout the Middle East. It did not take long before requests came to him from around the world. "Come and teach us," they asked.

Not being a man who sought fame and being one who eschewed publicity, Nasief resisted the invitations. During 2000, travelers from eighty-one nations visited him. Each day brought stronger and more urgent pleas. Soon local leaders bowed to the inevitable. "It is your duty. God has given you special insight. You must share it."

He agreed initially that cameras from abroad could televise his studies. Nasief had personal misgivings about the cameras zooming in, the bright lights, the distraction caused by media workers, but he had agreed on two conditions.

First, that his teaching not be used for fund-raising, and second, his personal income would come only from donations by local followers. Any other monies would go to charitable causes.

Nasief himself could not understand this overwhelming interest. He believed he had a message to teach, but he recognized that other gifted teachers taught better. His slower pace of speaking, he knew, did not compare with the faster cadence and better-planned services of others. He did not like being singled out as an authority.

One world-renowned evangelist who had escaped the purge of Christian leaders visited him and said afterward, "Nasief, this is the message that God intends for the world to hear."

"Then why doesn't he give it to you? You're an evangelist."

The silvery-haired church leader, an American from the Deep South, bowed his head slightly and mumbled, "God couldn't trust me, I guess."

Henri duPre at the World Health Organization lived in perpetual confusion. New diseases appeared, spread over a wide geographical area, and took the lives of many. By the time scientists isolated the cause, the disease disappeared. The SP (Spanish Prostitutes) disease disappeared after taking the lives of more than three million people in fifty-six countries. Every kind of research predicted a globe-wide epidemic. Then no new cases. He noted that no country had had a reported case of SP for 140 days.

DuPre hated to hear reports these days. The deadly diseases came and went often before they could appropriate research grants. Even his own staff could not keep the names of these diseases straight.

"It's another STD," Gertrude VanderHof sighed. "Different symptoms, different group, but just as deadly."

"All right," duPre said. "Let's have it."

"We're calling this one AIDS-X because it has all of the symptoms of the Acquired Immune Deficiency Syndrome that caused such a scare two decades ago." Gertrude laid the file across duPre's desk. "It's back, it's stronger, and, in its new and virulent form, it resists any standard AIDS treatment. As a matter of fact, the three most widely used drugs to combat AIDS seem to spread the disease more rapidly into the upper respiratory area."

DuPre listened, wondering what came next. "What can you tell me?"

"Because of its similarity to AIDS, we isolated this one easily enough. We know from research done at Sanford University Research Center and at Emory in Atlanta that it is passed through semen."

DuPre recalled that AIDS spread through the unsterile needles of drug abusers and, in the beginning, through blood transfusions. "Exclusively?"

"Absolutely." Gertrude walked to the window and, with her back turned to her supervisor, said, "Henri, maybe we ought to leave this one alone. For now."

"Leave it alone? Aren't people dying from AIDS-X?"

"Yes, within weeks of multiple exposure. It requires several sexual partners. A minimum of six, our research shows."

"Then why—?"

Gertrude turned around and stared directly at duPre. "Isn't it time we got rid of all kinds of perverts in the world? Let them kill each other off."

"But what happens when AIDS-X gets to the general population?"

"If people had decent moral standards—"

"Gertrude, we have no right to make moral judgments. We are scientists."

An argument ensued and Gertrude apologized. Instead of forgetting the issue, she called two newspapers and gave them information, with the understanding that they would not quote her.

The next day the story of AIDS-X burst into every

newscast everywhere. A sentiment similar to that expressed by Gertrude VanderHof arose. When the facts became widely known, the world learned that it had been confined to one population group. They also knew that eventually it would spread beyond the homosexual community.

The first proposed solution came from Zambia's President Philip Kayubi. "We need to find a place in the world where we can segregate such people. Let them kill each other but not infect the rest of us."

International leaders ignored Kayubi's suggestion until others spoke up. The Premier of Chad called for the immediate killing of AIDS-X carriers. The Amir of Kuwait and the Prime Minister of Canada proposed that each nation set aside specific segregated areas for such people. Savvy politicians, hearing of the growing fear of their constituents, supported Kayubi's original suggestion.

Within weeks, leaders from around the globe met in Teheran for three days. They proposed that all known sexual deviates (which they went into minute detail to categorize) should be isolated from the rest of the world's population.

They agreed that they must place them in one geographic place and in total isolation. After hours of strenuous debate, they narrowed their choices down to three: Australia, New Zealand or Malagasy Republic.

They ruled out Australia and New Zealand because they comprise vast lands and it would be difficult to evacuate. Tempers ran short as representatives from those two nations pleaded not to take their land. In the end, they selected the Malagasy Republic, returning it to its former name of Madagascar.

"Approximately ten million people live on that island," someone pointed out. "What do we do about that?"

"Simple," said Philip Kayubi, "we inform them of our decision. We give them one month to evacuate. At the end of the month, we send military strength to the island."

The arguments started again, more for the sake of publicity than anything. They agreed. In one month's time, planes would land at Tananarive, the capitol, to take the evacuating members. Military transports from Malawi, Zaire, Greece, Italy, Argentina, and Peru would be on alert to land their soldiers and kill without question anyone left on the island.

Henri duPre had found the whole business disgusting. He could not prove that Gertrude VanderHof had leaked the initial information but he had no question in his mind that she had done it. Instead of showing compassion, or at least remaining objective and concerned for other human beings, she had helped turn world opinion against homosexuals.

"If it starts there, where will it end?" he asked her. "Don't you see what you've started? Who knows what will happen next? Perhaps next year anyone with brown eyes faces extinction."

"Henri, we are not exterminating these people. We are isolating them. Nothing more."

"You are sentencing them to death."

"No. They sentence themselves."

The day after the finalization of the Teheran Pact, Henri duPre resigned. "I am a man who cares for the people—all people. I do not advocate these sexual practices of the victims of AIDS-X, but I do plead for compassion and tolerance."

Only stations in Switzerland aired his comments. Not one newspaper carried his statement. On page two of *USA Today* it stated:

> Dr. Henri duPre, forty-nine, head of the World
> Health Organization, resigned yesterday in Geneva.
> He cited ill health and heavy pressures.

Gertrude VanderHof became acting director for three months and then she received permanent appointment.

She sat in her office, pleased that it had worked so efficiently. When the long-distance call came on her private line, she thanked her sponsor profusely.

"I have other things for you to do," he said. "I am pleased with your performance."

"Thank you," she said, "thank you. I am ready, King Joshua."

T·W·E·L·V·E

Nasief's first instruction class, held five mornings a week at 6:00 in the ballroom at the newly completed King Joshua Hotel, always found a crowd of people waiting at the door before 5:30.

Nagila Levy and Shaheen Ahmed regularly attended this early meeting. Nasief reserved sixteen chairs in the front row for them and other special friends. "It inspires me to see you, my dear Nagila and Shaheen. You listen with eagerness written across your faces. You take notes. You flip through your Bible to read each of the passages I quote. Every teacher needs students like you."

"I'm so ignorant," Nagila said, "and you have such a vast amount of knowledge to share with us."

"Then listen carefully. My days are short. I shall not be able to do this much longer."

"I don't know how you hold up now—"

"No, Nagila, not because of my physical condition. God spoke to me through a dream last night." He smiled at her. "Do not let that surprise you. As you continue to read, you will discover that throughout the pages of the Bible God used dreams as one method of communicating to his own people. Sometimes to those outside of the faith such as Pharaoh of Egypt in the days of Joseph or King Nebuchadnezzar of Babylon."

"And God has shown you that—" Nagila could not finish her sentence. She had grown to love the old man. He was as dear to her as her own father had been.

"They shall destroy my body—the enemies of God. Right here in this city." He brushed tears from her eyes. "Don't be saddened. The end is near. My spirit shall live forever."

Nagila wanted to protest his talking that way, but Nasief had such a serenity about him, she would later say to Shaheen, "I think I stood on holy ground when he spoke. It was a touching moment for me. He is ready to die. Even looking forward to it. I hope I shall be that ready when my time comes."

"You will," Shaheen said. "For those who are faithful, God makes them ready." The determined lines on his face momentarily disturbed Nagila. She felt as if he also knew an ominous truth about the future and held it from her.

On a Tuesday morning in May 2002, Nagila arrived at Nasief's early teaching session a few minutes later than usual. Shaheen had already gone inside. She approached the door where the attendant would recognize her and tell her to go through.

For the past week the 1200 chairs filled the room, and people stood around the sides. Others sat on the floor in the center aisle, and the management had added fifty chairs at the back of the room.

Nagila stared at the size of the crowd still queued up and waiting in an orderly manner. They had their choice of waiting for the 7:30 class or remaining in the hallway to watch the class on closed-circuit television.

"Ms. Levy—"

She turned to see who in the crowd around the door

had called her name. Her face immediately registered surprise and she called, "Ivor Kalinin! I never expected to find you here."

Ivor pushed through a group of people and came up close to her. He laughed self-consciously. "You are not more surprised than I am."

"I'm so pleased you decided to come—"

"I decided the day after we talked. I have been coming to these teachings since then. Much I still do not understand. Yet this man speaks the truth. It is as if he listens in *that man's* bedroom and office and hurries here to tell the King's secrets."

"That frightens me," Nagila said. "The things Nasief predicts for the next few months. Especially after all that's happened so far—"

He nodded and lowered his voice. "It seems it must get worse. That is as the King has planned it to be." He shook her hand. "So happy to see you again." He turned to go back to his place in line.

"No, no," Nagila said as she clasped his hands. "Please come inside with me. I am sure we can find a place for you in the reserved section."

He shook his head. "That would be wrong. I am willing to wait and take any empty place I can find."

"Not today!" She pulled his arm and led him to the door. "I have a special guest today," she told the attendant. "Can you put in an extra chair?"

"Take mine," the man said. "I'll find another." He handed Ivor a plastic folding chair and allowed them to pass through the door.

"This is most gracious."

"I am so pleased you decided to come, Ivor."

"I came because . . . because at last I am ready to search for truth and to accept it. Please do not laugh at me."

"I'm not laughing."

"I have walked in fear for many years—most of my life it now seems. I am no longer afraid of Joshua. My mind is free to think. To choose. To make my own decisions."

She kissed his cheek. "You'll find what you seek. I'm sure of it."

Nasief sat on a large chair while a member of the video crew adjusted his portable microphone. At the appropriate moment, Nasief prayed a simple prayer for guidance for his speaking and for openness so that the people would understand.

Nasief paused and let his eyes roam across the audience for a few seconds. "Today I want to talk to you about a mysterious number in the Bible. It is the number six. We have many ways of interpreting this. For all ancients, numbers had symbolic meanings." He spent several minutes explaining the significance of each of the numbers through five. "The number six is the number of humanity, and it is this number we must watch carefully during the next few months. Six is only one short of seven. Seven is the number of perfection.

"Among the ancients, when they doubled any number it called attention to it, as if to underline it and say, 'read carefully.' When they trebled the number, it raised it to its highest power, and emphasized it was a matter of the gravest importance. I hope you grasp this simple concept because it will open to you the next great event to take place in our world."

Nasief paused, opened his Bible and read:

> "And he (The Beast) causes all, both small and great, rich and poor, free and slave, to receive a mark on their right hand or on their foreheads, and that no one may buy or sell except the one who has the mark of the name of the beast, or the number of his name. Here is wisdom. Let him who has understanding calculate the number of the beast, for it is the number of man: and his number is six hundred and sixty-six."

"Friends, this is the next thing that must happen in our world. I cannot tell you precisely the meaning of the number 666, but I can tell you that you will know soon. As I have continued to study, it becomes clear to me that it will soon be upon us."

While Nasief continued to explain about the power the beast would exercise over the entire world, Nagila glanced at Ivor Kalinin. His mouth open, he sat in shock. "No, no, no," he whispered. "How can he possibly know this? How can he know?"

T·H·I·R·T·E·E·N

In late 1994, King Joshua established a medical research center in Jerusalem. He engaged the top researchers in the world and provided them with the newest and best facilities. The complex covered fifteen acres in a twelve-story structure.

These scientists stunned the world with their break-through treatments for a wide variety of diseases. In 1995 one such group conquered obesity. They perfected a drug that required one daily injection with virtually no contrain-dications. This drug depleted the body of fat cells.

Patients received treatment only from recognized doc-tors who specialized in the field. The World Health Organ-ization set up complex charts showing ideal weights. They would allow a variance of 2 percent body fat and ten pounds in weight. By 1996, no obese people existed in the world.

This led the Jerusalem scientists to further their re-search. They promised the elimination of debilitating factors including death from the effects of diseases such as diabetes, renal failure, and hypertension.

Another team isolated the cause of AIDS-X and provided inoculation. The eight million people exiled to Madagascar remained on the island. Once the disease stopped, the people prospered. They allowed immigration to the island.

Madagascar became the world's leader in unrestricted sexual practices. They allowed marriages between family members. Polygamy became a common feature of the wealthy. Divorce laws dissolved a marriage by one party asking. They legalized child prostitution.

As a nation, they prospered financially. They led the world in their mineral production of uranium and thorium, both valuable sources of nuclear energy.

Leaders and ordinary citizens praised the humanitarian efforts of King Joshua.

"He is determined to wipe out all disease by the year 2010," said a report in *Pravda*. The article quoted sources from the World Health Organization that said malaria, chicken pox, and measles were now extinct. No new reports of these diseases had appeared in one full year. No new cases of polio had occurred in eight months.

Nagila leaned over to Ivor. "What is it?"

"I cannot believe it! Only—only one hour ago—Joshua told me this himself."

"Told you about the use of three sixes?"

"Nagila, no, no. I know what the professor means. You see, this New Testament he reads from comes originally from Greek, does it not?"

"Yes—"

"And in Greek, a number corresponds to a letter of the alphabet, if I recall correctly."

"I think so."

"By any chance, would the letter that corresponds to six be the letter *s?*"

Shaheen, sitting on the other side of Nagila and who had overheard, whispered, "Yes. If you use letter value instead of numbers, you could just as easily read that as SSS."

"Then it is happening. It starts soon. Very soon." He turned to Nagila and lowered his voice to a bare whisper. "I must leave and I do not know if I shall see you again. I can tell you this much. Your friend Nasief Habib speaks more truth than he can possibly realize."

Ivor left his seat and walked hurriedly through a side door.

When Nagila returned to the palace at 8:30, she found a message that the King waited for her in his private quarters. Two guards escorted her to the King's residence and closed the door behind her.

Nagila stood at the door and Joshua stared at her. She wore a gray suit of blended cotton. Her pink blouse, of fine quality silk, was tied with a large bow at the neck. He stood in the middle of the room and his eyes moved from head to foot several times. "You are so lovely, Nagila."

He came closer and touched her gleaming hair. "When I see you, I want to touch your hair and feel its softness in my fingers. I want to press my lips against yours. I want—"

Nagila stepped back, but Joshua took her hands. "Don't move away from me. I had to talk with you, Nagila. I cannot wait any longer."

"You see me every day—"

"You know what I mean, I think. To see you alone. Here."

"I'd like to get to my desk. I am expecting—"

"No! That can wait! This cannot."

"All right," she said. Nagila tried to assess her feelings toward the King. When he had spoken to her months earlier she had mixed emotions. Now she had no uncertainty. She despised him for the evil he planned and executed.

"Nagila, it has been a long time since I talked to you

about—about this love I feel for you," Joshua said. "It has become like a disease to me. Each day I find myself thinking of you, desiring you—"

"Joshua, please. I don't want you to talk that way to me."

"I love you. As much as I understand what it means to love a person. Is that so complicated?"

"I don't love you. It's that simple for me."

"As King, I could take you. I could command—"

"You could do those things, but I hope you have more sense. I despise what you are doing. I would soon learn to despise your presence."

"Nagila, I want you to understand. My kingdom—the goals for which I have worked all my life—are within my grasp. I can truly and literally place the entire world at your feet. Isn't that the way suitors are supposed to talk to the women they love?"

"I don't want the world." She took a deep breath and said evenly, "I don't want you either."

Joshua came closer, his lips only inches from her own. Nagila turned her head.

With his fingers he cupped her chin and pulled it forward. "Look at me. They tell me that I am handsome. I know I am brilliant. I have everything to offer. Yet you don't want me. I don't understand—"

"You are more like a—a robot than a man. Except when you talk to me. In this one single instance you feel love—"

"That's true."

"What about the eight million people who died across the world from starvation or the victims of the Green Plague? Did you feel anything for them?"

"That is another matter. This planet is overpopulated."

"So you eliminate them this way. Does that make you a great humanitarian?"

"It makes me a pragmatist. Would you prefer that I set up firing squads and shoot eight million people? Or perhaps select one country such as Uganda, wipe out the entire population and that would make the total numbers about right."

"Joshua, you *murdered* human beings!"

"You may not understand, but I did what I believed to be reasonable and for the world's best interests. I calculated this carefully. I made that decision more than thirty years ago. Don't you understand I didn't do it because I hated the human race or any group of people? I chose logically and fairly."

"What if my blood type had been O? Would you have allowed me to die?"

"I would have given you the vaccine."

"You mean—you mean you had a vaccine? A cure? Even before the disease struck?"

"Of course. That is why the plague stopped. I always had the vaccine before any new disease appeared. As soon as the Green Plague eliminated the proper number, I put a stop to it."

"That's monstrous!"

"Monstrous? You would prefer that in ten years we would starve because of overpopulation, underproduction, and increasing disregard for the balance of nature? Creating such unlivable conditions that the whole race would die off? No, Nagila, I would not call that monstrous. Can't you think of it as an act of kindness? I sacrificed eight million to die for the benefit of five billion."

"Do you think you are God?"

"Not God—"

"Yet you choose. You decide who lives and who dies?"

"That is precisely what I am doing."

"You speak so callously—"

"Perhaps. Call me any names you want because your words of insult don't hurt me. When I was a child in Russia, people often yelled at me. I felt nothing then. I feel nothing now from the intended insult. I feel nothing—nothing except my love for you."

"This can't be," Nagila said. "It just can't."

"Stop fighting me. No one else fights me. Even if you

don't feel what I feel, I would accept that. I would teach you. I know I could help you to feel—"

Nagila pushed him away. "No."

"No? You are saying that to me?"

"Joshua, I think it will be better for you and for me if I leave my job."

"Don't do this to me—"

"I don't love you. I don't want to be around you. I don't want to work for you."

Joshua grabbed Nagila and said calmly as his fingers dug into her arms. "I'll tell you when you may leave. I cannot force you to love me. At least I do not as yet know how to bring that about. But you will not leave here. There is nowhere you can go without my permission. Not in Jerusalem or Israel. Not in the whole world. Don't you understand that? I have become the most powerful man on earth!"

The realization of what he said struck Nagila. She wanted to scream, to kick, to shout in anger and frustration. Instead, tears slid slowly down her cheeks. "Yes, I do understand."

"It will be easier if you submit to me—I can make life beautiful for you, Nagila. I can offer you so much."

"No."

"Let me touch you, hold you—"

A calmness spread through Nagila and her voice hardened. "You can take me by force. You can rape me. You can kill me, but you will never, never have my love."

"Your love is the only thing I want," Joshua said. He walked to the door and opened it for her.

King Joshua Gad-Erianko spoke on national television. The Knesset required all citizens of Israel to listen to this broadcast unless involved in emergency service. For those excepted, the government required employers to arrange special showings of the speech.

King Joshua's television broadcasts became a weekly event. The significant portion of his first message said:

"We have formed an elite society in Israel. From Israel it will spread throughout the world. It is a society of mutual benefit. It is an organization that will bond all good and honorable people together because we share common goals.

"Beginning tomorrow all citizens of Israel will have the opportunity to join the noble organization that unites us together. I have called it SSS or Triple S. The letters stand for Solidarity, Superiority, and Salvation.

"I have called it by this simple term, the Triple S, because I want everyone to understand our goals.

"First, *Solidarity*. We shall work together. Together we shall wipe out injustice and poverty from the world.

Second, *Superiority*. We shall not rest on previous laurels or goals. We shall excel.

Third, *Salvation*. We shall set all peoples free from oppression. We shall save the world from the oppression of slavery, of religion, of both capitalism and communism . . ."

Within hours the streets of Israel filled with what appeared as spontaneous celebration. "We shall rule the world," one man yelled to a crowd.

"God has appointed us to save the other nations!" a woman proclaimed. "Together! Triple S!"

"Triple S! Triple S!" the people chanted as they marched through the streets of Jerusalem, Tel Aviv, Capernaum, and as far as the Golan Heights.

Once the demonstrators had done their initial work, "spontaneous" parades broke out with placards and signs to tell the world that they stood behind their wise and gifted leader.

One of the signs read:

JOSHUA, EARTH KING
JOSHUA, MORE THAN A KING

Soon others painted more decorative signs and banners. Marchers came from across Israel, marching through the streets of Jerusalem. Day by day the signs elevated the role of King Joshua.

The King stood on his private balcony and waved when he saw the banner for which he had been waiting. Printed in large red letters, it covered the full width of the street and required eight people to hold it upright:

JOSHUA!
THE WISDOM AND POWER OF GOD

Few observers paid special attention to the banner that day. Newsreels captured the enthusiasm and ended each broadcast in Israel and abroad with that banner.

In the days ahead that slogan would become increasingly significant.

F·O·U·R·T·E·E·N

At twilight, Joshua burst into the office allocated to Ivor Kalinin. "You old fool! What have you done? How dare you interfere?"

"Interfere?"

"You cannot stop me. You think that by opening your mouth you can change anything?"

"I have only tried to correct."

"You authorized the vaccine to go into production. I did not give you the authority. How did you dare to do this?"

"Because people are dying, Joshua. People the vaccine will save."

"You know my plan, and not enough people have died yet. Too many people still live on earth. We must decrease the population much more"

"Are you God, Joshua Gad-Erianko? Is that what you have become? You hold the power to live in your hands? Who will you destroy next now that you can withhold life?"

Joshua grabbed the old man's frail shoulders. "Someone else asked similar questions recently. Nagila Levy. You have discussed me, haven't you?"

"Some things, yes."

"You are a fool, Ivor." He gazed deeply into the old man's eyes and then pushed him roughly backward. Ivor's back hit the wall, and he did not move for several seconds because of the pain.

"You are not afraid anymore, is that it?"

"No, I'm not." He straightened and said, "Joshua, if it will do any good, I plead with you. Do not take more lives. Stop this inhuman thing you have started."

"You do not tell me what to do. Now. Ever." Joshua grabbed his former teacher and wrapped his hands around the thin neck. "I don't need you. You have betrayed me. To whom else have you talked?"

The light of fear had already died in Ivor's eyes and he smiled. "Press your fingers more tightly, Joshua. Squeeze the life out of this body. Let me die and then, at last, I shall have peace. You have made me live in the torment of Hell for all these years. I want no more."

"No more? You don't know the meaning of torment. When I am through with you, then you'll know." His fingers tightened, and the old man did not resist. His eyes stared in defiance.

Joshua had never personally killed a man before. As his fingers clutched the old man's throat, he felt a pleasure in what he was doing. The fingers tightened and the pressure cut off the air supply. Ivor's eyes bulged, but he made no effort to resist.

When he knew Ivor was dead, he released the body and watched it fall lifelessly to the floor. He walked out of the room and shouted at a guard in the hallway. "Clear this out."

He felt no remorse for his action. However, Ivor had his uses and he would have to go through the process of finding someone to replace him.

Joshua returned to his own suite of rooms and sat down. Ivor's actions had stirred him inside. He experienced a sense of anger that he had never known before. It was a new emotion.

Until he killed Ivor, Joshua had made every decision and completed every action without emotional consideration. He had simply decided on the best plan and carried it out. It was a simple way.

Now he had experienced anger. His anger had so possessed him that he seemingly had no control until he squeezed the life from the old man. Joshua reflected on what he had done. He felt no regrets. Ivor Kalinin was nearly seventy and had become quite useless. Seventy years was long enough for Ivor Kalinin to live.

From the Senate chambers the President of the United States scheduled a major address to the nation. Because the word leaked out that he would make a "strategic, drastic change of foreign policy," the visitors' gallery had filled by 6:00 although the President would not enter until 7:30 exactly. TV cameras and microphones cluttered the podium.

The President, contrary to his usual method, had given no hint of the content of his message. Other than the one phrase, no word had leaked to the press. Reporters grumbled, plied their informers with promises or raged with threats, but no one could or would provide information.

"Only the President and the Secretary of State know the contents of his message," said Larry Dean in announcing the press conference. This had never happened before during President Whilhite's administration. He had carefully worked to gain the most advance publicity and favoritism toward any policy or program he advocated.

Washington's pundits argued that it would be a get-tough message against America's enemies or a step toward detente with the powerful Chinese. Yet even they admitted, "This is purely an educated guess."

Security, as usual, was tight. No one carried packages into the visitors' gallery. Because of the President's appearance, guards also checked purses and searched anyone who aroused their suspicion. With all their careful search, guards did not question one paper bag that contained two un-opened packages of sugar-free chewing gum and two large-sized chocolate-covered coconut bars in a woman's purse.

The guard who assessed the young woman smiled and said, "You can't eat the candy in there, you know."

"Of course not," she said, dazzling him with the bright-ness of her gleaming smile.

He did not realize that both candy bars were actually C-4, a plastic explosive. Together the two bars weighed 1.7 pounds. By themselves they would not do a lot of damage. The combination of fifteen such bars, placed strategically around the building would have the desired effect of de-stroying the entire Senate Building.

Earlier that day, two men posing as employees of CBS and NBC substituted microphones for the ones the network sent. The men had carefully prepared the substitutes so that each hollow base contained C-4.

Two other bars came in the clearly recognized enve-lopes of Federal Express. The first, addressed to the Hon. Douglas Bonner, senior representative from California, went to his office first. A phone call, half an hour before the arrival, instructed Bonner's secretary that it is "of the utmost importance that Mr. Bonner have this envelope before the President speaks. It contains highly significant information."

The secretary, recognizing a voice who had provided similar material of great value to the President's top foe, did not open the parcel. She placed it on his desk.

The second envelope arrived minutes later, addressed to the Speaker of the House, Stephen MacBryde. On the front, in bold red letters it said URGENT AND CONFI-DENTIAL. A page brought in the unopened, bulky enve-lope. Stuck on top was a note from MacBryde's personal aide with the words scribbled, FOR MAC'S EYES ONLY.

Neither man was present at the time of delivery. They were delayed in a minor car accident at C Street, right outside the State Department Building. During the discus-sion over the mishap with the driver who rammed their vehicle from behind, spectators appeared and a crowd collected. Voices filled the air as they tried to explain what happened—all giving conflicting statements. The two politicians, attempting to get back inside the car, were bumped by spectators. Both men received injections that took effect within three minutes. The purpose was to make them confused and so physically relaxed they had trouble standing.

The police officer in charge noticed the strange behavior of both politicians. He assumed they had drunk too much. However, he radioed for an ambulance, concluding that the hospital could make the decision regarding their condition. Both men protested—mildly because of the effects of the drug—going to the hospital. They would fully recover within twelve hours.

Mukta, the leader of the newly formed group known only as Free World, had laid out the plan carefully. She had methodically rehearsed her people. "You must know exactly what you are to do. You must also be prepared for any contingency."

All fourteen members of Free World had worked together on other terrorist activities, using other group names and in other countries. They recruited only one new person, a beautiful twenty-year-old student named Yazmin from Calcutta, who had not engaged in terrorism before. With her innocent appearance, her soft voice, and by wearing the traditional sari, they assumed she would be able to get past any inspection unless the guards decided to hold a strict body search.

Mukta had successfully engineered and participated in eighteen assassinations. She had become the most highly paid freelance mercenary in the world. The few who talked to her in person assumed she was part Oriental because of her skin hue and almond-shaped eyes. No one knew she was actually Russian.

Known for her thorough professional approach, Mukta had recruited her assistants (as she referred to them), and drilled them for months before they ever participated in a "project."

Had she not needed another person badly she would never have allowed Yazmin to participate. The girl had panicked twice in drill. Mukta, who seldom made mistakes about the people she chose, had misgivings about Yazmin.

"Let her go," her second-in-command said. "Even if she fails, we have more than enough explosives to do the job."

"I suppose you are right," she said. "I simply dislike doing a project unless I can put every factor in our favor."

Yazmin, unaware of Mukta's low regard for her, had arrived at the Senate at 5:00 and waited in line until they opened the gallery for visitors. Mukta had instructed her to sit in the fifth row from the left, right side.

Yazmin failed in the first instruction. She did not get the seat in the fifth row. A family of five grabbed the seats. Yazmin hesitated. She considered asking them to move down. Yet Mukta had drilled into her, "Never do anything that will call attention to yourself. Never speak unless addressed by another." She sat instead in the sixth row. Mukta had instructed her not to place the first explosive until 7:25. That would give her five minutes to complete her work and be out of the building.

As the minutes slowly lapsed, Yazmin tried to convince herself that one row made no great difference. It would matter to no one except Mukta, who had to have everything perfect or she went into a rage. Mukta worried too much.

Yazmin sat down, laying her purse in the seat next to her to indicate that she was saving it for a friend. Had anyone observed her, they would have noticed that she carefully smoothed the multiple folds of her sari. In the process, however, Yazmin untied the knots that held blocks of C-4 that she had concealed between her legs. The released string brought them slowly to the floor. She had only to attach the explosives to the bottom of the seat next to her. She had done that so many times in practice she did not worry about it.

It was a relatively simple process for her because Mukta's supplier had coated the plastic explosive with a sticky substance. She peeled off the thin strip of paper that covered the top of the first.

Yazmin squirmed, twisting her body so that she could glance occasionally for her late friend. Anyone watching would have been aware only of her anxiety in waiting. The crowd grabbed all other seats within five minutes of the opening of the gallery. Yazmin decided that she had another two minutes before she would demurely remove her purse, showing her disgust and allowing someone to occupy the seat.

Yazmin allowed herself a sigh, knowing that the first explosive had stuck properly. All she had to do now was place the second bar and her work would be completed. She felt perspiration gathering on her forehead and under her arms.

She bent to her left, twisting around as she searched the crowd of people. With her right hand concealed by the sari, she pulled on the paper. Instead of pulling off clean, it tore, leaving a strip on either side. For a moment Yazmin felt panic rise within her. What should she do? She tried pulling off the rest of the paper, but it did not cooperate. In order to get all off, she'd have to place it in front of her and look at it.

Large beads of perspiration formed around her forehead and face. Her body quivered because of her now rapid-but-shallow breathing.

"Excuse me, miss," the man said behind her, tapping her on the shoulder. "Are you feeling all right?"

Yazmin jumped at his touch, dropping the explosive. To her ears it sounded as if the impact thundered through the balcony. No one looked her way.

Yazmin stared at the man, forcing herself to speak calmly. "Yes . . . I am well."

"I didn't mean to interfere, but you looked . . . well, sick."

"You are most kind. I am . . . I am well."

Yazmin turned around, faced the front, and looked at the face of her watch which she wore on a chain around her neck. It was 7:26. She was now one minute late. At this moment Mukta had instructed her to start walking out of the room.

What do I do now? Leave it on the floor? No, I can't. I can't take it with me either.

Perspiration soaked through her light-weight cotton blouse. She twisted her body so that she faced the man who had spoken to her earlier. She had only to keep him looking at her face while she used her hands to position the plastic. "You are kind to be concerned."

He said that he was a medical student, and Yazmin hoped it appeared that she listened. She smiled as the plastic stuck. "Thank you for being concerned. I—I do feel a little sick."

"Would you like me to help you?"

"No. I am fine. If you would be so kind as to save my place here, I think I only need a little air. With so many people—"

"Can get stifling," he said. "And some people get this way around crowds—"

Yazmin forced herself to walk slowly toward the exit. The guard held the door for her. "Better hurry back. In a few minutes I'll have to keep this locked until after the President's speech."

"I am not feeling well. Someone may have my place." She pointed to the sixth row and started for the open door.

"Miss! Miss! Wait! You dropped something!" The man sitting in the seventh row had picked up the bar of C-4 and was holding it in his hand. Yazmin clearly saw the paper that had not come off and, consequently, the bar had not held.

She shook her head and knew she should run. Instead she froze. She kept shaking her head, the only physical motion she seemed capable of making.

The man rushed to the end of the aisle and started toward her. Then he looked at the solid bar. It read "Charge Demolition, Lot TKK-9788." He paused, staring at the object in his hand.

Fear filled his face and he screamed, "Explosive! It's an explosive! She's trying to kill us all!" He lurched forward and grabbed for the edge of her sari, missed and stumbled.

His action made Yazmin spring into action and she tried to run through the door. The guard grabbed her by the shoulders and spun her around.

At that moment, the Marine Band began to play "Hail

to the Chief." The man, still holding the plastic explosive, stared at Yazmin, sensing it was too late to do anything. He threw the bar at Yazmin. It struck her hands at the moment Mukta detonated the first of the explosives.

An ear-shattering explosion filled the room as the microphone exploded, striking the President with a powerful blow on the head. He was dead before his body hit the floor. An explosion from the other microphone went off one second later. For the next thirteen seconds, one by one, Mukta detonated each explosive. At the end of fifteen seconds, forty-seven people were already dead. In the flames, falling debris, and the panic that ensued, another eighteen people lost their lives. A total of sixty-five dead and many with serious injuries. Eight more would die in the hospital before the night ended.

The President, Vice-President, and all members of the Joint Chiefs of Staff died in the first two explosions.

Beginning the next afternoon, Mukta and her assistants continued their reign of terror in twenty-one state capitals of the United States. They recreated similar scenarios in each. They all went perfectly.

Stephen MacBryde, Speaker of the House and now the senior person alive to succeed to the Presidency, declared a state of national emergency. National Guard and all military personnel went on instant alert.

The second day 300 people perished when bombs exploded on Liberty Island. Seconds later the Statue of Liberty crumbled and fell into the Atlantic Ocean.

On the fourth day, Stephen MacBryde, now officiating as the President of the United States, sent a message to King Joshua of Israel. When decoded it read: Everything according to plan.

F·I·F·T·E·E·N

The SSS began in a frenzied but well-planned blaze of patriotism and continued to build. Each person who joined received a uniform to wear at official functions. At other times, they identified themselves with a scarf. SSS instructions allowed them to wear scarves made of silk, cotton, or any "suitable material." The scarf carried a singular mark, a yellow triangle that enclosed a black "S" in each corner.

All adults between the ages of twenty-five and sixty-nine who joined the SSS wore red. The SSS Youth Corps, sporting royal blue, designated anyone fifteen to twenty-four. The SSS Children's Brigade received gold. No child could join before age seven. The Senior SSS (Retired) wore scarves of red, blue, and gold stripes. Eventually, as King Joshua pointed out, faithful citizens would wear each of the scarves during the appropriate period of their lives. As part of the indoctrination ceremony, called Rites of Passage in World Citizenry, the government hosted a party and welcomed them as guests of honor. King Joshua explained that the Triple S would take the place of former religious practices such as Bar Mitzvah and Confirmation. "This will unite us to each other and eventually make us at one with the entire world."

The government allowed a wide flexibility in the wearing of scarves, except for official occasions when the regulations clearly explained that they must be worn as armbands, three inches above the elbow. The regulation stated only that they must be clean and visible at all times. Members of the SSS could also wear their cloth around their necks or waists, or tied to an ankle. It became fashionable for young men to wear them around their right leg at high level.

Ninety-eight percent of all students in Israel enrolled in the program before the first week ended.

Few adults resisted. Even those who had personal reservations and would have defied governmental pressure did not stand up against social coercion. "You don't want to make this a better world?" taunted members of the SSS at reluctant joiners.

"Is our king asking us to do anything immoral or illegal?"

"Aren't these wonderful goals for the whole world?"

"We are fortunate to offer the rest of the world the blueprint for humanity."

When social pressures did not break down the resolve of holdouts, employers hinted at loss of jobs, cajoled, and, in rare instances resorted to firing. No employer openly fired workers for not participating in the SSS program. They always found other reasons, and the dismissed understood.

Nagila Levy and all government employees automatically found themselves enrolled and given rank. Aside from national occasions and celebrations, King Joshua declared that all government employees would wear their uniforms every Wednesday. On that day he made his weekly speech to the nation and to the world. The cameras panned the audience, showing most of the listeners wearing the SSS uniform. Others wore the scarves. No one was admitted to the palace courtyard who did not wear at least the scarf.

Nasief heard the news of the formation of the SSS on television. As he listened, tears glided steadily down his cheeks. *It has come at last. The beginning of the ending. I do not know what I can do to stop this. Yet must I sit by, do nothing, and allow it to take place?*

In his next study hour, the old man reminded his listeners of the prediction he had previously made. "This is the fulfillment. I can do nothing to thwart this plan. It must take place. God recorded this truth two millennia ago." That Nasief could not change.

"What can we do? How do we resist?" asked a faithful disciple.

Nasief shook his head. "I do not know." Tears again welled up inside Nasief. He could not tell them that this would be one more step in bringing about the death of millions of people. Worse, he had an immediate understanding that most of them in the hall would be martyred by the hands of the Triple S.

Nasief dismissed the study early. "My heart is too heavy to continue. I wish to go home and pray for guidance for me and mercy for all of us."

He prayed throughout the rest of the day. No peace came to him. Nasief went to bed with a troubled heart. "It must not be this way," he kept saying. "God, don't let this happen. I can't give in and not fight against it."

Long after midnight he fell asleep and he had a dream. In the dream, Nasief walked slowly, aimlessly down a street in Jerusalem. A loud shattering noise, like millions of window panes breaking, filled his ears. Then he heard human screams. He raced toward where he heard the agonizing cries for help. He stopped. In front of him he saw a large building engulfed by smoke and flames. On the street, a crowd watched, but seemed unconcerned. A few hecklers called, "Just jump. Perhaps you'll die from the injury so that you won't burn!"

Nasief barged through the crowd, raced inside the building and grabbed the struggling people. "This way. Follow me." He led some, others he carried, making trip after trip, then hurrying back for more victims. The flames intensified and the smoke nearly blinded him, but he kept going back. A few that he had brought to safety, now fully recovered, ran back inside to help others find their way to safety.

Finally, unable to get back inside again, he sat on the street and buried his head in his hands. A woman kicked him. "You try to spoil everything. If we let these people die, it'll bring down our taxes and get rid of more useless people."

When Nasief awakened, he understood clearly. He did not have to sit in silence and watch it happen. He must do what he could do. People might misunderstand him and hate him, but he had to do what he could.

In those moments of meditation and comprehension, Nasief felt a strangeness come over him and he knew the voice of God was speaking to his understanding.

He got out of bed. "Yes, God," he said.

Nasief had one task left. He did not know how long he could work or how much opposition he would encounter. He knew he must not think of those things. He must concentrate only on his single task.

Shaheen, pressured to join, held back. Because he was not officially a government employee, he had to make his own application. On the surface, none of the requirements of joining the SSS bothered him. King Joshua had outlined his program for achieving each of the three goals in his telecast.

As Shaheen read the specially prepared brochure, he realized it contained the same information, with slightly different wording. Again, he could find nothing to object to. Still, he knew that Joshua had conceived of the SSS to cover some diabolical scheme he had not yet revealed.

King Joshua had magnanimously given thirty days for people to join the SSS. Within twelve days after the announcement, more than 85 percent of the people in Israel had become members of the SSS. Of the remaining hold-outs, Joshua had devised other means to handle them.

Shaheen discovered how powerful Joshua intended membership in the Triple S to become when he went to The Paradise for dinner. Nagila would meet him there. The Paradise, considered Jerusalem's best restaurant for international cuisine, had been a favorite of Shaheen for years. The maitre d' and all the waiters greeted him by name. He never made a reservation.

Shaheen walked into the low-ceiling alcove and greeted Noel, the maitre d', and added, "A table for two."

The French-born citizen stared at him blankly and then looked away. "I see you do not have your SSS scarf as yet."

"I have not joined."

"Please do it soon." He smiled, leaned closer, and lowered his voice. "By the end of this month, we shall not have tables available for those who do not support our country."

"Thank you for—"

Noel moved away. He clicked his fingers and a waiter appeared to show Shaheen to his table.

"This way," said Fayez, the waiter, in a monotone. Normally he smiled and chatted with Shaheen. Tonight, when he saw the absence of the SSS scarf, his features took on a frown. He threw the menu on the table and walked away.

Shaheen selected his own chair and sat down. His eyes followed the waiter, dressed in his well-fitted Paradise uniform. The young man stopped, turned slightly, making certain that Shaheen noticed. He tugged on his blue armband, as if to adjust it. He glared at Shaheen and disappeared.

Fayez did not approach Shaheen's table while he waited. He sat in silence, taking note that he was the only customer in The Paradise without the SSS identifier. During the fifteen minutes he waited for Nagila, one couple walked past his table. The woman said loud enough for Shaheen to hear and, he assumed, for his benefit, "Soon we shall get leeches and unpatriotic people out of our land."

"I hope they do more than exile them," the husband

answered. As he spoke he turned and let his eyes search for Shaheen's nonexistent scarf.

Noel himself escorted Nagila to the table. She wore her SSS emblem, tucked like a handkerchief in her belt. As Noel pulled out her chair, he said, without looking directly at Shaheen, "You understand that things are different now."

"I understand," Shaheen said.

"It's the beginning, isn't it?" he asked Nagila.

"I wore this tonight, Shaheen, because I was afraid not to." She tried to smile at him. "It shows I'm not much of a believer, doesn't it?"

He took her hands. "We do what we must do. If you are not able to resist, don't."

"You know," she said, "this reminds me of one of the many films we used to see about the rise of Nazi Socialism. Hitler began on a simpler level, but eventually he had all Jews registered and wearing a Star of David." She freed her hand and pulled out her scarf. She laid it on the table with the bright insignia on top. "If I remember my history, by wearing the Star of David, Hitler excluded them from public places and social functions. Now it's reversed. Without the Triple SSS, they exclude you."

"One small step at a time," Shaheen said, "Our King Joshua has only given it a new twist. Worse than the Triple S, I keep asking myself, 'What is coming next?' I don't know, but I have a premonition of great disaster ahead."

Nagila nodded. "I can't give you any specifics about his next move, but I know this is only the beginning. He won't stop, Shaheen. He won't stop until he controls the whole world."

Shaheen tried to change his mood, to forget the turmoil in the world, while they had dinner together. He had wanted the evening to be a special time for him and Nagila together. But he could not stop thinking of what lay ahead.

"He's going to murder more millions of people, isn't he?" Shaheen said.

"I think so." Nagila contemptuously rolled the scarf into a ball and laid it on a dirty plate.

"He could kill you for doing that," Shaheen said.

"He could. He might. I'm not afraid anymore."

Shaheen leaned back in his chair, thinking. He had made a decision shortly after Nagila joined him at The Paradise. He wanted to rethink it and to be certain.

Shaheen decided that he must kill Joshua.

S·I·X·T·E·E·N

"The simpler the plan, the fewer things can go wrong," Shaheen said as he discussed his plan with four trusted friends. "We must do the unexpected. This is not the time that he would expect trouble."

"What if we get caught?" asked Momar, the oldest of the group and their spokesman.

"We have to consider that we might be caught. If caught, we must expect to receive instant death if they choose to be merciful—"

"Or agonizing torture first and death later?"

Shaheen nodded. "That's why I want you to consider carefully what we're doing. He is a beast, a man without conscience, a man determined to destroy anybody who opposes him or who stands for godliness."

"But you know, Shaheen," he answered, "we are all caught in a moment of surprise that this plot should come from you. I can remember since childhood, you have always opposed violence."

"I still do."

"But that troubles us even more. Your plan. You want us to help you kill a man."

"I may be wrong in what I want to do," Shaheen said. "I have agonized over this decision for three days. However, I have finally concluded that the killing of one evil man who has already murdered eight million people is not murder. It is justice. Call it divine vengeance. It is deserved retribution because no human power on earth can bring him to justice."

"We think you are right in what you say about him, but," Momar persisted, "it seems difficult for us to understand. Once we could have killed for much less reason. Once we were men of action and we believed in killing our enemies. We are no longer the same because now we believe in the God who teaches us to love."

"Isn't God the only one who has the right to take a life?" asked Abdul.

"Perhaps what I plan to do is wrong." Shaheen's normally placid features showed the strain of the past few days. Although physically tired from lack of adequate sleep, a sense of despair plagued him. He could never do the assassination alone. He hated to involve others. He rested his head in his hands and closed his eyes. "I cannot sit by and do nothing. If I take no action while knowing what the King is doing, I am participating by my silence. He murders millions and I do nothing. Surely the taking of his life is the same as going to war against our enemies."

"Come, brother, surely you take this too hard on your own shoulders," Momar said.

"If King Joshua walked down the street and murdered every person he saw, wouldn't you do something to stop him?"

"Of course!"

"The difference is only in Joshua's method."

Shaheen spent more than an hour presenting evidence of Joshua's masterminded plans of destruction, famine, governments overthrown through Joshua's financial backing.

"You have to say this much for Joshua. He does not spend a lot of time covering up what he has done," Momar said.

"He does not need to. Who has tried to stop him?

What world power would dare? Besides, unless we do something, no one will ever oppose him."

"I know you are right," Momar said. "We are unsure only if we should join you."

"I understand," Shaheen said. "Perhaps this will help you decide. It's my final argument." He displayed a copy of an order, signed by King Joshua, for the cessation of the manufacture of L-12-L, the cure for the Green Plague.

After the four men had read it, Shaheen pointed to the date. "He wrote that order months before the first reported incident of the Green Plague. Don't you understand the implication of this paper?"

"You mean he had the cure before anyone ever knew about the Green Plague?" Momar's fingers shook as he held the paper.

"More than that. He caused the Green Plague to strike. He set up the conditions for those deaths." Shaheen's eyes moved from one man to the other and back to Momar. "He made certain that the world knew that scientists had no way to halt the spread of the lethal disease."

"Yes! Yes! That's right!"

"We were so gullible," Shaheen said. "The King appealed to all religious groups, encouraging us to pray for the researchers to discover a breakthrough drug."

"He had the cure before he released the plague," Momar said, shaking his head. "Monstrous."

"And announced the miracle breakthrough—"

"Only after millions had died," Momar said.

Zidik, a thin man who seldom spoke, began to pound the wall with his fist. "He did it! He planned to kill people, didn't he?"

"Yes—"

"My wife as well as my mother and father died of the Green Plague!" He stepped forward, pushing Momar aside. "Until this minute I hesitated. But now—"

"You're ready to help me?"

"I am ready to do anything to destroy this destroyer!"

"A wise English Prime Minister once said that all it takes for evil to triumph is for good men to do nothing,"

Momar said. "If we sit by and do nothing, King Joshua will devise a new means to take away another eight million lives. Then another. Where does it end?"

"Only with Joshua's death," Shaheen said. "No matter how often I've looked at this, I can't come up with any other answer." He shook Zidik's hand. "I'm glad you're with me." He turned to Momar. "What about the rest?"

"Before we answer, Shaheen, we must talk it over in private and then decide." Momar stared at the others and they nodded agreement.

"Let's talk," Zidik said.

The four men went out of the room to talk privately. They had grown up together, all Muslims born in a village in northern Galilee. All of them had converted within weeks following Shaheen.

Outside they said nothing. Over their years of comradeship, they had fallen into the habit of discussing important matters without the use of words. Each man pondered in silence. Through gestures, indicated by a blink, a bare nod, a raised eyebrow, or a movement of the hand, they communicated their opinions clearly to each other.

When they returned to the room, Momar said, "Three of us are willing to help you without reservation. One says that his conscience will not allow him to take a life, even that of a man as evil as this beast. He will assist so long as he does not have to kill."

"I understand," Shaheen said. "It's not that easy. If we are caught, the authorities will consider us equally guilty. I want him to understand that." Shaheen paused and waited while the signals passed between them.

The fourth man waved his hand and silently left the room. "He has decided that since he cannot cooperate without reservation," Momar said, "he believes his presence would only hinder us."

"That's his choice," Shaheen said, "but each of you is ready to work with me?" Shaheen purposely stood directly in front of each man, faced him, and asked, "Momar, are you ready?" He moved to Zidik, and last to Abdul.

All men nodded in agreement.

"I am ready to go ahead with my plan."

"Agreed," said Momar.

"Yes," said Zidik.

"Agreed," said Abdul.

Shaheen opened a briefcase, took out a large sheet of paper, and unfolded it. "This is where we do it." They saw a crude drawing. "This is the interior of the palace. I have been there a number of times and I have also checked its accuracy." He explained how they would go to the palace three nights from then because there would be no moon.

S·E·V·E·N·T·E·E·N

Mike Hege had grown up as a religious person. He had not questioned his faith in God. When the Triple S program started, he had no hesitation in joining. His widowed mother Cecile begged him to renounce the Triple S.

"Mother, you lived your life in the old world. We are a new generation. We have new values."

"Some things don't ever change," she said. "Right is always right. Wrong is wrong—"

"No more lectures. No more preaching. Those things are now obsolete," he said. Mike Hege walked out of the house his father had built when he was eight years old.

Now at age twenty, he decided to make his own choices. He found the Triple S appealing. By being the first to join in his age group, and by showing diligence, he gained the notice of his team captain. Within the first months of his membership, Mike Hege advanced to Colonel, Junior Grade—the highest level he could attain.

Mike privately admitted that he did not like everything the Triple S did, such as destroying religious relics, icons, and statues. Since one of the purposes the Triple S was to do away with all religious groups and to unite them, his organization tore down the two synagogues in his hometown.

It disturbed him the next day when he read that five elderly people had been inside when their barrage of Molotov cocktails went through the windows. Fire blazed quickly when one of them struck the menorah, knocking it over and catching the carpeting on fire. Within minutes flames engulfed the building.

"They wouldn't obey the law anyway," his commander said. "None of them wore the SSS emblem. They defied the law, and lawbreakers must always be willing to pay the penalty for their acts."

Mike Hege consoled himself with that explanation. He wanted to believe and he wanted nothing to disquiet his newfound "religion."

He visited his mother less often after that. Although she never asked him about the destruction of the synagogue, he felt the accusation in her eyes and in her voice.

Later they rounded up a group of Hassidic Jews and made them lie on their backs while they forced pork down their throats. As soon as one attempted to spit it out, whoever spotted him first got to shoot him.

Mike had led the group that night. He himself had shot three of them. One Jew was about his own age. But again he reminded himself that they sealed their own fates by refusing to obey the law.

The next morning Mike visited his mother. When he came into the house, she laid down the front page of the newspaper for him to see. The photograph showed Mike shooting the young man. The article told of the vagrant disregard for law by Hassidic Jews. It praised the bravery of young men and women who would zealously uphold the principles of the land.

Her accusing eyes held his. "Mike, do you wish to kill me now? I do not wear the Triple S scarf. I do not intend to wear it. Will you and your hoodlums come here next?"

Mike turned and walked out of her house. He did not understand the overwhelming sense of shame and confusion that flooded his mind. Presently, however, he pushed the thoughts from his mind. His mother was old, set in her ways. She would never change.

Three days later, Mike and his band, along with a number of others throughout the city, surrounded a private college. Reports had come that none of the students or faculty had joined the SSS.

"You know your orders. I expect you to carry them out and make me proud of you," the commander had said.

Mike led the first assault team. They burst into a classroom. The woman teacher stopped in mid-sentence and stared. She said nothing as Mike advanced. She watched him with eyes that dilated as her instincts began to rise in horror. Her hand went to her mouth.

"We come here today in the name of the SSS. You have violated the laws of this country. None of you is wearing the required scarf."

"And we shall not," she said quietly.

Mike slapped her and her head jerked backward. The shock was so extreme she betrayed no visible reaction. She stood straight, her eyes fixed on him. Her expressionless face seemed to mock him. Mike felt the hostility as if it oozed from her pores.

"Mike Hege!" she finally said. "It took me a few seconds to remember your name. I taught you in Sunday school when you were a boy—"

Mike slapped her again. "Be quiet! We do not live in the past." He whirled around and faced the students. "We have a supply of blue scarves for you to wear. Your refusal to comply will result in your immediate death."

Two recruits under Mike's command stepped forward holding the scarves. Students stared at each other. No one moved.

"Who will be first?" Mike pulled out his Magnum .357 and advanced toward the first row. A blonde with brown eyes looked up at him. Her lips quivered.

"What's your name?"

"Ann."

"Ann, listen." He put the barrel against her temple. "You have three seconds to choose."

She sobbed and screamed, "Give me a scarf! Give it to me!"

Her defection brought about similar results for all but three others. Mike nodded and his soldiers killed them on the spot.

Mike faced the teacher again. "Now will you change your mind?"

"Never."

"You know the penalty."

"Then carry it out."

Mike called Helene, his assistant. "You take care of her."

"No!" the teacher shouted. "You must do it, Mike. You, a child I have known since infancy. I want you to shoot me. I want my death to be a reminder to you as long as you live."

Mike pulled the trigger.

The next morning the custodian discovered the body of one of the students. She had hanged herself from the ceiling in a classroom.

He knew her. A nice, quiet girl named Ann. She had used her Triple S scarf.

As much as possible Nagila Levy had avoided contact with her Aryeh friends since the beginning of the SSS program. She had no doubts that Joshua had her followed anywhere outside the palace. Her presence would only endanger others.

Because she and Shaheen could not trust the telephones or the mail system, they devised a method of contact. At six in the morning and eight at night, one of Shaheen's people sat on a hillside that faced Nagila's window. If she wanted to come out of the palace and see them, she gave three short signals with a flashlight. It was answered by three. If Shaheen wanted to see her, the person on the hillside started the signal. If she did not respond to the signal, the person waited until the next half hour and tried again. If still no response, he returned at the next appointed time.

Nagila failed to respond twice. Both times she had been a prisoner of work for Joshua for four days. Today she signaled at eight o'clock and received the answering response.

Nagila put on a hooded navy-blue sweater, black slacks, and black sneakers. She pulled the hood tight so that little more than the top of her head showed.

Outside her room, she tiptoed across the hallway and down the back stairs. No one liked to use the narrow spiral staircase. Joshua had designed it so that it retained the look of a castle and could be used for emergency evacuation. She had used it twice previously to slip out.

The staircase ended near the kitchen. Joshua ate lightly in the evening and had imposed this eating style on those who lived in the palace. Kitchen employees vacated by 7:30 unless it was a state occasion.

Nagila listened. She could hear the muffled sound of music from a room she knew belonged to the assistant chef. She stepped forward and to her surprise heard noise coming from the kitchen. Stepping from the staircase, she could see the chef through the glass door. He was baking bread. Nagila remembered that fourteen heads of state would arrive the next morning and surmised the chef had not finished his final preparations.

She hesitated to move. From her position, hidden in the darkness of the hallway, he could not see her unless he turned his head while she passed in front of the glass door. If he saw her, she had a strong suspicion that he would report it immediately to Joshua.

While Nagila hesitated, the chef turned and looked in her direction. She gasped and pulled back into the darkness. He came to the door, pushed it open and screamed, "Miriam! Miriam!"

No one responded.

"Asleep I suppose! That is always the way when I have to work late! I'll not make the desserts for you this time!" He screamed her name louder than before.

Miriam's room, three doors down, still did not open.

The chef stood in the hallway and screamed his assistant's name a third time and still received no answer. "She plays that music so that she won't hear me call!"

In the doorway he stopped and screamed her name again. He stood close enough that he could have touched Nagila had he moved only a foot to his right. She breathed as softly as possible, trying not to make a sound. *Oh, God, make him move on or else go back into the kitchen.*

He stood in the dark hallway, hands on his hips and yelled for Miriam again, but still no response. He muttered a string of profanity and marched down the hallway. She heard him banging on the door.

Nagila moved from her place, stepping carefully. His banging and screaming at the door covered up any other sounds. At the door, she turned the knob slowly and it opened noiselessly. From there the corridor led into a short hallway that ended at a flower garden.

Nagila walked cautiously, keeping close to the building until she reached the far wall. When she touched the cold brick, she paused, listening for the guards who stood on the other side. Hearing nothing, she climbed up the wall, using indentations between stones. Having done it on two previous occasions, it seemed an easy part of the exercise. Nagila moved expertly, doing nothing to disturb the soft noises of the night.

Once she reached the top, she lay flat on her stomach, keeping her face away from the guard's side. She crawled across the two-foot-wide top for another forty feet until the wall turned. Just beyond the turn, she came to the place where gardeners tossed the dead flowers, plants, and leaves, making their own mulch pile.

Nagila sensed she was now close to the turn. Cautiously she turned her head and saw the bare outline of the mulch. Had she not seen it, her keen sense of smell would have told her anyway. Once over the refuse, she lowered her body, feet first until they touched the solidness of the pile. She moved one step at a time now, carefully working her way to the edge of the pile.

She had reached the edge and had poised to run when she heard voices coming from the guard's post. She dropped to the ground and lay immobile.

"I heard something. Like a scraping sound."

"Then we ought to check it out," the second voice said. "Better safe than sorry, they keep reminding us."

Their voices grew louder and she decided they had turned the corner. "Who would want to sneak in or out of here?" the first voice said. "They would never make it."

"Of course. That is why they have us on the outside! We deter anyone who has an idea of getting inside."

The two men laughed. They stopped next to the mulch pile that rose nearly four feet from the ground.

"This pile of garbage needs removing. A few months and it will be as high as the wall."

"You report it. I've complained three times. Sometimes I think the King wants it left here just to tempt people to try to sneak inside."

"Ha! Not much chance of getting anywhere."

"It would make great target practice for us." He kicked contemptuously at the pile. "Let's go back."

Nagila remained flat, unwilling to move as long as she could still hear their voices.

"Or maybe," laughed the other, "the King wants it left here just to test our own people to see if they can sneak outside."

Nagila wondered about that pile. Would Joshua really do something like that? He was capable of it. Was it possible that he knew she had sneaked outside the gates before and was doing it again?

He could not possibly know. She repeated that to herself several times. As she lay in the darkness, Nagila knew she wanted to believe her own comforting words. She wanted to believe them very much.

E·I·G·H·T·E·E·N

Shaheen waited in a cave-like section of an embankment. In his concealed spot he watched her scurry across the square and into the wooded area. He stepped out and grabbed Nagila's arm. She gasped. "I didn't realize you were so close."

He pulled her inside. "I have been staring at the darkness so long, I could see you coming this way." He stopped talking and embraced her. Their lips met in a long kiss that neither wanted to stop.

"You're shivering," he said when he released her. "It's not cold tonight. Something wrong?"

"I'm a little nervous. I have a kind of premonition, Shaheen. A feeling that no matter how secretive we are, Therion knows what we're doing."

"If he does, we cannot do anything about it right now."

"No, I suppose not."

"Right now it matters only that you are here. With me. Now." He kissed her again. Slowly Nagila relaxed, and he held her in a tender embrace.

Even though no one was around, they continued to

whisper as if someone could interrupt them at any minute. Shaheen told her of Nasief's continued recovery. "I cannot believe the strength of that old man. He does little else beside teach, sleep, and study for more teaching. But he will not quit."

"Can't you make him slow down?"

"You do not know how stubborn he can be. When I say anything he answers me from the Bible. 'I must work while it is day,' he says to me, 'for the night comes when no man can work.' How do you answer him?"

"Maybe we're not supposed to answer him, just be thankful for what he's taught us, for what we've discovered through our mutual faith."

"Nagila, I need to tell you something," he said. "It is important that you listen and that you not argue with me."

"You sound like a demanding husband."

Ignoring her statement, except for a light kiss on the forehead, he asked, "Is there any way you can get away from *Therion* for three or four days?"

"Why?"

"I want you out of Jerusalem for a few days, that is all I want to tell you."

"You mean some official reason for being gone?"

He nodded. "If possible."

"If I have to—and if you'll tell me why."

"It is better if you do not know."

"You're planning to assassinate him, aren't you?"

"Nagila, the less you know—"

"I sensed that you were going to try. Don't do it, Shaheen. I don't think you can get away with it. But if you survive, I don't want his blood to be on your hands."

"Do not argue with me about this. If this man does not die, he will kill more. Millions. Half the world's population. Who knows how many?"

For a long time Nagila offered every argument against killing she could think of. Finally, exhausted, she admitted that part of her concern was fear for Shaheen. "If you die, Shaheen, I don't know if I would want to go on. I suppose I would have to, but I wouldn't want to. I've only recently found you and known what it means to love you. I don't want to lose that."

Shaheen held her, and neither spoke again for a long time. He had a hundred things he wanted to tell her, but words would not come. He had never known he could love another person so fully. No matter what he did throughout the day, thoughts of Nagila intruded constantly. He admitted to himself, however, that as much as he loved her and hoped that one day they would marry, he had a higher commitment in life. God was now number one, and he did not know how to explain that.

As he held her, a host of conflicting thoughts filled Nagila. She loved this Arab. She understood his strength, his zeal. Right now she only wanted happiness for both of them. And peace. *Why can't we be like normal people? Why can't it be just the two of us getting away from all this turmoil?* She knew she could not escape life as it was. The very thing that brought them together—their faith—was the very thing that also kept them apart. Their commitment to follow Jesus Christ had become more powerful than anything else.

"I won't fight you on this," she whispered. "If you believe this is the right thing—"

"I believe I have no choice," he said simply.

Shaheen went over the entire plan in his mind one more time. If every man did his job properly and at the right moment, they would accomplish their goal of eliminating Joshua Gad-Erianko. Once convinced the plan would work, he consciously pushed every element that might go wrong from his mind.

He checked his watch again, the only outward evidence of uncertainty about his manner. He lay quietly in the wooded area to the east side of the palace until 2:30. By then everyone would be asleep. The guards changed at 2:00, and this gave his men the time to overpower them, tie and gag them. They would not be missed until 4:15 when the captain of the guards phoned each post.

The only element of chance lay in the activity of the captain of the guards. Most of the time he remained in his fortified chamber inside the palace basement. He rarely walked along the patrol routes to check out the guards. Most of the time, however, he lay in his bunk and read, occasionally slept, and often ate or drank non-alcoholic beverages. His personal alarm reminded him five minutes in advance of his call-in to each of the posts.

Shaheen stationed Zidik outside the captain's office. If the officer came out for any reason, the assailant had orders to "put him out of action." Shaheen's order had meant they should do anything short of killing. He had decided to leave it up to each volunteer to do what he deemed best.

The crescent moon had remained behind the clouds through the night. Only enough light penetrated the earth for sharp eyes to catch the barest glimpses every once in a while, and then only for a moment. Exactly the way Shaheen wanted it.

It was now time. He inched forward and started to crawl toward the palace. No voice raised itself in alarm. No challenge. Another ten feet. He crept forward, keeping low, ready at any moment to drop flat. He heard no out-of-place sounds. He allowed himself a smile, knowing it would go well. The inner knotting of his stomach had lessened. He could feel released energy pump into his body as his fingers touched the wall.

Shaheen, now blocked from any light, felt from left to right for ten paces and touched nothing. He moved to the left ten paces and tried again. This time his fingers scraped the edge of the ladder. Exactly as he had planned.

Moving only on the balls of his feet, Shaheen stepped upward. Twelve rungs and he topped the wall. He lay flat, waiting and listening. It was 2:34. He had another minute to wait until he started down the other side.

On the south side, Momar and Abdul, whom Shaheen assigned to eliminate interference from guards within the palace, did their work well. They had sneaked up on those guarding the side entrance, overpowered them in seconds, and left their alive but neatly trussed bodies hidden from view. They moved down the corridor, having only one other objective to fulfill their assignment. They had to make certain that no one could reach the alarm system.

Although on the opposite side of the building from that of the captain of the guard, it could be activated from the south side of the palace as well as from his office.

Momar, the taller of the two, quietly inserted the key that Shaheen had mysteriously provided and opened the control box. He stared at the switches before him, not wanting to make a mistake. His hands trembled as his long fingers moved down the panel. Second switch on the left along with the fourth switch on the right. It had been rigged for such situations as this. Pulling either switch automatically set off the other. They had to move at precisely the same moment.

Momar's hands touched the small bar and he counted a military cadence to himself. *One, two, three, four. One, two, three—*. He pulled simultaneously.

He froze for four seconds, half-expecting a piercing alarm. Nothing. He exhaled slowly. *I did it. Just as Shaheen told me. I did it.*

Meanwhile Zidik waited outside the captain's fortified office. He struggled with mixed feelings about his mission. On the one hand, it was likely going to be the least eventful and he did not expect to move from the passageway until Shaheen signaled an all-clear by a triple dimming of the lights.

Zidik heard nothing, but in one dreadful second he sensed that someone had come up behind him. He hesitated and in that fraction of a second, the butt of a machine gun struck him behind the ear. So expertly placed, Zidik had fallen unconscious before his body touched the floor.

At that moment, Shaheen stood at the entrance to the palace, one floor below Joshua's sleeping quarters. He now faced the most dangerous part of the mission and especially the most dangerous for him.

Pressing himself against the wall, he waited and listened. He heard nothing except the faraway echoes of an occasional car or truck moving along the highway. He strained his ears for any hint that the others had not done their work properly.

Satisfied that he could enter the palace, he began the tortuous ascent. He climbed the four-foot stepladder that had been left behind the neatly shaped thornhedge. He set it up, reached the ledge of the ground-floor window and pulled himself up. It reminded Shaheen of his fitness exercises when he had to do fifty chinups at a time. He had done them, grumbling and straining. Now he was glad the instructor had insisted.

The stone ledge above the window provided enough space for good footing. He inched to the far side of the window, hugging the stone building, smelling the dust and scraping his face against the stone.

By standing on tiptoes, he barely reached the bottom ledge of the next level. This would be the real test for him. He hesitated, took a deep breath and lunged sideways. For a split second his left hand clutched air and then miraculously it caught. His right hand automatically grabbed and he hung from the bottom ledge.

In the distance he heard a dog barking, followed seconds later by the answer of a second canine. It had been years since he had practiced his chinups and gymnastics on the bar. He had also put on twenty pounds and he felt the strain of every ounce in those seconds.

Slowly, careful not to jerk, he raised his body by the sheer power of his arm muscles to waist high. Momentarily releasing his left arm and putting all weight on his right, he swung his legs in a wide arc from the right to the left. As they came up on the left side, he gave his left leg an extra push and it landed exactly as he had hoped, on the ledge.

Perspiration poured from his face and he rested a moment before pulling his right leg up. He felt for the seam of the double windowscreen and moved upward. The lock on the window lay at midpoint, set half an inch inward. Having to guess at the spot and using a quick slashing motion, Shaheen's powerful fingers cut the wire a full twenty inches.

To his surprise, the window was not locked. He sighed, thankful for not having to force it open and the noise perhaps awakening the King. Using caution and careful to allow no noise, he ripped the screen from its frame. A clean job now would make it easier for him if he left the same way. He pushed the screen inside, wanting nothing showing from the outside.

Shaheen's body dropped on the sill at his waist. He slumped forward and downward with his arms extended. He judged it was three feet to the floor. He inched forward, allowing his body to glide noiselessly downward until both hands touched hardwood. It felt surprisingly cool. Shaheen retained his snakelike approach until he lay prostrate. He paused once again and listened. He was in what the palace plans called the King's dressing room. He lay in the darkness, his eyes closed, waiting.

Shaheen opened his eyes, but he did not move. He waited until he accustomed himself to the darkness. Satisfied that he could see the outline of objects within the room, he crawled slowly toward the door. He knew it was easier to encounter objects from that position than if he stood. He could also see a dim light from the King's bedroom. Any movement or light and he would instantly alert the King.

When he reached the far side, he stood silently erect, allowing his fingers to move along the wall until they touched the corner of the light switch. Careful not to touch the switch and accidentally fill the room with light, he eased himself against the door. He listened. He heard only his own rapid breathing.

He turned the handle slowly, pushed the door inward and took his first step into the bedroom. He closed the door behind him. Shaheen pulled the Walther from his inside pocket. From another pocket he took out the silencer. He had screwed it to the gun in the dark a dozen times so that he could do it quietly. He took two steps forward.

"Do come in," a voice said.

N·I·N·E·T·E·E·N

Shaheen froze. His fingers tightened around the trigger.

"I can see you perfectly. I also have a gun aimed at your heart," Joshua said without emotion. "You might try firing at the sound of my voice, but it will be the last physical movement you will ever make."

Shaheen dropped the gun. It crashed to the floor, filling the room with such loudness, he momentarily thought the gun had gone off.

"Wise of you."

Shaheen heard movement in the room but saw nothing. A light snapped on and Joshua sat in a chair, a gun aimed at him. "Kick the gun under the bed so that it will be out of your way and provide no temptation for bravery."

Joshua sat quietly waiting for Shaheen to do as he was told. Shaheen kicked the gun once and it struck the bed leg. Another kick and it disappeared.

Joshua pressed a buzzer on the table and the door opened instantly. Two armed soldiers entered the room, their automatic machine guns pointed at Shaheen's chest.

"Your companions are dead," the King said.

"Are you going to shoot me, too?"

"Perhaps." He pulled open a drawer and laid his gun inside. "First, I wanted to look you in the eyes before I decide what to do with you." He stood and walked across the room to Shaheen. Over his shoulder he told a guard, "Turn on more lights. I want to see his face more clearly."

Shaheen fought the impulse to tighten up. He had failed his mission. It did not matter greatly what happened now. It had been his chance to help the world and he had failed. "You knew we were coming."

"Suspected only," the King said. "I have a sense of those things. I always obey my impulses because they never fail me."

He stared at Shaheen. "You are the man Nagila Levy loves."

"She had nothing to do with this."

"Nagila is not the topic!" He stared at Shaheen. They were nearly the same height, both with the typical Middle-Eastern features and coloring. "It has amazed me that she loves you. When I met you before I couldn't understand what she saw in you. You are a follower of that man Nasief."

"He taught me the truth. About a lot of things," Shaheen said.

Before Joshua stared into the deep-black eyes, he knew that this man, too, could resist him. He stared anyway. He saw nothing. A second before he decided to turn away, Joshua perceived a mental image.

That was how it worked with the others. Yet this image was different. Theirs came to him veiled in darkness, sometimes along with a sense of shame and always fear. With Shaheen he perceived an image of peace. This man had no fear of the King, no fear over secret wrongdoings of his past. "Why are you not afraid of me?"

"Should I be afraid?"

"People always fear when I come close to them."

Shaheen shook his head. "I'm not afraid of you because I know who you are."

"And who am I?"

"Therion. The beast."

"The powerful man who opposes the faith? That's high flattery."

"No, it is truth."

"You think that is who I am?"

"I *know* it."

"I see," Joshua said. He motioned to the guards. "Take him. I shall decide how to dispose of him later."

Shaheen walked toward the guards. "However, you lied to me. You did more than suspect. You knew. Someone told you."

"Excellent guess."

"More than a guess. I know."

"Wait," he told the guards. "How did you deduce this fact?"

"Nothing like that. I just know."

"But how? Who told you?"

"You did. I mean—when you stared into my eyes, I saw something—not really saw, more like felt—"

"And?"

"You knew before we finalized our plans. Zidik betrayed us, didn't he?"

"Zidik's wife, actually."

"You have had quite a little game of this, haven't you?"

"As a matter of fact, yes," Joshua said. The smile etched in his face belied the confusion going on inside him. *This man, this nobody named Shaheen Ahman, had done to him what no other human being had ever done before. What could this mean? Would Shaheen attempt to control him? Would Shaheen use the tactics on him that he himself had used so well on others?*

Joshua felt as if his feet had frozen to the spot. He had to ask the next question, but already he knew the answer. "You know other things about me, do you?"

"I think—yes. Yes, I do."

"You're not afraid of me?"

"Not in the least. Am I supposed to be?"

"Most people tremble—if that doesn't sound too old-fashioned. Why are you different? Why are you not affected this same way?"

Shaheen thought for a moment. Common sense indicated that he ought to be scared. He was a prisoner. Joshua would likely have him killed. Yet he had no fear. Shaheen turned from the guards and took several steps toward the King. The two guards hesitated, unsure of what to do.

"Wait outside," Shaheen said. "The King and I wish to speak in private."

Joshua hesitated only a second and waved them out. When the door closed behind them, Shaheen took two more steps forward. The men, only inches apart, locked eyes.

"You know other things about me?"

"Yes," Shaheen said. "I cannot explain how this knowledge came to me, only that everything inside me says it is true."

"Such as?"

"I know your plan for world dominion. I know your heart is filled with hatred and evil. You are a man without a conscience. Other things—too many to take into my mind."

"Most profound." Joshua touched Shaheen's shoulder, and the prisoner recoiled.

"You are evil. Even your hand on me communicates that. You are more evil than I thought possible."

"Remarkable," Joshua said. "I understand. I have a similar gift. I can do this also. Or at least I can do it with people who have evil, hidden secrets. Tell me, Shaheen, how long have you known of this special ability?"

He shook his head. "This is the only time. It has never happened before."

"I see," Joshua said and turned away. "What will happen to this great knowledge when I kill you?"

"Until now I expected you to kill me. Now, I think you will not. When I looked into your eyes, I understood something else. You are afraid to murder me."

"Afraid to kill you? Why should I be afraid?"

"I am not sure. I think it is because I represent the one power on earth you can never defeat. I represent God."

They stopped speaking, their eyes focused on each other as if mesmerized. Shaheen stepped forward and Joshua instinctively moved backward. "Now you have made it clear that I have only one weapon I can use against *you*. You use fear to control and to destroy others. I intend to use your fear of God because it is my only weapon against you."

"I only have to give a command—"

"But you will not," Shaheen said softly. He sat down and stared at the King. "You are afraid. Not because of me. After all, I'm only a human being. You fear Aryeh whom I serve."

"Aryeh? God? You try to speak of God? I am the only god on this earth."

"No, King Joshua, you are not. You know that it makes you afraid. I am a follower of Aryeh, who defeats men like you. He is the only power you cannot control or destroy. And you fear Aryeh."

"Afraid? I? Don't you realize that right now—at this very moment—I hold the destinies of all people in the world in my hand? I am the one who decides who lives and who dies? Only I."

"Another ruler boasted something like that in the days when Jesus walked the earth. You know what Jesus told him? He said the man could have no power except what God allowed him. Things have not changed much in two thousand years, have they?"

"You mock me? You dare to mock me?" Joshua's fist pounded on the night table again and again. His hand struck so fiercely the lamp bobbed and finally tipped, falling to the floor. "I can have you tortured! You and Nasief and any other of you religious fanatics! One word! One single word and—"

"You could, but you will not. I know that now." Shaheen stood. "I'm leaving. I also warn you that so long as I am alive I shall oppose you every chance I can. I am only one man, but you must remember that Aryeh is on my side!"

Shaheen opened the door. The guards snapped to attention in front of him. He pushed them gently aside. "Our King is allowing me to walk out the front door."

The guards turned their eyes toward the King. Joshua, oblivious of them, stared out the window. The first rays of light crept across the horizon. Morning would soon arrive.

Until this moment, Joshua had never doubted the fulfillment of his plan. It had come to him in a single moment, dictated step by step. Now, more than three decades later, the first threat to its fulfillment faced him.

Joshua wanted to kill Shaheen himself. With a venom-filled heart he wanted to run after him, lunge for his neck and choke the breath of life from Shaheen. He wanted to destroy this man. But he could do nothing.

He stood before the window watching the streaks of light broaden until they filled the eastern sky. By the time all shadows of night disappeared, Joshua had revised his plan. It was so simple. It required little change. He had only to intensify what he had already started.

He pressed the buzzer for his secretary. "Send me General Liebmann of the SSS."

He could not personally touch Shaheen. He could put his plan into action so that others would destroy his enemy.

Joshua smiled.

B·O·O·K
T·H·R·E·E

O·N·E

When the first tidal wave swept across Hawaii's southern coast, it made the evening news. Reporters gave the usual facts of damage estimates in dollars and the number of lives lost. Within a week it had become a forgotten item in the rest of the world.

One week later a similar tidal wave struck Singapore.

Two days later, North America was hit. A startled world heard the report of Jerry Richardson on CBS-TV. He flew over the coastal area in a helicopter. Waves lapped so high that viewers could not distinguish the landmass.

"The Bay of Fundy, located between New Brunswick and Nova Scotia, has experienced tidal fluctuations before. In the spring citizens have reported tides as high as fifty feet.

"Our plane is flying over the Bay of Fundy right now. Tides are reaching more than 100 feet. Experts estimate that they may reach an unheard of 200 feet.

"We explain this by the term resonance. Suppose you sit in a small swimming pool and start a wave at one end. It travels to the far end of the pool, is reflected, and returns. With careful timing you make a second wave at the instant the first wave starts to move away from you the second time. The second wave moves in time with the first, and this is resonance. The first and second waves reinforce each other. If you continued to make new waves that move in time with the others, the movement of water gets larger and higher with each new wave.

"We cannot explain why this is occurring. Nor can our experts tell us why such tidal waves have struck across the world.

"Reports have come to us that the tidal bores—walls of water—have appeared along the Amazon River in South America and the Tsientang Kiang in China. In both these instances tides from the oceans are funneled into the mouths of the rivers and they create a hugh wall of water—a tidal bore—that moves quickly up the river.

"Previous records indicate that the Amazon's tidal bore has reached sixteen feet. Currently it is forty-two feet high. The Tsientang bore has a record of twenty-seven feet, set in 1988. Today it reached ninety-three feet.

"We have no way of knowing the amount of damage, property loss, or the number of people who have perished. This is Jerry Richardson reporting live from the Bay of Fundy."

The TV cameras switched to Susan Cothran reporting from Nairobi, Kenya:

"An unexplained natural disaster struck the Great Rift Valley at 4:30 yesterday afternoon. The valley, located west of Nairobi, cuts across the rolling plateau from north to south and stretches westward to Lake Victoria. The Great Rift Valley varies between thirty and forty miles wide and is 2,000 to 3,000 feet below the level of the surrounding plateau."

Ms. Cothran paused and the camera focused on the plateau's peak and then slowly panned down the eastern wall. Viewers saw the steep and sometimes dramatic escarpment. "On the floor of this valley is—or used to be—a chain of lakes—Naivasha, Elmenteita, Nakuru, Hannington, Baringo, and Lake Rudolf.

"Yesterday the rift opened wide, like a giant break in the ground, swallowing all the lakes and rivers. Within the hour it closed again.

"Sometimes referred to as a graben, a German word for trench, the rift closed during the night. No one has been able to explain this natural disaster. Here is the report of one eyewitness."

Susan Cothran held a microphone in front of an African, perhaps ten years old. "His name is Gore Oko. He stood where I am now and watched the earth open up below."

The boy pointed. "I heard a rumbling sound, like thunder in the far distance. Then I saw a long crack in the ground that got wider and wider. Fire leaped from inside the crack and I heard the voice of thunder again. Everything fell into the hole. I watched, unable to know what was going on. Then it started to close."

Susan Cothran took the microphone. "We have yet to determine the damage encountered. With the loss of these lakes that provide water for all of western Kenya, we can predict famine for certain.

"Lake Victoria, the world's second largest freshwater lake, and the largest in Africa—some 250 miles long—chief source of water for the Nile River, is all but dry. Previously the source of fresh fish for Kenya, Tanzania, Uganda, it now resembles little more than a large mudhole with a water covering of no more than three feet at any one place.

"The continent of Africa has seen much famine, civil war, and disease in the past forty years. Nothing, however, compares with this latest natural disaster."

Shaheen walked the streets of Jerusalem until midmorning. The knowledge thrust upon him so overpowered him that his head ached. His thoughts raced from grief over the loss of his friends to specific moments of the aborted mission, but they always came back to that scene in Joshua's bedroom. Momar and the others had sacrificed their lives, and he had lived. The plot to kill Joshua had been his idea, yet they paid by their deaths.

He tried to console himself with the reminder that Momar, Zidik, and Abdul had known of the danger and had gone anyway. This knowledge didn't absolve him. He had known these three men a long time, but more than that, they had become brothers in a common faith. Young men. Good men. Even if Zidik betrayed them, he did it thinking it was the right thing to do. He probably did it to save all their lives. Yet they had died and he had lived.

Tears filled Shaheen's eyes. The inner pain did not let up because he could not forgive his mistake. He tried to push the events from his mind. He hated what had happened to them, but it was done, over. He tried to convince himself that they had all done their best. Their faith also convinced them that they were going to a far better place than earth. Even knowing those facts did not immediately ease his grief.

The gentle tap on Nasief's door went unheard until Shaheen pounded louder. "Open up, Nasief! It's Shaheen!"

He finally awakened the old man, who made his way slowly to the door. His eyes brightened at seeing his friend. "Shaheen! It has gone well?"

"How did you know what I went to do?"

"Nagila came to see me, greatly troubled. She feared she would never see you again. It warms my heart that you are alive."

Shaheen walked past the old man and collapsed in an old but worn stuffed chair. "Nothing went right."

Nasief closed the door, followed Shaheen inside, and sat down beside the younger man. He listened without interrupting while Shaheen recounted the whole incident. Occasionally he nodded. Twice he picked up his Bible, flipped to a section, read it, closed the book, and continued to listen.

"I walked and walked, exhausted but not able to sleep. I do not understand what is happening. Please, Nasief, help me—"

The old man leaned back in his chair and held up his hand for silence. He closed his eyes and for a long time he said nothing. Shaheen wondered if he had fallen asleep.

"Now we know," Nasief said. "Now we know the truth. We must fight, but we must do it in a different way."

"No more attempts to kill—"

"We fight with something more powerful than guns and bombs. We fight with the one weapon that must always prevail. The weapon of truth."

"I hear your words and I know it ought to comfort me and to give me hope, but—"

"We will prevail!" Nasief leaned forward and his lined hands clasped those of Shaheen. "Think for a moment. We have Aryeh on our side. Even if we lose our lives, we win. Aryeh will give us the ability to die with dignity if such a time faces us. For now we need to remind ourselves that we are fighting the most deadly evil in the world today."

"We are so few, Nasief. Even if we cooperated with all the other believers, we would still be only a few hundred or a few thousand." He shook his head wearily. "It seems hopeless . . . I know you are right . . ."

Nasief's eyes blazed and the lines of age seemed to erase themselves. "You think of numbers, of victory going to those who are strongest. Aryeh doesn't work that way. David used only a slingshot against a giant. A few against the many—that's how God has always worked."

"I am so new at this," Shaheen said. "And a little weak in faith."

"Oh, Shaheen, I'm only urging you to take heart. We are living in The Last Day. It is here. It is happening now."

"I know you believe that. And maybe you are right."

"I have waited for this to happen. I knew it would come in my time."

"You taught us that godly people going through persecution and torment have frequently felt the same way."

Nasief smiled. "You learned well. But, Shaheen, I have a story to tell you . . . a story I have told only one other human being in my life. But now you must hear it because you can understand."

Nasief went into the kitchen, returning minutes later with a pot of tea. As he poured a cup for Shaheen, he said, "Sit back and relax. It is not such a long story, but I think you will better understand if I hold back nothing."

Nasief closed his eyes, moving backward, remembering his own childhood days in what they then called Trans-Jordan. The continued uprisings between Muslims and Jews. The hatred that erupted from time to time. No one knew anything of neutrality.

T·W·O

Nasief Habib, a nominal Palestinian Christian, lived a life full of hatred for his enemy. They would destroy the Jews. "Push them into the sea!" He had heard that slogan all his life.

During his fifteenth year, Jews attacked the settlement of mud-and-wattle houses in which he and his parents had lived for the past three years. They were refugees in their own land.

He awakened one morning to the booming of cannons in the background. He had heard them before. Perhaps not quite as close but just as real. Sometimes the Jews started the attack. On other occasions the Palestinians struck first or made a surprise blow of retaliation. No one kept track. It did not matter who started each skirmish.

Nasief rolled over, wanting to sleep a little longer. The sun had barely awakened for the day, and he had not felt well the night before.

"Nasief! Up! Out of bed! Run! Run for your life!"

He heard the voice call his name and the words. He did not recognize the speaker. Yet he instantly obeyed. He grabbed his shirt as he hurtled from the single room and out the back door. He raced onward and did not stop until the houses were well out of sight. Gasping from lack of breath, he fell to the damp earth and lay prostrate. He had badly winded himself and breathed through his mouth, willing new energy to return.

Ahead a few feet he saw a clump of scraggly trees surrounding a large jutting rock. He sat up in the exposed area, not sure if he ought to hide behind the trees. He had heard no more bombing since he first left the village.

As he pondered the question, Nasief heard the whizzing of a bomb, a sound he had long recognized. This was followed seconds later by the detonating explosion. His body shook in rhythm with the trembling earth. A second explosion followed, then a third. Nasief lost count, knowing only that the enemy timed them close together and they were striking close by.

Nasief looked around and he was alone. Where were his parents? The other villagers? He thought immediately of returning to them. Or at least going back far enough so that he could figure out what happened to them.

"Nasief! You have stopped too soon! Hide behind the trees! Quickly!"

Nasief, trained to obey such commands, raced ahead and dove to the ground. He discovered a hole big enough for him to lie in if he curled into a fetal position. Although the attack did not last much longer, to Nasief it seemed as if it would never end. At one point, he lost all sense of hearing. Only when the mortar fire lessened did he once again experience the vibrations of sound in his ears.

A total silence that lasted several minutes caused Nasief to stir. Then machine gun blasts filled the air. Nasief had heard them often enough. The staccato bursts of dozens of such deadly guns vied with each other as they filled the morning.

He smelled smoke, like wood burning. That meant that at least some of the houses had received hits. Or even that the foot soldiers with their machine guns had burned them. Then the stench of burning flesh bit into his nostrils, an all-too-well-known odor to inhabitants of Trans-Jordan. No matter how long Nasief lived, the acrid odor would never be erased from his memory.

Occasionally he heard a shout, indistinguishable except to understand that human beings screamed to one another. The machine guns gave way to short blasts or single shots. An occasional scream of pain followed.

He heard the tramp of boots. Soldiers coming his way. That could not mean anything but Israelis. He tightened himself in a ball as if he could make himself invisible.

"Nasief! You have nothing to fear. Lie still and make no sound. You will not be hurt!"

Once again he obeyed and lay in his protected spot. The soldiers came closer until he could hear them call to each other in Hebrew.

"The trees over there! Check them."

"Yes, surely there must be an army hiding there, waiting to ambush us!" answered a voice.

"Go anyway! Look! No survivors this time!"

Nasief heard the soldier's footsteps coming toward him. He felt no fear. The strange voice had told him he would be safe. He lay quietly, trying hard not to move.

The soldier grasped the limb of a scrubtree and pulled himself up. He stood, his feet only inches from Nasief. By a slight turning of his head, the boy saw the soldier clearly in his gray-green uniform and heavy boots.

"Nothing here except five thousand Israeli soldiers!" he shouted. "Should I give them medals or kisses?"

"Give them your gun! Let someone get use out of it!" yelled back the other voice.

The soldier did not look down. He stepped over the hole in which Nasief lay. If he saw the boy, he gave no indication. Seconds later Nasief heard the retreating footsteps. He lay in his cocoon and strained his ears. He heard only the snap of dead wood burning and breaking. As he stared upward, spirals of black smoke rose to the heavens.

"It is safe, Nasief. You may come out. They have gone."

He struggled out of the hiding place and his eyes could

detect nothing but billowing smoke. "Mama! Papa!" He raced ahead until he came to the settlement he had known as home.

He approached the small hill that overlooked his old village and stopped. It was useless to go any further. Nothing remained. It was only a place of death.

The direction he had gone had been the only way of escape. The Israelis would have covered all the other directions on their approach. He alone had survived—he and one other man in the village. At the moment, Nasief could not think about the other survivor. He thought only of his loss.

Nasief sat on the burned grass, lowered his head between his legs and wailed. His mother and his father. His three sisters and two brothers. All of them had perished either by fire, bombs, or guns.

His stomach twisted and a wave of nausea came over him. He raised his hands heavenward, his fists doubled. "I swear by God the Almighty that I shall avenge—"

"No, Nasief! No vengeance."

The voice. It had come again. Nasief whirled around, but he saw no one. At that moment he realized that he had not seen anyone at any time the voice had spoken. Had he imagined the voice in his head? Surely not.

The voice had been loud, speaking with urgency and authority. A man's voice—strong, powerful, deep. Yet it lacked the harshness of his father's tones.

"Don't be afraid, Nasief. I am with you."

"Who? Who are you? Where are you?"

"Nasief Habib, one day you will know who I am. For now, you need to know that you will not seek revenge. I have preserved your life. I have a purpose for you."

"What purpose?"

"Go from this place. Go to Jerusalem. You must learn in the university. Receive your education. One day I will call upon you to use it."

Nasief stood. He stared at the devastation around him. He was not even sure how to get to Jerusalem. He had no idea how to get into a university and he wasn't totally sure what a university was. He could read and he had been good at numbers. Father had said that was enough for him to know.

Now the voice had told him differently. He must follow that voice. He walked alone, across the heated plain to the next village. They fed him and allowed him to sleep in a home. They offered to let him stay. "No," he told them, "I must go on to Jerusalem. A voice has spoken to me and I must go."

For weeks Nasief traveled from village to village. Each time he asked questions. Most commonly, "Where is Jerusalem? Which way is it?"

For months he wandered onward, getting closer, never fully sure why or what he was doing. He knew only two things. First, that he must go to Jerusalem and, second, that he must enter the university.

On a day in May he arrived at the city for which he had searched for a long time. He walked slowly up the long winding road toward the city. No one had described Jerusalem, yet when he saw it he felt a keen sense of disappointment. It looked like dozens of other towns he had seen, only larger. More people and higher buildings. The city buzzed with the noise of people and motor vehicles. The country had only been officially handed over to Israel as their nation a year earlier.

Nasief wandered through the streets. He had no money and no food. He had eaten with shepherds and farmers on his travels. Sometimes he stayed long enough to work until he had new shoes or clothes, but he never lingered.

Today as he wandered through the street, he silently asked the voice to speak again. *I have come here. I have done what you have told me. What happens now?*

The voice did not speak to him. For the first time, Nasief questioned his purpose in coming to this city. In the beginning the voice had been strong in his memory. It gave him something to do and helped him to assuage his grief. Now he had arrived.

During his travels, Nasief had turned sixteen. He had

entered manhood, and his bronzed body and taut muscles showed his fitness as he walked aimlessly through the broad streets. Because he did not hear the voice again, a feeling of despondency arose within him. I should have stayed in my village and died, he thought. Now I am alone and hungry, and I do not know what to do next.

A short distance ahead, Nasief saw a tour group, recognizing only that they were strangers and did not look like Arabs or Jews. They wore bright clothing, different from the cool garments of shepherds. Many of them had light-colored hair and fair skin.

Momentarily forgetting his own plight, he drew forward out of curiosity. A thin, hawk-nosed man with a high-pitched voice motioned to people as they slowly stepped out of a large bus and tended to wander away from the group.

Nasief, having a limited knowledge of English, decided to tag along behind them. They stopped outside what he later understood was the tomb where they laid Jesus after the crucifixion.

Nasief Habib had never seen such finely dressed men and women in his life. The deep-colored dresses of the women and the fine material of the men's trousers gave him a great urge to touch the cloth and to discover for himself if it was as soft as it looked.

The one with the high-pitched voice finally stopped gesturing and speaking. The people grouped around a second man. This one raised his hands for everyone to keep silent, and began to speak in a language totally foreign to Nasief.

Nasief, bored with the scene, started to move on. He heard the voice again. "The voice"—the same voice that had spoken to him and sent him to Jerusalem. Nasief whirled around and listened.

He heard the voice, but he did not understand the words. His eyes peered through the crowd, and the man who had raised his hands had the same voice he had been hearing. Although Nasief had no way to know, the man spoke in French, paused, and then said essentially the same thing in English. He concluded with, "Here! This is the place!"

Nasief heard the voice speak in English, but still understood nothing but an isolated word or two. *That voice. That is the voice that spoke to me. He is the one to whom I have come. But why does he speak in a language I do not understand?*

Nasief did not know the answers to his questions, but he felt at peace. He had done the right thing. He had obeyed and come to Jerusalem. This man would show him what to do next. His journey had been worth the trouble. It was right for him to be here.

After a fifteen-minute lecture, the man with the voice stepped back. The hawk-nosed man led the procession of people to the tomb. Each bowed slightly and entered the tiny room and, seconds later, came back out. The deep-voiced man watched from a distance.

Nasief walked up to him. The man was gray-haired. Wrinkles bit deeply into his swarthy skin, making it appear as if he had been born that way.

"Pardon me . . .." Nasief said haltingly in Arabic.

"*Na'am* (Yes)," the man answered, also in Arabic. His teeth gleamed when he smiled, and Nasief thought he had never seen a happier man in his life.

"I have come," he continued, "as you told me."

"I don't know what you mean." His speech, although excellent and precise, had not overcome the heavy accent that convinced Nasief he did not speak Arabic as a native tongue.

"At the village. You spoke to me. You saved my life." Nasief's words raced wildly on, and the facial expression of the man made it clear that he did not understand. "You told me I must come to Jerusalem and—"

The man stared in confusion as if he debated whether to reason with the half-crazed boy or walk away.

"Please," Nasief said slowly in Arabic, "you must listen to me because I heard your voice. It was your voice that saved my life. My life only out of the entire village."

"I do not understand—"

"I have come here as your voice said. I am ready to go to university as you also told me. I have walked for many months to find you."

The man, still as confused as ever, peered into the face of the young man. Nasief's intensity and sincerity moved him, and he wanted to understand. He laid his hand on Nasief's shoulder. "Let's sit down and you explain everything to me. Slowly." He told the hawk-nosed man something in English, and the tourists left.

Nasief told the old man of his experience, leaving out nothing. Because he recited with such detail, it took an hour before he came to the end of his account.

The old man interrupted only occasionally when he did not understand a word or was unsure of Nasief's meaning.

"Nasief, this is the most unbelievable thing I have ever heard in my life. I believe you because it is too incredible to be other than the truth."

The old man, Armand LeTour, a French-born missionary linguist, had lived in the MIddle East for thirty-four years. "I came here to teach about God."

"I know God, of course. In our family, we observe the feast of Christ's birth and—"

"No, I am talking about Jesus Christ. I have come to this land to tell of his love for all people—to Muslims, to Jews, to anyone."

He shook his head. "I do not understand that. I know only that I heard your voice and I have come to study at the university because your voice told me I must do so."

The dark-blue eyes stared at Nasief until he assured himself that the boy spoke the truth. He nodded slowly. "Yes, you have come. I have waited a long time, but I did not know it would be someone like you—a—an Arab."

LeTour had his own story. This time it was Nasief who listened. The two sat on a wooden bench. People passed in front of them and the heat of the day struck them. Neither paid any attention to the world around them.

LeTour explained that when he first came to the Middle East, he had learned Arabic and Hebrew and spent his life teaching people about Jesus Christ. "One night, perhaps ten years ago, I had a dream in which I heard the voice of God speaking to me."

"Armand LeTour," said God's voice, "you are old. You want to go home and rest until you die. The time has not yet come. Not until I send you the man who will continue your work. You will teach him. He will be like a student's empty exercise book and you must fill in all the lessons. Then you may return to your home. He will stay. He will be here, in this land until The Last Day."

"The Last Day? What do you mean?" LeTour asked.

"Until Jesus Christ comes in the clouds. That is The Last Day. This one who follows you will remain here and alive. He will prepare many to receive Jesus Christ."

LeTour's dream ended, but he could never forget it. He knew that God had spoken to him in a dream in the way God had spoken in the days of the Bible.

"When God said you would be an empty exercise book, I had no idea how empty of knowledge you would be, Nasief."

"I can learn fast. I promise you—"

"You need to promise nothing. I have waited for you and you are here. You must come with me to my home. We shall begin your lessons today."

For four weeks LeTour explained the Christian faith and Nasief listened intently, responding with insightful answers and provocative questions.

At the end of that month Nasief said, "My good friend, I now believe in Jesus as my Lord and Savior. At first I believed in you because of your voice that spoke to me. Now I have come to believe for myself."

LeTour, a gifted linguist, taught Nasief English and helped him perfect his Hebrew. It amazed the scholar how quickly his protege picked up everything. "You are not only an empty book," he said often, "but eager to be filled. Never have I seen anyone grasp languages so quickly."

LeTour introduced Nasief to American missionary

friends and arranged for him to live with them for a brief period. He stayed four months and absorbed the language so thoroughly that he began to read English texts. The Americans, attached to an organization that also operated a school for the children of American missionaries in the Middle East, provided him with the use of their textbooks.

To everyone's amazement, Nasief read with an almost photographic memory. Within one year he had mastered every textbook available in English. One missionary loaned him classics of literature, and he read them as rapidly and as thoroughly as he had the texts.

During Nasief's eighteenth year, LeTour and the Americans arranged for the young man to travel to America. He received a scholarship at Princeton University and completed his undergraduate program in two years by reading widely and asking for both oral and written examinations.

From there, he went to seminary, completed the three-year program in one year, and continued on for the doctoral program. At age twenty-two, Nasief Habib, as educated as any other man in the world, who spoke and read eight languages fluently, returned to Israel.

LeTour met him in Tel Aviv on May 14, 1956. It appalled Nasief to see the aging that had taken place in his friend and mentor. They embraced warmly and talked continuously for three days.

On the fourth day, Nasief taught his first Bible class. LeTour sat in amazement as he listened to the young man. Tears streamed down his eyes when he stood to dismiss the class.

"This is my spiritual son. I have prayed often for him and expected great things. Never did I dream of such a gifted teacher. He is now ready to take my place, and I shall return to France within the month."

Nasief raised no objection. Although he loved the old man and he felt the intense pain of losing the one who had become a second father to him, he also knew that LeTour had completed his life's purpose.

LeTour returned to Nice, France. He lived six months

with a widowed sister. One afternoon he lay down for a nap. He never awakened, dying peacefully and at home.

Shaheen slept through most of the day. In the late afternoon, Nasief shook him. He awakened and blinked as he realized where he was.

"You must clean up and eat. We leave for our first service in one hour."

As Shaheen stretched and roused himself, Nasief explained that he had arranged for teaching sessions in six locations. "It will be past midnight when we finish, but we must do it tonight. If all goes well, we shall do it each night."

"I'm ready—"

"Not quite. You listen carefully, study on your own, and soon you will be able to conduct these sessions also. I shall then go to new places and teach until someone is ready to replace me. This is how we must do it."

"What about Therion? Won't he try to stop us?"

"Of course he will try," Nasief said. "He will try."

T·H·R·E·E

Fourteen major revolutions took place across the world in the first six months of 1996. A previously unknown virus killed more than two million people in the South Pacific. Although no official figures ever appeared, experts estimated that more than twelve million people died of starvation in the Asian subcontinent of China and India.

Fred MacDaniel, a reporter from the BBC, doing an in-depth study of America, broadcast and telecast simultaneously the following report:

"In the United States, three years ago, John Speaks of Alabama began a pro-white campaign that saw him elected to the mayoral office in Birmingham. The Anglo-Saxon population in the Deep South is now 43 percent. With 12 percent Oriental, that leaves 45 percent black. With the white population declining and the black growing, population experts project that within the next decade Caucasians in Alabama and the Deep South will be a definite minority, approximately 34 percent of the population. In the United States itself, they project the figure will run slightly higher, more like 36 percent Caucasian.

"During the past four years, blacks have all but taken

over the political offices in the South, beginning with minor mayoral positions. Fear among Anglo-Saxons has increased in recent months. Two years ago, by rallying white voters and appealing to the fears of Orientals and blacks, John Speaks landed in the Governor's mansion. Within six months of his election, not one person of African or Asian descent lived within the state. Unverified reports of brutality, mass murder, and lynching circulated, but nothing has come to light that proves such allegations.

"The honorable John Speaks has received outstanding press support across the nation. One elderly Senator said, 'I never would have believed that 140 years of progress could be wiped away so easily.'

"Polls indicate that Americans support the measures proposed by John Speaks. The Gallup Poll indicates that 98 percent of Anglo-Saxon Americans favor banishing all illegal aliens, deporting anyone who has not either been born in America or naturalized there. A record 97 percent believe that Americans should allow no new immigrants into the country.

"This attitude has arisen since 1992, uniting Caucasians with a wide variety of political positions. They cite their militant stance because of rising unemployment, increased taxation, and chronic food shortages that now plague that nation."

On the televised segment, the camera focused on a group of people bearing signs and banners, "America for Americans." One of them stepped forward and took the microphone in his hand.

"My name is Malcolm Brown. It's time for some of us to stand up and to speak up. We have become foreigners in our own land. I am a staunch supporter of Speaks and anyone else who stands for the right."

He started to hand back the microphone, changed his mind and screamed, "Our forefathers came to this country for freedom and the right to live and worship *and work* freely. Then we let all these outsiders come in and take over. I'm not going to stand for it any longer!"

The camera cut to MacDaniel:

"The states of New York, New Jersey, and Tennessee passed laws that limit employment to native-born Americans. These three states, along with twenty-two others, enacted some form of legislation that demands all citizens to carry intra-state passports on their persons at all times. Local police force members round up those unable to obtain these identity passports. If they cannot establish their citizenship within twelve hours, they receive extradition papers and must leave the continental United States within an additional twenty-four hours. Two states have imposed the death penalty, without trial, for those who refuse to leave.

"Those who receive extradition papers usually end up shot. They can find no country that wants to accept them.

"Nine western states have passed miscegenation laws. Four states in the south that previously had such laws have restored them to the lawbooks."

The film showed MacDaniel, standing with his back to Liberty Island where the Statue of Liberty once proudly shone her torch, reminding the world of the words that once emblazoned the pedestal. He read the last portion of the sonnet:

. . . Give me your tired, your poor, your huddled masses yearning to breathe free, the wretched refuse of your teeming shore. Send these, the homeless, tempest-tost, to me. I lift my lamp beside the golden door!

The scene changed and the reporter stood in London's Trafalgar Square. He concluded with these words:

"We here in Britain face many of the same problems as our American cousins. We now have a population that we cannot possibly support with our limited land and resources. Since Australia, Canada, and other parts of the former Commonwealth have closed their doors to immigration, Parliament is debating on its next step.

"Among the long-term measures likely to come up for debate and that pundits insist will pass without incident include mandatory sterilization after one child, voluntary euthanasia, and the death penalty for habitual criminals. Should all such measures pass, and that appears likely, critics say they will only postpone the inevitable for us here at home.

"What do we do next? Follow the example of the United States? Anthropologist and professor Robert Ramey of Oxford suggests that we must also eliminate all nonproductive citizens such as the mentally retarded and the mentally ill. His ideas, first espoused in 1979, were generally laughed at. Today, many former critics now find themselves in agreement with Professor Ramey."

Joshua Gad-Erianko, King of Israel, continued to appear on worldwide television weekly. Despite revolutions, famine, and racial disturbances, the people in the world viewed him as a moderate, compassionate, concerned international leader. Sentiment had already spread throughout the world's major population centers to elect Joshua Gad-Erianko President of the world. The King himself never made mention of this. His silence added fire to the growing cry of the nations.

Nagila, at work in the palace, watched his latest broadcast. All television stations in Israel automatically activated when their King spoke. She listened to him a few minutes and then went to the window. From there she saw the whole spectacle as it took place.

The street, packed with ecstatic young people, broke into what seemed like spontaneous applause as speaker after speaker came to the podium. Joshua had gathered eighteen international leaders in Jerusalem. Half of them spoke on behalf of uniting the world using the SSS concept.

Nine of them said essentially the same thing, urging the support of everyone to make the world a safe place. "We must eliminate those who bring dissension and weaken our nations." Those who followed echoed the words of that speaker.

After all the leaders had spoken, Joshua Gad-Erianko walked slowly to the platform. He paused, and his gaze surveyed the crowd. On the television screen millions of viewers would later say, "I felt as if he looked right at me when he talked. And when he spoke, it was if no one else existed but me."

Nagila listened, realizing that if she did not know the truth about Therion, she would be cheering with them. The masses in the street, along with viewers across the world, were hypnotized by Joshua's forceful voice, his clear logic, and, most of all, by his unique ability to speak to millions as single individuals.

When the wild cheering died, the crowds did not disperse. They stood, waiting silently as if to move would break a magic spell.

Six men filed across the platform. Each carried an instrument, and they lined up, ready to play. They needed no introduction. The Gang of Six, as the world knew them, burst into a song of tribute to Joshua. Although it had been released as a single record eight months earlier, it remained as the number one best-selling single in the world.

When the first notes from an electric guitar, a violin, and a French horn rose from The Gang of Six, the crowd burst into applause. They played a lengthy introduction as they waited for silence.

"The world belongs to us . . ." sang the soloist. Before he finished the first bar, the airwaves filled with the thunderous echo of listeners.

> . . . we are making the world for us,
> Leaving behind the old.
> We have a new world aborning,
> A new world for us to mold . . .

Cameras focused in on the crowd. They stood at attention, as if they sang the national anthem of their land. Tears glided down many cheeks. Their voices raised to a crescendo as they sang their final chorus:

> A fine world that blends us all
> In strength and in salvation,
> and noble superiority.
> A world that never let us down.
> A world for all in equality.

Eighteen world leaders attended a private luncheon following the broadcast. The food, placed on six buffet tables, provided for every kind of appetite and taste. Joshua nodded to the head waiter and dismissed all the servants from the mammoth dining room. Joshua remained alone with the eighteen guests.

"I have invited all of you to be with me on this special day," he said. "Today the new world has been born. I am inviting you to join with me in ruling it."

Joshua paused, and his eyes moved from one face to another. He confirmed his original assessment in selecting them. They were all men and women of immense greed, unbridled ambition, and extreme capability.

"I have only one problem remaining. I share that with you now, and you will then know the next step of the plan." Joshua pressed a button, and a large screen came from the ceiling. A second button and a map appeared on the screen.

"This is the new world. You will not recognize any boundaries. I have set aside Israel as the place of my personal domain, not subject to any of the ten kingdoms. Under the new boundaries, you will recognize me as supreme ruler. You will rule your sphere of land. You may call yourselves Regents, Kings, Princes—it does not matter." He moved aside so that the guests could view the restructured nations.

"King Joshua," Ning Huo from China blurted out, "I count only ten nations. We are eighteen here."

"Exactly," Joshua said.

The members stared at him and a few glanced at the others nearby. These perceptive leaders immediately understood his meaning, yet they waited for him to clarify.

"From this point onward, we require only ten Regents. You are exactly correct."

"But what about the rest of us?" the Russian Frolov asked.

Joshua leaned forward. "When only ten of you remain in power, the new world plan goes into effect."

F·O·U·R

"Wait. Do I understand you clearly?" The American, Governor Speaks, asked in his cultivated drawl, "You mean you want us to eliminate eight people from our midst?"

"I do not care how you do it. Perhaps eight are willing to take subservient positions. You may persuade eight of you to step to the position of Vice-Regent. It does not matter to me."

"It matters to us," Speaks said. "It involves our lives!"

"Exactly. That is why you must make the decision."

"You're setting us up to kill each other off? Is that your plan?"

All trace of warmth disappeared from Joshua's face. He walked over to Governor Speaks and grabbed his lapel. "I am not deciding your future. You decide your own. I have planned for the ten strongest, wisest, most ambitious and cunning leaders of the world to rule with me. You must decide for yourself if you are among the ten."

Joshua stepped back; the friendly face millions recognized from television stared back at them. "You have hardly eaten your luncheon. I am leaving you now. The map will remain. Please study it carefully. It may help you in your decision-making process."

After Joshua exited, a spirit of confusion and despair filled the room. The eighteen studied the map carefully, memorizing the boundaries, all wondering what they might do to ensure one of the positions.

Governor Speaks intuited immediately that he had two choices. He could eliminate either Helmut Dronen of Western Europe or Mateo Del Rio who already ruled Mexico and all of Central and South America.

He made his decision immediately.

Shaheen slept less than four hours a night. He felt a compulsion to travel throughout Israel. Wherever anyone would listen, from a single person to a hundred, he taught the message of Aryeh.

Desiring to extend the message beyond Israel, Shaheen applied for visas to the other nations in the Middle East, doubting that any government would issue them. To his surprise, he immediately received permission to visit Jordan, Egypt, and Iran. For once Joshua was unable to keep track of his whereabouts.

Shaheen went to any settlement, town, or community he encountered. Each time he asked, "Who is the most important person or family?" He went to them first.

In most instances, they listened. It surprised him that Muslims flocked to receive his message. At the same time, Shaheen recognized that he now spoke with an authority and an urgency that he had never experienced before.

"When you speak, Shaheen, your eyes burn with zealous intensity," Nagila said when she met him in Egypt. He had entered the country days earlier. Nagila came on official business that kept her in Cairo for nine days. During most of those days she managed to spend some time with Shaheen. "Your face, the way you stand, your voice—all those things show a conviction more eloquent than your words."

"Because I am doing what Aryeh wishes me to do," he said.

Shaheen usually stayed in one place two to three weeks. On those occasions, he spoke each morning and evening until he developed a cadre of disciples. Once he could count upon at least six devout followers, he took them through a ten-day intensive course of instruction. When he left, these leaders, both men and women, carried on the teaching.

"Nagila," Shaheen said on their last evening together, "I have so many things I want to say to you. I love you more than I ever thought it humanly possible to love."

Nagila stared at his dark features. "I never thought I would love again. Ever. You have changed everything—"

"Aryeh has changed it. Now we fit together," he said. They stood on the balcony of her suite at the Cairo Hilton. He took her hand in his and kissed it tenderly. They stared momentarily at each other before Nagila fell into his arms. For several minutes he held her in silence.

"You know, Nagila, I loved my first wife Zaynab dearly. I thought I could never love again after her death. I determined that I would be loyal always to her memory. But," he paused and kissed Nagila's cheek, "I think if she knew what is happening in our lives, she would be pleased. Zaynab once said that she wanted me to be happy. Yes, I think it would please her very much."

They turned and their lips met. They held each other tightly, savoring the warmth of each other's embrace. Neither wanted to stop.

"Where will it end?" Nagila asked. "When will it end? Will people like you and me ever have the chance for a normal life together?"

"I do not know," he said. He kissed the top of her head. "I doubt it."

Nagila pulled back so that she could see his face. "I think I've known that for a long time, Shaheen. I'm a woman and perhaps we women think more of the tender moments, the togetherness. We long for a home and a place where we share our love—"

"Nagila, we have now. Today. Maybe a few more weeks. Months at most."

"The end is coming, isn't it? The end of this world?"

"Yes."

"I should be happy. And I am, of course. I believe and I want Aryeh to return to earth . . . but . . . I love you, Shaheen. I wish . . . I wish . . . that things could be different—"

"As much as I love you, Nagila, this is not our time. We have no time for us."

"No, Shaheen. We have little time. Precious little but still—"

"Yes, as we are right now."

"Sometimes I want to be your wife. To stand by your side. To be with you all the time. I think I wouldn't mind the end coming so much if I could only be with you."

"Then be with me."

"How? I'm a virtual prisoner."

"Do not go back. Stay with me and we'll move across the land together."

"If only—"

"It can be done, Nagila. If you want to."

Nagila turned away and stared into the darkness of the night. Below, the muffled sounds of evening traffic provided no distraction. Nagila wanted to think through the consequences of such a drastic action.

Joshua had threatened her. If she left, he would kill her if he caught her. She realized that didn't trouble her greatly. She began to ask herself what was important. What she wanted to do. *If all I have in this life is right now, then this is the one person I want to spend it with.*

She turned to face Shaheen. "It's not the same context, my darling, but, as Ruth said to her mother-in-law Naomi thousands of years ago, I say to you with new meaning: 'Entreat me not to leave you or to return from following you; for where you go I will go, and where you lodge I will lodge; your people shall be my people, and your Aryeh my Aryeh; where you die I will die . . .' "

Shaheen pulled her close. "It will be this way. Together we shall stand against Joshua and every evil force as long as Aryeh is pleased to keep us alive."

"As long as Aryeh is pleased to keep us alive," she repeated.

Governor Speaks maneuvered so that he and Mateo Del Rio left the dining room at the same time. "May I offer you a ride to the airport?"

"I am sure I can arrange—"

"You aren't afraid, are you?" Speaks said. A tall, broad-shouldered man, his horn-rimmed glasses and soft voice often made people underestimate his cunning. "In broad daylight?" He took Del Rio's arm. "My car is parked at the rear of the palace."

Del Rio hesitated only a second and then walked with Speaks. The American governor's chauffeur waited next to the Rolls Royce until he saw the two men coming his way. He put on his hat and opened the door for them.

Speaks entered the car first and Del Rio bent down to get in beside him. He did not see the Python .357 that Governor Speaks pulled out of a special compartment in his door.

"Thank you for making it so simple," Speaks said and pulled the trigger four times in rapid succession.

The impact of the .357 at close range knocked Del Rio backward and he fell to the ground. The chauffeur looked at Speaks, waiting for instructions.

"Apparently Presidente Del Rio has suffered a stroke. Would you inform one of the guards as we drive off?"

"Certainly," the man answered.

"I hope no one gets upset over the blood on the upholstery." He leaned forward. "As soon as you get me to the airport, will you see what you can do about cleaning it?"

"I shall certainly do that, sir."

Speaks leaned back in the car. He had now assured

himself of being one of the ten—not that he had doubted it—but now a new ambition came to him . . . One day he might even be the single ruler of the world. One day . . .

Speaks smiled to himself. It was time to lay his plans to make certain.

F·I·V·E

The Chinese officially broke with the Russians and Arabs and lent their support to the coalition headed by John Speaks of the United States. A rash of international assassinations of leaders and heads of states took place over the next four days, all of them effectively carried out. These deaths included not only eight members of the eighteen who had attended King Joshua's luncheon, but widened to take care of any threats to power. New leaders immediately proclaimed allegiance to a new government that joined them with another power.

John Speaks was now undisputed head of the entire North and South American continents. Vitali Frolov shot into the place of supreme control in the entire Communist bloc that included eastern Europe.

The lesser rulers emerged exactly as Joshua had foreseen. Each day he counted the movements of national loyalty. From eighteen to fourteen in two days. On the third day, only twelve world leaders. He waited almost a week before the news came that Baya Marach Jullu from East Africa eliminated her South African counterpart and, within hours, grabbed control of the Republics of the Pacific.

Joshua decided to watch Ms. Jullu carefully. He had underestimated the cunning of the tall woman from Africa who could kill as easily and as frequently as she could smile benevolently. The world recognized her as happy, smiling constantly, concerned for the welfare of the continent. She had moved into the foreground sooner than he had anticipated.

Joshua put the next step in his plan together. He provoked the Russians by making them believe that the Americans had stolen nuclear test results. This involved more than the normal theft of information. Whoever perfected these results would send the first permanent colony to the moon.

He contrived again so that the Chinese blamed the Russians for the leakage of the scientific breakthrough in human cloning. This had been the most carefully guarded secret the Chinese had ever held. They were ready to clone their own selected world-class leaders, those of charismatic ability and brilliance.

Joshua felt his triumph coming closer. He began to make phone calls around the world to put the next step into motion. The ten nations, now evenly aligned, had only to focus on a common goal. He had selected leaders of unparalleled greed. He had only to provoke them to seize the vast supply of malgamite. Joshua appeared on television on a Wednesday morning. The live address would be taped and shown around the world at least 7,000 times within a twenty-four-hour period. He made his shortest address on television. He wanted one message to go to the top ten survivors, and this would achieve it.

"Today I stand up to the leaders of the nations who have violated human rights and denied citizens the right of choice. In collaboration with the Knesset, we have passed the following measure *unanimously.*

"As of midnight tonight, we shall export no more malgamite to any nation in any part of the world until they can bring us incontrovertible proof that they are not denying human rights according to the conditions of the Geneva Convention.

"In Israel, we have always stood for the rights of all people and of all races. We shall not tolerate racism, sexism, ageism, euthanasia, enslavement, or any form of economic injustice."

King Joshua's bold announcement stunned the world. The oppressed nations of what had once been called the Third World applauded his measures. Politicians hurriedly met with their constituents, wondering what to do.

Within hours the leaders of each of the ten amalgamated nations knew they had only one choice: they must take control of the production and distribution of malgamite. Each leader saw that whoever controlled malgamite controlled the destiny of the world.

Messages poured into Joshua's office. All ten leaders had begun an offensive move. Six had already ordered their troops to move toward Israel. Others, attempting to be more diplomatic, rallied their people, filling them with fears of being denied malgamite. Within weeks their entire transportation industry would be at a complete standstill.

For the previous four years, King Joshua had provided malgamite at a low figure, assuring the rest of the world of the bountiful supply for transportation. Behind the scenes, he had systematically closed down oil production for transportation and even destroyed the fields, making the remaining oil nearly impossible to reach.

At the time of Joshua's announcement about malgamite restriction, the former oil-producing nations became aware of the trap they had been led into. The leaders, more angered than ever, determined to wipe Joshua and Israel out of the picture.

The leaders individually agreed upon their primary target. Once they destroyed Joshua and Israel, they would find an equitable way to produce and distribute the valuable mineral malgamite.

But first the ten leaders faced a great difficulty. Before they could swoop down and take over the malgamite, they had either to make peace with the other half of the world or to best them in war.

John Speaks never hesitated. He hated Vitali Frolov and, if given the opportunity, would personally have enjoyed killing him. Fifteen years earlier, Speaks had visited the Kremlin. Most of the officials had treated him respectfully. Frolov had insulted him by his indifferent attitude.

The final insult came to Speaks on his final day in Moscow. Frolov, who controlled the transportation industry, had refused to provide a special car for Speaks. He himself had a new Zoita—the elite sports car of the Soviet Union. Frolov displayed the Zoita in Speaks's presence, but never allowed him inside of it.

On the morning of Speaks's departure a driver appeared. Speaks went outside and saw an American compact waiting for him. As he hid his anger, he vowed that one day he would destroy Frolov.

Frolov had not particularly disliked Speaks. He had acted on the instructions of Joshua Gad-Erianko.

Within forty-eight hours, most of the world had gone into a state of military mobilization. Every available fighting unit headed toward the Middle East. Secrecy no longer mattered. Each country grasped the fact that their existence depended on their prevailing against the other nations. Pacts and treaties, hammered out with great time and energy, now remained nothing more than papers with words written on them.

Each nation in the conflict knew that one great allied army would defeat Joshua and the Jews and crush them forever. They assured themselves and their people that they would equitably control the world's supply of malgamite. "Share and share alike," Speaks announced.

Television coverage from across the world showed the armies on the march. Planes flew troops to the Middle East. Carriers filled the Mediterranean. Even though rival powers saw each other's military forces and could have started fighting, they all restrained themselves because of orders from the top.

No world leader knew that Joshua Gad-Erianko surreptitiously issued specific orders to each head of each of the ten nations. Each leader acted under the assumption that he or she alone had direct assistance from King Joshua. Because of the King's favor, they knew they would not fail.

"It has finally happened," Nasief said and snapped off the television. The sadness on his face emphasized the tired lines around his eyes. "I knew it was coming and that it had to happen—" His voice broke and he cupped his head with his hands.

"You've known all along," Nagila said lamely. "That ought to make it easier."

He nodded. Finding his voice again, Nasief said, "Knowledge is one thing. To know in advance of the suffering of millions of innocent people is a burden—a heavy burden. Nagila, the worst has not yet come."

"It can get worse?" Shaheen asked. "By more repressive measures against us? Outright persecution against anyone not belonging to SSS?"

"More than that, much more," Nasief said. "Inhuman brutality, unparalleled persecution, mass extermination. Joshua Gad-Erianko and his people have learned well from the records of Hitler, Stalin, and other great mass murderers."

"What more can we do?" Nagila asked. She laid her arm on the old man's shoulders. "We have to do more than wait for the inevitable to happen."

"We intensify our activities," Nasief said. "The more Joshua and the SSS work against us, the stronger we grow." He paused and took several deep breaths. "My heart is saddened for those who must suffer. At the same time, we have the greatest opportunity in the history of the world.

Don't forget that, in one sense, human destiny is in *our* hands! We must save others from imbibing these lies and seductions." He pounded his fist. "We're going to forge ahead because we're right! Aryeh is with us and that makes us a majority!"

Nagila thought of the implication of Nasief's words and shuddered. She had already seen some of the forms of persecution followers of Aryeh went through. The telecast had reinforced much of what she had already known about.

She kissed Nasief's cheek, picked up her purse, and walked toward the door. "I'm going back to the palace now. For the last time."

"I wish you would allow me to go with you," Shaheen said.

She shook her head. "We've been through that. If all goes well, I shall return this afternoon. If I do not re-turn . . ." She shrugged and attempted a smile.

"It is not wrong to be afraid," Nasief said. "Aryeh will grant you the strength and the wisdom at the moment you need it."

"I know you're right," Nagila said. "That's what gives me the courage to do this."

"You do not have to go back," Shaheen said weakly. "You do not have to face Therion again." He had used that argument for hours the night before.

"I believe in an Aryeh who is all-powerful," Nagila answered. "Not in a Therion who wants us to slink away. I must face him before I am free."

"I cannot understand that," Shaheen said. "You owe him nothing."

"No, I must. Hasn't Nasief said that we owe the truth to everyone? That we must show concern for their eternal welfare? Doesn't that include a man as beastly as the King?"

"At least let me go with you. With a witness, he will surely not harm you at the palace."

Nagila shook her head. She took Shaheen's hand and clasped it tightly. "When I was a young girl, my mother told me of the terrible times she and father endured. They were the fortunate ones. They escaped Germany, both of them. My mother told me that what gave her the most strength was a story her rabbi told her. During the days of the dispersion of the Jewish people, Nehemiah, the cupbearer of the king, wanted to return to Jerusalem and to rebuild it.

"The king gave him permission and offered to send an armed guard to protect him on the dangerous journey. Nehemiah faced a dilemma. He wondered how he could allow that protection and still speak about a God of great power. He refused.

"That's how my parents and grandparents survived, Shaheen. My parents and my mothers' parents went by themselves, traveling mostly at night, using back roads, sleeping in fields. The other Jews in their community decided to go together. A kind of caravan. The safety-in-numbers idea. Of that group of 300, not one soul made it to safety. The Germans detained them, confiscated their money, jewelry, and a valuable art collection. Then, conveniently, all 300 died of some mysterious plague that affected no one else."

She laid her head against Shaheen's chest. "I cannot take a coward's way and run. I must do it this way. I must face Joshua and I am willing to do that. My life is in Aryeh's hands."

"It always has been anyway," Nasief said.

"Yes, I know that," Shaheen said. "But, Nagila, darling, I cannot let you go—"

"You can and you must!" Nasief said. "This is what Nagila believes Aryeh requires of her. We shall have a final prayer for her and commend her life to Aryeh. Then she leaves."

Shaheen released her. He stared at the soft features of the woman he had come to love. He lightly touched the blonde curls, now cut short, and his hand stroked her cheek. He knew that while Nagila's going to face Joshua was her most courageous act, his was in letting her go.

S·I·X

Joshua smiled as he paced his office. He now had everything in place, ready for the final act of history. He wanted ten great world leaders. It had taken only days for the redistribution of leadership to take place. Exactly as he had planned back in Russia.

He paused to stare out the window. Only a few crucial events and then he would realize his ultimate aim. He had been patient a long time, careful never to hurry. He had done everything right—everything except take care of those dreaded Aryeh people. He was now correcting that one error with new measures and greater power in the hands of the SSS leaders.

A knock at the door interrupted his thinking. "Yes," he said, turning around.

Nagila opened the door and came inside. As she closed it behind her, Joshua stared at her white cotton dress and her matching pumps. Her face glowed with a radiance he had never seen before, making her even more lovely. He felt again the longing ache for her. A hundred times he had considered forcing her into bed. Each time he gave it up, willing to wait. Willing for her to understand what he, and he alone, could offer her.

His eyes followed her as she crossed the room. He liked to watch her smooth stride that was feminine but not coquettish. He sometimes thought of her movement as more of a glide, or the poise of a well-trained dancer.

"How good to have you back from Egypt," he said. He walked toward her, his hands stretched out toward her.

Instead of accepting his effusive greeting, Nagila sat down. She place her matching white purse on her lap. "I have already written a lengthy report," she said. "It is being retyped now."

"You did an excellent job, as I expected. Even those who resent the presence of women have had to acknowledge that you carried the negotiations for worldwide distribution of water—"

"That's not what I came in here to talk to you about."

"You must tell me then," he said. His spirit had been so buoyed by the latest triumphs, he did not pay particular attention to the seriousness of her mood. "Shall I ring for tea?"

"No."

"Something else, then?"

"No."

Joshua pulled himself straight up and sat facing her, his knees barely touching hers. He leaned forward and took her hand.

"I have something important to say to you," Nagila said. She squirmed slightly, moving away from him.

"You sound so solemn—"

Nagila withdrew her hand. "I can no longer work for you. I have decided to leave the palace. This morning."

"I told you once that I would decide when you leave." The evenness of his tone did not disguise the strength of his threat.

"No," Nagila said. "You no longer have that choice. You can incarcerate me or kill me, but I refuse to continue working here. If you use physical force on me to stay, I promise that I shall do everything I can to sabotage your projects."

Nagila had been shaking inside when she approached Joshua's office. Now she sat before him, perfectly calm. She felt an inner strength entirely new to her.

"It is that way, is it?"

"Yes."

"And you are throwing in your lot with the Aryeh rabble?"

"Then you know what we call ourselves."

"Of course I know. But a peculiar name—why did you select the Hebrew word for lion?"

"Jesus our Messiah descended from the tribe of Judah."

"Ah, yes, of course. The tribe of the lion."

"Joshua, I came here to face you in person because I wanted to explain why I must do this. It is precisely because I believe in Aryeh. May I tell you about—about this faith?"

"You want me to listen to your foolish talk of terrible days ahead? Of the end of the world? The punishment of the wicked? The destruction of people like me? I know what you teach and I forbid you to speak about it."

"Then I want you to know something else," Nagila said. "I am convinced that you are evil. Totally, completely, fully evil. I am further convinced that you are the person predicted in the Book of the Revelation as the Antichrist." She took a breath and said in a low voice, "And as long as I have breath in my body, I promise to oppose you and your evil forces."

"You speak with great courage, Nagila."

"Because I believe in what I am saying and because Aryeh gives me this courage."

"I see," Joshua said. "I want to make you a counter-offer. Today I am signing a new bill. It establishes a world-wide police force. They have a singular purpose: to eliminate all members of Aryeh wherever they find them. All other nations will automatically adopt this bill and offer the fullest cooperation. Do you believe I can do that?"

"I believe you. It does not surprise me."

"You followers of Aryeh have now been categorized as undesirables and placed on the elimination list above the mentally retarded, the physically disabled, the mentally ill."

"As you choose," she said. "I am aware of how powerful you are and the behind-the-scenes games you play."

"But you have not yet heard my counteroffer." He clasped both her hands in his and held them tight. "I can spare you and your friends."

"No. The price is too high."

"You have not yet heard my offer."

"Joshua, I don't need to. You're about to offer to spare them if I'll marry you or sleep with you or live with you or something like that."

"That is exactly my offer."

"No."

"I thought you were a great follower of Aryeh."

"Because I am, I cannot do such a thing. I cannot do an evil thing to bring about good."

"Evil? Good? Those are relative terms."

"Again I disagree. Right is always right and wrong is evil, no matter how you attempt to twist—"

"You have become quite strong in your feelings since Nasief and Shaheen brainwashed you—"

"Furthermore, I don't trust you. Even if I submitted to you, you would find a way to destroy them. Not just people like Nasief and Shaheen, but all the followers of Aryeh. As long as any of us live, we shall always be a threat to you. As long as any good people survive, your kingdom stands in danger!" She stared defiantly at him. "No, Joshua, I take my place with them."

"The blood of forty million followers of Aryeh will be upon your head, Nagila."

"You cannot lay that burden on me. If they die, it will happen because you chose to murder them."

"Let's say eliminate—"

"Let's say murder. You conceived of the idea and you are the one who will have it carried out."

Nagila knocked his hands away and pushed her chair back as she stood up. "I have a few personal items in my office. I'm going there. If you want me arrested, send your soldiers for me. Otherwise, within twenty minutes I intend to leave this palace for good."

Nagila did not wait for his answer. She walked rapidly across the room and slammed the door behind her. She continued down the hallway to her own office. She felt no fear or uncertainty.

Nagila did not know if Joshua would send his soldiers for her. It did not matter. She had learned something valuable in the meeting with Joshua. Nasief had talked many times about Aryeh giving people courage at the moment they needed it.

Nagila had indeed experienced an infusion of courage. She could face anything.

S·E·V·E·N

The deserts of the Middle East virtually disappeared with the continued movement of military personnel and armament to the area. Troops lined up side by side until they fully surrounded Israel. The armies of five countries grouped together along Israel's northern border. These five nations, ready to attack, awaited only the arrival of their leaders: Speaks, Jullu, Frolov, the Premier of the Democratic States of Asia, and Ali Mokhtar who now led the United Arab Nations.

John Speaks, President of the United Republics of America, arrived by malgamite-propelled jet and landed at a hastily constructed airstrip on the Syrian border.

Vitali Frolov had flown into Damascus the morning before. He had planned to meet with President Speaks. He would have accomplished this except that Baya Marach Jullu argued against it. "Who are you to represent half of the world's population? Because you Russians control great land-masses you think you must always be the speaker?"

Frolov, at sixty-five, looked every year of his age, but his stamina and razor-sharp mind equalled that of any young man. He was eight inches shorter than the tall, athletic-built Ms. Jullu. At forty-three, Baya Marach Jullu had risen to one of the top positions in world leadership. A woman of great self-confidence, she determined that no Russian would represent her and her people.

For six hours they argued, trying to reach a compromise by having neither attend and one of the other three represent them. Neither Frolov nor Jullu agreed to the latter solution.

"I am younger. I am better informed. And I am capable," Jullu insisted, smiling all the time she spoke. "No one is more qualified."

"You are young—too young," spat Frolov. "You have yet to prove how capable you are against that devil Speaks. I know him and I can force him to surrender to us. I am the only sensible and logical choice."

By nightfall, they had not resolved the issue. Finally, Eman Mustafa Bari of the Democratic States of Asia, the only other woman among the five leaders, demanded the floor. "I am tired of this wrangling. Personally I am as capable as any of you men. However, I know that in this I must defer. I remind you, however, that my time will come! For this matter, I can come to one conclusion only. You both must go and speak as one voice."

"Impossible!" Frolov said.

"This old man would be only a handicap," Jullu said.

"Stop!" Premier Bari said. "Unless the two of you agree to this, I tell you that by midnight I shall commit my troops to move southward and join the other side. We will outnumber you and aid in your defeat."

Frolov stared. "You would—you would do this?"

"I must be on the winning side. If I cannot work with you, then I will switch sides and change the balance of power."

"Agreed," Jullu said.

"Yes," Frolov added without enthusiasm.

The following morning Frolov and Jullu met with Speaks on a yacht sixteen miles off the coast of Israel. A small navy encircled the yacht during the two-hour negotiation.

Neither side was willing to share malgamite with the other. None of them knew the others' secret orders from Joshua Gad-Erianko.

"If it must be war, then," Speaks said, "we are ready." He faced Frolov and swore. "I have been waiting a long time to do this to you."

"You say strong things now. In a week, we shall see."

"If you two men want to have a fight, go ahead and then I'll take on the winner," Baya Marach Jullu said. "You hate each other. I hate you both. Now we decide some issues and then I leave. I have many armed troops prepared and eager to blow up American and Russian bodies."

The summit meeting, called by Speaks, had been convened to agree upon conventional weapons of war. The other two, although they would not admit it, were pleased that Speaks had taken the initiative. They also had secret instructions that under no conditions were they to use nuclear arms against the other side.

Once they agreed upon the limits of weaponry, they discussed token warfare more as a gesture than a desire. Speaks suggested that a limited number of soldiers engage in the actual fighting, and that whoever conquered won the right to take over Israel.

"Not unless you march at the head of your soldiers," Frolov said. "I would take supreme pleasure in firing the first shot. I assure you, I would need only one bullet."

Speaks laughed, dismissing the statement and infuriating Frolov. He turned to Jullu. "If you choose to change sides, you are a woman of considerable ability and I would welcome you to work by my side."

"Would you?" Jullu said. "You would make me your assistant or deputy and then we'd spend years plotting against each other."

Speaks whacked Jullu on the back. "I don't like many people. You're one of the few. We might get along."

"Perhaps," she said.

"One question," Frolov said. "We win or you win, is that not so? Or we whittle our forces down so that we work out an agreement—"

"That will never happen—"

"Anything can happen," he said to overcome Speaks's interruption. "It is a winner-take-all game. Where does Gad-Erianko fit in?"

"The meeting is over," Speaks said. He walked out of the room. Upon seeing him emerge, his four-man bodyguard stood at attention and signaled for his launch.

Speaks had been thinking about Joshua Gad-Erianko for the past three days. He knew he could defeat Vitali Frolov. Joshua had secretly communicated that to him. He had wrestled with the more important question that Vitali Frolov had raised. Speaks would never to be content to walk two paces behind Joshua Gad-Erianko.

Joshua had aided him in reaching the top. He could discard Joshua as he had discarded dozens of others on his way up the tallest ladder in the world.

Jullu and Frolov finished their tea before departing. They had agreed at the beginning that whoever left first, the other party would wait a minimum of ten minutes before proceeding, thus ensuring themselves that no entrapment awaited.

Jullu knew that Frolov hated King Joshua as much as she did—and wondered for what reasons.

"When we win," Jullu said, "and I assume you know that we will . . ."

"I have no doubt whatsoever."

"When we win, I suggest that you rethink your ambitions. To rise to the top and to have power over nearly half of the world is surely enough, isn't it?"

"For some men it is enough."

"That will be your downfall, Vitali Frolov. You reach too high."

"Do I? We shall see."

Jullu took her final sip from the cup. "Brilliant people know their limitations. Only fools and those of lesser ability never know when to stop."

"I know when to stop," Frolov said. "I know exactly when to stop." The harshness of his voice contrasted sharply with Jullu's smile.

Nagila had chosen to walk out of the palace, leaving the Maserati that King Joshua had given her for her personal use. She went on foot until she could hail a taxi. From there she went directly to Nasief's house.

Shaheen had waited for her. That afternoon they planned their activities for the weeks ahead. Making use of Nagila's classified information, the two of them would travel throughout Asia and Africa for seven weeks. They planned their trips separately for the sake of safety, yet coordinated their schedules so that they had a few hours together when they moved from one location to another.

At best, Joshua's people kept a partial surveillance on Nagila and Shaheen. In order not to have problems with King Joshua, they falsified their reports. Nagila and Shaheen had become expert at outwitting members of the SSS who tried to follow them inconspicuously.

Travel conditions became increasingly difficult because neither of them wore the SSS band. They discussed wearing them as disguises when they wanted to move unobtrusively.

"I could not do that," Shaheen said. "It would be a form of compromise that I am not prepared to make."

"I tried to talk myself into using one to make it easier to travel," Nagila said. "I decided that if any of the members of Aryeh saw me with the SSS band, it might lead them into making concessions."

"Our strength," Shaheen said, "lies in the fact we are free in our consciences. We do not resort to the use of anything but speaking the truth. Surely this is the way Aryeh wants us to behave."

Joshua timed his next step to coincide with the beginnings of the battles on Israel's borders. The SSS had infiltrated every nation of the world. Although ostensibly independent in each country, province, or city, the SSS were all linked in Joshua's computerlike mind which kept everything in focus. He personally controlled more than 7,000 SSS leaders worldwide.

He allowed the initiative to come from the United Republics of America. The Joint Congress of the now-eighteen sovereign nations in the two continents passed public law A-7734 which read in part:

> Only members of the SSS will work for any national, regional, or city governments. No one will serve in the Armed Forces who is not a member of the SSS.

In itself the public law did not disturb religious and dissenting groups. Their concern and growing fear was that it would be the first of a growing number of laws prohibiting anyone from working, buying, or selling who did not hold membership in the SSS.

They guessed correctly. Within four days, lawmakers introduced similar legislation to their constituents and in each case passed it unanimously.

News items and columns next grabbed public attention. Without exception, all apprehended criminals admitted that they were with dissident organizations and their goal was to subvert the objectives of the SSS.

In Naples twenty-five dissidents, all members of a subversive religious group, admitted that they would never give allegiance to SSS. One of them spit upon the Book of SSS which every court now used to administer oaths. All twenty-five received the death penalty.

Their crime: refusal to register their church with the government. Registration meant that state inspectors regulated worship so that it functioned "with dignity and decorum" and that it espoused the major tenets of SSS.

In Manila, a newly erected wooden structure used for

worship burned on a Sunday morning. The worship service had started at 11:00. By 11:20, the SSS blocked off every entrance and window, allowing no one to exit. A group escaped by knocking holes in a second-story window and climbing down the drainpipe. Another handful raced into the basement of the building and forced open a back door. No one saw them leaving—the only reason they survived.

Of the more than 500 people in attendance, only eight escaped the fire. The authorities captured four escapees, beat them until they lost consciousness, then laid their bodies across the main road. Patriotic marchers trampled upon them.

Their crimes: more than a thousand violations of individuals within the congregation who assisted and encouraged nonmembers of the SSS to defy regulations.

The most serious charge: the pastor introduced a new hymn and taught it to the members. They had not sent this hymn to the Bureau of Religious Affairs for their approval. Inspectors produced tape recordings of worship services on two consecutive Sundays when they sang the illegal hymn.

Part of the words went:

> Storm the palace of darkness
> Pull down Therion's kingdom
> Where'er he holds dominion.
> Storm the palace of darkness . . .

Women sang these words while men broke into a descant with these words:

> Bring it down, bring it down.
> Pull it down, pull it down.
> Ruin his pow'r, ruin his pow'r.
> Bring it down, bring it down.

E·I·G·H·T

Outside Atlanta, along the Chattahoochie River, soldiers lined up, scrutinizing the ninety-one adults who came to undergo the ceremony of baptism. It had started quietly as the black followers of Aryeh met beside the river. Four pastors went first, followed by the eighty-seven new converts who stood momentarily at the edge of the water. At a given signal, they started forward to receive baptism.

Along the shore, members of the Community Fellowship of Aryeh sang the hymn that had circulated around most of the world through the efforts of leaders such as Nasief Habib. Nagila and Shaheen had written the hymn and sent copies to every church leader they knew in more than twenty countries. They, in turn, made copies and mailed them to others.

Nasief remarked one day that a love ballad had become the uniting song of the French resistance movement during the Hitler days. "It was a sentimental ballad called 'Lilli Marlene,' but because the Nazis forbade them to sing it, it became a rallying message for those who refused to submit to tyranny." That stirred the couple to compose a hymn to unite all followers of Aryeh.

Along the riverbank the four pastors and their converts sang the forbidden words. Marvin Simmons, decorated commander of the troop, willing to allow this indiscretion, hoped nothing worse would happen. However, the next movement incensed him.

All eighty-seven converts, wearing white robes with the required SSS bands of their designated color, received baptism. In one long line, they stood before the watching congregation, the soldiers, and onlookers and sang "Storm the Palace of Darkness." At the beginning of the second stanza, the senior pastor raised his hands over his head.

Immediately, and in choreographed motions, all eighty-seven touched the band with their left hand as they sang the first measure. On the next measure they pulled the band loose. On the third they held the cloth high in the air above their heads. As their voices reached a crescendo with the final line, "Storm the palace of darkness," each released the cloth and it fell into the river.

As soon as it touched the water, each person grabbed the wet cloth, rolled it into a ball and threw it backward over their shoulder. They made a precise left face and marched toward the shore.

Captain Simmons screamed, "Fire! Kill them! Every one of them!"

His men, all carefully selected Caucasians, did not hesitate. Their shots rang out. The new converts of the Aryeh congregation, foreseeing it might happen, remained in orderly file and fell only when they could no longer stand. One of the pastors with four streams of blood flowing down his white robe started the hymn once again. They sang over the barrage of the repeated firing.

It was over within two minutes. The dead bodies lay in the muddy river. None of the onlookers moved. To do so, they knew, would seal their own deaths.

Fourteen-year-old Dan Rosenberry had received his

blue SSS band in school a year earlier. He had not only worn it with pride, but frequently sang, "The future belongs to us."

He was also a member of the Aryeh congregation. He had argued many times saying that one could be a true follower of Aryeh and be loyal to the SSS.

As he watched, horror filled his mind. His father had been right. It was a choice of Aryeh or Therion and the SSS. He turned around and saw his father standing behind a grove of willow trees. Because of his refusal to join the SSS, his father constantly faced the risk of being discovered and dragged off to prison.

Revulsion filled Dan's heart. He tore the now-hated band from his arm and waved it at his father. None of the soldiers witnessed his action.

He stepped toward the river and did not look back. He heard the voices of the soldiers asking their commander what they should do. Dan felt a pang of fear trying to cripple him, but he went forward anyway. As his feet touched the water, an infusion of courage and peace strengthened him.

He walked over to the body of his pastor who lay face-down at the edge of the water. He knelt down and with his SSS band wiped the blood from the dead man's face. He turned toward the crowd. Everyone was watching him.

"I am only a boy. I do not understand much of what goes on here and elsewhere. I have been a faithful member of the SSS and argued many times with my father. I wanted to believe in Strength, Solidarity, and Salvation. I wanted to uphold these principles because I believed they were right.

"Today I came here confused, unsure. I prayed for Aryeh to show me the truth and to give me the courage to obey, no matter what." He held his cloth high above his head. "Now I know the truth."

He dropped the blood-streaked blue band. A light breeze made it flutter before it struck the water of the Chattahoochie. He bent down and wadded it into a ball and tossed it over his shoulder.

His face creased with a beatific smile as he raised his hands high. "I have found true peace."

Dan backed up a few steps and clasped the limp hands of his pastor on one side and the lifeless hand of a woman on the other. He stared at the commanding officer of the soldiers. "I know that you follow orders, that you must do what you must. I also must do what I must do. But I forgive you for your wrongdoing toward me and my friends."

He bowed his head for a moment and when he lifted it, he started to sing in a strong, melodic tone, "Storm the palace of darkness . . ."

"Fire! Fire! Fire!" screamed Captain Simmons.

Three soldiers responded. All of them hit Dan. Several uniformed men gaped in unbelief.

"He was only a boy!" whispered one soldier.

"He was our enemy!" Captain Simmons walked in front of his men and shook his head. "No one can defy the laws of the state and remain unpunished. If I command you to fire, you must fire, or I shall have you shot as well!"

He wanted to point out that they had killed only blacks. They should be grateful for the opportunity. Instead, he walked to the far side. He was ready to dismiss his troops.

From the corner of his eyes, he saw a black man coming down from behind a clump of trees. He wore no SSS band. The commander hesitated. They had already killed so many and he knew this crazy fool was going to go down to the water. He wanted to plead with him, Go back! Go back!

He faced the newcomer, and their eyes met momentarily. The black man broke into a run and did not stop until he reached Dan. "This is my son. I tried to teach him the way of Aryeh. Today he taught me a lesson in courage . . . and faith." He picked up the inert form and held him out as if to offer him to the people.

"Dan made his choice today for Aryeh. They have killed him. They will kill me also. But I am not afraid. I remember the words of our Lord who told us not to fear those who could destroy our bodies. I do not fear. I stand before you and proclaim to you that with my last breath I have chosen to give myself only to Aryeh!"

He took a deep breath and then shouted, "Storm the palace of darkness . . ."

Before the commander collected his wits to give the command to fire, four spectators arose and walked to the shore. One elderly woman moved slowly with her walker, almost fell twice on the muddy shore, but kept going.

". . . Pull down Therion's kingdom . . ."

Another handful of people filed down behind a father. Four of them were children.

A soldier dropped his rifle and grabbed the two children. "No! No! Come back and I'll take care of you."

The boy, who looked about eight years old, said, "You think because I'm black or that I'm little I don't understand. I would rather die with them than to live with people like you who shoot and kill with your guns." He jerked his arm away.

Another child, a girl of about the same age, said, "I think you want to help, but you are not helping." She walked ahead.

The commander, struggling for composure, screamed, "Fire! Kill every one of them!"

The soldiers stood as if they did not hear. One by one those who sat on the banks and had watched the massacre rose to their feet and turned toward the crooked path. As if following a signal, they walked toward the water's edge. Each one went through the ritual they had seen earlier.

> ". . . where'er he holds dominion.
> Storm the palace of darkness . . ."

A woman with a lyric soprano voice started the second stanza of the human and others joined her. At the chorus, everyone sang boldly.

"Don't you hear my command? Fire! Kill them!"

The soldiers stared at each other, confusion overwhelming them; they appeared mesmerized by the singing. They heard their leader barking commands, but his words did not penetrate their consciousness.

The officer grabbed the rifle from the nearest man. He pressed it against his chest and fired. The impact knocked the soldier backward in death.

"Who is next? I am ready to kill everyone if you do not do as I command!"

The soldier who had tried to grab the two children threw his rifle to the commander. Saying nothing he raced to the water. He grabbed the two children's hands. "Please, I've never been a very good man, but I want to be one. Will you let me stand with you?"

"Sir," the girl said, "Aryeh accepts anyone. Aryeh loves us all." She squeezed his hand. "Sing with us. This is your song, too."

The solider's eyes had filled with tears so that he hardly saw anything for a few seconds. He let go of the boy's hand long enough to wipe his eyes. In that moment, he smiled at the dozen of his fellow soldiers who marched or raced into the river. Those already in the water reached for the new-comers and they clasped hands.

The black followers of Aryeh moved aside, making space for the soldiers. "Welcome!"

"Won't you stand by me?" someone asked.

Captain Simmons shot two soldiers after they dropped their rifles. His wild gaze moved from the river back to his men. In stark horror, he saw that only three still remained with him—the three who had fired upon Dan.

No one remained on the bank. Aside from the four military people, everyone stood waist-deep in the water. Simmons watched as they joined hands and sang the chorus one more time.

"Kill every one of them!" he barked.

The three soldiers began to fire, picking them off one at a time. As soon as one gun ran out of ammunition, the soldier picked up a discarded gun of his former comrade.

It took another twenty minutes before they fired the

last bullet. Because he was a soldier and a commander of troops, Captain Simmons demanded an accurate body count. The three men counted twice.

Aware that some bodies had already floated downriver, they counted 247 bodies present.

As the commander marched his loyal troops toward the four trucks they had come in, he could not erase the scene from his mind. He was not a religious man. He had rejected the faith of his parents when he was a boy. Now, middle-aged and wearied with life, Marvin Simmons wondered what he would have done if he had been a follower of Aryeh.

I shall never know, he told himself.

That evening when darkness fell, twenty people met for worship at the Community Church of Aryeh in Norcross, an Atlanta suburb. They came to hold a memorial service for their fallen comrades.

They knew they endangered themselves by congregating. The eighty-seven converts and four pastors came from that church. They assumed that the SSS knew of their meeting, as they always did. The SSS also had their names and addresses on file.

They knelt in the chancel area and began by singing softly "Amazing Grace," and without pausing a voice would lead them into another hymn. They did not hear the front door open.

Captain Marvin Simmons tiptoed up to the building and stepped inside without anyone's awareness of his presence. Tonight he carried a fully loaded submachine gun. He moved his weapon into the firing position.

A new hymn started, "What a Friend We Have in Jesus." Simmons had not heard that since childhood—a favorite hymn of his parents.

An elderly man turned then and smiled at Captain Simmons. "If you have come to worship, we welcome you.

If you have come to ridicule us, we cannot stop you. If you have come to kill us, we are ready."

The others, now aware of Simmons' presence, stared at him. He expected to see fear written across their faces. They smiled at him—the smiles of compassion and kindness. They smiled as if he had come to worship with them. None of them showed fear over the weapon he gripped.

Simmons moved his finger to the trigger, but he did not fire.

The older man reached for a hand to help him stand. When he got to his feet, he said, "Children of Aryeh, we have a commander of the SSS here. A captain, I believe."

Simmons nodded.

"Captain, we are going to stand before you. We are going to sing again of the peace and happiness that Aryeh gives us—even in the moment of death."

The old man's gaze moved among the members present with him. When their eyes met, each nodded as if to say, "We are ready."

"Harris," he said and nodded to a man who then picked up a violin.

The young man played a few measures and put down his instrument. "I prefer to sing with you." He cleared his throat and began, "Storm the palace of darkness . . ."

The others joined him. They formed a line by linking arms.

The commander stared but said nothing. He rested his hand on his submachine gun. He knew his duty. His superiors would decorate him for his heroism, and he would likely receive a promotion.

He waited in silence until they sang their rallying song. He pointed his gun, ready to fire, when the young violinist again picked up the instrument and played, "What a Friend We Have in Jesus."

Before he had finished the first bar, the others started to sing. Their arms still linked, they looked upward. Marvin Simmons saw a glow of happiness on their faces he could not understand.

*They face death and they sing! They're waiting for me
to pull the trigger and yet they show this—this serenity.*

> . . . Do thy friends despise, forsake thee? . . .
> Take it to the Lord in prayer!
> In his arms he'll take and shield thee,
> Thou wilt find a solace there.

Hearing them sing that final stanza felt like a knife plunged into Marvin Simmons' heart. He closed his eyes momentarily and saw his parents sitting in church on either side of him, singing with vigor.

Hardly aware of what he was doing, Marvin Simmons dropped his submachine gun, and the worshippers heard the crash as it struck the floor. He walked toward the old man who had spoken to him when he came in.

"May I—can I—?"

"Welcome," the old man said. "There is joy in Heaven right now for what you are doing."

"Help me," he mumbled. "Help me. I have—I have killed many of you good people."

"What you have done in the past is over. When you come to Aryeh, your past is gone. You are clean like a newborn infant."

The violinist played a stanza on his instrument, and the people listened. When he started a new stanza, their voices rang with impassioned zeal. None of them sang more forcefully than the commander.

N·I·N·E

The first earthquake in California caused no great alarm, although it covered a larger area than any previously recorded quakes. In an area used to such natural disasters, even a rating of 6.5 on the Richter scale did not unduly disturb residents of the Big Sur. Estimated damages ranged in the area of $85 billion.

A second quake followed hours later. The entire area from Palo Alto to Foster City disappeared from off the map. That evening people noticed a mud-and-soil slide beginning along Southern California's Pacific coast.

By morning seventeen inches of coastline had disappeared into the sea. The next day saw the loss of double that amount. By then residents along the coast tried to bolster up the shore to prevent further loss.

Nothing they did made any difference. Despite the technology and the best scientific evidence, California lost a strip of oceanfront more than two miles wide. It simply slid into the sea, taking everything and everybody with it.

Thirty days later, a similarly powerful earthquake shook Japan. World media focused on the immediate effects such as the loss of 4,500 lives and millions of dollars in property. Two days after the quake, Kyushu, the southern-most of the four major islands of Japan, disappeared within a period of twelve minutes. Occupants of the island sent out word that a tidal wave had struck. A photojournalist, riding in a helicopter above the city of Nagasaki, snapped startling film that showed the occurrence. No tidal wave struck. The land simply fell as if the foundation gave way and the water rose.

"It's like watching the bathtub when it's already full and you can't pull the plug," one expert said. "The water level continues to rise because nothing's going out."

Across the Soviet Union and throughout the northern portions of eastern Europe, experts detected a high radiation level. "Another Chernobyl?" asked French newspaper head-lines.

Russian experts, aided by the top nuclear scientists in their part of the world, could find no cause for the high radiation levels.

State officials banned the further use of milk or dairy products, but the high levels had already been ingested by millions. Without exception, every newborn above the thir-ty-eighth parallel suffered severe birth defects. On the basis of government orders, doctors, nurses, and midwives al-lowed none of them to live.

The same high radiation levels appeared over most of the South American continent. In examining domesticated animals, they discovered toxic levels of radiation, and an immediate order went out to kill all cats, dogs, and farm animals. Argentina, the worst province affected, lost 54 per-cent of its human population and 99 percent of its farm animals.

Across China, Nepal, Pakistan, and India a previously unrecorded disease broke out. It became known as the Rice Plague because it affected only people who subsisted primar-ily on rice. In other areas where it struck, such as Saudia Arabia, Iran, Iraq, and Libya, they termed it the Black Foot Death.

Those infected noticed that one day the soles of their feet turned black. Within hours they lost all feeling in the bottom of their feet and their hands. Soon afterwards the disease struck their lungs, filling them with fluid. At that point they could no longer breathe, and they died. Most victims succumbed within two days; no one lived more than five.

Bodies piled up in the streets and along country roads. Nobody made any effort either to bury or to burn them. Most people stayed away from other human contact.

A stomach virus broke out among the soldiers who surrounded Israel's northwestern boundaries, felling 400 soldiers on a Tuesday morning. By nightfall, all of them suffered from some symptom such as internal bleeding, weakness, low-grade fever, or a slight case of vertigo. Two deaths occurred the first week.

The virus did not go away, but moved from platoon to platoon. Frolov, who monitored the reports and passed them to Jullu, said, "We can predict where it's going next, but we have no idea what to do about it. It moves from one army to the next, even when they have no direct contact."

It took three weeks to affect the entire army. By the end of the three weeks, a second attack began with those first afflicted. Although the effects were not much worse, they had not recovered their strength.

At first Speaks thought his soldiers were immune from the affliction, only to have it cross the lines and strike his personnel. If this virus followed its previous course, Speaks had a four-week lead on the other side before his own troops would be worthless to fight.

The armies had agreed that on October 7 they would formally begin to fight each other. They would not destroy anything in Israel if possible. Since most of the malgamite came from the Negev region, they carefully avoided any skirmishes in that area.

In preparation for the great battles, armies practiced military maneuvers. In Israel the citizens became used to the sounds of firing in the background. It often lasted days without a letup. The gun blasts became so frequent in such a small area that one reporter admitted, "If you have any pictures of Lebanon, I hope you will remember what it used to look like. Nothing will be left but holes and pits after this war."

Egypt and Saudi Arabia, the only two Arab nations that had remained with the western forces, received the worst bombings and shellings, all done while the troops underwent target practice. A reporter said, "I have not seen a single tree, shrub, or plant in twelve days of travel. Temperatures have risen to 87 degrees during the day and they drop to sub-freezing at night. Never have we known such strange weather."

In Israel, King Joshua continued making regular telecasts to the nations. By use of satellite, the messages went to the rest of the world.

"The world's forces are at our borders. The warmongering leaders are intent upon self-destruction. They have no concern for the earth. Each intends to wipe out the other. In the process they shall only destroy themselves.

"Peoples of the world, I implore you to stop this madness. Your leaders have entered into a war they cannot possibly win. If they continue, they will not only destroy each other, but the rest of our world."

This speech, which lasted fifty-three minutes, outlined the destructive policies and condemned those in power on both sides. He concluded with these words:

"I have advocated only peace—peace for all nations and for all peoples. I have avoided entering into the conflicts between nations. Israel and Israel alone has maintained neutrality.

"This neutral stance will continue no longer. I now appeal, not to leaders, not to royalty, not to the prominent, but to the common people, those of you at home around the world. I can save you from world destruction. I and only I can destroy and defeat those who have waged war and carelessly disregarded human lives.

"If I have your loyal support, I promise you that I, Joshua Gad-Erianko, King of Israel, will use power I have never shown before. I have received supernatural powers given to me for the good of the world. I shall use these powers only for good and will save you and our world.

"If you will protest the war and the killing, the destruction and desolation, I promise you that within three days I shall stop the diseases and earthquakes now afflicting our world."

A stunned world listened to the last portion of his speech. Virtually every television and radio station on earth played and replayed the speech.

In New Delhi the first protest against Frolov and Jullu began. In Lesotho, Africa, every physically able inhabitant took to the streets and demanded Jullu's resignation. Other cities followed their example.

In Rome, Brasilia, Chicago, and Montreal protesters demanded not just the resignation of John Speaks, but offered a million dollars for anyone who killed him. Their boldness sparked other cities. By the second day, the common people had raised a reward of $20 million for the death of John Speaks.

Desertions from all armies began. Hundreds of soldiers dropped their guns and raced from the battlefield. In some instances, they ran to the other side to surrender. Mostly they ran from all military installations and battle stations. Mutinies occurred on most ships. All levels of personnel from admirals and captains to the lowest seamen participated. They wanted only to get away from the ravages of war.

In Jerusalem, Joshua did not listen to the reports. He had planned each strategy carefully, and he derived no particular pleasure in hearing after-the-fact reports. He had worked it out so expertly, it involved no suspense.

He stared at his watch and quickly converted to London time. He would have to wait only three hours for the next event. This was the crucial one. He would read those reports.

When the first messages came from London, he read them and smiled. The first of a handful of bulletins came from the BBC and the reporter said:

"King Joshua has referred to unleashed supernatural

powers at his disposal. He has shown over the past four years that he is more than the King of a small nation. He is the symbol of what is good and right about our world.

"By all means, let's turn to him. No one else has anything to offer but platitudes and mottos to keep a stiff upper lip. We are living in a time of great desperation. We urge the rest of the world to appeal to King Joshua: 'Save us, King Joshua. We are no longer too proud to beg for your help.'

"If King Joshua can save the world, as he says, we ought to fall down and worship him as Joshua, our God."

Joshua smiled. This was the great moment in history for which he had planned nearly fifty years earlier.

"Today I fulfill my destiny," he said.

T·E·N

"I don't expect to see you alive again," Nasief said as his eyes moved slowly from Shaheen's face to Nagila's. He wanted to imprint the memory of their faces for the next few days that lay ahead of him.

"You're looking better than you have in years," Shaheen said.

"A remarkable recovery since that terrible beating," Nagila added. "You look like you could live another fifty years."

"I want you to understand what I mean," Nasief said. "I am going to die. This week. That's all that I know."

"Old friend," Shaheen said, "do not talk that way—"

"I must tell you that today is the last time I expect to see either of you alive again."

"Oh, Nasief—" Nagila said and choked back the tears.

The old man laid his hand on hers. "My time has come. I have finished my work here and I am ready to leave."

"You are sure?" Shaheen asked.

He nodded. "I have waited a long time for this moment, as you know, Shaheen. I am ready. It will happen soon. Today, tomorrow. Soon is all I know."

Shaheen and Nagila, aware of the gravity of his words, sat in stunned silence. For the predicted Last Day finally to come so overwhelmed their minds they staggered at what this information meant.

"I have finished the work Aryeh gave me, but both of you still have many things you must do. I cannot tell you precisely your roles. I can tell you that Aryeh will guide you."

"I have never had any kind of guidance," Nagila said and laughed self-consciously. "I've heard you and others talk about it. I've always assumed I didn't have the capacity for direct communication—"

"You will receive it. Soon. I promise you."

"But what? How?"

The old man struggled inwardly, not certain how much to say to them. Finally, he sighed. "All right. Last night I had a dream in which the clouds of Heaven opened. I saw Aryeh himself sitting on a throne of pure ivory, with thousands of angels surrounding him. The most beautiful music the human ear has ever known filled the air."

The couple instinctively held hands, focusing their attention on the older man. Nasief took on a glow and his features became ageless.

"Never had I had such a dream in my life. Never has a dream been so real as that one."

"It must have been an overwhelming experience," Shaheen said.

"But I don't see how you understand from that dream that you'll die and that God will show us what to do."

"I shall tell you the entire dream," he said.

Nasief's Dream

I stood near the wailing wall and I heard a voice say, "Nasief! Come!" I looked around, but I could not see who called my name. Then billowy clouds floated down from the sky and surrounded me, and my body started to rise. I had no fear, only a sense of deep peace. The clouds stopped suddenly and parted. I looked around and saw that I was standing in space above Jerusalem, and I could see the rest of the world at the same time. Angels sang hymns of praise for a long time. They stopped abruptly. The music moved me deeply and I started to cry.

"Why are you crying, Nasief?" a deep, kind voice called to me. "You have no need for tears now."

"Because I have heard nothing so beautiful in my life and now it has stopped."

"Come closer."

I saw the figure clearly on the throne and arcs of light emanating as if they outshone every diamond in the world. I closed my eyes because of the brightness and I fell to my knees.

"You have done well, Nasief," he said. "You have endured. You have done what I required of you. The Last Day has come to earth and I am ready for you to be with me here."

I felt as if I needed never to speak again. The One upon the throne knew every thought before I knew it myself. Then I thought of my failure and the many times I had not lived up to what I knew was right. I fell prostrate, and as I lay on the ground I felt as if I were suspended in air. I could think of nothing else but my failures. I wept loudly and I couldn't staunch my tears.

"No tears here," he said. His hand touched my head, and a warm light went through my entire body. My tears stopped and I couldn't remember why I cried. I tried to think of my failures, but the light had erased them from my memory.

"How is this possible?" I asked and looked at him.

"All things are possible with me," he said.

I kept trying to peer at his face, but his eyes shone with such brilliance I found it impossible. At the same time, I felt loved. *He understands me. He loves me completely.*

"That way, Nasief." He pointed and I saw an ornate oak door, inset with rubies and diamonds. "You are wearied from your struggle. Rest now."

I got up and walked toward the door. Angels flew around me and sang again the songs of peace and joy. Just as I reached the door, I remembered the terrible things still happening on earth. I paused and turned around. "I want to stay with you, but so much remains undone."

"I have other workers. You trained them well. Shaheen and Nagila will carry on for a little while. When they have done what I have called them to do, they will join you."

Joshua sat on the recently constructed throne of ivory and gold, facing the Knesset. "I have one piece of legislation for you to pass. Leaders from around the world are presenting similar measures to their legislative branches. Since we began the SSS, we have had splendid results, but not perfect. These perfect results will come about only when every person accepts the basic tenets of the SSS."

Joshua spoke for another fourteen minutes, reiterating the principles of SSS to the Knesset. The richness of his voice and the charisma of his personality destroyed any resistance. Once satisfied that he had them totally with him, Joshua came to the real purpose of the meeting.

"I want it enacted as a law that anyone who refuses to wear the SSS emblem will be put to death. Immediately. Any citizen will have the right—the duty—to execute any person who refuses to show allegiance to the government by the wearing of the Triple S emblem. We will not tolerate the use of tax money for trials and appeals. These people are troublemakers. They threaten peace and unity on the earth.

"It also comes to my attention that the single largest resistance to SSS are the people who call themselves followers of Aryeh. When they disappear from the earth, then will come peace, prosperity, and unity. As part of this legislation, I want the death penalty for anyone who professes faith in Aryeh."

Joshua stood, nodded to the assembled members, and left the Knesset. He did not need to stay. He knew exactly what they would do. A few would debate the issue only because they wanted to speak. They would vote unanimously for its passage. Joshua knew that the same legislation, no matter how they worded it, would pass in every other country in the world.

Joshua felt a keen sense of elation. He was at the apex of his career. By noon tomorrow he would reach the goal for which he had planned since his boyhood in Russia.

One hour later, with TV cameras set up, King Joshua captured the world's attention.

"I am now able to tell you great news. The earthquakes in California have ceased and will not return. The Black-Foot death will claim no more victims from this moment forward. Those still alive and afflicted will be perfectly well and strong within twenty-four hours. None of the death-causing viruses will claim more lives after today.

"From now on, deaths will result from murder or accidents. I can now inform you that a scientific research branch here in Jerusalem has perfected an antiaging serum.

"We have tested it on animals and on humans. It has no adverse effects or contradictions. This serum, known as SSS-J, will prolong the human life span. Most of you will live to be at least 150 without infirmities. We have prepared sufficient quantity to inoculate every law-abiding citizen.

"Even as I speak, our laboratory is preparing to ship these vials to every nation in the world. I have arranged with cooperating countries for 200 centers across the world to open today. Governments have already received instructions on how to do this in an orderly fashion.

"This serum is for every citizen of the world. Loyal citizens have only to appear at designated places, produce their passports with the SSS stamp, and receive their injections. It requires one injection now and a follow-up injection after two years.

"Despite the blockades around our nation, I have appealed to the military and government personnel of the world to allow the exportation of SSS-J to all nations. They have assured me that they will not prevent the exportation of SSS-J. Soldiers on the field in and around Israel will receive their inoculations as well.

"I have had this antiaging agent perfected because of my love for every citizen of the world. This goes far beyond border disputes or concerns over the control of natural resources."

Gideon Wittstein had known Nasief Habib for years. He had not liked the teacher, although he had always respected the man's integrity. But, he reminded himself, it did not matter how he felt about Nasief. He had a task to perform.

Two of Gideon's assistants attended Nasief's classes for a week. They sat in a prominent position so that Nasief would recognize them. The teacher knew they worked for Weinstett.

At the end of the week, they lingered after the meeting to talk to the old man. "Our superior would like to have a private appointment with you," he said. "We have told him everything you have taught."

"We think he wishes to convert," said the second. "He certainly listens with eagerness when we tell him about your classes."

"I am ready to meet with Gideon at any time and anywhere he wishes. But," he said, staring directly at them, "you are up to no good. You sit and you listen, but nothing penetrates the hard protection over your hearts, does it?"

"I believe you. I believe everything you say," the first one said.

"You do? And what about you?" he asked the second man.

"I won't lie to you," the second one said. "I don't believe your teaching. I think you're a good man. You teach what you're convinced is right, but you're wrong."

Nasief nodded. "I can confront honest disbelief better than outright lies." He laid his hand on the man's shoulder. "You are closer to the kingdom of Aryeh than you realize."

"Mr. Wittstein would like to meet you in front of the Wailing Wall. Tonight. Midnight?"

Nasief arrived at the Wall a few minutes early and walked slowly back and forth. Although the wall was well-lighted, no one came there at this time of night. He thought of the millions of prayers of honest and honorable people through the years.

Nasief heard footsteps behind him, and he turned to face Gideon Wittstein and his two assistants. He walked toward them.

"Hello, Nasief," Gideon said. "It has been a long time."

Nasief extended his hand, but Gideon ignored it. "As you like," Nasief said.

"I asked you here to warn you," he said. "Joshua wants you dead. He's determined that you won't live to see another sunrise."

"And you, Gideon? Do you also want me to die?"

"I want you to go with me where I can keep you safe. For a while. I have a car down the street—"

Nasief shook his head slowly. "No hypocrisy, Gideon. You want to kill me. Why should it matter if you do it here or in some far-off place? Do what you have to do. I'm ready."

"Who warned you?" Gideon asked and stepped closer.

"You would not believe if I told you."

"One of these two men?"

The two associates began to protest their loyalty and Nasief interrupted. "Neither of them. And does it matter? I've done nothing to protect myself."

"If you are ready to die," Gideon said, "I can think of no good reason why it should not be done here." He had been standing with this hands in his pockets. He pulled out a .25-caliber Baretta, holding the small gun in the palm of his hand. He checked the clip and pointed it toward Nasief. "Not a powerful weapon, but sufficient, I think."

Nasief looked upward at the sky. With the full moon

he could see the cumulus clouds stretching lazily across the horizon. He felt at peace. "I am not afraid, Gideon. I am ready."

Immediately after the telecast announcing the antiaging serum, Joshua received the three leaders, Speaks, Jullu, and Frolov, at the palace.

"You planned it this way," Speaks yelled as soon as Joshua came into the room. "You deliberately planned for us to weaken and to kill off each other. I can't even go home. Millions of people are waiting to kill me."

"Is that how you see it?" Joshua said.

"Now I understand why they call you Therion," Jullu said.

"And you would have done the same thing."

"Any of the three of us would have," Jullu said. "That is why we are here. You are no better and no worse than we—"

"Only more talented," said Vitali Frolov. "Perhaps you are a little more cunning as well."

"Finally we understand each other. Now I am ready for the final phase of my plan. And it does include you—all ten leaders, of which you three will be the most prominent." He paused and gazed directly at Speaks. "Have no further concern about those who seek your death. In a few days, they will praise your heroism and gallantry."

Speaks nodded and managed to mumble, "Thanks." His eyes, however, burned with hatred.

"I played my little game because you must realize how little it will take for me to destroy any of you. I hold the power—the total power—and you must understand that."

"Of course we do," Frolov said. "We are ready to do whatever you say. We cannot fight against you."

"Excellent," Joshua said. "First, both armies will choose to withdraw. You must do this anyway because of the heavy desertions—"

"Anything about us that you don't know?" Speaks asked.

"Nothing." He focused on Speaks. "That also means that when you think you are ready to plot against me I will know before you have put the first step into action."

Speaks rocked in his chair, laughing. "I think I can work under you after all."

"You have no choice." His eyes moved from one to the other. "Many years ago I chose all ten of you, but especially the three of you. You have no scruples. Nothing is beyond you. You are exactly the kind of people I want."

Joshua outlined for them his next and final action. He would become worshiped as Joshua, the eternal god. He explained that he had already begun to implement the move toward his recognition as being superior to other human beings.

"I am superior, you know," Joshua said simply. "I have resources of which you do not know. I have an empowerment, a wisdom that transcends that of others."

Frolov said, "Coming from anyone else it would sound like idle boasting, but from you—"

Joshua held up his hand to silence Frolov. "I do not need your flattery. The sooner you resort to your true behavior, the easier we work together. You have been selected because of your ruthlessness. Understood?"

"Yes," he answered.

"Excellent. You three must first do one thing for me. You must fully, totally, and completely wipe out this religion of Aryeh."

"And then?" asked Baya Marach Jullu.

"By then I shall be exalted to my rightful place. You will function as my three Regents, with the other seven immediately below you in authority. We shall rule this world for at least a thousand years."

"A thousand—?"

"Precisely. My personal scientific researchers have perfected a more powerful serum, called SSS-JK. Injections of this serum guarantee unlimited life. When taken properly it is completely antiaging. Once you begin your injections, you will never look or feel any older than you are on the day your first receive it."

The three leaders, not used to showing their true feelings, beamed in both amazement and pleasure.

"That explains your agelessness," Baya Marach Jullu said. "You have not aged a year since I first saw you on television ten years ago."

Ignoring her remark, Joshua said, "I restrict the use of this serum. I keep it safely under my personal control. You must come here to Jerusalem to receive your annual injection. Only the three of you. No one else."

"Our wives?" Speaks asked. "And our children—?"

"Are expendable. You will have fifty wives, a hundred—"

"Ah, yes," Jullu said. "You do know our true natures. You know that with only a small regret, we can walk away from our present families."

At that moment, Speaks's devious mind began its first steps toward wresting control of the formula. He would never need Joshua again.

E·L·E·V·E·N

On May 14, 2008, King Joshua stood on top of the Mount of Olives. Dignitaries from around the world attended the elaborate ceremony. The seven lesser world leaders, wearing robes of silk trimmed in silver, sat on ornate chairs made especially for the occasion.

Above them sat the three World Regents. Each wore a robe of silk trimmed with gold. On each head rested a crown of a special alloy that was both strong but lightweight. The crowns contained a diamond at the center point.

In a final tier above them, the crowd awaited the presence of Joshua. With TV cameras poised, the 120-piece orchestra began to play a new hymn written in honor of Joshua. The words flashed across a screen so that everyone could sing:

> Gracious Master Joshua, ruler of all nature.
> Great one of God, yet human still.
> You do we worship, you do we cherish,
> To none else do we bend our will.

Joshua walked the length of the newly constructed pavilion and up the steps to the throne. Constructed of forty-two types of hardwood, all two inches wide with no nails or glue used, it had a simplicity that made the chairs below appear gaudy. He wore no crown, but an attendant handed him a brass scepter. Joshua held it high as he sat down.

At that moment, all those present bowed their heads.

"True God!"

"The Only God!"

"The only one worthy of worship!"

"The Eternal One!"

Joshua sat quietly and listened to the outbursts of praise directed at him. This, he said to himself, is the moment for which my whole life has come into being. This is the moment for which everything has come to pass.

As the hymns of praise continued, Joshua found one thought disturbing him. Shaheen and Nagila were together. They loved each other. Nagila had rejected him, had rejected all of this. She could have sat on a throne next to him for a thousand years.

Joshua's pulse raced. He would never be happy, he realized, with Shaheen alive. He must destroy that man. Yet he did not want him to have an easy death.

And Nagila? He felt nothing but hatred toward her now. He wondered how he could ever have wanted her. He did not need Nagila. He needed no one for anything.

Joshua was king.

Joshua was divine.

T·W·E·L·V·E

Nagila and Shaheen, along with forty followers of Aryeh, gathered outside old Jerusalem near the Kidron brook. They held a memorial service for Nasief.

He had disappeared the day he spoke with them, and they never saw him alive again. They heard rumors that Gideon Wittstein had either killed him or had him killed. They also heard that Gideon had completely destroyed Nasief's body so that the followers of Aryeh would not display it and make a martyr of the man.

On that fateful night, Gideon had played his charade to the end. He held a scarf with his left hand and the Baretta in his right. "Choose."

"I made my choice long ago."

"You know the law. If you refuse to wear this, we can kill you. It is our duty to kill you."

"You must do what you must do," the old man said. He fell on his knees and started to pray silently.

"You think God will answer your prayers and send someone to save you?"

"No one will stop you, Gideon. I want you to know

that I bear no evil thoughts toward you. I wish only that you could understand the love and the peace I have known from following Aryeh."

Gideon flew into a rage. He tossed the Baretta to one of his assistants and grabbed the Czech-made machine gun from the hand of the other. Using the butt, he knocked Nasief to the ground. Gideon then pushed the trigger and riddled Nasief's body from head to foot.

"We have one problem," John Speaks said to Joshua by phone. "We have arrested thousands of these Aryeh people, and most of them have died instead of renouncing their beliefs."

"Then what is the problem?"

"These Aryeh people come from noplace. When my men kill them, often those who executed them end up joining the Aryeh people. If they don't join, they complain that their crimes torment them and they can't sleep. Within days of any major executions, the members of SSS help to form new groups of Aryeh worshipers. I can't understand this."

"Exterminate them! Every one of them! Allow none of them to speak and to spread their poison. It is not their deaths that cause the contagion. It is their words."

"I propose an idea," Speaks said. "Suppose we issue a universal order. On June 30, every follower of Aryeh must come to a central place. Our governments will provide free transportation. Once they are in one place, we can exterminate them all at one time."

"Yes," Joshua said, "an excellent idea. They must come here to Jerusalem. This is their holy city. We shall allow them to gather at the Mount of Olives."

"Where they recognize your *divinity?*" Speaks sneered as he pronounced the last word. "Do you think that wise?"

"You choose to question me now?"

"Certainly not. Just asking." Speaks felt the perspiration breaking out all over his bulky body. He carefully obeyed, choosing to wait his time because he had already determined that one day he would destroy this man.

Joshua had uncovered Speaks's past, a past Speaks thought he had covered well. Since King Joshua had declared himself a god, he had made it clear that Speaks ruled only as long as it pleased him. For the first time in his long rise to fame and power, Speaks developed a morbid fear of being eliminated. Joshua only had to refuse to give him injections of the antiaging serum. He could set one of Speaks's rivals against him. One of his own assistants might assassinate him.

"I apologize," Speaks said. "I did not mean—"

"On the contrary, you did. I understand your hatred for me, Speaks. That is what makes you useful."

Speaks, eager to change the subject, asked, "If you issue an order that calls them to Jerusalem, will they come? They know how you hate them."

"Your job is to see that every follower of Aryeh comes to Israel. Offer them any inducement. They'll come. This is where their religious superstition started."

"Of course you can count on me to do my best. I'll figure out something—"

"Tell them anything. Speak of amnesty. Freedom to worship as they choose. *Anything,* providing you get them here."

Joshua hung up the phone. He liked the sound of fear in a man's voice. Even through the long-distance phone call he perceived that Speaks was already conspiring, trying to figure out how to steal the serum. At present he feared Joshua too much to make any attempt. It did not matter. Joshua would be ready for him.

At that moment, Joshua had one thing to take care of before he issued an order for the gathering of the followers of Aryeh. He dialed Gideon's private number.

"I have one more task for you," he said, "and then you shall retire from royal service with immense wealth. You may then live anywhere in the world you wish."

"I'm ready," Gideon said.

Joshua liked the way he could control Gideon. In the beginning he discerned that Gideon's secrets were much less than those of others. As a young man he had roamed across Lebanon with a gang, beating and robbing non-Jews.

With Gideon it had not been his great crimes as much as his potential that intrigued Joshua. This man had an infinite capacity for evil, especially violent evil. The more tasks Joshua gave him, the more Gideon's true nature came to the fore.

The respected former minister of the Knesset, the head of the Taba delegation, the leader in cultural affairs had hidden his true ruthlessness until he came under Joshua's control. Joshua liked to think that he had liberated the man to be his true self.

Shaheen parked his Merkab in the street in front of his eight-story apartment building. He had fitted it with a burglar alarm that went off if anyone tried to force open a door. He had never considered that a professional might want access to his car without stealing it.

In the early hours of the morning, a van pulled up next to Shaheen's Merkab, shielding the vehicle so Shaheen could not see it if he looked down from his apartment.

A woman jumped out of the van, deftly unlocked the door, and shut off the burglar alarm. She methodically released the hood and planted an explosive next to the engine. As soon as the engine heated, the explosive would go off.

In less than two minutes she had closed the car's hood, reset the alarm, locked the car, and drove the van down the street.

The next morning Shaheen got into his car and turned on the key. Nothing happened. He had needed a new battery for weeks, but kept putting off buying a new one. His neighbor, also a follower of Aryeh, had used a jumper cable to get the car started twice before.

Shaheen knocked on his neighbor's door, and the man followed him out. Shaheen promised himself to replace the battery today.

When the neighbor opened the hood, both of them saw the explosive, although it took Shaheen several seconds to figure out what it was.

"Aryeh looks out for us, doesn't he?" the neighbor said.

One of Gideon's men, posted three hundred feet away in his own car, saw them take the explosive from the car. He wondered how Shaheen had known. He drove away and reported to Gideon.

That afternoon Gideon paid an expert to plant a simple bombing device in Shaheen's apartment. The opening of the door pulled a string that held the pin on a grenade-type bomb. It would kill anyone within twenty feet in three seconds.

Unfortunately, the man made one simple mistake. On the way out of the apartment, he accidentally brushed the handle of the deadbolt and it hit the frame when he tried to close the door. He opened the door only far enough to push the bolt back.

The expert had done his work so well that the slight tension pulled the pin. He had gone two steps when the explosion occurred. The wall collapsed on him, and a sharp piece of glass from the chandelier cut through his windpipe.

Joshua heard the report of the two failed attempts. He flew into a rage as Gideon explained what had happened both times.

"Excuses you give me! I want results and you give me more excuses!"

"I'll try it one more time," Gideon said, fear welling up inside of him.

"Another chance to fail?"

"This time I won't fail—"

"But you will! You will! That man! Aryeh must have some kind of protection over him!"

"You believe in that stuff?" Gideon asked. The question had exploded before he realized what he had said.

Joshua glared at him and struck him with his fist. Gideon fell backward and his head hit the wall. He flattened himself against the wall, his eyes opened wide in fear. Joshua struck him a second time, with greater force, and Gideon fell to the floor. Joshua kicked him again and again, as if unable to stop himself. He screamed as he kicked. "How dare you say such a thing! How dare you accuse me of that!"

Long after Gideon died, Joshua kicked his bruised and bleeding frame. He did not stop until exhaustion overcame him. As he walked away from the body, he screamed, "Aryeh, you have protected him this time. The next time I shall have his life!"

Nagila and Shaheen heard the first announcements on television directed to the followers of Aryeh.

Joshua said, "We have now moved into an unending era of peace. In consultation with the ten Regents, we decree that all followers of the religion of Aryeh must register their allegiance to their faith on June 30 of this year in the city of Jerusalem.

"Being governments composed of the people and for the good of the people, we grant total amnesty for any who follow this teaching. After June 30, we shall place no restrictions upon this religion or upon its registered followers. We also grant to them the right to teach their faith without hindrance. We ask their leaders to choose a scarf or other identifiable means to protect them because we will not require them to wear the Triple S."

Joshua's announcement further stated that the one-world government would provide free transportation, lodging, food, and any other expenses incurred.

"This must be a trick. Joshua would never capitulate that easily," Nagila said. "What do we do?"

"We do it anyway," Shaheen said. "And of course it is a trick."

"Our brothers and sisters from the entire world will be

present," Nagila admitted. "What if he calls us all here to—to destroy us?"

"Then that's what he will try to do. And if Aryeh allows it to happen to us, then—"

Nagila shook her head. "I don't know, Shaheen. That seems to me like giving up and saying we'll let Joshua do whatever he wants."

"Has it occurred to you that Aryeh might want this to happen? Could it not also be possible that Aryeh wants all the faithful to gather in one place?"

"Has it occurred to you," she asked, "that Aryeh doesn't want it to happen?"

"Perhaps we both need to think and pray about this," Shaheen said. Minutes later he left Nagila.

Nagila went outside and walked through a small park. *What should I do? What should all of us do?*

"I have planned this to happen," a voice said to Nagila. For a moment she thought it came from outside and then she realized it came from within her own head. Its forcefulness and power made Nagila realize that she had heard Aryeh speak to her. She hurried back inside to tell Shaheen.

"Nasief said I would," she told him. "Nasief said Aryeh would guide me."

After she recounted her experience she said, "I can see that the event could provide us with a wonderful opportunity to encourage each other in our trials."

"Just so we remember that as long as Therion lives, he will work toward destroying us."

Shaheen and Nagila discussed the matter thoroughly before she said, "I know the best way to bring our gathering about. I am going to the palace. I shall personally contact our leaders and urge them to come."

"I'm going with you then."

"Good. I think that hearing from both of us would make the appeal stronger."

Since Nasief's death, the followers of Aryeh across the world informally recognized Shaheen and Nagila as the leaders of their faith. Neither sought such honor or responsibility, but they accepted it because they believed Aryeh had brought it about.

They went immediately to the palace and asked for an audience with Joshua, whom the entire world now called Joshua the Divine. A platoon of soldiers escorted them to Joshua's office.

"I have experienced few surprises in life," Joshua said. "This is one of them."

"We have come regarding the announcement," Nagila said. "We will help you by urging all leaders we know to come."

"Very wise."

"I have one question," Shaheen said. "What is your real purpose in this?"

"I thought the announcement made it clear," Joshua said. "Regent John Speaks came up with the idea—"

"Which you gave him first," Shaheen said.

Joshua felt the same discomfort in his body that he had sensed the time he met with Shaheen in his own bedroom. It had not lessened. He avoided looking directly at the man's face. He went to his desk and said on the intercom, "We shall have tea now. For three."

"Not for us," Nagila said.

"Surely one cup—"

"You make all of this appear so civilized," Shaheen said, "and all the time you have the worst of intentions toward us."

Joshua shrugged. "People change. An old saying from America goes, 'If you can't beat them, join them.' I do not intend to go that far, but I am willing to acknowledge your right to exist."

"Even though we'll continue to speak against your evil doings," Nagila said.

"That is your privilege. Free speech. The right to worship. We offer you all of these."

Joshua felt a pull toward Shaheen as if invisible wires slowly guided his body back to where the other two stood. He put his hands on the desk, clutching the sides. To move closer meant that Shaheen would look into his soul once again and he could not allow that to happen.

"If you do not wish to drink tea with me, I think our business is concluded. You may go to the international news room and make your appeal."

Joshua turned to the window, keeping his back toward them. No longer seeing them eased that magnetic pull, but did not destroy it.

"May Aryeh have mercy on you," Shaheen said.

"Mercy? From Aryeh?" Joshua swore at him. "I need nothing from this God of yours. I am my own God!"

As soon as Nagila and Shaheen left the room, Joshua sank into his chair. His fingers trembled so badly he could not control them. A churning pain erupted in his abdomen and nausea filled his stomach, moving upward toward his throat. He pounded his desk, silently screaming curses on them, on the dead Nasief, and mostly upon Aryeh.

Believers in Aryeh arrived from around the world. Beginning June 27, all airlines into Israel contained only non-SSS passengers. Busses, trains, and private vehicles streamed toward Jerusalem.

By June 29, more than eight million had arrived in Palestine. Hotels accommodated only followers of Aryeh. By order of Joshua the Divine all other business, except essential matters, closed for June 29 and 30. All non-essential service workers evacuated the city to allow for the influx of Aryeh disciples.

Stores, halls, private homes filled with these pilgrims and still they came. Regent John Speaks arranged for temporary housing in the Negev desert and arranged transportation for all of them to converge on Jerusalem the morning of June 30.

From the time the first visitors came, they held continuous worship services throughout the city. Members of the SSS could walk noplace within the environs of Jerusalem where they did not hear "Storm the palace of darkness" or voices lifted vocally in prayer.

By late evening of June 29 it became obvious that the twenty-two million people could not fit into Jerusalem. Speaks flew Nagila Levy by helicopter to the Negev where workers had constructed an amphitheater. Giant temperature-control saucers, placed in strategic areas, kept it a pleasant 74 degrees. TV hookups and mammoth screens provided coverage of both spots so that Nagila and Shaheen could converse.

Speaks announced, "After your morning worship, you will receive forms for new passports. When you turn in the old passports, you will receive new ones within one day. These passports will provide you with unrestricted travel rights. Until you return to your homes, the governments of the Ten Kingdoms will continue to pay all expenses."

Shaheen listened to the words, wanting to believe what Regent Speaks said. Deep within his heart another voice said, You will never need the passports. They'll see to it.

Shaheen would have tried to still that inner voice except he knew it spoke the truth.

T·H·I·R·T·E·E·N

Baya Marach Jullu and Vitoli Frolov examined the stadium, deciding where they would sit the next day. Both of them vied for the spots where the tele-monitors and TV cameras would focus on them most often.

As they left together, Frolov suggested, "A victory celebration. What do you think?"

Jullu thought for a moment before she said, "The followers of Aryeh haven't died yet."

"Can you conceive of any way they will escape?"

"None!"

"Then—"

Baya Marach Jullu agreed quickly. It would give her the opportunity to take care of Frolov. She had expected to wait until after the destruction of Aryeh. She smiled. "Yes, I think a celebration now would be an excellent idea!"

"I've left word for Speaks to join us when he returns this afternoon from the Negev."

"Yes, that makes it even better, I think," Jullu said. She had not expected to have access to both of them so soon. "Yes, a celebration is exactly what we need."

In the chauffeur-driven limousine Frolov and Jullu rode to a house located between Jerusalem and Bethlehem that Joshua provided for their use when they were in town. Not having been to the house before, they hardly knew what to expect. They had stayed in special suites at the luxurious Palace Hotel the previous nights. During that day, someone took their luggage to what Joshua referred to as the "little place."

Frolov approved the drive that made three complete circles around the hill as the road snaked gradually upward. At no point could a car travel toward the house without being observed from above.

The driver parked, jumped out of the car, and opened the door on Baya Marach Jullu's side. He gave her a half-bow, then held out his arms to assist her. Once out, the driver opened the door on the opposite side for Vitoli Frolov.

The two paused for a moment before walking up the steps. As they approached the intricately carved solid oak doors, a servant opened the double doors slowly and stepped back.

"I am Randolph. The staff and I will attempt to provide for every need while you are here." He was a tall, nondescript Oriental. He nodded and backed away two steps.

"We shall explore on our own," Jullu said and dismissed him.

The two guests stepped into a large, marble hall. On the north walls hung two landscapes by Monet that few people knew even existed. A genuine smile lit up Frolov's face. He stared unbelievingly at the masterpieces. He had tried to follow their trail after their theft from the Louvre in 1988. The last evidence pointed to Vienna three years later and he never heard of them again. He assumed they would never surface again.

Frolov reluctantly turned and gasped as his eyes beheld two ornately framed works on the opposite wall. He paused as his practiced eye scrutinized Gauguin's splendid landscapes done during the artist's year in Martinique. Rumors in the art world claimed that the bombings near the end of World War II had destroyed these priceless paintings.

Momentarily he wondered if Joshua knew of his weakness for the Impressionists? He smiled again as he visualized how these lost treasures would look in his own palace, now being built in Moscow.

Jullu scarcely noticed the paintings because of their primitive quality. She stared at the ornate rococo ceiling. Even though Jullu was essentially aesthetically illiterate, the intricate carvings on the high ceiling impressed her.

As the two Regents surveyed the rest of the house, she took note of the inlaid floors, the crystal chandeliers, the long windows that provided an excellent view of a well-kept flower garden.

While Frolov stood mesmerized by the paintings, Jullu browsed through the rest of the main floor. She entered a large living room. At the far side, she noted that four steps led down to a sunken living room, dwarfed by a magnificent fireplace. Beyond that room, she discovered a library with a modest collection of rare books in top condition. Jullu, who knew nothing about art, did know about books. Her long fingers caressed the covers, and she could not resist pulling them from the shelf one at a time.

Jullu not only had a weakness for books, but a special love for the American writers of the first half of the twentieth century. She stared at names like Sinclair Lewis, Pearl S. Buck, and Margaret Mitchell. She gasped in utter delight when her eyes fell upon the collection of John Steinbeck's works. Hardly aware of her action, she snatched *The Grapes of Wrath* from its place and held it against her breast. Her own copy had cost her thousands. Her hand trembled when she pulled out *Of Mice and Men,* which she regarded as Steinbeck's best. Opening it up, she saw that he had scribbled his name in fading-blue ink. The author's early novel *Cup of God* also contained his signature. Baya Marach Jullu almost fainted from the experience. For years she had tried to obtain a first-edition of that book. She knew only four perfect copies still existed, none of them for sale. This was one she did not know about.

Jullu replaced them while her nimble mind figured out then how to carry all of the Steinbeck volumes with her, discreetly hidden among her luggage. A simple rearranging would hide the theft from all but the most astute observer. She had to have them.

When Frolov joined her, Jullu had moved on to the twentieth-century English writers. Frolov nodded at the books and continued walking. She reluctantly left the room with him. Across from the library they found a smaller, more intimate room, each piece of furniture original Queen Anne. As they went up the marbled steps, they saw kitchen, living room, and living quarters for servants. The top floor held three huge bedrooms, each with its own balcony.

They chose the smaller room on the main floor for their celebration. Servants immediately provided a plentiful amount of food and laid it on a table in silver dishes. Both ignored the food, still too excited from the events of the day to think of eating. Another servant wheeled in a portable bar, and the two began their celebration.

Frolov picked up one of the glasses and noted its delicate design and light weight. It was the most beautiful crystal he had ever seen.

"To us! May we live forever!" With her eyes gleaming and her smile wide, Baya Marach Jullu lifted her glass.

"To us! The victors!" Vitoli Frolov raised his drink and the glasses clinked. Frolov, a phlegmatic type, allowed himself the freedom of a full smile that gradually crept into a deep laugh.

"Something is funny?"

"I said 'To the victors' and my parents originally called me Viktor—which I changed before I started to school. But today I can say 'To Viktor.' Or if you like, 'Victory to Viktor.' Don't you think that appropriate?"

"Of course," Jullu said through narrow eyes. "You have earned your victory." In that moment, she sensed that Frolov had not fully satisfied his greed. Then she permitted herself a chuckle. Neither had she.

"To make this more special," Frolov announced, "I have brought a small flask of brandy which I have carried with me just for this special occasion." He took it from his breast pocket and held it up to her. "You will join me? Yes?"

"Of course."

Frolov turned his back on Jullu to pick up the snifters from the lower shelf of the bar. From another pocket, he clasped a small pill and palmed it nicely. From the back Jullu would never notice that he dropped the odorless pill into the glass. It would dissolve within seconds. Frolov filled both glasses halfway to the top, emptying the flask. By the time he faced Jullu the poison had left no trace of its existence.

"Here, Madame Jullu! I share my great moment of victory with you!" He raised his glass. "In Russia we handle our liquor well and we swallow this in continuous action. Like this."

Frolov raised his glass to his lips and tilted his head back. The brandy oozed over the top and into his mouth. He took several breaths, but kept the liquid flowing.

"Yes, I see," Jullu said and attempted an imitation. She sputtered twice but kept on. She held up the empty glass in defiance.

"Good! Very good!"

Jullu grabbed at her heart. Her eyes stared at him in unbelief. Too late she realized what he had done. She opened her mouth to speak, but no words came.

In three more seconds, she lay dead.

The three Regents had planned to meet for dinner at the house. Frolov temporarily disposed of Jullu's body by locking it inside the downstairs bathroom.

When Speaks came into the room later that afternoon, Frolov suddenly felt a moment of fear that he could not explain. Pushing his emotions aside, he extended his hand. "Come! Join me in celebrating!"

"Of course," Speaks said. "Where is Baya?"

"She cannot drink like a Russian. She has already re-tired." He smiled and shook Speaks's hand. He led him into the room. "May I pour you a drink, my friend?"

"Frolov, I am not your friend. I have never been your friend." Speaks's soft-spoken drawl hardened.

"As you say." The older man shrugged. "At least let us have a drink together." He turned his back on Speaks and pulled two champaign glasses from the shelf. "One drink that unites us in celebrating our mutual victory—"

He had not anticipated a direct approach by Speaks. As he turned around with the glasses, he saw the man directly before him, holding a Webley .38-caliber pistol.

"What is going on? We are working together. We are comrades—"

"No, Vitoli, we are not comrades. We are what we have always been—enemies. Only one of us will survive." Speaks pulled the trigger four times.

Frolov's body flipped backward, the glasses flying and breaking when they hit the inlaid floor. Speaks's perfect aim had found its target on the first shot.

It took him another twenty minutes to find Baya Marach Jullu's lifeless body. Speaks said, "Frolov, thank you for making it more convenient." He carried the now-stiffened corpse back into the room where he had shot Frolov.

At that moment one of the servants came to the door and knocked discreetly. Speaks whirled around.

"Excuse me, sir, but I would like to clean the room," Randolph said. His hooded eyes betrayed no expression. "That is, if you are now finished." His eyes swept past Frolov's body and rested on the far wall, spattered with both blood and brandy. "I wish to remove any stains as soon as possible, you understand."

"I'm finished."

"Very good. And, sir, Joshua the Divine left a message for you. I placed it on the hall table." He walked past Speaks and started picking up the pieces of broken glass.

John Speaks walked into the hallway and saw an envelope with the royal seal of Joshua imprinted on the back. He slit it open with his index finger.

Congratulations, John Speaks!
I anticipated that it would come to a parting

of the way between the three of you. I fully
expected you to eliminate the others.
Please join me at the palace at your
convenience.

Speaks arrived at the palace an hour before sunset. An
armed escort took him immediately to Joshua's office.
When he walked inside, he saw Joshua standing in the middle of the room. He held a glass of wine in each hand.

"Do come in. I just poured this for us. For our celebration—yours and mine, Speaks."

The American's eyes moved from Joshua's face to the
glasses and he hesitated.

"You think I have poisoned one of them?" Joshua
smiled. "Frolov's method and the way he killed Jullu. Ms.
Jullu, on the other hand, liked the boom-boom kind of
violence such as bombs and whole buildings destroyed to
eliminate one person. She had planned to murder Frolov in
his sleep. By the way, your marksmanship with a gun im-
presses me. I understand your first shot killed Frolov."

"One of my minor accomplishments," Speaks said. "I
learned to shoot rats and other wild animals when I was a
boy."

"So I understand. You have not lost your skill."

"And you, Joshua?" Speaks said as he took the glass.
"What is your favorite method of elimination?"

"I use other people to do my work for me."

Speaks broke into a hearty laugh. He raised the glass.
"To our triumph!" He swallowed half the glass.

When they finished their drink, Joshua said, "Now you
are ready for your first injection of SSS-JK." He took
Speaks's arm and guided him toward the back of the office.
The wall, paneled in a variety of wood, contained a door,
fully invisible until Joshua pushed at the right spot. It swung
forward.

"This is my private entrance to our research laboratory," he said as he ushered his guest forward. They walked
down a well-lighted hallway and came to a large laboratory.
Two armed guards stood at the door.

"Here they produce SSS-J, now being distributed to the population at large." He nodded to the door at the far end of the hallway. "In there we keep SSS-JK."

"What's the actual difference between the two serums?"

"Quite simply, SSS-J, which I offer to everyone, retards aging but does not prevent it." Joshua paused and allowed him to watch the white-coated workers at work inside the room. "Human beings are genetically programmed to live approximately 120 years. Disease, stressful living, improper diet, lack of exercise—these things have gradually lessened the life expectation of the population."

"So this serum slows down the process?"

"Precisely. Instead of dying at age seventy-five of multiple diseases, the serum keeps glands and genetic factors productive longer. For example, in most men over fifty, the prostate gland becomes quite troublesome." He smiled at Speaks. "You're barely forty but already having trouble urinating. Am I correct?"

"You read my medical history, too?"

"Of course." Joshua started to move on. "With regular injections, you would find considerable relief for the next thirty to forty years, perhaps as long as fifty. It merely prolongs the length of life."

"And SSS-JK?"

"I have reserved SSS-JK for you and for me, John Speaks. Yes, even in the beginning I assumed you would eliminate the others. Greed works like that, does it not?"

"Yes, it does—"

"And, before you concern yourself too highly about how you will take the antiaging drug from me, I will tell you that you cannot possibly do that. I suggest you forget about trying, but you will not."

"Oh? Sounds like a strong boast. And a challenge."

"An impossible challenge."

"Possibly."

"I'll show you why." They walked to the door. "Notice I have not posted guards here. I do not need them." He turned the handle. "The door has no lock either, you have noticed."

"Yes—"

"Proceed." He stepped back.

Speaks turned the handle and pushed the door open. He saw a room approximately fifteen feet by ten. It contained two straight chairs and a large stainless steel cabinet.

"The serum is in the stainless steel refrigerated unit. It must stay at a regulated temperature. You may take it from the container, John."

Confused by the way Joshua was treating him, John eagerly walked toward the built-in unit. Three feet in front of the unit, his body struck a wall—an invisible wall. With his hands, he felt a hard substance he could not see. "A shield of some kind? Invisible but impenetrable?"

"Exactly. And you can never penetrate it, John. Never." He took Speaks's shoulder and pulled him back. "Watch." Joshua went to the shield, opened his hands and pressed the palms against the invisible shield.

Both men heard a swishing sound that lasted four seconds. Joshua stepped forward to the unit. "Open it," he said.

John turned the handle and nothing happened. He turned it harder and still nothing, yet he could discern no lock. He shrugged.

Joshua went to the unit, pressed his palms above the door and said, "Joshua Divine." The door swung open.

"Very clever," Speaks said. "Print and voice-activated unit."

"You need only to duplicate both and you have access to the serum." Joshua reached inside and pulled out a metal tray. It contained a cotton ball, a bottle of disinfectant, a vial of pale-red liquid and one syringe. "If you will roll up your sleeve, please."

John Speaks complied. The King swabbed his arm with the disinfectant, extracted .2cc of the liquid, and injected it in the fatty tissue of the upper arm. He returned the vial to the stainless steel container and laid the tray on top.

"Oh, John, one more thing. Knowing how your devious mind works, I have another built-in precaution. You cannot leave the room without me. The shield is already in place again."

"Is it? I didn't hear it close." Speaks turned and felt it. "So I see."

"You concentrated on the serum and my voice or you would have heard it. Oh, should you attempt to use anything to block the space so that the panel does not close . . ." He paused and looked upward. A dozen tiny pipes protruded four inches from the ceiling. "It activates a gas that will destroy your lungs within five seconds."

"Another safety factor? You are thorough."

"You need to feel honored. I would not resort to all of this if any other person were involved. Next to me, you are the most dangerous man on the earth."

"And so—"

"Only two more precautions. One, you cannot open the door to exit except by matching my voice print. But the best idea of all, and I am sure you can appreciate it, you cannot leave the palace with a vial of the SSS-JK."

"Surely you are not going to tell me that the vial will self-destruct when it comes into contact with outside air."

"Not quite. Each entrance—including windows, incidentally—emits microscopic rays that detect the serum. If serum attempts to pass, no matter how well hidden, laser beams destroy it immediately—along with whoever or whatever carries it. Would you like a demonstration?"

"Not necessary. I believe you."

"I thought you would."

Joshua used handprints to lift the shield and his voice to open the door. They went back into the King's office.

"Before you leave, John, we now need two Regents to replace those two who were just killed. I have decided to allow you the privilege of appointing your two most promising leaders."

"I shall give you their names by tomorrow."

"It is unfortunate, isn't it, that fanatics from Aryeh poisoned the food that killed our two splendid Regents?

Isn't that what happened? That's the way we have already released the story."

"But, of course," Speaks said. He dropped to his knees. "I bow—literally—to the most corrupt wisdom in the world. You rightfully control the world. I am willing to remain in second place—"

"For now, anyway." Joshua took Speaks's hand and pulled him to his feet. "But not for always. You will continue to think of this. Every time you return for an injection, your evil and devious mind will ponder how to take possession of the serum. I hope you will wait several hundred years before you try . . ."

"King Joshua, how could you—?"

"I know you. I know you as well as I know myself."

Speaks left minutes later. A Mercedes-Benz awaited him in front. For the first time, he began to feel a sense of liking for Joshua—the only person who had bested him in life. "Ah, well," he sighed, "what must be must be."

As the car drove slowly out of the palace grounds, John Speaks yawned. It had been a long day and he felt tiredness come upon him, the aftereffects of a strenuous day when adrenalin is pumped at top level. His eyes felt heavy and he lay his head back.

King Joshua did one merciful thing for John Speaks. The poison mixed with the serum would not cause him any pain. Speaks would drift into a peaceful sleep from which he would never awaken.

F·O·U·R·T·E·E·N

At 6:38, the first full rays of the sun came from the east, lighting up the sky. The followers of Aryeh gathered in the two locations in preparation for worship.

Nagila stood with her microphone at the amphitheater and hooked up electronically with Shaheen in Jerusalem. She began to sing the first stanza of "Storm the Palace of Darkness." Before she finished the first measure of the chorus, millions of voices blended with hers.

They sang the five verses and their voices filled the air in the final chorus.

At that moment, two significant events began to take place. In Jerusalem, machine gun-carrying soldiers appeared. They surrounded the millions of believers standing together in the city. Each soldier carried a five-gallon can of malgamite. At a given signal, each soldier turned the can upside down, letting the odorless liquid spill to the ground. They took four steps backward and each soldier threw the near-empty containers into the crowd.

One of the Regents, observing on the north side, lit the

first match. Seconds later another Regent lit his on the south. Both men's eyes sparkled as they watched flames licking up the liquid and moving inward, followed by the first screams of pain.

In the Negev, the mammoth temperature saucers shut off the cool breezes. Nagila, assuming they had shut down because of such heavy use, wondered how long it would take for their repair.

The next moment flames shot from the center of the major saucer and it spun lightly over a 45 degree angle. Each of the saucers did the same. For the first time she saw the rows of armed soldiers in the background. They had their machine guns trained on the crowd.

"They have brought us here to murder us!" Nagila said. "We cannot escape. We must not try. We shall show them how we can die with peace and the praise of Aryeh on our lips. Storm the palace of darkness . . ."

The crowd picked up the song and Nagila watched, her eyes filled with horror as she saw burning bodies. The flames sped through the crowd like a drenching rain. "Keep singing! We shall never yield as long as we have a breath left!"

From the palace, Joshua the Divine watched the proceedings through tele-monitors from both places. He experienced a moment of anger when the crowds did not panic. Not one follower of Aryeh scrambled for safety.

They die singing? They go to their deaths with songs about Aryeh on their lips?

Joshua the Divine walked to the window and opened it. He looked up and screamed, "I defy you, Aryeh! I now eradicate you and all of your followers from this planet! I have won! You are defeated!"

Everything had gone according to the plan—down to the last detail. The followers of Aryeh had almost upset everything, but in the end Joshua had destroyed them as well. He knew that pockets of Aryeh adherents still existed, most of them now leaderless.

Reports told Joshua of fifty-three such groups in the world that had not complied with the order to assemble in Jerusalem. It did not matter, he reminded himself. He would wipe them out within days. He had destroyed those who led. The rest would either follow him or die. Their choice made no difference. He would have total obedience from the entire world.

Joshua would continue to function with the ten Regents. With the appointment of three new leaders, he felt satisfied. All of them were controllable. None of them had the insidious capacity for corruption of Jullu, Frolov, or Speaks. They would not fight among themselves because Joshua held the SSS-J. But that would not prevent underlings from usurping their positions. In time these leaders would fall to the greed and ambition of their underlings.

Joshua looked forward to those changes. He would begin the manipulation within the year. He wanted no leader to feel too secure. Earlier that morning he had completed his world-plan for the next hundred years.

Joshua ruled the world. He was the Earth King at last. He had wiped out the only serious threat, followers of Aryeh. No one could defeat him now. He was untouchable. He would live for hundreds of years, perhaps thousands, maybe even forever.

"I am supreme! I am infallible! It has all taken place exactly as I planned!"

Joshua walked calmly to the balcony. A crowd of several hundred had gathered. "There!" a woman shouted as she pointed to him. She waved a banner that read, "Joshua the Divine!"

The people fell on their knees. He heard their words clearly and waved in return.

"Joshua the Divine!"

"Joshua, King of Kings!"

"Joshua, the only eternal one!"

He continued to wave for several minutes. Instead of the crowd disbursing, others joined them. Soon the entire area surrounding the front of the palace filled with grateful citizens. All of them waved their SSS scarves. They burst into song, praising Joshua the Divine.

"I am your ruler!" Joshua raised his voice. A hush fell over them and they knelt. "You shall have nothing but prosperity from here on! Do you believe this?"

"Yes! We believe!" a man's voice screamed, and the people took up his words, repeating them again and again, growing louder and more intense.

Joshua held up his hand and a hush fell over the crowd. "I have destroyed death! I have overcome the hated followers of Aryeh! I am the only one, the eternal one!"

"Yes, Joshua the Divine!"

"True God and Divine!"

Joshua's heart beat faster as he heard the deserved praises. He had waited a long time. Now it was his—all his.

He turned his head upward momentarily. "Aryeh! You have lost! I am the winner!" He turned back toward the people below. "Yes, I am with you always. I will protect you and guide you forever!"

Joshua did not notice the movement in the sky. Cumulus clouds floated peacefully across the horizon and then, as if propelled by a driving wind, the isolated billows floated toward each other, joined together, and hovered directly over the palace.

Suddenly the piercing, moaning wail of the shofar filled the air. Joshua had not heard that mournful sound since a boyhood visit to Israel when shepherds blew the ram's-horn. The noise built to an ear-shattering shriek and continued without a break. The people in the courtyard and street, paralyzed with fear, stared upward or looked at each other.

One man fell on his knees and cried out, "God, forgive me! Forgive me!" The words moved like a shock wave through the crowd as one after another took up the cry and fell on their knees. The courtyard became one huge writhing mass of humanity, and the deafening roar of thousands screaming in anguish and torment competed with the sound of the shofar.

In the Negev, Nagila infused new courage into the followers of Aryeh. "Storm the palace of darkness!" Nagila's voice rang out, the microphone amplifying her voice across the desert. In Jerusalem, Shaheen urged the people to sing with all their might and to ignore the inevitable death that would touch them in seconds.

All attempts to panic the believers had failed. They remained steadfast, everyone joining in the singing of the Aryeh anthem. A member of the SSS cut the power from the microphone, hoping to break their spirit, but Nagila continued to sing at the top of her voice. Then she jumped down off the platform and began to move among the people. She kept singing and other voices, refusing to yield to panic, sang with her.

In Jerusalem, the giant screen showed the Negev scene, but they heard nothing. The people stopped, fear spread among them, and they screamed.

"No! Hold on!" Shaheen pleaded. He, too, had stopped momentarily, but gazing at the screen, he saw Nagila's image. Her face, filled with a radiance he had never seen before, infused him with new courage. He picked up the words,

> . . . Pull down Therion's kingdom
> Wher'er he holds dominion . . .

He dropped his mike and moved toward the center of the crowd. A body fell against his and the first flames scorched his flesh. He felt a stabbing pain and his body recoiled in shock. Flames lapped at his clothes and skin. He sensed he had only seconds to live.

"Storm the palace of darkness!
Pull down Therion's kingdom . . ."

All at once the sound of the shofar filled the air, blotting out the triumphant singing. The followers of Aryeh stopped. Momentarily they stared at each other while the trumpeting continued.

One elderly woman's face blazed with glory. "Just as Aryeh promised!"

As the piercing tones of the shofar ceased, a young boy pointed skyward. "Look!"

"I see it! I see it!" said a second voice.

The people huddled close together and watched the clouds coming closer. A rushing wind swept through Jerusalem and the Negev, instantly putting out the flames from the malgamite. Those who only moments before screamed from the torturous pain felt nothing, as if the fire had never touched them.

Every eye turned upward. Every face glowed.

"It has happened!" Shaheen cried out with tears streaming down his eyes. Instinctively he raised his hands. The clouds parted and he saw a man, suspended between Heaven and earth.

"Even so, come . . ." Shaheen whispered.

At the palace, the sound of the shofar stopped as suddenly as it had started. The ensuing silence disquieted the crowd there more than the shrill horn. All of them stared upward. Some pointed, others fell on their knees or were prostrate. No one spoke.

A tremor ran though the courtyard, beginning with a faint rumbling. On the balcony, Joshua felt a slight shaking, increasing with the tempo of the rumbling. The foundation began to sway and the reverberation intensified into a roaring and pounding that filled his ears and blocked out all other sound. Joshua gasped, horrified as the magnificent palace slowly disintegrated. A sound like a giant sledgehammer erupted and the far walls, as if struck with one massive blow, crumbled into rubble.

He looked down and the floor disintegrated, sucking him into a giant vortex of swirling rock.

Before he fell, Joshua the Divine shook his fist again. "I curse you, Aryeh, now and for all eternity!"

He plunged downward till his body struck the ground. Twenty tons of marble and stone fell on top of him, entombing his body. The room containing the serum burst open, and the precious liquid spilled across the ground. Debris covered every drop with a dusty coat.

The clouds parted as if a giant hand separated them. Joshua the Divine did not live long enough to observe the final scene of history.

E·P·I·L·O·G·U·E

For the Lord himself will descend from heaven with a cry of command, with the archangel's call, and with the sound of the trumpet of God. And the dead in Christ will rise first; then we who are alive, who are left, shall be caught up together with them in the clouds to meet the Lord in the air; and so we shall always be with the Lord.

St. Paul's First Letter to the Thessalonians, 4:16-17

Then I saw a great white throne and him who sat upon it; from his presence earth and sky fled away, and no place was found for them. And I saw the dead, great and small, standing before the throne . . . Then I saw a new heaven and a new earth; for the first heaven and the first earth had passed away, and the sea was no more. And I saw the holy city, new Jerusalem, coming down out of heaven from God, prepared as a bride adorned for her husband; and I heard a great voice from the throne saying,

"Behold, the dwelling of God is with men. He will dwell with them, and they shall be his people, and God himself will be with them; and he will wipe away every tear from their eyes, and death shall be no more, neither shall there be mourning nor crying nor pain any more, for the former things have passed away." And he who sat upon the throne said, "Behold, I make all things new . . ."

The Revelation of St. John 20:11-12; 21:1-5